MW01257426

BEYOND RUIN

Kim—
O'Kane for life!

Kit Rocha (signature)

kit rocha

Beyond Ruin

Edited by Sasha Knight

ISBN-13: 978-1530099993
ISBN-10: 1530099994

For everyone who celebrates love, no matter what shape it takes or how it comes to people.

Again.

F ROM THE TIME he was old enough to understand words, people had been assuring Mad that he was blessed. He was the cosseted grandson of the Prophet, a holy prince adored and anointed by God himself. Everything he wanted should fall into his open hand. It was his destiny to do great things.

For a blessed man, he had terrible timing.

He paused on the threshold of the garage as Scarlet scowled at the broken-down amplifier on the bench in front of her. Shitty timing or not, the sight of her still kicked him in the gut as she pulled the wires away from the circuit board to get a better look.

She was wearing beat-up jeans and an even more battered tank top. Her newly blonde hair had a bluish tint and was twisted on top of her head in a messy ponytail. The cigarette dangling from her lips emphasized her frown, which did nothing to diminish her overall impact.

Scarlet was hot. Not in spite of her clothes and her attitude, but *because* of them. Because Scarlet was unapologetically herself.

And because of who she was—protective, dangerous, *stubborn*—she was going to be trouble.

Mad had hoped to slip out of Sector Four without attracting attention. Dallas had always granted him a certain amount of autonomy, a choice driven by politics and cemented by trust, but tonight he was treading a line dangerously close to disobedience.

She pulled the cigarette from her mouth without looking up. "Hey."

"Scarlet." He pushed off the doorframe and headed for his bike. She sounded distracted, so maybe luck was with him after all. "You're working late."

"Amp's got a short in it. The garage has the best tools, but you have to use them when some motherfucker's not banging them on an engine." The soft glow at the tip of her cigarette flared as she took another drag. "What about you?"

"I have an errand to run." Close enough to the truth.

"Alone?" Scarlet rolled her stool away from the workbench and propped one solid boot on the shelf. Her brows came together in a severe slash over her clear blue eyes as she looked him over. "I thought O'Kane had *rules* about that these days."

These days had started the moment Eden tortured one of Dallas's operatives. Well, started all over again. Mad could still remember the early years, when no O'Kane ever ventured out of the compound without a partner to guard his back. Success and relative safety had made them all cocky, careless.

Now wasn't the time for cocky and careless. But he couldn't ignore the unsettling rumors coming out of Sector Two, either. "I'm just bending the rules, not breaking them." Just like he was bending the truth when he finished, "I'm meeting a friend in Three."

"Uh-huh." The corner of her mouth tipped up in a sly smile. "Sure, Saint Adrian."

The nickname made him tense instinctively, though he preferred the faint mockery in her voice to hearing the words whispered in earnest. "You can't become a saint until you're dead, sweetheart. That's not on my agenda."

"I bet." She rose and crossed the garage, passing within inches of him before circling his bike. The proximity sparked heat all over his skin, and her low, husky laugh was even hotter. "Be careful anyway. And if—*if*—you happen to make it all the way into Sector Two, do me a favor?"

That was the sexiest thing about Scarlet—her clever brain. "It never hurts to ask for a favor."

"Mmm. Avery Parrino."

There was only one person in Four besides Dallas's queen who cared about Lex's baby sister. "Jade's worried about her?"

"Of course. They're friends."

Somehow, Mad thought Jade might worry even if they weren't. She'd won her freedom from Sector Two, but she still carried the place inside her, the same way Mad carried Sector One. A duty and an obligation. A painful scar.

At least Jade had Scarlet. Protective, dangerous, *stubborn* Scarlet. Whatever crazy shit was going on with Two, Jade wouldn't have to face it alone.

"That's why I'm going," he said, reaching for his helmet. "We all know there's trouble over there, and it can blow back on too many of our people. We need to be ready."

"Spoken like a good little soldier."

There was the mockery again. It dug under his skin this time, scraping at wounded pride he didn't want to acknowledge. He *was* a good soldier. Damaged and worn down, maybe, but he held the line for his brothers and got the job done. "You got a problem, Scarlet?"

"A problem? Nah." She crushed her cigarette out on the sole of one boot and tossed the butt on the workbench.

"Just seems like you talk a big game about teamwork and brotherhood, but when you get right down to it? You're gonna do whatever the fuck you want. You always do."

She was leaning against the bench again, mere feet away. He crossed the garage in two long steps that brought him into her personal space. Their bodies almost touched as he reached past her to jab the switch that opened the big bay door.

Her ponytail brushed his cheek. Her hair smelled like vanilla and cinnamon. Like *Jade*, and the reminder of their relationship was a distraction Mad couldn't afford.

He pulled back far enough to get a good grasp on his sanity, then smiled. "I'm gonna do whatever the fuck needs doing. Count on it."

"You're offended." It wasn't an accusation, just a statement of fact. "I meant it as a compliment, you know. O'Kane doesn't need a bunch of blind followers. He needs men who can think for themselves." She brushed a lock of hair back from his cheek. "Men like you."

Her fingertips were soft. So was her touch, gentle and easy and nothing like his fantasies. And she could *not* be touching him right now—not with where he had to go and what he had to do tonight.

He caught her wrist and eased it away. "I'll ask my contacts for news about Avery."

"Thanks." She turned away, but he could hear the smile in her voice. "You're a prince."

She was back to poking him, but it was almost a relief. The poking and the scratching and even the mockery were easy, safer than soft touches that tempted him to want what he couldn't have. "Since the day I was born."

Scarlet ignored him as he swung a leg over his motor-cycle. He returned the favor as he shoved his helmet into place and roared out of the garage—maybe faster than was advisable.

He told himself it wasn't running away if you had someplace to be.

The sector was mostly dark. When he shot past the final line of street lamps, the only light came from his bike and the moon. He could still tell when he crossed the invisible border between Four and Three. Sector Four was rough around the edges, but Three was a mess. It had been nearly a year since Dallas claimed ownership, but long hours and determination couldn't roll back the clock on total destruction.

Once upon a time, Sector Three had been a thriving business hub. An industrial center full of bustling factories that turned out the electronics and technology desperately needed by a civilization trying to drag themselves back from the brink of annihilation. But with raw materials hard to come by, profits were narrow—even when you paid your workers a pittance. And when you stopped paying them at all...

Mad could remember his grandfather talking about the strikes. A noble cause, he'd proclaimed. The people rising up to demand their due. A cause sure to shake Eden to its very foundations.

His grandfather might have been the Prophet, but he had no gift for prophecy. Eden's foundations had stayed intact. And all eight sectors learned the price of disobedience when the sky filled with fire and Eden's drones turned Three into rubble.

It remained rubble for more than a decade. None of the petty leaders who had risen to power in the sector had bothered expending time and resources to make things better. When the O'Kanes finally took over, half the roads were still impassable, and some were straight-up death-traps.

Progress didn't happen overnight. It would take years to turn Three around completely and rebuild what had been lost. But for now, at least Mad had a clear path through the sector as he guided his bike north toward the East Road that marked the boundary between Three and Two.

The road wasn't the only boundary. Even before the bombing, Sector Two had their wall. Ten feet high and running nearly a mile out, it encircled their paradise and did its best to keep out the undesirables on both sides.

It also did its best to keep girls like Lex's sister—*girls like Jade*—inside.

The man waiting on an idling bike in the middle of the East Road was one of the ways those girls got out. Mad pulled to a stop next to him, rested his boots on the cracked pavement, and tugged off his helmet. "Deacon."

"Mad." The nickname still tripped clumsily off Deacon's tongue, like a man speaking a language he'd learned to sound out but didn't understand.

For good reason. Addressing a member of the Rios family casually approached blasphemy. Deacon might not have been the truest of true believers, but he was high up in the leadership of Sector One, the commander of the sector's police force, and fiercely loyal to Mad's cousin, Gideon. And this was why Mad hadn't brought another O'Kane with him tonight. The way Gideon's men looked at him—the way they *treated* him, with a hint of reverence and lingering deference—was too stark a reminder of all the things he'd fled.

But right now he needed Deacon and his connections.

"Another night might be better," the man said slowly, squinting into the darkness surrounding them. "My friends in Two say security's thin on the ground these days. Someone must have pissed off the MPs."

Only one person could irritate Eden's military police that much—the leader of Sector Two. "Cerys is usually more careful than that."

"Guess she's feeling the strain."

They all were. But if Two had lost the support of the city, Dallas needed to know, and soon. "We can handle any trouble that comes our way."

For a moment, Mad thought Deacon might argue. But he only bowed his head in submission.

Responsibility was a heavy weight. Sometimes he wasn't sure how Dallas carried it every day. Mad felt it pressing down on him as they stashed their bikes and headed for the easiest place to slip over the wall.

Deacon went first, launching himself with a half-jump off the bottom of the wall to grip the top of the brick. He pulled himself up with no other leverage, then reached down from his perch atop the wall. Mad sighed and let Deacon haul him up.

They hit the ground on the other side together, their boots digging into the soft grass. The trees lining the river made this the best place to slip in undetected, but by the time they'd eased out of the sparse woods and into the shadows of one of the larger warehouses, Mad realized it didn't matter.

Security wasn't just thin. It was absent. So were the people who were usually going about their business, even at this late hour. He and Deacon made it two blocks without encountering *anyone*, and that was chilling enough to make Mad stop in a sheltered alley with his back against a brick building. "What the hell is going on?"

"No fucking clue." It must have unnerved Deacon just as much, because he seized the opportunity to check the pistol tucked into his shoulder holster.

The shadows were deep, but Mad's eyes had adjusted enough to pick out the tattoos winding down Deacon's left arm. Every man who joined Gideon's Riders was given the same initiation tattoo on his left shoulder—a sparse, leafless tree growing out of a skull. Deacon's shirt sleeve hid most of it, but not the little black ravens spilling down toward his wrist, each one signifying a life taken in his quest to protect Sector One.

Gideon was tattooing his men long before O'Kane formed his gang. Maybe Dallas had been inspired by the memorial tattoos—there was no denying the intimidating impact of a Rider with an arm full of ravens. But Mad preferred the promise of brotherhood inked around his wrists to the silent penance etched into Deacon's skin.

Too many reminders of why he'd left. His shoulders tight, Mad checked his own pistol. "Let's go see Lincoln so we can get the hell home."

They made it only a few blocks before an unmistakable sound drifted out of the darkness—a blade clearing a leather sheath.

Mad spun, but his companion was faster. As the figure rushed from the shadows, Deacon surged in front of Mad. Silver glinted, but Deacon didn't even grunt as the knife slashed across his chest. He gripped his attacker's head, whispered something low and unintelligible, and snapped his neck with a vicious twist.

Just like that—in less than a heartbeat—it was over.

"Looks like Three." Deacon kicked the knife away before kneeling beside the dead man. His jacket had fallen open, revealing a tangle of gold chain, credit sticks, and the occasional jewel. "Must have gotten cocky, with none of the fancy folks fighting back."

He spoke so casually, as if he wasn't bleeding from an entirely preventable wound. As if he wouldn't be going back to Sector One to receive another little black raven tattoo, penance Mad owed for dragging him over the wall to begin with.

Mad retrieved the credit sticks and a couple of pieces of jewelry that looked easy to fence and shoved them in his pocket. Lincoln could use the credits to save a few more lives, to give a few more girls like Jade a chance at a future of their own choosing.

Triage. That was all it ever felt like. But he kept trying, even in the face of relentless hopelessness.

Maybe he was still a Rios at heart after all.

2

THE ONLY BAD thing about his new place was how empty it was.

Dylan stood in the center of his loft and surveyed it critically. It was essentially one giant room—only the bathroom was separate from the rest of the cavernous space. There were no half-walls delineating the kitchen or sleeping areas, just an endless, open room nearly the size of the entire floor.

It wasn't fancy—nothing in Sector Four outside of Dallas O'Kane's private bedroom was—but it was entirely livable. It didn't leak, and just one of the numerous windowpanes had been broken and repaired with tape instead of replaced. It had endless possibilities. It would be good for entertaining. He could set up weight machines and mats, even a boxing ring, a whole gym right in his living room.

But somehow, as he paced in his bare feet over the

scarred wood floor, all Dylan could think was how useful it would be as a morgue. There was plenty of room to lay out bodies, and everything more than six feet away from the fireplace was freezing cold. The only thing missing was the smell—chemicals and disinfectant. Death.

He fumbled with the tin in his pocket. The metal was warm from his body heat, comforting, but not as comforting as the tiny tablet he slipped under his tongue. A half dose, and he mentally tallied them as the tab dissolved.

One before breakfast. Two after lunch. One just now—four. Only two doses in an entire day. A personal record.

He laughed.

"Dylan?"

The voice startled him. Not with fear, but with a shiver of heat down his spine. "Mad. I didn't hear you come in."

And it was no wonder. The man could move silently when he wished, which was often. He stood just inside the door, dark. So dark. Dressed in black, his motorcycle helmet dangling from one gloved hand.

Dark and haunted. His gaze was blank, but tension bracketed his eyes and showed in his stiff posture. "I know it's late…"

"No. I'm glad you're here." He was just a man, one man, but he filled all the empty space somehow.

Mad crossed to the table and set his helmet down with exaggerated care. "I was in Sector Two tonight."

That always upset him, but this was something more. Dylan reached for Mad's jacket and eased it off his shoulders. "What happened?"

Mad's shirt stretched tight over tense muscles as he clenched his fists. "One of my cousin's men was there with me."

"Why?"

"We were meeting a contact." Mad rolled his shoulders and didn't turn. "It was necessary. There's intel Dallas needs."

"And you didn't answer my question." Dylan threw the jacket across the back of a chair and waited.

Mad knelt to jerk at the laces on his boots. Disheveled black hair fell over his forehead, hiding his eyes. "I got the job done. Without a fucking scratch on me, because a Rios never has to bleed or kill when there's a Rider left standing."

"It's a good thing I'm not competitive." Dylan gripped Mad's forearm and hauled him to his feet. Their faces—their *mouths*—were only inches apart. "Self-loathing is my thing, not yours."

Mad took an unsteady breath, and *finally* something beyond empty blankness sparked to life in his gaze. Heat and hunger and a deeper, darker need. "No, it's mine," he whispered hoarsely. "Yours is self-destruction."

"An excellent point." There were goose bumps on his arms, and Dylan traced them lightly. "Chilly?"

"Aren't you?" Mad skated his fingers up Dylan's arm, then curled them around the back of his neck in a rough grip. "Why do you keep it so fucking cold in here?"

Because he had to feel something, and the cold was safe, easy. He could endure it without having to reach for the tiny tablets of oblivion stashed in his pocket.

Dylan bit back the words. "I was waiting for you to come and warm me up."

"Liar," Mad rasped, before cutting off any chance of reply with a brutal kiss.

Some nights were soft and slow, full of long, helpless groans and warmth. Others were like this, sharp bites and indrawn breaths, hard and punishing. Desperate.

Dylan craved them all.

He opened his mouth, seeking the wet heat of Mad's tongue as they moved toward the bed. No stumbling, because they both knew the way by now. It was second nature to cross the room blindly, too wrapped up in the pleasure of touch to break away.

Mad twisted both hands in Dylan's T-shirt and jerked,

tearing the fabric. Fingernails raked over his stomach, higher as Mad's lips found his ear. "You're just as bad as the Riders. You'd let me do anything to you."

"Is that what you want? To ravage me?" He wound his fingers in Mad's hair, clenched tight, and pulled his head back. "Or do you want to be ravaged? Pinned down and fucked until you forget everything else?"

Mad flexed his hands on Dylan's shoulders. Still rough, still pushing, but the words that tore out of him were more plea than command. "I want your lips around my cock."

The words pulsed through him, heating his blood. Dylan shed his ruined T-shirt and reached for his belt, his gaze fixed on Mad. "Take off your clothes."

He was as violent with his own clothes as he'd been with the T-shirt. His shirt ended up ripped and discarded. He kicked his boots off without breaking eye contact, then attacked his belt with clumsy hands.

He was shaking by the time he stripped off his pants. He stood there, naked and hungry, and Dylan watched, mesmerized by the play of golden skin and ink over muscle.

He stepped closer. Mad's cock jutted out, hard and ready, and Dylan soothed him with a single firm stroke. Mad hissed in a breath, but he didn't resist as Dylan shoved him back onto the bed.

The fireplace was close enough to the bed to cast flickering shadows over Mad's skin, and Dylan stretched out beside him and gave in to the urge to trace the dancing shadows with his tongue.

"Dylan—" Mad twisted a hand in his hair—tense, as if he wasn't sure whether to tug his head up or push it down.

"No." Dylan arched away, relishing the zing of pain when Mad held tight. "You don't control this. Not tonight."

Mad closed his eyes and dug his head back against the sheets. "What am I? Self-loathing or self-destruction?"

"Neither." He was a chance to escape both, if only for a little while, a truth Dylan realized with a jolt. Words wouldn't do, so he tried to convey it through touch—a kiss to Mad's collarbone, a slow, leisurely lick over his hip. His hand wrapped around the thick, rigid base of his cock.

Groaning, Mad thrust up into his hand. "Then stop torturing me."

Torture seemed like a strong word, at least until Dylan squeezed tighter. Mad's dick throbbed in his hand as a drop of moisture pearled at the tip. He licked it away, teasing more than soothing, and bit back his own groan when the man's salty, musky flavor spread over his tongue.

"*Yes.*" Mad's fingers tightened at the back of his head. "Harder."

Dylan licked him again, from base to tip, then stopped with his lips an inch away, so that Mad could feel his breath as he spoke. "I'll give you what you want, but only if you tell me which one you're thinking about."

A snarl vibrated up out of Mad's chest. "Fuck you, Dylan."

Yes, fuck me. "Tell me, love."

This time his groan was pure surrender. "Scarlet. I saw Scarlet tonight."

Of course. Scarlet and her lover were sexy as hell, and both appealed to Mad—and, if he was being brutally honest with himself, to Dylan, as well. But Jade was softer, sweeter. Lusting after her, *longing* for her, never seemed to put this vicious edge on Mad's hunger the way Scarlet did.

Dylan hummed encouragingly and sucked Mad's dick into his mouth.

Mad's hips jerked up, and he bit off a curse. "You're an evil bastard."

Dylan tightened his hand but lifted his head. "I guess you want me to stop, then."

"God fucking *damn*—" The firelight clung lovingly to

the muscles in Mad's arms when he clenched his fists in the blankets. "She smelled like cinnamon and vanilla. She smelled like she'd just crawled out of Jade's bed."

The scent was as familiar to Dylan as Mad's or his own. Thinking about it made his balls ache as he turned his attentions back to Mad's dick and grazed his teeth lightly over the head. "And?"

"And she touched— *Fuck*." He was trembling already, need and guilt twisting him up so tight he was helpless as Dylan swallowed him deep. "She touched my face. I had her backed up against a bench. I could have fucked her on it."

Could have—but didn't. Between the denial and the guilt, no wonder he was so wound up, close to coming even though Dylan had barely touched him.

He didn't have to prompt anymore. Mad knew this game and only resisted it with the first touches. He was lost in it now, breathing heavily, his eyes closed. "Fast. Fast and hard. She wouldn't let me go slow the first time."

Not a fucking chance. She did everything that way, wide open, and sex would be no exception. Dylan found himself sucking harder, matching the quick rhythm Scarlet would demand.

Mad lifted his hips, pushing deeper as his hand found the back of Dylan's head again. "I want to hear the sounds she makes. I want to hear—"

Dylan pulled free but kept his fist pumping over Mad's cock. "She already has a lover."

"I *know*." Mad's groan was desperate. "Just like I know her lover's the one you want in your bed."

Jade, with her endless curves and her sweet scent. Her haunted eyes. He'd found out by accident—with a murmured, offhand command while she was helping him tend to a patient. But something had flared in her then, a single moment of relief so bright and palpable that it had followed him for weeks.

He wondered if Scarlet ever gave her that subtle,

quiet domination. If she even knew Jade needed it.

He leaned up and stared down at Mad, whose dark eyes were full of hesitation now as well as lust. "And Jade wants you. She must. Or don't you know why Scarlet tries to tempt you?"

It was a line too far—or one temptation too many. Mad upended them in a surge of strong muscles and slammed Dylan back to the bed. He settled astride him, his hands rough and hurried as he dragged open his pants. "This is a twisted fucking game."

"You get off on it." Mad's erection ground against his thigh, still slick from his mouth, and Dylan reached for it.

"Maybe I'm twisted, too." Mad shifted out of reach, sliding down Dylan's body, hauling his pants with him. He tossed them off the bed and crawled back up until his mouth hovered over Dylan's aching cock. "Isn't that what you like about this?"

"If it helps." Dylan tangled his fingers in the other man's hair. Sex was a way to pass the time. Games could be fun or frustrating. But *Mad*—he was beautiful. He burned with life and righteousness, burned so hot you could feel it even through the anguish and guilt.

Tonight he burned with something else, too. He was determined as he closed his mouth around the head of Dylan's erection. No teasing, no patience. Just lips and tongue and sucking hard as he worked his way lower.

The drugs could numb Dylan to everything else, but not this. Not the sheer animal pleasure of Mad's mouth or the heat of his desire. He welcomed both, let the waves roll over him until he couldn't stop himself from thrusting up, seeking *more*.

Mad moved up with him, staying tauntingly out of reach. "Tell me which one you're thinking about."

His answer tore free, uncensored. Raw. "You."

With a groan, Mad surged up his body and claimed his mouth. Hot, deep, his teeth scraping Dylan's lip as their tongues met, tangled. It was perfect, an intimacy even more gut-wrenching than the man's mouth on his dick. Dylan wrapped one arm around Mad's flexing back, holding him close, and slipped his other hand between them. "Come with me," he whispered.

Mad's fingers joined his, warm and eager as they wrapped around Dylan's shaft. They stroked together, faster and rougher, until Mad stiffened and moaned into his mouth. His grip tightened almost painfully, and Dylan followed him into oblivion, coming all over Mad's belly, his own, and their desperate, grasping hands.

"Fuck." Panting, Mad pressed his forehead to Dylan's. "Fucking hell."

"Stay." It came from that same raw place, the place where Dylan couldn't close his eyes without hearing Mad's quiet voice.

"I shouldn't," he replied, the words wrapped in reluctance. "Dallas needs to know what's happening in Two."

"Tomorrow."

The fight went out of him, and that was how Dylan knew it was bad. Mad never stopped fighting. "Okay."

"You deserve this." Dylan caught his chin and forced him to meet his eyes in the dim light. "One night that's just yours."

The smile was slow to come, but it softened Mad's expression and warmed his gaze. "Will you turn on the damn heat for me?"

"Mmm, for you." He fumbled for the control on his nightstand and flicked the screen. It took only a few seconds to activate the heating system, and a handful more for the chill in the air to begin to dissipate.

Soon, the loft was as warm as the bed, and Dylan let it wrap around him, blocking out the rest of the world. There was no more suffering, no political maneuvering, just the steady, reassuring thump of Mad's heart.

It was enough. More than enough. It was everything.

3

L EX WAS THE only person in the meeting room when Jade arrived with a basket of warm muffins and her tablet. "These are from Lili." She set the food down in front of the tired-looking queen of Sector Four. "She and Jared got in late last night."

Lex didn't look up from the map spread across the table—a perfect representation, drawn in Ace's meticulous hand, of Sector Two. "Did you ever think you'd get out, and then have to spend this much time thinking about that fucking place?"

"No," Jade admitted, because it was the truth. Getting out and never looking back had been the plan from the first day her mother had returned to Rose House, broken-hearted and slowly dying, with Jade's tiny hand clutched in hers. Only seven years old, and Jade had already been too aware of how little security life in Sector Two offered.

Too aware, and still not aware enough.

"Eden wants something," Lex murmured. "They've pressed Cerys before, but it's never gone this far."

Jade slipped into the chair beside Lex's and reached for a muffin. "Two years ago was the worst," she said as she carefully peeled the paper liner from her breakfast. Focusing on the small, meticulous details of the task gave her the distance to keep her voice flat. "Eden cut our network connection for two weeks, until Cerys agreed to...compromise on their request."

"What did they want that time? More money, or more girls?"

It was always one or the other. "More girls. The second-tier bureaucrats wanted the same quality of free companionship that the Council enjoyed." They wanted *her*, or other girls like her. Jade had been forced to watch, sick with dread, as girls without her emotional protections were marched into Eden like lambs sent to nothing as merciful as a quick slaughter.

"Of course they did." Lex's chair screeched over the floor as she pushed it back and rose. "Cerys managed to keep that quiet. The fact that we're hearing so much shit now has me worried."

"Cerys had more control two years ago." The muffin smelled delicious, but Jade's stomach was too unsettled to eat. She set it down and looked up at Lex instead. "How many girls have left now besides me, besides Mia? Cerys keeps her power because of the secrets her girls collect, and there are fewer left who can do the job than ever before."

"Maybe. But Two's real security has always run deeper." Lex stabbed one red fingernail down on the map, right on the checkpoint coming out of the city. "It's a little bit of Eden out in the sectors."

"It was," said a low voice from the door. Dallas stepped into the room, his expression grim, but it was the man behind him who made Jade's pulse stutter.

Adrian Maddox was a beautiful man by the standards of almost any time period. Jade recognized that the same way she objectively recognized her own attractiveness.

Classic bone structure, symmetry of features—meaningless things they'd both been born with. They even shared similar coloring—black hair, brown eyes, brown skin, though Mad's was lighter than her own, and so much of it was covered in vivid, beautiful ink.

His beauty wasn't what made her heart skip. It was the look in those deep brown eyes when their gazes clashed, the intensity that burned there, the hunger he tried to fight.

So much heat. Subjective. *Personal.*

After only a moment, he looked away, reminding her that his desire for her could never overcome the shame he felt for wanting her. It had been that way from the beginning, and it still had the same devastating impact on her.

Stiffening her spine, she shifted her attention to Dallas. He wasn't classically beautiful, but he had the sort of presence you couldn't teach, the kind that came from knowing your own power, owning your place in the world.

"Was?" Lex asked expectantly.

Dallas tilted his head toward Mad, who nodded slowly. "Security has been pulled from Sector Two. *All* of it."

Ice filled Jade's veins. "The military police are gone?"

"Seems like." Dallas took a seat. "They're squeezing Cerys hard. What would keep her fighting like this?"

Lex stared blindly, her hands on her hips, her expression torn between anger and amusement. "What else? Her own power."

Raw truth. Jade's own body was proof of that. Long months of recovery had returned her appetite, and the face she looked at in the mirror was hers again. Not starved and gaunt, not lined with pain. But the shadows were there, in her eyes and in the occasional hollow ache inside her. One mistake in judgment had almost killed her—the mistake of overestimating her value to Cerys.

Cerys would sacrifice anyone if the price was right. "She'd give them money or girls—"

Lex cut in viciously. "But she'll never give them Sector Two."

No, that was the twisted morality—or simple vanity—at Cerys's core. She could have tolerated handing her empire over to Lex because she still harbored the delusion that she'd been responsible for the powerful woman Lex had become—and the greater delusion that Lex would someday embrace her for it. But she'd *never* give it to a man.

"The sector's locked down." Mad braced his fists on the table, his gaze riveted to the map. "A few opportunists jumped the wall from Three, and no one's bothering to chase them out."

"Everyone with half a brain will be hiding in their safe rooms until this blows over." Lex leaned over the table and frowned. "The city will have to give. Cerys won't. Not this time."

"They need Two." Dallas traced his fingertip over the outlines of the buildings just inside the far edge of the wall. Warehouses, mostly, full of treasures from other cities. That was the lifeblood and necessity of Two—the willingness of its men to take risks and their skill at forging connections. As valuable as Jade had been to Cerys personally, the secrets she'd coaxed from a councilman were nothing compared to consistent trade.

"They want Two," she corrected. "The Council's weakness has always been their inability to make the distinction between *need* and *want*."

Dallas acknowledged her words with a rough laugh. "They've never had to learn there *is* a distinction."

Because no one had the power to teach them that harsh lesson. Not even Dallas. "Lex is right. Cerys would burn Two to the ground before handing them the keys."

"I almost wish she would." Lex sank back into her chair and pinched the bridge of her nose.

"I know, darling." Dallas dragged her closer and dropped an arm around her shoulders. His lips found her temple in a kiss so tenderly intimate, Jade averted her gaze.

She found Mad doing the same, and that only made it worse. She didn't want to share someone else's intimacy with him. She didn't want to watch the fantasy come to life in his eyes, to know he was imagining holding her, touching her, kissing her—

Gently and softly. That's what he'd expect—no, *demand* from her. A fragile, fractured creature who trembled and shook. A woman who was broken because bad people had hurt her. Who needed a savior, not a man.

Sometimes, she wondered what would be worse—giving in and playing the victim just for the chance to have him once...or watching him bolt when he discovered her spine had always been more steel than spun glass.

In her darkest moments, she didn't care how much it would hurt to pretend.

She forced her attention back to Dallas and Lex. "Lili said Jared was going to meet up with you. Have they heard anything about the situation in Two?"

"Not a goddamn whisper." Dallas eased away from Lex but kept his arm around her. "Even Markovic's got nothing. Or if he does, he's not sharing."

"The silence goes both ways," Lex agreed. "Cerys doesn't want anyone to know she's being pressured, and Eden doesn't want anyone to know they can't make her buckle."

Dallas nodded. "Cerys is running short of friends on both sides of the wall. She relied too heavily on advantages she doesn't have anymore."

Mad flinched. Jade refused to. "You mean she relied too heavily on my ability to sway Gareth Woods." She offered Lex a tight smile. "I hope you don't mind that I got all the credit for his death."

"As long as he's dead, honey. That's all I give a suntoasted shit about."

In that, Jade fervently agreed with her. For seven

endless years, she'd played whatever games necessary to keep Councilman Gareth Woods addicted to her presence. One hundred and seventy-eight alternating weekends. She'd given him innocence and fear, she'd given him wide-eyed sexual awakening. Sometimes she'd given him pain—or had taken it in return.

One hundred and seventy-eight times—and for the first one hundred and sixty-five, she'd held him in the palm of her hand. Her eager, willing victim, blind to how deftly she coaxed free his secrets or nudged his opinions to align with Cerys's best interests.

The most foolish thing Cerys had ever done was take away her control.

Remembering Gareth Woods didn't hurt. Not as much as the memory of the drugs he'd given her, drugs that had shifted their balance of power. Even nearly dying while she shuddered through withdrawal was less painful to re-call than the six horrifying months when her will had not been her own.

Just the thought constricted the room around her, and maybe her spine wasn't steel after all. She reached for her tablet and rose. "I have to meet Scarlet. I'll check in later to see if you need anything, Lex."

"Thanks, Jade."

She refused to look at the men as she turned and walked—*walked*, not fled—to the door. It didn't help. She heard the soft footsteps behind her before she made it to the end of the hall, and she knew it was him. She felt him all along her skin, an unwelcome tingle when she needed peace.

"Jade, wait—"

Mad's fingers closed on her shoulder, and she spun quickly enough to jerk away from his touch. He stood, fro-zen, his hand still in the air, and it was the look in those beautiful brown eyes that snapped her self-control.

Wary. Cautious. Like she was a skittish creature he was trying not to startle.

Jade stepped closer, into his personal space. So close that she had to tilt her head back to meet his eyes, and that was the point. To make him feel big, to make him feel dominant.

To make him feel *guilty*, because he was imagining her sliding down the front of his body. And she did, running her fingers along the outsides of his legs as she sank gracefully to her knees. "Is this what you want, Mad?"

If lust had been the only thing filling his eyes, she might have eased open his pants and taken him between her lips right there. She could already taste him, salty and warm, could imagine the noises he'd make as she took him deep and made him come.

And then, with the taste of him on her tongue, she'd have to listen to his self-recrimination and apologies.

She wrapped her fingers around the hilt of his boot knife. And when he dragged her back to her feet, the denial forming on his lips, she twisted her wrist and rested the tip against his balls.

His eyes went wide. "Jade—"

"No," she said, letting the chill of anger fill her voice. "I'm done being treated like some broken toy you wish you didn't want to play with."

His fingers tightened on her shoulders. "I'm not—"

She pressed a little harder, and he stopped. Good, at least he wasn't stupid.

"I don't want to hurt you," he said instead.

She hated the earnestness in his voice. It threatened to shake her resolve, because he *meant* so well. But his well-meaning solicitousness was killing her. "I spent seven years keeping a psychopath wrapped around my little finger. If you think you present a challenge after that, your ego is even bigger than your cock, and I'm happy to trim either for you."

Mad's chest heaved. Something dark flashed behind his eyes. He leaned in, even with the knife precariously close to his balls, and his warm breath danced over her lips. "I still don't want to hurt you."

"You can't," she lied.

He didn't challenge her. No, he did something so much worse.

He kissed her.

It didn't seem real at first. The softness of his mouth on hers, the sweetness of the contact. So careful, so restrained, but she couldn't blame it on his reticence this time. Not when she was holding a knife to pieces of him he'd rather not lose.

It was his tongue that undid her. The tiniest lick across her lower lip, as if he was testing her, tasting her, and her hand trembled. She'd shown him her spine, steel and all, and she wasn't prepared for his response.

She dropped her hand so she wouldn't cut him, and he rewarded her by cradling the back of her head, his strong fingers splaying wide as he tried to deepen the kiss.

It was the memory of Scarlet that had her pressing her lips together and turning her face. His mouth ended up on her jaw instead, and that was even worse. His teeth teased over her skin in the faintest of nips, and pleasure tingled all the way to her toes.

"I have to go," she whispered. "Scarlet is waiting for me."

"I know." Mad released her, letting his fingers slide through her hair before stepping back. "She asked me to check on Avery for you. Her patron's house is locked down, but secure."

To Mad or Scarlet, that might mean *safe*. Neither of them would understand that the greatest danger to Avery had always lived within the four walls of the estate—and within her own heart.

That, at least, was a vulnerability Jade never intended to share.

4

T HE BEST THING about Sector Four—and, in turn, about the O'Kanes—wasn't brotherhood or belonging or any of the other shit Dallas liked to trot out in his recruitment speeches. It was *space*.

Not physical space, though Scarlet would be the first person to admit that nothing would drive a person nuts faster than being crammed into two rooms with six other people. No, the most brilliant part of O'Kane's setup was that he gave people space to relax, to be themselves, to pursue hobbies and interests outside of work.

Which was why she was perched on the roof of the main building just before sundown, with a cold beer in one hand and the scent of grilled meat filling the air. Because what the O'Kanes liked to do more than anything else was *party*, even when the party in question was neither violent nor obscene.

Honestly, it was a bit of a marvel. Their collective reputation painted them as savage libertines, only content when they were fighting or fucking. Yet here they were, kicking back at a gathering that most people would consider harmless, even by Eden's rigid moral standards.

"I don't get it," Six said, cradling her own beer between her hands. "I've seen Trix brain a man with a fucking brick. How does she get squeamish over butchering a couple of chickens?"

Scarlet grinned. "Maybe she likes animals more than people. I know I do."

"Then you haven't met many roosters." Six leaned in and lifted her sleeve, showing off a pale, thin scar on the inside of her elbow. "I almost lost a fight to one when I was seven. Those things'll tear you up faster than Bren in a bad mood."

"But they're honest about it. They're never going to smile sweet while they stick a blade between your ribs."

"Fair enough." Six stretched out her legs and slumped back in her chair. "But they taste damn good. Didn't exactly have a lot of chicken in Three, did we?"

"Nope." They never had a lot of anything. Sometimes it was hard to really believe those days were over. It was even harder to let go of them.

"You'll have plenty now." Hawk dropped into the seat beside Scarlet and snagged a beer out of the bucket. "One thing you can count on chickens to do is make more chickens. Things are moving along nicely on the new farm."

Some of Hawk's family—a few sisters, along with a handful of women he'd called his stepmothers—had moved out to the edge of Sector Four and set up a farm over the winter. It was a surprisingly beneficial arrangement for everyone. Dallas gained easier access to the produce and meat he needed, and the women were paid handsomely for their experience and labor.

They were on their own, most of them for the first time, and loving it. Scarlet envied them. What would it be like to get your first taste of independence like that? Where failure meant fewer eggs or not enough strawberries for Dallas's favorite jam, but no one was going to get hurt or starve?

She'd never know.

"One thing I miss?" She winked at Hawk. "Bacon. Tell me your sisters know how to make it."

Hawk grinned. "The first pigs should be old enough in a few weeks. I'll tell them to save you some, if you keep Six from bringing anyone else out on butchering day."

Six made a face and a rude gesture.

Soft laughter came from behind Scarlet as a familiar touch brushed the back of her neck. "I'm glad I made it in time for the family squabble."

"If you missed it, we'd have another one just for you." She reached for Jade's wrist and tumbled her into her lap. "I missed you."

Jade smiled and slid an arm around her shoulders. "I got caught up with Dallas this afternoon. He has me and Noelle going through his files on the council. Again."

"Find anything new on the bastards?" She slipped her fingers into Jade's hair, relishing the feel of the thick, heavy strands.

"Nothing he can use right now." Jade stole Scarlet's beer and took a tiny sip. "Is this Rachel's latest batch? It's good."

"Mmm. I asked her for something a little—" A whistling noise tickled at Scarlet's ears, so out of place and *wrong* that it stopped her cold. "What the fuck is that?"

Jade frowned. "What is what?"

Across the roof, Cruz shot to his feet. "Inside!" he barked. "Everyone get the fuck inside. *Now.*"

Beneath the scrambling footsteps and startled questions, the sound grew louder. It pulled Scarlet to her feet, her away from Jade's frantic hands, toward the edge of the roof.

In the distance, something was tracking through the

wispy clouds, dark against the deep blue and gold of the sunset. Scarlet watched, petrified and cold, so cold, as it arced through the sky.

"Scarlet!"

A scuffle sounded behind her, followed by a soft grunt of pain. Jade reached her side as Cruz shouted, "I've got them. Go!"

The tallest buildings in Three were squat compared to Four, and her vantage point offered her an unobstructed view of the first strike landing in the center of Sector Two. It flared with dust and debris, a giant cloud billowing up with surreal speed. Spellbound, Scarlet stared as hungry fire flickered to life beneath it, traveling out in a perfect circle of blazing orange and red destruction.

Cruz hit Jade first, shoving her into Scarlet before bearing them both to the rough surface of the roof. A split second later, the blast hit with deafening force, rattling the tables and chairs. Scarlet clamped her hands over her ears, not to block out the sound, but the sick chill creeping up her spine.

There would be more. There were always more.

Cruz dragged them both up and to the door. Scarlet scrambled down the stairs in a numb haze, Jade's hand clenched in hers. They stumbled against the wall when another explosion rocked the building, and she met Jade's terrified gaze for one heart-stopping moment.

"Basement," Cruz said tersely, already herding them down the last flight.

Downstairs was chaos. Worried conversation formed an incoherent hum. The cries of Flash and Amira's baby rose above it, loud and scared even though they tried to soothe her.

Movement in the corner drew Scarlet's attention. Mad had both arms locked around a struggling, wild-eyed Lex. "You can't—"

"Adrian, I swear to Christ, if you don't let me go, *I will kill you.*"

Jade's fingers clamped around Scarlet's wrist like iron. "We have to go. The girls in the houses—" Her voice cracked.

"We can't," Dallas said, brushing past Scarlet to reach Mad and Lex. He gripped her shoulders. "They're still dropping bombs."

Lex went still, her expression one of agonized torment. "Declan."

"I know, darling." He shifted his touch to her face, cupping her cheeks. "Cruz and Bren are gathering supplies. As soon as the skies clear, we'll be over there."

"No." She clawed at his wrists, though she didn't pull away. "It'll be too late. You know they'll only stop when it's too late."

Dallas dragged her into his arms and held tight.

Scarlet recognized the look in Lex's eyes—the hopelessness, the sheer, impotent rage. She'd lived it before, and it tugged at her now, reaching straight through her shock to wrap an icy hand around her throat.

Her vision wobbled and went black around the edges as the memories rose like a wave of nausea. The first jarring impact that had startled her out of her bed. The shock wave that had shattered the windows, slicing her face and arms. Fighting through streets as bright as day, alight with the sick, hot glow of burning buildings. Screams and sobs, terror and confusion.

Standing outside the factory where her father worked—or the hole where it once had been. Looking up into a solemn, wrinkled face, wet with tears. *Don't look*, the old man had told her gravely. *It's nothin' you need to see.*

The blackness swallowed her, blotting out the world for a moment. She swayed, and strong arms enveloped her, along with the scent of leather and wood and whiskey.

Mad. "Breathe for me, Scarlet."

She couldn't. The darkness was closing in, cinching around her.

"Scarlet." Jade framed her face, her hands comforting and familiar. "Look at me."

Oh, Christ. Jade grew up in Two. She had *friends* there, and Scarlet was the one giving in to weakness. "I'm sorry," she mumbled, her voice cracking. She steeled her voice and tried again. "I'm sorry, baby."

"Shh." Jade leaned in, burying her face against Scarlet's throat. Mad's arms tightened, leaving Scarlet surrounded by warmth. "How old were you?"

She couldn't talk about that, couldn't *think* about it. "I have to get out of here."

"You can't," Mad said softly. "Not yet."

The door scraped open, and Bren came in. Six met him in the doorway, and he embraced her before lowering his voice to speak to Dallas. "The drones have withdrawn."

"Is it safe to go out, or could they come back?"

"They can do whatever the fuck they want," Bren growled, then sighed. "Sorry. I don't know. Maybe they'll come back for a second wave, maybe they won't. It's impossible to tell."

"They didn't in Three." Scarlet's voice cut through the tense silence, startling even her. "They dropped the bombs and never looked back."

Dallas hesitated another heartbeat before releasing Lex. "Mad, get to One. Talk to your cousin. We're going to need help. Jas, organize teams. And send someone to find Doc and sober him up. Lex—"

"*Declan.*"

"*Alexa,*" he replied, voice firm. "You, Bren, and Six gear up. We're going to get your sister."

She stared up at him, naked adoration warring with gratitude. "Together."

"Damn right, darling. Now move."

She hurried out of the basement, with Bren and Six hard on her heels, and Dallas turned to face Scarlet and Jade. "You know that sector, Jade. We could use you there, if you think you can do it."

Jade straightened and nodded, cool and collected except for the painful grip she still had on Scarlet's hand. "I can handle it."

If she could set aside her fear, so could Scarlet. "Me, too."

"Good." Dallas squeezed Scarlet's shoulder.

She suppressed a wince. The last thing she wanted to do was walk into hell. She was a selfish fucking asshole, but she couldn't help it. She'd fought so hard to put the darkness behind her, and now here it was, threatening to swallow her whole.

But Jade was going, and more than ancient history awaited her in the burning rubble. The least Scarlet could do was be there for her, to help make sure the memories she found today could turn into scars, not nightmares.

 lex

WHEN AVERY WAS little, no more than four or five years old, she'd fallen while running—she was always running somewhere—and skinned her leg. The abrasion wasn't deep, but it was wide and ugly, welling enough blood to terrify a child.

She refused to try and walk on such an impressive injury, so Lex carried her, even though she wasn't much older. Nearly half a mile, with Avery's tiny, trembling arms wrapped around her neck.

Lex heaved another shattered slab of cement out of the way, and a sharp edge sliced her palm. Her fingers had already been scraped raw, but the pain was inconsequential. Unimportant. All that mattered was finding Avery.

It had taken them far too long to find her patron's small compound in the midst of the sector. Even knowing its exact location didn't help, because such total destruction completely changed the landscape. There were no trees or signs left, no streets that weren't buried in two feet of rubble from the collapsed buildings on either side.

By the time they found Gordon's house, the minutes had already ticked into hours, and Lex could feel their chances slipping through her bleeding fingers.

Dallas tugged her away from the huge piece of rubble she was trying to lift. "Let Bren and Flash move that one. You're going to hurt yourself, Lex."

"Hurt." She laughed. Nothing hurt as much as not knowing.

Dallas wrapped his arms around her and pulled her back a few steps, giving Flash space to slip past her. Heavy gloves protected his huge hands, and he didn't have to wait for Bren. With a grunt and a heave, he lifted the concrete out of the way.

"Let him dig for a minute." Dallas forced Lex to face him. "Let me check your hand."

"It's fine. Nothing a little med-gel won't fix. Later." Later, when she wasn't consumed by dread, by thoughts of what lay under the shattered remains of Gordon's house. When she wasn't scanning every inch of the debris for a hint of life.

He pried her fingers open anyway, and wiped away the blood with his thumb. "We'll dig until there's not a damn stone left to move, darling. But if you keep hurting yourself, you're going back to Four over Flash's shoulder."

He'd do it, too, she had no doubt about that. So she opened her mouth to agree, but a shout from Bren cut her off. "Over here!"

Her heart didn't leap into her throat or sink into her belly or any of the other flowery phrases she'd always heard. It seized, shuddered to a stop, and only seeing what Bren had uncovered—the probably *terrible*, *awful* thing he'd uncovered—had even a chance of starting it up again.

Avery's patron lay there in the shattered glass and pulverized brick, facedown, still and pale under the fine coating of ash that clung to his skin and hair. But the sight didn't kick-start her heart—it *froze* it.

One of the man's hands had been crushed, and his fingers curled at odd, unnatural angles, stiff and rigid. Lex stared, consumed by the memory of watching those fingers drift lovingly through her sister's hair.

She sank to her knees and started to dig again. "She's close," she choked out. "She has to be. She wouldn't leave him."

Dallas dropped next to her and silently began to help. Flash and Six joined them, forming a line that shifted rubble faster. They freed Gordon's body, and Lex squeezed her eyes shut as Bren and Flash carried him toward a clear area at the edge of what used to be the street.

A thud jarred her eyes open. It was muffled, so faint that it sounded far away, but it shook her hard enough to snap her teeth together.

"Lex!" Six swiped debris away with her leather-clad arm and rapped on the surface beneath—not concrete or wood but steel. "There's a vault or something down here."

A floor safe, the kind popular in the city as well as the more affluent sectors. It was the kind of security measure people used to protect their most prized possessions from theft and loss. And Gordon had shoved her sister into one.

Her morbid, relieved humor evaporated when she realized it wasn't just shut. It was *locked.*

"No." Once upon a time, she'd survived by breaking into safes exactly like this one. And she was damn good at it—when she had her tools. But her sensors and drills were back in Four, shoved into the depths of a closet. It would take time to send someone for them, time—and air—her sister might not have.

Lex pounded on the dented metal and screamed.

"Lex—" Six nudged a tattered, leather-bound book off the door's surface. "Look."

Beneath the book, shielded from the dust and debris, lay tacky smears of blood. At first, it looked like Gordon had been clawing at the door, but when Lex examined the

surface more closely, she could make out a series of numbers—smeared, shaky, but still legible.

"Oh my God." She punched the numbers into the key-
pad, but her hands were shaking so badly that she fucked
it up, and the lock buzzed angrily. She took a deep breath
and tried again, more slowly this time, and the bolt gave
way with an audible *click*.

"Let me." Six gripped the handle. Bracing her weight,
she pried the door up.

Avery clung to a narrow ladder, her pale face inches
from the door, her bare feet slipping off the rungs. When
she spoke, it was on a ragged sob. "Alexa—"

Lex hauled her up, spilling them both back on the
ground. Glass cut through her jeans and into her legs, but
Lex didn't care. Her sister had survived, and that was all
that mattered.

5

"You're all right, Olivia." After fifteen hours of breathing the dust in Sector Two, Jade was hoarse, and it was a struggle to keep her tone soft and soothing. "I know it hurts, but he's almost done."

Fear lined Olivia's young features, but she dug her teeth into her lower lip and turned her face away from where Dylan concentrated on stitching up the gash on her arm.

They'd run out of med-gel two hours before dawn. The painkillers were long gone, and no one knew how quickly Finn would be able to coax more out of the new leader of Sector Five.

Hours of digging out the rare survivors—and the far more frequent dead—had left everyone in a state of numb exhaustion. Half the O'Kanes had gone back to Four to recover enough for a second day of rescue operations.

But Jade couldn't stop. She couldn't leave. Not when

the girls she'd known since they were children were bleeding and suffering and *dying*.

Olivia sucked in a pained breath as Dylan started on
the next stitch, and Jade touched the girl's cheek with a
soothing murmur. She'd scrubbed her hands clean so
many times they were raw, but that was a minor discomfort, one she'd stopped feeling a lifetime ago.

"It hurts," Olivia whispered, squeezing her eyes shut.

"I know, honey, but you're doing so well." She stroked
the dusty hair back from Olivia's forehead and tried not to
remember the girl the first day she'd come to Orchid
House. Nine years old, with huge eyes and the shyest,
sweetest smile Jade had ever seen.

Unprotected and defenseless, just like all the girls
who ended up in the four Houses.

Except Jade.

She didn't have to close her eyes. The memory was as
vivid as the day it had happened, burned into her heart as
much as her mind. The long, curving walkway lined with
rosebushes that ended at a massive wooden door carved
with even more roses. Her mother's hand, tight around her
own. The tension in that beloved voice as she knelt and
gripped Jade's shoulders.

*"This is not home. This will never be home. Remember
that, Jyoti."*

"I'll remember."

"And what's your name while you live here?"

"Jade."

It had taken her years to understand why her mother
had insisted on giving her a new name. At seven, she'd
simply been afraid. Afraid of losing the comfortable house
she'd been born in, afraid of the pain in her mother's eyes
when she asked about her father.

But she'd taken the new name, and with it a new iden-
tity. She'd wrapped it around herself like armor, and by
the time she was fifteen and mourning her mother's death,
she no longer questioned.

When your name was the only thing that belonged to you, you held it as close as your heart.

In the years that followed, that armor solidified around her. She achieved what her mother had planned for her all along—enough wealth to secure independence, and a freedom beyond anything she'd known in Sector Two.

But the armor wouldn't come off.

"Jade."

That's not my name.

"Jade." Firmer this time, accompanied by a strong yet gentle hand on her cheek.

She blinked and found herself staring up into Dylan's warm brown eyes. Her hands were limp in her lap. Olivia was gone, and she couldn't remember her departure.

Honestly, that was for the best. She wasn't sure she could survive remembering this night anyway.

She licked her chapped lips. "Who's next?"

"No one," he answered heavily. "You need to rest."

Scarlet had said the same, and Jade repeated her answer. "The girls know me. I can keep them calm."

"This isn't optional." His voice turned into pure steel as he rose and fetched a blanket from one of the packs the O'Kanes had brought. "You're going to eat and lie down for a while, or I'll haul you back to Four and make you do it there."

She couldn't even feel the cold. She'd skated past numb with her first glimpse of Orchid House—or what was left of it. As they'd dug through the debris, she'd talked herself hoarse soothing terrified girls who were trapped, trying not to think about the fact that there were three more houses filled with equally scared children.

There wasn't time to rest. But when Dylan returned, she couldn't fight past her numbness to argue. "I could use something to drink."

Dylan placed one hand on the small of her back. "The Riders brought water."

The bikers from Sector One had arrived on the scene at the same time as the O'Kanes, and they'd come prepared. Within half an hour, they'd erected tents and organized triage stations before turning their seemingly endless determination toward unearthing survivors.

The nearest tent was only a few hundred feet away. Jade gathered her strength, which was really nothing more than stubbornness at this point, and stood as gracefully as she could manage. Dylan's hand blazed on her back, hot enough to make her wary.

If she staggered, if she stumbled, he would catch her. And when that solid warmth wrapped around her, her numbness would fracture.

The Rider in charge was standing outside the tent, counting rolls of bandages. Deacon was a tall man, broad through the shoulders, with brown hair shot through with hints of red—and a permanent frown etched between his eyebrows.

The muscles in one arm flexed as he heaved a box out of the way and lifted another into its place. "You okay?" he asked Jade.

Telling men what they wanted to hear was as reflexive as breathing, and most men revealed their desires with every breath. But not Deacon, nor any of the other Riders. They were shrill dissonance, a jarring mix of selfless pacifism and ruthless violence.

Mad scraped at her that way sometimes, too.

"I'll manage," she said finally, willing it to be truth. She had to manage. She simply would allow no alternative.

"You look like shit."

Dylan stepped between them and smiled at Deacon, the charming, lopsided grin he only used when he wanted something. "Is this tent free?" Instead of waiting for an answer, he pulled Jade toward one of the smaller rest tents.

Inside was a stack of cases of bottled water, some

boxes of rations, and a single cot. He snatched up one bottle, opened it, and held it out. "Gideon's people are
assholes."

Deacon could undoubtedly hear him, and Jade
frowned. "Obviously you agree with him, or you wouldn't
have forced me to stop."

"You're exhausted, and you're starting to exhibit
symptoms of an acute stress reaction." He pointed to the
cot. "Sit."

It wasn't a seductive word. It was sibilant to start and
cut off harshly, but Dylan's voice wrapped around it with
implacable gentleness. Even worse was the knowledge in
his eyes, his awareness of the weight of this moment. He
knew what the command would do to her, how it would
sing to her.

Raw and exposed, she sat.

He crouched in front of her, so that she had to look
down at him. "You're going to want to push yourself," he
began, his voice even lower, gentler. "Because there's so
much to do, so many people who need help. But you can't.
If you don't take care of yourself first, you'll burn out, or
worse."

He was right. In his place, she'd be saying the same
thing. Preservation of resources was logical, and she was
a valuable resource when it came to Sector Two. But when
she closed her eyes...

"They're just girls," she whispered hoarsely. "Children. Why would Eden kill *children*?"

His answer was flat, as if it was simply a fact he'd
learned long ago and was repeating by rote. "Because they
can."

She reached for him blindly. Her forehead bumped his
cheek, and she turned her face into his throat, as if she
could hide her tears.

So much life. So much potential. So many bright lights
snuffed out before they'd had a chance to taste freedom,

all because Eden couldn't tolerate having less than everything.

"Shh." His lips brushed her temple, and he folded his arms around her, anchoring her against the solid strength of his chest. "We'll do what we can, Jade. *Everything* we can. I swear it."

If anyone else had witnessed this fracture in her control, it would have been intolerable. But there was nothing left to hide from Dylan. He'd watched her claw her way back to life through the agony of drug withdrawal, a withdrawal everyone had assumed would kill her.

Those weeks were blessedly blurry. Fevers and nightmares, day after day when she threw up everything she tried to eat. She'd grown weak by the end, hallucinating people who were long dead—her mother, one of the girls from her classes who'd taken a razor blade into the communal bathroom and ended it all, even her first trainer, who'd been turned out of Rose House for trying to teach the girls some measure of inner strength.

But the fingers running through her hair now were achingly familiar. She'd wondered sometimes if she'd hallucinated his kindness, too, because Dylan was always so cool and detached during her lucid periods. Sometimes he was even high himself.

But she knew his touch. She knew the soft warmth of his fingertips on her cheek, the way his voice rasped when he lowered it to whisper reassurances.

Maybe that explained her terrifying weakness for him, the way her body thrilled at his tender commands. After seven years of playing flawlessly at submission, she'd been so sure she understood the nuances of power games. But she'd only ever played for survival.

Dylan would demand something she'd guarded more closely. Her trust.

After two days, *search and rescue* was turning into *search and recovery*.

Tendrils of damp hair had escaped her ponytail. Scarlet finished washing her hands and brushed her hair off her face as she surveyed the base camp Dallas and Gideon had set up. At least the sight didn't kindle that familiar, choking panic in the back of her throat. When fire had rained down on Three, there were no coordinated efforts, no men and women with tents and boxes of food and collapsible jugs of clean water. Just a few scattered individuals, helping out as best they could.

Coming here, she'd been so worried about how she would deal with her memories, only to find that there were none, not for her.

Jade was another story. Scarlet had watched her, helpless, as every passing hour had drawn her tension and agony tighter and tighter, until it looked like she might break, fold in on herself until she vanished completely. She'd been on the verge of taking Jade away herself—even if they had to leave and keep going, away from the sectors altogether—when Dallas had sent Jade on to One to help set up the temporary hospital.

As long as Jade was away from all this, Scarlet would stay and move bloody bricks and busted cement forever.

"Here." Mad appeared beside her and held out a bottle of water. "There's stew at the main tent."

"I ate already." Just a rations bar, but it fit the bill. She wasn't hungry anyway, so let the people who were have a hot meal. "What about you?"

His smile was a sad echo of his usual grin. "Lili wouldn't give me the news from Eden until I'd had two bowls."

The mention of Eden did what the rubble couldn't. Scarlet's heart started thumping painfully, and she forced herself to slowly count to three before replying. "And what is the news?"

"Nothing." When she didn't take the water, he twisted

off the cap and took a long swig. "It makes me nervous. I figured they'd be clogging the vid network with propaganda before the dust settled."

"Probably scrambling to think of a way to spin a bunch of hookers and kids as an imminent security threat."

"They'll find a way." He drained the rest of the water. "But something must have happened to spook them, or they wouldn't have gone forward without all that in place."

He had far more faith in the city and its leaders than she ever did. "Are you—?"

"Excuse me." A man stood a few feet away, his reddish-blond hair dirty with soot, his blue eyes fixed on Mad as if he were staring at the gates of heaven. "Can I get you another bottle of water?"

Mad's expression froze into a polite mask. "I'm fine, thank you."

The redhead shifted his weight nervously. "I could take the empty one away for you."

After a moment's hesitation, Mad extended his hand and offered him the bottle. "Thank you."

"It's an honor. An honor to serve." The man thrust out his right arm in obvious pride. His shirt was rolled up past the elbow, and an elaborate tattoo covered his forearm—a woman with ethereal features and wild, flowing black hair entwined with roses. Her hands met in front of her vivid blue dress, cradling a glowing heart between them.

At the sight of it, Mad's jaw tightened. But he only smiled stiffly. "It's beautiful work. Del's, isn't it?"

Beaming, the man nodded. "Sponsored by Maricela herself."

"If you did her a service, then I'm grateful."

"It's an honor," he said again, and for a second Scarlet thought he was about to drop to his knees in front of Mad. Instead he touched the tattoo, his eyes worried. "Our youngest wife... She's having a difficult time with her first pregnancy."

A muscle in Mad's jaw worked. He reached out and

covered the other man's hand. "I'll ask her to look after your wife."

The redhead dropped into a low bow. "Thank you. Thank you, bless you."

The man hurried away, almost stumbling in his haste. Scarlet held her tongue until she was out of earshot, just barely, and then the words exploded out of her. "Okay, what the fuck was that?"

Mad laughed harshly as he turned. "That was a man with a tattoo of my dead mother on his arm, asking me for her blessing."

Scarlet had teased him about the blessings—mercilessly, even—but the tense scene that had just played out before her was anything but funny. "I'm sorry."

He shrugged one shoulder. "Whoever he is, he deserves a little comfort. Maricela's my cousin. If she paid for his tattoo, he's a good person."

"Yeah, that's not the part I'm sorry about." If people followed her around all eight sectors, waving tattoos of her dead father in her face, she wouldn't be so casual about it. Something told her Mad wasn't, either. "Hey."

He didn't look at her. "Can we find a tent? If I stand here, more people will come over."

With most of the survivors already moved to Sector One, there were plenty of tents. Scarlet had claimed one away from the aid stations. She dragged Mad there, zipped the flap behind them, and shoved a flask into his hand.

He stared at it for an endless moment before taking a drink. "All they want is a few seconds of my time. I'm the only one in the family who resents them for it."

Because it hurt. He didn't have to say so, not with the pain etched across his face. "If you're the only one who resents it, then I think you're the only one who's human."

"Maybe just the only one who knows any other kind of life." He passed the flask back to her. "Sometimes I want to go back there and smuggle Maricela out. Gideon would murder me, but I still think about it."

Scarlet drank, too. "Does she want out?"

"No." For the first time, his smile was real. "She's stubborn. She wants to protect the world."

"Must take after you, then."

He reached for the flask, but his fingers wrapped around hers, rough and warm. "I don't want to protect the world. Just my corner of it."

Gods and saints didn't limit themselves to tiny corners. She opened her mouth to tell him so, but he was *staring* at her with those dark, dark eyes, watching her with an intensity that prickled over her skin.

At first, she'd told herself that flirting with Mad was a way to keep him humble. When that excuse fell apart, she figured that Jade was interested, so any way she could get under Mad's skin was preparation for the inevitable day he tumbled into their bed.

It was all bullshit. Scarlet flirted with him because she wanted to flirt with him.

Because she wanted him.

Mad tugged the flask toward his lips without releasing her hand. His gaze held hers as he slowly drank.

Don't, Scarlet. The words echoed in her head, but they seemed far away. Trivial, because Mad was so close, so warm. His eyes promised sheer pleasure, and after two days of numbness punctuated by despair and terror, she needed it.

She reached out with her free hand and pulled his hair.

He hissed and tossed the flask aside. Before it hit the ground he had an arm around her waist, dragging her against the hard bulk of his body. "You like to fuck mean, don't you?"

"I'm not afraid of it." His hair was so damn soft, and her vicious tug somehow turned into a caress.

Mad stroked a hand up her side, ruthlessly gentle even when it wrapped around her throat. "You like it. Does

Jade?"

Of course it came down to that. Scarlet sympathized—you'd have to be dead, fucking six feet under, not to want to get your hands on Jade. "She likes sweet." Scarlet slid her hands over his shoulders, matching her movements to her words. "Soft."

He leaned closer, his warm mouth almost touching hers, his fingers tightening on her neck. "So be mean to me."

Not tonight, maybe not in a million years. Definitely not until Jade was there to take over when Mad had had enough of her being rough. "No."

"Damn it, Scarlet," he murmured, just a whisper of breath that barely formed words before he kissed her.

Soft. Sweet.

But only for a heartbeat. Then he tilted his head and drove deeper, gliding his tongue over hers, and the tiny flutter in Scarlet's belly turned into a clench of need. She moaned and gripped his shoulders harder, using the leverage to wrap her legs around his hips.

He broke away with a groan and pressed his forehead to hers. "We can't do this. You know why we can't do this."

"Because of Jade?" Their bodies were still pressed tightly together, so she eased one hand between them and slid it down toward his belt buckle. "Jade wants to be right here."

His fingers flexed on her hips. "Did she tell you?"

"She didn't have to." Scarlet wrapped her fingers around the leather. "I know what gets my girlfriend off."

"Did she tell you I kissed her?"

She blinked at him. Not because she was shocked that it happened—sooner or later, it was bound to—but because Jade hadn't said a word. "When? How?"

"The day they dropped the bombs." His lips brushed her cheek, and she couldn't understand why he was smiling until he murmured, "Well, first she held a knife to my balls."

"Should've known that would turn you on."

His hands settled at the small of her back. "But she stopped. I figured it was because of you. I don't want to screw up whatever you have going on."

"That's sweet." Scarlet arched an eyebrow. "But if that was a thing, Jade never would have let you kiss her. And I wouldn't be in your lap right now."

He shrugged. "The world's falling apart. Again. Sometimes, when that happens, people do things they end up regretting."

Oh, but he was so quick to assume he fell into that category. "Is that what you and Dylan are doing—stockpiling regrets?"

"I only regret it when I hurt someone." His thumb edged under her shirt, warm against her skin. "I don't know what Dylan regrets. Sometimes I think he's in love with Jade. And sometimes I don't think he gives a shit about anything."

Scarlet had always leaned more toward the latter, though it was getting harder and harder to dismiss the man outright. Sometimes, a glint of agonized humanity broke through his nonchalant façade—and the drug haze—and her heart ached for him.

The rest of the time, all she knew was that he was a time bomb, primed and ticking.

Mad continued, as if he heard her doubts. "He's good on the inside, better than anyone. But I'm not enough to hold him together."

And Mad wanted to save him, because Mad wanted to save the world. She snorted. "If you're thinking Jade and I can get it done, just stop right now. Doc and I aren't exactly on the same page about...well, anything."

"You might be right now," he murmured. "I have to go to Sector One soon. You should come with me. Dylan needs help protecting Jade from herself."

It would have been nice if he'd wanted her to come along because he liked her company, but Scarlet would take what she could get. "Okay."

"If we go to One…" He took a deep breath and exhaled slowly.

She filled in the silence. "Don't sweat it. I'll stay out of your way."

His hands tightened again, dragging her closer, and he buried his face in her hair. "Don't," he whispered hoarsely. "Jade's hurting, Dylan's focused on work. You'll be the only person in the damn sector who sees *me*."

The naked need in his voice shook her. It wasn't physical, like the erection still pressing between her thighs. It came from someplace deeper, more vulnerable.

So she held him. "All right. It's all right. I'll be there for you *and* Jade."

"Good." He pulled back and gave her a lopsided smile. "Someone's got to keep my ego deflated over there."

Somehow she didn't think that would be a problem. He could joke about his ego, but there had to be a reason he was in Sector Four. It seemed like a place where he could forget the fact that he was destined for sainthood, that there were people who worshipped him as the living embodiment of their god's will on Earth.

Maybe even forget that he hated all of that, ego be damned.

6

A S HEARTBREAKING AS the makeshift Sector One hospital was, Mad would have given anything to stay there with Scarlet and Dylan and Jade.

Duty had other plans for him.

Mad clenched his hands around the steering wheel, acutely aware of Lex's presence beside him as he started up the gravel drive that led to the Rios estate. Trees lined either side of the path, trees planted before Mad's birth. They towered now, only letting light through in teasing patches, hiding the orchards and gardens that circled the estate.

They couldn't hide the residence itself. Mad tensed as they pulled into the open drive in front of the main building—three stories and two wings of stucco and stained glass. An embarrassment of luxury.

"Goddamn," Lex muttered under her breath. "We're in

the wrong business, Declan. Looks like being a self-proclaimed prophet is what really pays."

Dallas laughed. "I'm wounded, Lex. If I wanted a pretty house, I could convince people to build me one. I just have better priorities."

"So does Gideon," Bren said. "This place was here long before he took over."

"My grandfather built it," Mad confirmed as he parked the car. "The rule of Sector One is pacifism. So murderers are banished or executed, of course, but killing in self-defense is still a mark on your soul, like a million other sins. The only way to remove it is by doing penance. Seven years of service to the Prophet or the temple." And the continuing supply of unpaid labor had built the many marvels of Sector One.

Lex peered up at the towering front entrance as she pushed open her door. "Well, Grandpa made out like a bandit."

He'd done more than that. He'd ingrained the idea of loyal work washing a soul clean into the culture of Sector One so firmly that Gideon had been unable to abolish the practice. His boldest attempt had resulted in a panicked month of supplicants arriving at the house, begging to be set to a task.

In the end, he'd used that to his advantage. He'd gathered his flock at their most holy of shrines and congratulated them for passing the test given to them by God. By refusing to set aside their penance, they'd proven themselves worthy of forgiveness. One year was the new standard, and Gideon had done his best to use their willing labor for things that benefited the sector as a whole.

Mad still couldn't tell if Gideon had planned it that way from the start. Underestimating his cousin's capacity for quiet cunning was a good way to get played.

By the time Mad slipped from the car, the double front doors had opened. Maricela came running out, a flash of white against the Saltillo tile. "Adrian!"

For a brief moment, the weight on his shoulders lifted. He opened his arms and caught her as she barreled into him, and even though she was too old for it now, he couldn't resist lifting her off her feet and spinning her around.

Gideon's youngest sister had been just a sweet-faced child when Mad left Sector One behind, and sometimes she still was in his mind. But she'd grown up in between his sporadic visits, and the woman he set back down on the driveway had all the dignity of an adult who knew her own power—and the responsibility that came with it.

Mindful of that dignity—and the fact that this was her first time playing hostess to other sector leaders—he bit back the urge to ruffle her hair. Instead he released her and turned them both around. "Dallas, Lex—this is Gideon's sister, Maricela."

Lex held out her hand. "It's nice to meet you."

Maricela stared at her, awestruck. "Lex Parrino. It's such a pleasure to finally meet you. I mean, the things you've done, especially for the girls in Two—" She cut off and clapped a hand over her mouth. "I'm sorry! Before. I meant...before."

Only an O'Kane could have noticed the tension in Lex's eyes as she smiled. "Gideon told me that his baby sister is adorable. Looks like he's an honest man."

Dallas held out his hand and waited for Maricela to extend hers. Instead of shaking it, he bent and brushed a kiss over the back of it, effectively diverting attention from the verbal misstep and the pain it had caused Lex. "He didn't do you justice."

The full force of Dallas's most charming smile slammed into Maricela. She blushed violently, and it took her a moment to speak. "Please, come in. Gideon's expecting you."

They followed her through the wide doors, into a foyer that managed to be even more opulent than the exterior of the house suggested. Delicately woven rugs covered the tile floor, and every bit of furniture and decor had been lovingly handcrafted. Nothing scavenged, nothing pre-Flare—and nothing that required electricity.

Gideon waited for them at the base of the curved staircase with a smile that seemed effortless and genuine. "Dallas, Lex. Bren. Welcome to my home. Jim and Ryder are already upstairs, if you'll follow me."

They started after him, but Mad hung back and turned to Maricela. "Is there a guest suite free?"

Her brow furrowed. "I've already set them up, Adrian."

This was a bad idea. His skin crawled at the idea of having Dylan and Jade and Scarlet under the roof his grandfather had built on the backs of the devoted. But it was the most secure place in the sector, and it was even worse to imagine them anywhere else. "Not for Dallas and Lex. I have some friends helping out with the refugees who need a place to stay."

"Oh. Yes, absolutely." She brightened, a little of her awkwardness from outside fading. "I get to meet your friends?"

Guilt sliced deep. It took so little to make her so fucking *happy*, and he hated himself for letting his shame over their grandfather's actions come between them. "Yeah, you do. Has Gideon told you about Jade?"

This time, she wrinkled her nose at him in exasperation. "I don't need to be told. Everyone knows about Jade and her houses."

Everyone except him, apparently. "Houses?"

"The ones she built for the girls who left the Garden. Two so far, with a third planned." She bit her lip. "We'll have to speed up work on that one now."

Mad's focus had always been on helping the Riders smuggle the girls out of Two. He knew that Jade had given Gideon money to help them start new lives, just as Lex had done before her, but Gideon had never mentioned the extent of Jade's involvement in those new lives.

It was something he'd have to ask her about—later. "Well, she's one of them. And her friend Scarlet, and a doc- tor, Dylan. I have to get to this meeting, but can you send someone over to the hospital to bring them here when they're ready?"

She laid a hand on his cheek. "Anything for my favor- ite cousin. I'll send my personal guard, and everything will be ready for them when they arrive."

"Thanks, love." He swooped down to kiss her forehead before turning and taking the stairs two at a time.

Gideon's meeting room was on the north side of the house. It was graced with floor-to-ceiling windows that af- forded a breathless view of the back garden and let in as much natural light as possible. Solar panels on the roof stored energy in battery packs that could be used in an emergency, but most of the Rios estate remained as their grandfather had originally built it—safely off the grid and reliant on candles and manpower over electricity and ma- chinery.

It was sunny out today, leaving the office bright and welcoming. The group gathered around the long polished table was less so. Gideon sat at the head of the table, his expression still pleasantly relaxed, but stress showed in the creases around his eyes.

To his right sat Ryder, the newly proclaimed leader of Sector Five. He had black hair, brown eyes, dark brown skin, and chiseled features so perfectly formed he gave Jared stiff competition. His attractiveness was enhanced by the quiet power of his presence. He'd dressed in black slacks and a crisp white shirt, and the only flaw in his out- fit was a slightly rumpled collar, indicating he'd already tugged off a tie.

Next to him was Jim, the long-time leader of Sector Eight. Jim was wearing a suit too, though not as effort- lessly as Ryder managed. He had more silver in his hair than the last time Mad had seen him, along with more lines bracketing his eyes. Jim's sector had benefited from the destruction of Sector Three by becoming Eden's only source of manufacturing—too vital to destroy. He had to be wondering who benefited from *this* destruction...and how it would hurt him.

Dallas and Lex sat across from them, with Bren a silent shadow behind them, and Mad slipped into the chair next to Lex's as Gideon finished his summary of events. "I judged the current situation too pressing to wait for Colby and Scott to overcome their internal issues. If anyone has a problem with this..."

Dallas made a rude noise. "Their votes have been cancelling each other out since they climbed into their daddies' chairs. We'll get more done without their bickering bullshit."

Jim regarded them with a mild expression. "They do seem determined to render themselves ineffective, don't they?"

"Unfortunately." Gideon studied them all with an aura of unflappable calm that Mad had never been able to emulate. "We each have our well-guarded sources of information. I suggest now is the time to share anything we know about why this happened."

Jim's features hardened. "The one person who could tell us is gone."

Lex leaned forward in her chair. "We don't know that. We still haven't found Cerys's body—"

It was Jim's turn to snort. "Body? You won't find one. Cerys was in the wind before the bombs fell."

Dallas raised an eyebrow. "Is that speculation or inside knowledge?"

"I had an agent in Orchid House. Does that surprise you, O'Kane?"

"Not really." Dallas glanced at Ryder. "It's a habit of yours."

Jim only smiled. "What they wanted is irrelevant. What matters is that they were willing to wipe the Council's personal playground off the map. If they'll go that far, none of us is safe." He paused. "That means it's time to act."

"You ready to lead the charge against the walls of heaven?" Dallas drawled, before tilting his head toward Gideon. "No offense."

"I'm not offended." Gideon shrugged easily. "Heaven is beyond the reach of men who slaughter innocents. Eden is earthly, and very, very mortal."

"And I was ready forty goddamn years ago," Jim growled. "The problem then? Everyone wanted to wait and see how things shook out before making a move. I think we've answered that question."

Mad knew Dallas agreed with him. Everyone in the O'Kane inner circle understood, though they left it unspoken. Sometimes Mad thought the reason they all lived and loved so damn hard was because they could feel it just around the corner—the end of the eternal party. The moment when everything changed, because they were balanced on the edge of a cliff and a gust of wind could send them tumbling over.

"That's dangerous talk," Dallas said slowly. "Way more dangerous if you don't sleep surrounded by all the factories that make the pretty baubles Eden can't live without."

"That's an excellent point." Even when he spoke quietly, Ryder's voice filled the room. He rose, walked to the window, and stared out at the gardens. "Jim and I are the ones with sectors Eden will want to preserve. But you're the ones who can hurt them the most."

"How do you figure?"

Ryder turned. "We have goods they want. Factories they can use. But all they have to do is get rid of us, take over our facilities, and no one would notice. You? You're a legend. If they shoot you in the fucking head, *everyone* will notice."

Lex stared at him with a dawning look of comprehension. "And Eden will have made a martyr."

He nodded. "With Gideon, that may as well be literal. Can you imagine how the faithful would rise up?"

Gideon didn't have to imagine, and neither did Mad. The faithful had risen up once before—not against Eden, but against detractors within their own sector. They'd torn through their enemies in a holy rage, seeking vengeance on those who'd spilled the blood of their beloved Adriana.

And Gideon was looking thoughtful.

"No," Mad rasped roughly. "Don't put those ideas in his head."

"Mad—" Gideon began.

"*No*," he repeated more forcefully. "Before you decide to walk into a hail of bullets for the good of the revolution, you better pick your successor. Because it won't be me. You'll be dumping this sector and the whole damn war on Isabela. Or God, on Maricela. Is that what you want?"

Gideon lifted one hand in a placating gesture. "I'm not planning on dying."

Which didn't mean he wouldn't take advantage of the first damn opportunity. He was as crazy as his Riders, with one foot already in the grave.

Before Mad could say as much, Dallas rapped his knuckles on the table. "Listen, martyrs and holy revolutions are nice and all, but while our loyal followers are trying to take the wall apart with their bare hands, Eden will be dropping bombs on them. Talk about taking a knife to a gunfight."

"Painfully true." Lex shrugged. "We may have dreams, but they have a well-trained, well-supplied army. One that just laid a sector to waste."

"That's something we'll have to figure out," Jim allowed. "Look, I'm not asking you to suit up tomorrow. What I need to know is, when the time comes, are you in?"

Dallas looked at Lex for a long moment. "We're sympathetic," he said finally. "But I'm not Gideon. I run a gang, not a religion. They didn't sign on for war, and I refuse to make that call without talking to them first."

"Someone should be here to speak for Sector Two," Gideon said. "Lex?"

She shook her head. "They can't think about anything like this right now. They're just trying to survive."

Gideon inclined his head. "What do we tell Scott and Colby?"

"We don't," Jim said. "Eden has increased tithes on Sectors Six and Seven again, and the farm workers have done the math. By the time they give the city their portion of the harvest this fall, there won't be enough left to carry them through. They're already rebelling, refusing to sow the fields, and I don't blame them. They're staring down death either way."

Dallas tapped his fingers against the polished wood. "You don't sound worried. Can I assume you made plans for this eventuality?"

The man's frown deepened. "Of course I did. But I'm not looking forward to watching two sectors full of people starve to death."

"You going soft on us, Jim?"

"Dallas," Gideon chided.

"Sorry." Dallas leaned forward. "What if I said I have someone? He has enough sway to talk people into putting crops in the ground...*if* he could tell them they might get a chance to keep some of the harvest."

"That gives us a timeline," Ryder noted.

"Yes, it does." Jim rose and buttoned his suit jacket. "I'm willing to make that promise."

Dallas got up as well. "Then maybe we should meet again in a week or two. Make a list of our respective assets so everyone knows where we stand. And then I'll make some promises of my own."

Ryder sighed. "In the meantime, I'll be sending medical supplies for your hospital, Gideon."

"They're appreciated." Gideon extended his hand. "If your men need an escort, mine are available."

"We'll make it, but thanks."

"Good." Gideon waved an arm toward the door. "I'll walk you out."

As soon as the echo of their footsteps had faded, Dallas dropped back into his chair with a groan. "Jesus Christ."

Lex stared at the polished surface of the table. "Not to freak anyone out," she said faintly, "but did we just sit here and plot a fucking revolution?"

"Nah." Dallas let his head fall back and closed his eyes. "But we sure as fuck got recruited into one already in progress."

"How long do you think he's been preparing for this?"

Mad had seen the steely glint in Jim's eyes. The satisfaction. "You heard the man. For the last forty years."

"That's Jim—getting ready for war while everyone else twiddled their damn thumbs." Dallas scrubbed his hand over his face. "I know we were planning to spend the night, but we can't. We've got to get our asses back to Four. Talk to Cruz first, see if this has a snowflake's chance in hell of working. He knows what Eden can bring at us."

"We all do, Declan." Lex stood. "And it isn't pretty."

"No, it isn't." He sighed and straightened. "So we finish coordinating with Gideon—"

"I can do that," Mad interrupted. "You guys have Sector Four to deal with. I'll stay here and work with Gideon."

Dallas pinned him with an uncertain look. "You sure?"

Lex studied Mad for an endless moment, then took Dallas's hand and tilted her head toward the door. "Come on. It's a long ride back, and I want to check on Avery."

"Gideon has a network connection set up over in the Riders' barracks," Mad promised. "I'll send updates."

"All right." Dallas squeezed Mad's shoulder on his way past. "We'll see you soon."

Mad didn't walk them out. They'd meet Gideon in the hallway anyway, and Mad didn't need any more time with Lex seeing straight through him.

Instead, he left the office. The second floor had almost a dozen lavishly appointed guest rooms and suites, but the third floor had always been reserved for family.

His skin prickled as he turned left at the top of the stairs. He hadn't been up here in years, but it was like walking into his past. Nothing had changed—nothing but him. He was taller, older. More tired.

More cynical.

His goal was the door at the end of the hall, the door he'd run to as a child after every terrifying nightmare and with every proud accomplishment. He could smell the candles before he touched the doorknob. Rose and vanilla, a combination that still lanced the pain of loss straight through him.

Mad took a deep, bracing breath and opened the door.

The bed was gone. So was the giant, shabby chair, angled to catch the light from the window, where Adriana had sat and read Mad fantastical pre-Flare children's books. Those books had vanished, too.

Generations of dead family members stared down at him. Elaborate paintings of his great-grandparents, his grandfather, and two of the Prophet's wives who had passed away before him. Of Gideon's aunt, who'd died during the civil war. Of Mad's uncle, who'd taken a bullet meant for the Prophet.

Candles flickered in tall glass vases, and the stripped bookshelves beneath them overflowed with offerings. Flowers from the family garden, both dried and fresh. Jewels and statues and charms—so many charms. Not the painted plastic ones the temple sold to worshippers who wanted to leave a prayer on one of the shrines, but delicately shaped masterpieces in silver and gold and painted clay.

Mad's mother didn't have a painting. Instead, the design from the tattoo the red-haired man had displayed so proudly in Two was replicated here, painted over the large oval mirror on his mother's vanity. Her face stared at him, gentle and loving, as her hands cradled that damn glowing heart.

She wasn't the only Rios to rip out her heart for the people who worshipped her. But she would always be the first.

"The guests are gone."

Mad didn't turn to face Gideon, but traced his finger over one of the golden charms affixed to the wooden frame of the mirror. "Except me."

"You're never a guest, Mad."

Gideon was the only one in the family who called him that. The only one who'd ever acknowledged that Mad's break with Sector One ran deeper than a difference of opinion, and that Adrian Rios had died with his parents.

But accepting his repudiation of the family name didn't mean Gideon was ready to accept defeat. "If you say so."

"I do." Gideon came to stand next to him and studied the mirror. "It's the hardest thing we have to do, you know."

"What?"

"Share them." He touched the frame around Adriana's portrait. "It's the price of hope. But you've been paying it longer than any of us, and without the rewards."

"I'm an O'Kane," Mad retorted. "I pay a much lower price for some much sweeter rewards."

"So Dallas always claims." Gideon let his hand fall. "Isabela wanted to bring her family to see you tonight, but I told her you and your guests need a night to settle in. Think you can manage a family dinner tomorrow?"

Oh, Christ. The thought of introducing Scarlet, Jade, and Dylan to Maricela was tense enough. Gideon's middle sister Isabela was something else entirely—a true believer who embraced Sector One and everything it stood for. Her two husbands and two wives were breathlessly devoted, and Mad was pretty sure any of them would willingly walk in front of bullets if Isabela asked it of them.

His hesitation dragged on too long, and a chill crept into Gideon's gaze. As much affection as he held for Mad, any hint of disrespect toward one of his sisters would spawn a protective fury far more terrifying than God's wrath.

You could spurn the Prophet, the religion, even Gideon himself, but only a fool messed with Isabela or Maricela. "A family dinner sounds great."

"Good." Gideon swung an arm around his shoulders. "Maricela has the cooks preparing food for you to eat in your room tonight, and she's already sent a guard for your friends. Come out to the barracks with me. The Riders'll be happy to see you."

The Riders' barracks was the only damn place on the Rios estate where Mad felt at home, probably because it was the closest thing Sector One had to the Broken Circle. Casual brotherhood, intense loyalty, and a dedication to living hard while you still had a life to live.

Until his people were safely under one roof, it was as close to comfort as he'd get here.

T HE ONLY THING worse than being sober was being sober *and* out of your element.

Dylan surveyed the cavernous room through bleary eyes. The bed alone was the size of his first apartment, easily big enough to accommodate a dozen or more people. A nod to the plural marriages common in the sector, and undoubtedly something that Mad found useful.

The man did not like to sleep alone.

Dylan tossed his bag on the bed. The sounds of running water and splashing floated through the closed bathroom door, so he closed his eyes and imagined Mad under the sluicing water, golden wet skin and dripping hair. If the bed was the size of a fucking room, Christ only knew how big the tub would be.

He stopped at the door, his hand on the knob, when a feminine voice rose above the splashing. Not surprising— except there was something about the tone and cadence that Dylan knew as well as his own name.

Jade.

He was still turning over the implications in his mind—Jade, in Mad's bathroom, naked and laughing—when another voice joined hers, this one in song. The lilting notes prickled over the back of his neck, and his jaw clenched as he opened the door.

The tub *was* huge. It dominated one corner of the bathroom, big enough to swim in and so deep that four wide, tiled steps led up to the edge. Jade had her hair piled on top of her head and her eyes closed, and Scarlet arched an eyebrow at him as she continued washing Jade's back.

"Well," he said pleasantly. "This is awkward."

Scarlet blinked innocently. "Is it?"

"Scarlet," Jade chided. "Be nice. He's had a long few days." Her eyes drifted open, and she smiled gently. "Do you need the tub, Dylan?"

"Not at all." He propped one arm against the door-jamb. The water was clear, with no bubbles or bath milks to obscure his view, and he watched as the water rushed and flowed around Jade's breasts.

Her breathing sped. A flush that had nothing to do with the hot water spread across her chest, and she turned abruptly, splashing waves across the surface of the bath.

Scarlet touched her cheek. "Ignore him. It's the worst thing you could do. He gets off on control, but he doesn't deserve it if he won't ask for it."

The words stung, not because they were harmful but because they were true. "The world isn't one of your songs, Scarlet. People are complicated."

"People are simple," Jade disagreed. "We're selfish and we're scared. Coming together in a way that doesn't hurt is the complicated part."

"Impossible, even," Dylan teased.

Jade stroked her fingers through Scarlet's hair. "Not always."

He had mostly the O'Kanes to judge by, and not a single one of their golden couples had come together without hellish pain. "Am I wrong, Scarlet?" he challenged softly.

She lowered her eyes.

Jade glanced back at him, the shy arousal gone from her eyes. "I suppose I have a different threshold for pain."

Dylan shoved his hands through this hair. As satisfying as it was to poke at Scarlet, to test her limits, the hurt on Jade's face was unmistakable. An unfortunate side effect, and one he didn't care for. "Don't listen to me," he offered. "I'm an asshole."

One elegant eyebrow rose. "I'll remember that next time you're issuing commands."

Retreat was a perfectly valid, perfectly reasonable strategy. He took a step back. "Let me know when you're finished with the bathroom, would you?"

"Of course."

She turned back to Scarlet, and Dylan closed the door quietly behind him. Whatever Mad was thinking, he'd clearly lost his fucking mind.

But when Mad arrived a few minutes later, he looked sane enough. A tiny army of servants followed him through the door, carrying trays weighed down with steaming dishes of food. The double doors on the far wall had been thrown wide to reveal an equally spacious sitting room with couches and plush chairs on one side and a table big enough for ten on the other.

Huge as it was, the table was groaning by the time the final dish had been situated on it. The silent servants bowed to Mad, who thanked each one by name as they filed past. His pleasant, placid expression lingered until the last one was gone.

Mad closed the door and sagged against it, smiling wanly. "Welcome to Sector One."

Dylan cleared his throat. "I think *home* is the word you're looking for."

"Do you?" Mad's head thumped back against the solid

wood, and he closed his eyes. "You know me better than that, Dylan."

"What part of it bothers you?"

"The part where I actually knew my grandfather." Mad finally pushed away from the door and crossed the room. "At least Dallas is honest about pursuing his own pleasures."

So it wasn't the faith or the doctrine, but the perversion of it. That sounded right. "Gideon doesn't seem like the type to use people for his own gains, or at his whims."

"No," Mad agreed, tugging at the laces on one of his boots. "But what about the leader who follows him? Or the one after that? What about when there's no one left alive who remembers that my grandfather was a man with flaws and selfishness in his heart?"

"Then you'll have a true religion. Congratulations." Dylan dropped to the mattress and reclined on one of the countless pillows. "There are two naked women in your bathtub. But you knew that already, didn't you?"

"It's a suite, Dylan." Without looking up, Mad tossed his boot aside and started on the other one. "There's room for about ten of them in the tub, if I remember right. And the bed's big enough for half the O'Kanes to sleep in without bumping into each other."

"So this is a space issue?"

"It's—" Mad growled and threw his other boot so hard it thumped against the wall. "Do you want your own room, Dylan?"

"No." He leaned forward. "I want you to tell me why they're here. No bullshit."

"Because I wanted them here." Mad settled on the bed. "I assumed you would too."

And for good reason—but all the wrong ones. "A twisted fucking game," Dylan murmured. "That's what you called it. You sure you want to drag them into it for real?"

"Maybe it's only twisted if they don't get a chance to

play it."

It made a fucked-up sort of sense. Maybe it *was* twisted for him and Mad to tease one another with the idea of Scarlet's arousal or Jade's lust every time they crashed together. If so, the only way to put things on the level again, make them right, would be to open those fantasies up to the ladies in question.

"You're sure about this?" he asked.

"We're O'Kanes. If they want a little comfort, I'll give it. If they don't, that's okay too." Mad caught Dylan's wrist and rubbed his thumb over the naked, unmarked skin there. "It's simpler for us, I think. We can cling to each other just because we don't want to sleep alone."

"Is that all it is?"

"Sometimes." He moved his thumb in lazy, soothing circles. "Besides, when we're outside the sector, we stick together."

As if any of them needed the physical protection of safety in numbers while they were hidden away behind the well-guarded, palatial walls of Gideon's estate. Though Mad seemed to be talking about a different kind of protection. Comfort, not defense. "Is it so terrible coming here because you hate it, or because you don't?"

"Oh, is he giving *you* a hard time now?" Scarlet closed the bathroom door behind her and walked into the room. Her hair dripped onto her white satin robe, soaking the fabric until Dylan could see not only the outline but the shadow of her nipples beneath it.

Mad gave Dylan's wrist one last caress before releasing him. "I wouldn't know what to do with him if he wasn't."

"Liar." She knelt on the end of the bed and smiled wickedly. "You'd know exactly what to do with him."

"Maybe." Mad relaxed against the headboard and stretched out his legs with a smile, as if Scarlet's teasing soothed him. "Jade still in the tub?"

"Nah." Scarlet winked. "But she has four or five different oils and creams she has to rub on her skin after a bath. She'll be along."

The words did exactly what she'd meant them to—painted a mental picture of Jade's hands, slick and soft, running over her naked curves. Dylan swallowed a groan.

Mad made it worse by laughing, low and full of lust and secrets. "And you didn't stay to help?"

"Sometimes I do. But not tonight."

"How is she?"

"A little wound up. On edge." Scarlet shifted on the bed, her leg brushing Mad's as she moved. "It's not every day the guy who's been teasing you forever decides he might come through."

Mad shifted his leg as well, and managed to nudge her robe higher. "Come on now, Scarlet. There's been a lot of teasing going around."

"I'll own it." She moved again, only this time she straddled his knees and planted her hands on his thighs. The edges of her robe slithered apart, white satin baring one pale hip. "Can you?"

Dylan held his breath as Mad stroked his fingers up her arm and over her shoulder before sliding back down the inside edge of the satin, almost—*almost*—touching her skin. "Should we wait for Jade before we start owning things?"

"Scarlet knows what I want."

Jade stood in the open doorway, completely naked, her hair spilling down around her shoulders. Her eyes locked with Dylan's, and she smiled.

Slow, soft challenge.

"Told you," Scarlet whispered, then jerked Mad's shirt free of his pants.

He lifted his arms to let her strip the shirt free, then gripped her hips. Even with Jade approaching the bed, gorgeous and naked, his gaze never left Scarlet's face. "No more teasing. Whatever you need, you can have."

She turned her head and held out her hand. Jade climbed onto the bed, close against Scarlet's back. Her slender fingers skated over the silk covering her lover's body before settling on the knot that held her robe closed. "No more teasing, Scarlet."

Her hips arched, and Mad hissed as she ground against his leg. "Do I look like I'm teasing?"

"No." Jade kissed her ear as she loosened the knot. The fabric fell open, baring the top of one of Scarlet's breasts. "But Mad still is."

"Savoring," he corrected, tugging at the sleeve of Scarlet's robe until it slipped off her arm. "You may be used to admiring her, but we're not."

From afar, perhaps. You couldn't be in the same room and not look at Scarlet—at the soft hair that seemed so at odds with the steel ring piercing her brow, at the leather and lace she wore like a shield and an invitation, all rolled into one. Jade was beautiful, sweet-faced and classically gorgeous. Scarlet was...

Compelling. The inescapable pull grew stronger as she dropped her head back and let Jade draw the satin away from her body. Mad's hands replaced it, his fingers tracing a path from the hollow of her throat, down between her breasts, all the way to her navel. "She's impatient, isn't she?"

"I wouldn't know," Jade replied, the words muffled as she kissed Scarlet's shoulder. "I can never bring myself to make her wait for anything."

"Fuck waiting." She sank her hand into Jade's hair. "Fuck *me*."

Mad grinned and stroked his knuckles back up to her breast. "Is this all you can take, Scarlet? Really?"

"I can—" The words cut off when Mad bent to her breast, and she gripped the back of his head with her free hand. "*Yes.*"

Jade cupped her other breast, her thumb moving in soothing swoops even as she brought two fingers together to pinch Scarlet's nipple. "Not so gentle."

In response, Mad switched sides, driving a groan from Scarlet as he licked Jade's fingers, and a gasp from Jade as he continued to the delicate back of her hand. He caught her wrist, lifted it, and Dylan knew the slow way he drew two of her fingers into his mouth was as much a show for him as anything else.

Jade's ragged breaths filled the silence as Mad glided his tongue over her fingertips one last time. Then he guided her hand down Scarlet's body. "Slow," he commanded.

Scarlet sucked in a sharp breath when Jade touched her. Dylan watched Jade's fingers closely, watched them part Scarlet's wet pussy lips before flicking the tiny ring above her clit. Watched them glide and tease, but only for a moment before delving deeper. Thrusting inside.

Scarlet released her indrawn breath on a low, harsh moan. His gaze snapped to her face—and she was staring at him. He stared back, mesmerized by the elegant, torturous simplicity of the invitation burning there.

Watch, it said. *Want. But don't touch.*

Another twisted game, one he knew well.

"Jade." Mad's voice was low, chiding.

She laughed. "I didn't promise you obedience."

Her voice held a defiant lilt that made Dylan's dick hard. She hadn't promised obedience—but she would give it to the right person.

Scarlet rocked her hips, fucking Jade's fingers, and yanked at Mad's belt. His chest heaved and his muscles flexed under all that beautiful ink, and he turned to Dylan, his eyes blazing.

A different sort of invitation burned there. *Stay*, it whispered. *Be one of us.*

He reached out and cupped his hand around the back of Mad's neck. "I'm not going anywhere."

"You better not," Mad growled, then kissed him.

Dylan closed his eyes as heat invaded his mouth and

beyond ruin

his senses. Mad's tongue slicked over his, and his tormented groan vibrated through the room, evocative
enough to paint a picture of exactly what was happening—
Scarlet had his pants open, was dragging her red-tipped
nails over his hip, wrapping one strong, graceful hand
around his cock...

Dylan opened his eyes as Mad broke away with a hiss
and slammed his head back against the headboard.

Jade was the one touching him, her fingers still slick
from being inside Scarlet. She stroked him from base to
tip and laughed softly when he tried to thrust up into her
retreating hand. She nuzzled Scarlet's cheek and worked
her fingers back inside her, sinking them deep while the
other woman shuddered. "He's impatient, isn't he?"

Scarlet twisted her hand tight, pulling Jade's hair
with a growl. Jade moaned in response, her fingers moving
faster as she pressed the heel of her hand to Scarlet's
piercing.

She jerked—hard—and Mad had to steady her. He
kept one hand on her hip and curled the other carefully
around the base of her neck, not quite gripping, but that
could change at any second.

His thumb swept over the pulse throbbing in the hollow of her throat, and he waited until she stopped swaying
before smoothing his other hand up to cup her breast.
"Come on, Scarlet. Sing for us."

She choked on a laugh and froze when her gaze
clashed with Dylan's. For an eternity, she stared at him,
through him, as if she could see not just his soul but everything he'd ever tried to hide.

Then she reached for him. Her fingers brushed his
cheek, cool and calming, like the blessings people begged
from Mad on the street, then slipped into his hair. She
tugged, drawing him closer, closer, until her mouth was
only inches from his.

He held his breath, but she didn't kiss him. Instead,
she smiled slowly and pushed his head down until his lips

75

grazed Mad's fingers—and her nipple.

Mad moved his hand, giving him space to swirl his tongue around the taut peak. His fingers splayed across Dylan's back, caressing and possessive, all at once. "This is what it means to be an O'Kane. No fantasy off-limits if it gets everyone off."

It was the same dream Dallas O'Kane had been trying to lure him with for years, but nothing sold it as hard as the sound Scarlet made in the back of her throat when Dylan sucked her nipple deep into his mouth. It was heady, that desperate noise, just like Mad's hand on his back, like Jade's whispers of encouragement.

It was enough to bring a man to God, and it only got better when Scarlet pulled his head up with a sharp jerk and another low moan. "Your fingers. I want them inside me."

Words as rough as Jade's were soft. "Help me, Dylan."

Pulling away, losing this warmth, wasn't an option. Scarlet was wet, but with Jade's fingers already buried deep in her pussy, he almost winced as he thrust two of his inside her, as well. But Scarlet only nodded, a barely perceptible but utterly certain movement of *consent*.

Jade looked at him, her eyes huge and dark, as she flexed her fingers and shivered at Scarlet's moan. Dylan stared back at her, ensnared by the way Jade's hunger flared when he moved his fingers, sliding them against hers.

The moment shattered when Mad surged between them and dragged Scarlet to meet his open-mouthed kiss. She went rigid and slapped his shoulder, but a moment later melted into his embrace with a helpless shudder.

"That's it," Mad rasped, stroking her shaking body as she rocked her hips faster and faster. "Feel it all. All of us."

Scarlet's breath seized in her chest. She ground down against their hands, clenching so tight that it almost hurt. It *did* hurt to watch her come apart, because never in Dylan's wildest dreams had he imagined she would do it so freely, with nothing hidden. And he understood why Jade would come crawling back to this if she had to, *any-thing* for a chance to touch this sort of wild abandon, even from the outside.

Jade was no stranger to pleasure. She'd learned her own body long before she ever let another use it, and that knowledge had been as potent a weapon as anything else in her arsenal.

But sometimes, when she watched Scarlet shudder apart, she wondered if she really understood pleasure at all.

It wasn't as if the reason was a mystery. It was the armor, that impenetrable layer of steel and shattered hope that kept her trapped in her head. She savored release, adored the way Scarlet touched and stroked her, but the wild abandon that transported Scarlet as she came apart in Mad's arms was something Jade had only ever found in pain.

Not that she enjoyed pain. Not like sweet, eager No-elle, who came alive at the kiss of a whip. Not like Bren, who embraced it like a lover. No, for Jade, pain was a tool. A way of restoring her equilibrium when her armor grew so constricting that it threatened to crush her. She knew the biology of physiological responses. She recognized the role endorphins played. Those precious, rare moments of peace were hard won, because pain was a clumsy tool for someone like her.

But it was all she'd ever had.

As soon as Scarlet's shaking subsided, Jade slipped her fingers free. Mad was already gathering Scarlet tight to his chest, his hands strong and soothing, sliding all over her body as he murmured low words Jade couldn't even understand.

She didn't need to. His voice was warm and approv-
ing, because if the O'Kanes prized anything, it was the
courage of sexual abandon. Scarlet had earned his petting
and his stroking.

Jade likely wouldn't.

Dylan was still watching her. Worse, watching like he
could hear each thought as it flitted through her head. As
if her armor wasn't there at all, though the pressure of it
had grown unbearable over the past few days.

Her skin prickled all over. Warm arousal buzzed along
her nerves, heightened by Scarlet's release and sharpened
by her own jealousy at how easily it had been achieved.

Breathing unsteadily, Jade licked her lips. "You're
overdressed."

Dylan's fingers were still glistening and wet when he
lifted them to the buttons on his shirt. "How long?"

A question with so many layers. She could take the
easy way out and tell him that Scarlet had given her two
toe-curling orgasms the night before the bombs dropped,
pleasure so hot and sweet that even the memory raised
goose bumps.

But Scarlet was still lying boneless in Mad's arms, her
eyes glazed with an emotional release that had nothing to
do with her body, and Jade knew what he was really asking.

She knew the answer, too, with telling precision. "Almost three months."

He nodded. Jade knew what to expect from a man like
him—she'd dealt with enough of them over the years. He'd
hold out his hand, make her come to him while he decided
when and how to touch her.

But he didn't. He crawled across the bed with his shirt
hanging open, pausing only to stroke one hand across
Scarlet's calf and Mad's ankle before kneeling in front of
Jade. "Help me figure out how."

He was so close. His knees brushing hers, his entire
body within reach. She traced the edge of his shirt and let

her fingers drift past to the warmth of his flesh, all the way up to his collarbone. "I think Scarlet knows better than I do."

"Does she?" He laid his hand over hers, trapping her fingers against his skin. He guided her hand, not down to his belt, but to rest over his heart.

It beat strong beneath her fingers. It beat *fast*. She shivered and closed her eyes. "I don't know if it belongs here. Tonight. It's never been about pleasure for me."

"What is it about?"

She didn't know how to answer. She didn't have the words for it. But Mad did. "Catharsis," he murmured.

Jade glanced at him. He was still sprawled against the headboard, stroking Scarlet's hair, but there was nothing lazy about him now. He was wound tight with arousal or intensity or something else, something that stared out of his beautiful brown eyes with a dangerous edge she recognized all too well.

Being in Sector One changed him. It made him aware of the power he held, and of the heavy responsibility that came with not abusing it. Her power came from training in manipulation that had become habit. His was effortless, inborn—and inescapable.

Oh, yes. Mad understood the need to break free.

"Catharsis," she agreed softly, then looked at Dylan. "But I don't need it tonight. I want pleasure. I want to feel good."

"And those things don't go together." A tiny, knowing smile played at one corner of his mouth. "Do you trust me, Jade?"

Her hesitation might insult him, but any swift response would have been a pleasing lie. Trust had more layers than an onion, and most people who asked for it never clarified how much they wanted.

But Dylan wasn't most people. He wouldn't ask for what he couldn't give. Body, mind. Those were what he had to offer, and hers were safe in his keeping. "Yes."

He touched her chin with just enough pressure to tilt her head back. "I need you."

It took her a moment to realize he wasn't talking to her, but to Mad and Scarlet. The mattress shifted beneath her, mirroring the way her equilibrium tilted when Mad's voice washed over her. "Come on, Scarlet. Time to play."

She reached Jade first, gripping her upper thighs with familiar ease. She scraped her teeth over the curve of Jade's hip, then tumbled her back to land on the bed. "I've been waiting for this," Scarlet whispered, hot words against the inside of her knee.

"Me too." Mad settled at her side, his hand as warm and strong as she'd imagined as it trailed up the inside of her calf. "But you know that, don't you?"

"No," Jade retorted, sinking her fingers into his hair. Scarlet would have jerked roughly, but Jade twisted just enough to produce a warning tingle across his scalp. "I know you want me. But I never imagined you'd let yourself touch me."

Mad paused with his hand curled around the knee Scarlet wasn't kissing. "I trust Dylan, too."

"See?" Dylan unbuckled his belt, moving so slowly and carefully that the metal made no noise as he worked it free. "Catharsis, love."

Maybe she could have it. She was wet enough, *achy* enough, and the race of her pulse wasn't all simple desire. Adrenaline surged as she let herself feel the size and weight of Mad's hand, the roughness of calloused fingers, the *difference* between his grip and Scarlet's.

She'd fucked men before. She'd even fucked Bren, once, before she'd come to Sector Four. Before he'd given his heart to Six. He'd been a pleasant enough diversion. More skilled than the men she was usually assigned to climb on top of. But he'd been a job, and she'd gone crawling through his fantasies with her armor intact.

She'd never had a man go crawling through hers.

"Relax," Dylan murmured. He brushed the backs of

his fingers over the top swell of her breast as Scarlet's mouth and Mad's hand both inched higher up her legs. "Or don't, it doesn't matter. Either way, we'll give you what you need."

What she needed was oblivion. To be so full of so much sensation that her brain couldn't hold on to the horror of the past few days. "I can't stop thinking."

"I know." His fingers drifted up, a mere tease of pressure across the front of her throat before vanishing. "That's why we're going to make you stop."

Mad's fingers and Scarlet's lips were so close to colliding that Jade's hips lifted on their own, seeking *something*. A touch, a kiss, anything to shatter the anticipation twisting through her.

She whimpered, a sound that turned to a moan when Scarlet's breath blew hot over her pussy. "Please, Scarlet—"

"Shh." It was Mad, low and soothing, and she wanted to sob her gratitude when his rough fingertips found her clit. But the touch was fleeting, gone in the next heartbeat as he stroked down and parted her outer lips. "God, already so wet."

Scarlet hummed as she licked past his fingertips, flicking her tongue in spots she already knew well. But it was all different, transformed by the harsh, staccato breaths that punctuated Mad's filthy, encouraging words.

And then there was Dylan's silent, commanding presence, subtle but unmistakable, especially when he touched the back of Scarlet's head with one single, vibrating word. "Deeper."

Miraculously, Scarlet obeyed. She trailed lower, and Mad slid one leg over Jade's, parting her thighs wider, pinning her in place. She was trapped and open as Scarlet thrust her tongue into her.

Thoughts scattered in a hundred directions before rushing back in choppy waves. Each shock of pleasure was a rock dropped into a placid pond. She reached blindly for

Dylan, wanting to feel him, wanting to tell him—

"More," she gasped, tangling her fingers in his shirt. If they could shock her enough times, maybe she'd never have to think again. "Please."

He peeled off the shirt, leaving it crumpled in her hands as he pulled away. He slid off the bed, walked around the end of it, and stopped only inches from Jade— his hair tousled, his belt open, and his pants—

Jade extended a trembling hand and traced the erection straining the fabric. It seemed impressive even like this, and her heart stuttered as she stared up at him and waited for a command.

He drew in a slow, controlled breath and held her gaze as he opened his pants, freeing his cock. Then he gripped her wrist hard and guided her fingers to his shaft.

Smooth. Silky. *Hot.* She knew all the right ways to layer sensation, to build from anticipation to need to climax. But she'd never had to focus before with Scarlet's tongue thrusting into her, with Mad's fingers rubbing slow circles around her clit—clever, wicked circles that teased without relieving.

Breathing raggedly, she tried to focus on sliding her hand up his erection. And it *was* impressive, long and so thick her fingers barely met when she returned to the base. She watched his face as she stroked him again, gratified to see his jaw tighten and his eyes flare with lust.

His voice was burning, too. "Mad?"

That sweet, taunting touch vanished, and Jade would have moaned in protest if Mad hadn't shifted his weight to his elbow and leaned across her body. From inches away she watched, heart pounding, as Mad parted his lips and enveloped the first few inches of Dylan's cock.

Dylan laid his hand on the back of Mad's head and rubbed his cheek with his thumb. The gesture spoke of intimate familiarity, of something precious. "Do you know what he wants?"

"No," she admitted softly. "Every time I try to guess,

I'm wrong."

Dylan tugged her other hand to rest on the pulse pounding in the hollow of Mad's throat. "When I can't stand how good your sweet little fingers feel anymore, I'm going to come all over you. And he has to lick up every single drop before he can fuck you."

It was elegant vulgarity in a voice so casual her brain scrambled to process the image. Not the overprotective tenderness she'd always imagined Mad would require, but raw, lewd sensuality.

And his pulse racing under her fingertips made it true.

She was still reeling when Mad licked his way down Dylan's cock and over her fingers. He'd left enough wetness behind to let Jade slide her hand more easily, and she'd almost regained her balance when Scarlet leaned up and joined him. She flicked her tongue over the head, then lingered to slowly trace the crown.

Dylan's head fell back, his rigid control slipping, and Jade stroked her thumb along the underside, all the way to the base, before wrapping him tight in her fingers.

It was easy. Effortless. They found a rhythm as if they'd choreographed it—Jade's firm, slow caresses, Scarlet's hot, taunting mouth, Mad's demanding tongue. But it was so much simpler than coordination. It was purity of purpose, something she'd glimpsed when they had all finally gotten their hands on Scarlet.

There was freedom in not having to be everything, all by yourself. There was joy in sharing the victory of each tensing muscle, every noise they pulled from Dylan's elegant throat.

He looked down and closed his fingers around hers. Scarlet kissed the back of his hand, then slid back down Jade's body to lick her clit, jolting warmth through her that quickly turned to fire in her veins.

Then Mad touched her, too. "Show me," he rasped. "Show me what gets her off."

Scarlet kissed her way up his arm and bit his shoulder. "Start slow," she whispered. "Too many fingers, but easy. Careful."

Scarlet always started with three. So did Mad, but his were *bigger*, and Jade panted as they pushed against her, and then inside her. So slow, a fraction of an inch at a time, and sometimes she hated how much she loved that implacable advance. Too much, too fast, and she lost this moment in the rush of sensation.

Now she could only feel it, savor it, until she gave in to the inevitability of being utterly filled.

Dylan watched her, his hand tightening around hers, squeezing his dick, as her pleasure mounted. "Nothing hidden now, Jade. Nothing at all."

Regret cut through her, because it was a lie. She was still hidden—her name, her past, the raw, battered heart of her—but in the next moment it slipped away, buried under a jolt as Mad sank his fingers as deep as they would go. She gasped, shuddering at the fullness and the friction, and Dylan nodded and licked his lower lip.

She wasn't hiding her responses, and that was all he demanded tonight.

"Fucking hell," Mad groaned, rocking his fingers. "She's squeezing me so damn tight."

"Tight enough to hurt?" Scarlet breathed.

"Not yet." He turned his head to Scarlet's and growled his next words against her cheek. "How do I get her there?"

It didn't matter what Scarlet said. The question itself was almost enough to get the job done. The low eagerness of it, the fact that he would ask it at all. She'd thought sharing victory was heady, but it had nothing on being the focus of it.

"Harder." Scarlet's soft command was muffled against Mad's shoulder. He obeyed, and she reached out to help him by circling the pad of her thumb on Jade's clit.

The orgasm took her by surprise. She choked on a cry as her body clenched, the release of pent-up tension almost violent. Her back arched, and she dug her head into the mattress, struggling to manage the fire beneath her skin, the wildness threatening to overwhelm her.

Dylan moved their joined hands faster over his dick.

"Jade." Mad's voice held a thread of roughness. Of darkness. It dragged her gaze back to him, held her captive as he timed his thrusts to the rhythm of her release with casual, intimidating skill.

And when she thought he couldn't coax another shudder from her, he twisted his fingers. Curled them. She knew it was coming and she still let out a shocked noise and tried to twist away when he found her G-spot.

Scarlet splayed one hand over Jade's hips, holding her down. "Let it happen," she said, then sank her teeth into the tense, bulging muscles where Mad's neck sloped gracefully into his shoulder.

He hissed, but his eyes never left Jade's. "Easy, sweetheart. Just look at Dylan. You trust him, don't you?"

"Yes—" She barely had enough breath for the word. Everything was so tight, coiled to the point of agony and flaring with every expert stroke. She tried to focus on Dylan, but his fingers distracted her. It was their only point of contact—his hand over hers, his cock sliding beneath it.

She could still feel him all over.

"Look at him," Mad whispered again, and she did.

He was beautiful. Stern. His strong features were tense, pleasure so close to the surface she didn't know how he was holding back. But he was. She could see it in the stiff lines of his body, in his dark eyes. He would hold them like this forever if that was what it took to smash through her armor, and the pressure should have crippled her.

Instead, it set her free.

She stopped trying to still her struggles and trusted Scarlet to pin her in place. She stopped straining toward release and trusted Mad to take her there. She gave them the honesty of her reactions—even the graceless ones. The helpless squirming when the intensity proved too much. The broken moans.

And when Mad lifted his thumb to circle her clit in the rhythm Scarlet had taught him, Jade screamed and bucked.

And came.

The world blurred. Pleasure and relief squeezed tight enough to hurt for an endless moment before everything shattered, and time turned into an elusive, meaningless thing. She floated. She fell.

She gasped in her first deep breath in three months and wanted to sob at how light the world felt.

Dylan groaned and shuddered, his cock pulsing in her hand. Anticipation spun through her bliss-drunk mind, and for the first time in her life she *wanted* the proof of a man's release painting her skin.

She lifted her body languidly into the first spurt. Hot seed spilled across her breasts and stomach, and she tightened her hand and stroked him faster.

He shuddered again and gripped her wrist, pulling her hand away. He was panting for breath when he bent down, kissed her palm, and released her. "Mad. Scarlet."

She couldn't imagine Scarlet obeying the command— she could barely imagine Scarlet resisting the urge to knee Dylan in the balls for his presumption. But before she could protest Mad was on her, dragging his tongue over her too-sensitive skin, and sense slipped between her fingers. "Oh—"

"Greedy bastard." Scarlet traced one fingertip around Jade's nipple, then followed the same path with her tongue.

It was too much. Every touch set off a tiny cascade of shudders, and the soft throbbing between her thighs reminded her of Dylan's promise. She arched into Scarlet's touch and threaded her fingers through her hair. "Hurry."

Scarlet hissed in a breath. "Fuck what Dylan says, Adrian. Don't wait."

Mad rose on his knees, drawing his fingers up the inside of her thighs. "What do you think, Dylan?"

He touched Jade's face, the caress as gentle as the ones she remembered from the worst of her withdrawal. "Give her what she wants."

Mad hooked his hands under her knees and pushed them up. Out. His gaze swept over her body, lingering on Scarlet's tongue. "I thought what she wanted was soft and sweet, but that's not what she needs, is it?"

"No," Jade said hoarsely. His fingers bit into her skin, just rough enough to be a sort of promise, and she could get drunk all over again on that alone.

Adrian Maddox, looking at her like she wasn't broken.

He rocked his hips forward, sliding his cock over her pussy, but not into it. The shaft rubbed her heated, sensitized flesh, but this time she couldn't even try to wiggle. At her first attempt, he pushed her knees closer to her chest, his eyes blazing. "Help me, Scarlet."

She licked the corner of her mouth and smiled. "With pleasure." She wrapped her fingers around him, her knuckles grazing Jade's pussy as she twisted her wrist lightly. "Help you what, exactly?"

He growled and fucked into her hand, grinding it down against Jade. "Put my cock in your girlfriend's pussy."

"See?" She squeezed until he snarled and then guided the head of his cock down until he was almost—*almost*—inside Jade. "Greedy."

Jade shook as she awaited his first thrust. "Please, Scarlet. Give him to me."

Scarlet always gave her what she needed. A gentle nudge, and Mad was thrusting between her fingers, thrusting *into* Jade, and her moan of relief turned jagged when he kept advancing, inexorable and huge and filling her so much more perfectly than his fingers could have.

Slow, the first time. But only the first time. His hips rested against hers long enough for her to catch her breath…

And then he fucked her.

Hard.

Her nails raked down Scarlet's back before she groped for the sheets, for anything to cling to. Her overstimulated nerves veered toward overload, and she squeezed her eyes shut to block out the sight of Mad leaning over her, dark hair spilling across his forehead, muscles rippling with every thrust. But the *sounds* remained, the slap of their skin as he drove home, the little growls of pleasure he made every time he sank as deep as he could go.

Dylan's fingers wrapped around her wrists, and his lips brushed her forehead, her nose. Then he kissed her mouth, soft and sweet and hot and open—

Their first kiss, and she only had a heartbeat to savor the gentle warmth of it before Mad tilted her hips higher and found that spot that broke her world in half.

She didn't come fast this time. She was past the hot flashes of pleasure, too wrung out for the toe-curling bliss. The orgasm started deep inside her, shuddering up in waves that left her moaning helplessly against Dylan's lips. Her body clenched around Mad's cock, making him feel impossibly big—

—and making her pussy seem impossibly tight. His groan was loud, edged with a growl, and she savored her victory when his smooth, skillful thrusts turned short and jerky, when he thrust hard against her and froze, shuddering.

She savored the softness of Dylan's lips, too, kissing him while Mad came inside her. Warmth on her cheek had her turning her head, blindly tumbling into another kiss as Scarlet captured her mouth.

Faintly, she felt Mad lowering her legs to the bed. The burn in her muscles faded to a gentle ache as warm hands stroked her thighs, her calves.

"Come on, baby." Scarlet's words filled her ears, but Dylan's hands lifted her, and Mad's smoothed the covers over her after they'd settled her into bed.

Warmth surrounded her. Dylan on her left, hard and strong. Scarlet on her right, all sleek muscles and lush curves. Her eyelids were as heavy as they'd ever been, but she forced them open and turned her head to watch Mad lie down behind Scarlet.

"You were right," she murmured, letting her eyes drift shut as she pressed her forehead to Scarlet's. "He's good with his fingers."

She laughed softly. "Told you."

Jade laughed, too, only her laughter twisted and came out as a choked sob. She tried to swallow it back, like she had in the tent with Dylan, but all her walls had been demolished. The agony and grief of the past few days rose up from the darkest places inside her, and she struggled to sit up, to crawl from the bed, to find some safe corner to hide in.

"Shh, hey." Scarlet cupped her face. "You're okay. We've got you."

As if to prove the words, Dylan laid both hands on her back, just under her shoulders, steadying her. Mad caught her hand and wrapped his strong fingers around hers.

No escape. They surrounded her in comfort, in support, and it made things better *and* worse. Words tumbled from her lips, reckless and uncensored. All the guilt and pain, all the rage. "They were helpless. They didn't have a chance. All those girls—and I left them there. I *left them there*."

Dylan sighed heavily. "You couldn't have saved them all, Jade."

"If I'd been there, maybe I would have known—" The words broke. Tears scalded her cheeks, and they wouldn't stop. "I could have watched Cerys. I could have seen—"

"You could have died," Mad interrupted. "And all the girls you've helped since then would have been lost."

Nothing had ever felt so helpless, so hopeless, not even the day she'd walked into her last meeting with her patron, convinced that she'd soon be dead. She'd chosen death for the chance to take the bastard with her.

The girls in Sector Two had never been given a choice. About anything.

She sagged into their embrace, too wrecked to fight her tears anymore. But Mad had been right. The sobs tearing through her were catharsis. Painful and messy, shredding her heart—and leaving a blissful sort of peace in their wake.

But not emptiness. She clung to the soft touches and soothing murmurs, wrapped herself in borrowed strength, and floated toward oblivion secure in the knowledge that she wasn't alone.

jeni

J ENI STILL BELIEVED in fairy tales.

Maybe it wasn't smart. It certainly wasn't careful, seeing as how she'd come really close to having her heart broken by the leaders of Sector Four—not that it was their fault. Dallas and Lex were like stars, a beautiful constellation of two. Ace had talked about how bright they burned, and he was right.

Bright enough to blind a person, especially someone as hungry as Jeni. They'd welcomed her gladly, openly, given her things she'd never dared to expect—friendship, acceptance, desire, affection. Not to mention the kind of jaw-clenching sex that only came when you had all the rest of it.

They'd even given her love, maybe, in their own ways. But no matter how close she got, how much they cared, there was always an invisible wall, with Dallas and Lex on one side and the whole fucking world on the other.

She couldn't blame them for simple reality. In truth, it was on her, too. They'd done everything right, given her as much as they could, but she never felt that *spark*, the undeniable need that meant she'd never be whole without them.

She sighed aloud. "What a clusterfuck."

"What's that?" Rachel stretched past her to retrieve a bottle of tequila and upended it over a line of shot glasses. The amber liquid poured out of the metal spout, splashing down into the glasses and spilling over the rims. A guy standing beside her customer leaned up and licked the liquor from the bar, and Rachel shoved him back with a hand on his forehead and a look of disgust.

Jeni stifled a laugh. "Nothing, just...thinking to myself."

She could have told Rachel the truth, and she had a feeling the woman would understand. It was at least partially due to her that Jeni had pursued Dallas and Lex—because Rachel and Ace and Cruz had their own beautiful, epic *thing*.

But comparing them wasn't fair at all. It wasn't as if Ace had become part of Cruz and Rachel's relationship, or Rachel had fallen in with something Ace and Cruz already had going, or even that Cruz had stumbled into the middle of Ace and Rachel and their ongoing flirtation. None of that worked, because none of it could. The only way the three of them could be happy was to be together, as *one*.

Dallas and Lex would be fine without her. And Jeni would be fine without them, too. But she still believed in fairy tales. She had to, with so many of them walking around the compound in Sector Four.

Rachel turned to stuff a wad of cash into the register, and the bar licker hopped up again, his arm outstretched toward the row of bottles just out of reach. Before Jeni could get rid of him, he jerked back with a choked grunt.

Hawk stood beside him, one hand twisted in the back

of the man's shirt, holding him on his toes with no apparent effort. "Was he going for a bottle?"

It was the first time he'd really spoken to her, and his voice was like a solid thing, a touch, raising goose bumps on her arms. "Yeah."

The would-be thief made another frantic noise, but Hawk had already grasped his hand. Jeni looked away, but the crack of fingers snapping followed, almost drowned out by a howl of pain.

"Get the fuck out," Hawk growled, tossing the man to the floor. "Next time it'll be your neck."

The guy scrambled to his feet, clutching his wounded hand to his body. Jeni watched his retreating form as he ran for the exit. "Ouch," she whispered.

"You okay?"

Hawk was six feet of solid muscle and seriousness. Right now, he was eyeing her with an unmistakable expression of concern. "Better than that guy." She grabbed a clean glass and held it up. "Buy you a drink?"

He smiled, just the tiniest softening of those firm lips. "Sure."

Her heart stuttered, but the rest of her body lit up like she was made of paper and he'd struck a match. She poured him a double and pushed it across the bar, her fingers lingering on the glass.

He reached for it and froze when their hands touched. Even in the dim lighting, she saw him flush as he murmured an apology and hastily tossed back the shot.

She refilled his glass. "I'm Jeni."

"I know." The words came automatically, but he clenched his jaw as soon as they were out, as if he wanted to snatch them back. "I'm Hawk."

"I know," she echoed. "But I didn't know you were bouncing here at the Circle. I thought you were busy with the farming projects."

"I am. Busy, I mean. Not bouncing." He shrugged and jerked his head toward the door. "But I saved Six the trip."

"Then I owe you one."

He shrugged again. "Hey. It was something I could fix. Not a lot of that going around right now."

Tension left every line of his body rigid. She'd heard rumors about the problems back in his home sector—there were whispers of discontent, even of revolt, amongst the farmers in Sector Six. He had to be worried about his family.

She rubbed his shoulder, then brushed the back of her hand over his bearded cheek. "It'll work out."

The flush in his cheeks deepened, but he didn't pull away, and his eyes were oddly intent as he met her gaze. "I'm meeting Jas. You got any of Nessa's better stuff back there?"

"I think so." Jeni sorted through the bottles beneath the bar until she found one marked with one of Ace's special labels. She held it out, acutely aware of the way Hawk was watching her. "I get off at two. If you're free later."

His eyes widened, but his expression was unreadable as he took the bottle. "I have to head back out to the farm after this. I already promised." Regret colored his words, but so did more than a little nervousness.

"Another time," she told him easily. She'd never met an O'Kane who got flustered by an invitation to fuck, but it was part of Hawk's charm. Her attraction was inextricably bound up in finding out what kind of man he was beneath that impenetrable surface.

She'd always been good at reading people, but she couldn't read him. And holy fuck, did she want to.

8

ISABELA'S FAMILY ARRIVED in a caravan.

Five adults, nine children, and a small army of drivers and nannies piled out of the cars and into the atrium. Mad didn't have time to warn Scarlet, Jade, or Dylan before the children descended on them in a wave—five girls and three boys from three to fourteen, with the ninth child, a sweet baby girl Mad had never seen before, propped on his cousin's hip.

Isabela beamed at him as she yanked him down to plant a solid kiss on his cheek. "Adrian, I've missed you so. How are you?"

"Isabela." He kissed her in return and tickled the baby's cheek, smiling when she giggled. Isabela had the dark hair and coloring of the Rios family, but the little girl had black curls and the same adorable smattering of freckles as Isabela's older wife, Makayla.

Not that it mattered. Every baby born in the family

was an equal part of it, no matter who had provided the DNA. Isabela was a traditionalist, and her husbands and wives believed every bit as fervently.

The baby grabbed Mad's finger, and he laughed. "Who's this little sweetheart?"

"Rebekah Gabriela." Isabela arched one eyebrow. "You'd have met her already if you came home more often."

That didn't take long. It never did, but Mad didn't want to fight with her, not before he had no choice. "I've been busy. But I'm here now, and I brought some friends."

"Oh, really?" Her chiding tone turned decidedly interested. "Special friends?"

"O'Kane friends," he deflected, turning to where they stood.

The wave of children had washed past him and run into the newcomers. Jade was talking easily with the two eldest girls while one of the toddlers tugged at her fingers, trying to get her attention. Dylan was kneeling, surrounded, grinning widely at the rest of the younger children as they bombarded him with questions.

Shock froze Mad in place for several heartbeats. He couldn't remember ever seeing Dylan so relaxed and comfortable—not while he was sober, at least.

No, Scarlet was the one wearing the expression he'd expected from Dylan—sheer wariness, especially when one of the youngest girls toddled over to smile up at her.

That drove him to action. He swooped up the little girl and settled her on his hip before sliding his hand to the small of Scarlet's back. It was too revealing a gesture, too *possessive*, but now that he knew what it felt like to touch her for real, he had to steal every touch he could get. "Come and meet my cousin, Isabela. Matriarch of this madness."

"Hello." Scarlet stretched out a hand, still wary but attempting a smile.

Not content with a handshake, Isabela pulled her into an awkward half-hug. She widened her eyes at Mad over

Scarlet's shoulder and mouthed, *She's adorable.*

God, this was going to go so, so wrong.

But it was already going, so when Isabela released Scarlet, he turned her again. "These are Isabela's husbands, John and Leo. And her wives, Makayla and Victoria."

"It's nice to meet you all." Scarlet smiled again, but this time it almost looked like a grimace.

"Come on." Makayla touched Isabela's arm gently. "There's plenty of time for introductions. I think Maricela wants to speak with you."

Victoria reached out, and Mad handed over the toddler. John and Leo paused to nod at him—nods that stopped shy of being bows only because they knew better—and then helped gather the children and herd them deeper into the house.

When they were gone, Mad stepped closer to Scarlet and lowered his voice. "Sorry. I never know how to warn people."

"You shouldn't have to warn people about your family." She shook her head. "It's not them. It's me."

He wanted to touch her again, to tug her against his side and stroke and pet until the tension left her body. But they were still in the entryway, and if they didn't follow the rest of the family, someone would be back to find them.

He settled for an arm around her shoulders. "C'mon, Scarlet. Unless you grew up on one of the farms out in Six or Seven, that many babies is a damn unusual thing to see this close to the wall. *I'm* not even used to it."

Dylan joined them. His fingers skimmed Mad's arm, then dragged gently through Scarlet's hair. A brief touch, but one with purpose—after what had happened between them, there was no going back to casual indifference. "Holding up?"

Scarlet wrinkled her nose at him. "I'm *fine.* They're children, not zombies."

There was that charming smile again, quick and easy

enough to steal a person's breath. "Wasn't talking to you."

There were far worse fates than to have a family that pried and poked and just wanted you to come home to take your place as a pampered prince. There was growing up in Eden, like Dylan had. There was growing up an orphan, like Scarlet.

And Jade—she looked almost at peace this morning. Tired but steady, with all of her masks back in place. Her resilience mocked his brooding pain. She'd dug children she had helped to raise out of the rubble.

All he had to face were live, happy ones who wanted to love him.

"I'll be fine," he promised. "Unless we don't go into dinner, and then Maricela will have one of the guards strangle me in my sleep for ruining her first big dinner party."

Jade smiled. "I like her already."

The party was far from formal. Dinner was being served in the big dining room rather than the smaller, more intimate one Gideon usually preferred, but the table had been set with the colorful, casual family dishes. It almost felt like any other day, cheerful and chaotic—until Maricela steered Mad toward the chair at the head of the table.

It was only a gesture. Gideon had settled in the seat at the opposite end, the one Maricela usually claimed. If he resisted, he'd set the tone for the meal—tense and unhappy. But sinking into Gideon's chair was a reminder that too many of the devout in Sector One felt that Mad belonged in Gideon's place. Permanently.

At the other end of the table, Gideon lifted his glass with a tiny smile to acknowledge that truth—and the fact that he was utterly unthreatened by it. Gideon wasn't jealous of power. He didn't need to grasp at it like the other leaders or fight to consolidate it. If Mad stood up and announced he was coming home to take his place as leader, Gideon would welcome him with open arms.

Sometimes knowing that scared Mad more than anything else.

He hid it with a smile as he lifted his own goblet. The
wine was sweeter than he normally liked it, but maybe
he'd been drinking whiskey for so long, he'd lost the taste
for it. He drained the wine and refused to let his smile
wobble when Leo leapt to refill it.

Isabela eyed Dylan over the rim of her glass. "Are you
from Sector Four, Mr. Jordan?"

"Dr. Jordan," Rosa piped up from her perch on Makayla's lap. "He went to school and everything."

Dylan's smile wasn't quite as open as the ones outside.
"I grew up in the city, actually. In Eden."

Mad stepped in to save him from further interroga-
tion. "None of them are from Sector Four, in fact. Jade
grew up in Two, and Scarlet in Three."

"Jade's a princess," seven-year-old Susie said. "We
took plants from Mama's garden to the new house, and the
lady who runs it said Jade owns half of Eden."

It sounded like the sort of comment that hadn't been
intended for young ears. Hyperbole, maybe, except for the
way Jade's face froze. Subtle, and replaced in a heartbeat
by her pleasant, engaging mask.

Now Mad wondered how much of Eden she *did* own.

She answered Susie with a warm smile. "Not quite
half. And I was never a princess. I know a few, though."

"So do you, Susie," Gideon supplied. "Your mother, for
one. And your Tia Maricela."

"I'm not a princess." Maricela leaned closer to Susie.
"I'm a superhero. But shh." She laid a finger over her lips,
and Susie dissolved into giggles.

The laughter eased some of the awkwardness as the
food arrived. The children chattered excitedly, competing
for the attention of parents and beloved aunts and uncles
and even strangers. Dylan and Jade fielded most of the
questions, and when Mad snuck a hand under the table to
grip Scarlet's, she rubbed her leg against his and winked.

Maricela hadn't taken any chances. Dishes piled high with Mad's favorite recipes filled the table. Their grandmother's mole and stuffed poblanos, his mother's carne asada. Even a loaf of Irish brown bread fresh from the oven, and Mad remembered his mother's smile as she scoured pre-Flare cookbooks to find the recipe. Weeks of searching, all to give his father the comfort of a memory from his childhood.

Carter Maddox had married into the Rios family, but he'd never believed in the religion or the Prophet. He'd loved Adriana for herself. As a flesh-and-blood woman, not a princess or a saint.

And when the Prophet had forbidden his followers from organizing a party to rescue his daughter and grandson, Carter Maddox had disobeyed. He'd walked into certain death to give his wife and son a chance at life.

No one in Sector One got tattoos of Carter. No one praised his sacrifice or counted him among their saints. He might have saved Mad's life, but his disobedience carried a price. No one remembered him. No one spoke his name.

No one but the son who'd taken that name as his own.

The room felt too warm. Mad reached for his glass and barely felt it beneath his trembling fingers. He needed to be calm. He couldn't vent his anger, not here, in front of the children. In front of family who couldn't change the past. "The food smells good, Maricela."

She blushed, pleased. "I chose the menu, but the real surprise is the flan. I made it myself."

"She's becoming quite accomplished," Gideon added from the far side of the table. "Not just in the kitchen. You should take them into the gardens after dinner and show them your sculptures, Maricela."

"No." She covered her cheeks. "*Gideon*."

"Stop being so modest." Gideon's smile was proud enough to belong to a father instead of a big brother—

though with the difference in their ages, that wasn't surprising. Gideon was already nineteen when his mother brought Maricela home, an orphaned baby girl who had stolen everyone's heart with her first sunny laugh.

Jade was the one who stepped in to save her. "What sort of sculpting do you do?"

"Clay. I tried my hand at pottery, but the wheel makes me clumsy." She glanced at Mad. "Lately, I've been making milagros."

Scarlet tilted her head. "Milagros?"

"Charms that you leave on shrines or holy sites," Mad told her. "It's something my grandfather started. His grandparents came from Mexico..." He hesitated, unsure if Scarlet even knew what pre-Flare countries were. Plenty of sector orphans grew up ignorant of the world that had existed before the lights went out.

There was no confusion in her expression, so he continued. "That's where he got the idea. He was a scholar before the Flares. He studied world religions, so he knew exactly how to build one."

"Adrian," Isabela snapped. "Don't be uncharitable. It's blasphemous."

He didn't usually provoke Isabela, but he was still so *warm*. The room was impossibly stuffy, closing in on him, and his temper shredded around the edges. "So is refusing to call me by the name I chose."

"Apologize, *mi hijo*." His mother's voice tickled his ears. "I raised you better than this."

Mad froze, his heart pounding so hard the whole table had to hear it. He scanned the faces at the table—Jade's concern, Scarlet's confusion, Dylan's carefully blank expression. Gideon's steely disapproval—even if Isabela stepped out of line, he'd defend his sister. The children had fallen silent, picking up on the tension from the adults.

None of the faces matched that voice. He didn't know if he was relieved or not.

The next gentle whisper came from the empty space

to his left. "It's okay. You're going to be okay."

"Mad?" Jade asked softly.

He ignored her and looked to his left, and the space wasn't empty anymore.

Adriana Rios was radiant. The artwork never did her justice. Even if it captured her long black hair and warm brown eyes, her heart-shaped face and her open smile—even if it captured her beauty, it was never *her*.

The truth of Adriana had always been in the imperfections that art smoothed away. The scar across her cheek that she'd earned while protecting a younger cousin in the first days after the Flares. The lopsided eyebrows, one slightly higher than the other, so that she always looked like she had one arched.

Her hands. Not smooth and soft and cradling a heart, but work-roughened and strong. Adriana hadn't ruled her people from a comfortable distance. She'd dug in the dirt with them, taught the poor how to cultivate gardens to feed their families. She'd built them shelters with her own two hands. She'd celebrated their triumphs and mourned their tragedies.

And when they needed someone to fight for them, she'd done that, too. The gentle depictions never captured the fire in her eyes, the sharp bite of her temper, the depth of her rage when faced with cruelty and corruption.

She was more than what they remembered. And she was standing two feet from his elbow.

"You look like me," she murmured. "I always thought you'd look like your father."

The room swam. Mad clenched his eyes shut and wiped his hands over his face. They came away damp—he was sweating. Of course he was. It was so damn *hot*.

He opened his eyes, and his mother was still there.

"Mad." Wood screeched against the floor as Gideon shoved his chair back. "Something's wrong."

That was an understatement. Because Mad was seeing ghosts—again. And this time he wasn't even dying.

Maybe.

Hands touched his face—one cool and steady, the other soft and trembling. "He's burning up." His mother's voice joined with Scarlet's, like an audio recording laid over another.

He stared up into his mother's soft, sad eyes, and she felt like the only real thing in the room. The color had leached from everyone else, but she was so bright, so solid.

So *alive.* And the hand stroking his cheek was whole, as if she'd never begged him to take a knife and slice off one of her fingers. Their kidnappers had been too cowardly to touch her—even in open rebellion against the Prophet, they'd been afraid.

Adriana had feared nothing except losing him.

"I'm sorry," he whispered. "I'm so sorry."

Big hands knocked everything else aside, and light directly in his eyes blotted out the world. "Pupils are dilated. No response to light. Jade, get my bag. *Now.*"

A chair toppled over, clattering so loudly against the floor Mad flinched. The light hurt. His head throbbed. He tried to pull free of Dylan's hands. "I heard her. I *saw* her. My mother."

"He's having a vision." Victoria's voice held a reverential awe that made Mad's skin crawl, and it was the last thing he heard before their voices melted into incoherent buzzing, lost beneath the throbbing of his heart. Blood pounded in his ears, but Victoria's words chased around and around, cutting through his panic until he wanted to laugh.

When he died, they'd finally have what they wanted from him. A pretty new martyr.

Vision, my ass. Dylan gritted his teeth. He didn't have time to argue with half-baked assumptions. Whatever Mad was on, it sure as hell wasn't religious ecstasy. He was tripping—*hard*.

How was a question for later, along with *why*. All that mattered now was the assessment, but as Dylan lifted Mad's wrist, terror threatened to overwhelm him.

He'd trained for this. Years of lectures and labs, internship, residency. He could shut his emotions down in a clinical situation. Hell, it was the only time he *could* shut them down completely. But now, looking at Mad as Gideon and Scarlet lowered him to the floor...

Fear threatened to choke him. His vision blurred, and his first instinct was to reach for the tiny tablets in his pocket. Oblivion was so fucking close—

He ruthlessly shoved the thought away. He needed to be focused, clearheaded. He needed to be here—

For Mad. His pupils were huge, so dilated they nearly obliterated his gold-flecked irises. A sheen of sweat dotted his forehead, and his trembling worsened. Dylan slid his fingers over Mad's wrist, searching for his racing pulse, and another sort of panic rose.

His lover's heartbeat was erratic, but not racing like it should have been. Instead, his heart was thumping slowly, each labored beat taking longer than the one before.

Holy shit. "Jade!"

She appeared on Mad's other side, breathless and disheveled as she sank to her knees and pried open the bag. "What do you need?"

"Atropine. He's bradycardic." Maricela covered her mouth to stifle a confused sob, so Dylan gentled his voice and explained while Jade prepared the syringe. "His heart rate doesn't fit the rest of his symptoms."

"What does that mean?" Scarlet asked as she helped him cut open Mad's shirt.

"It means he's not just high." Dylan dug his transcutaneous pacemaker out of the bag. He peeled the backing from both pads and placed them—one high on the right side of Mad's chest, and the other on the left side of his rib cage.

He flicked on the tracker and watched the screen come to life with a series of beeps and trails that represented Mad's heart rate. A normal human heartbeat was poetry, a series of spikes and dips in just the right intervals, just the right times. Mad's was a mess, the intervals all fucked up, and the recovery times longer than normal.

His heart was failing right in front of Dylan's eyes.

"Push the atropine," he ordered, "and get ready to start pacing."

Mad's hand shot up, wrapping around Dylan's arm in a bruising grip. "Take me back—" He gasped in a breath, and his fingers flexed painfully. "Four. Bury me in Four."

Dylan's heart twisted. "You're not going to die, sweet-heart. Not on my watch." He couldn't afford to sedate him, not without knowing what drugs—*or poisons*, a tiny voice whispered—he had in his system. "When I start up this machine, it's going to hurt. I'm sorry."

Mad muttered something in Spanish. Gideon pried Mad's hand from Dylan's arm and closed both of his own around it. "He says he's ready."

When Dylan switched the monitor into active pacing mode, Mad stiffened and groaned through clenched teeth. Maricela and Isabela clutched at each other, weeping, while Scarlet looked on in ashen-faced silence.

Jade's expression was blank as she took a moment to twist her hair up out of her face. But her eyes were dark with fear when she met his, and her hands shook slightly as she rolled up her sleeves.

Dylan touched her arm. "The atropine and the pacing will get it done. We'll stabilize him, get him to the hospital. I promise."

"But what *happened?*" Gideon growled, his voice rough with a dangerous edge that was anything but holy.

Dylan's gaze skated past him and snagged on the gob-let Mad had been using during dinner. It was different from everyone else's, delicately wrought glass etched with scrollwork and flowers, rimmed with gold. "What's with the fancy cup?"

Gideon glanced at the table, his brow furrowed. "One of the glass crafters made it for me a couple years ago. I always—" He broke off, his gaze fixing on the carved back of his usual seat—the seat Mad had been in tonight—and his jaw tightened. "Shit."

"So it's yours."

"Yes." He whispered something too soft for Dylan to understand and brushed Mad's hair back from his forehead. "Could this be poison?"

What better way to get rid of the leader of Sector One? One showy religious experience followed by a heart attack? His people would be too busy building his fucking shrine to think about assassination plots. "It's a possibility. A good one."

Dylan glanced at Jade. She rose silently and crossed to the table to retrieve the glass. The pitcher of wine still sat in front of Leo, who paled visibly. "I poured the wine for him."

Isabela wrapped her arms around him. "We all drank it, love."

Which meant the poison had to be in the cup. Dylan clenched his jaw and checked the monitor. Mad's heart rate had steadied, but he'd slipped completely out of consciousness now—a blessing, maybe, when the cardiac pacer was sending regular jolts of electricity through his body to keep his heart going.

He turned to Gideon. "We need to get him to the hospital and find out *exactly* what he's been given. We can keep him alive in the meantime, but that's the only way to make him well."

"Maricela, have one of the drivers pull a car around." Gideon didn't look up from Mad's slack face as she rushed to obey. "I'll stay and question everyone who could have laid a hand on that cup."

"Not a bad idea, Gideon." The monitor was still beeping steadily, but Dylan had to press his fingertips to the spot below Mad's chin and feel the pulse thumping there before he could swallow past the lump in his throat. "Because it looks like someone's trying to kill you."

9

T HE PRINTOUT IN his hand made sense, but it wasn't the whole picture. Not by a long shot.

"Lysergic acid diethylamide." Dylan tossed the papers on the table in front of Jade and turned back toward the row of vials—the dregs of the wine remaining in Mad's goblet, divided into miniscule samples. "No wonder he was seeing dead people. Someone dosed him with LSD."

She frowned and studied the paper. "But that's not all. It can't be, can it?"

"No." He glared at the vials. "There's something else here, something quieter. Something hiding under the trip."

Soft fingertips brushed the back of his neck. A calming touch, warm and gentle. "You'll find it."

Her quiet confidence should have soothed him. It did, but it also left him feeling out of sorts, because she didn't understand the truth. None of them did.

The reason he was so damn good at healing was be-cause he knew every possible way to inflict injury. He knew every pressure point, every weak spot, every un-pleasant sensation that could make someone beg for mercy. He'd been trained as well as any of Eden's soldiers, only his battleground was the human body, and his weapon was knowledge.

He used his knowledge to heal these days, but he could never escape its origins in torture. He felt himself slipping into those old habits now, letting his mind sink into the depths of violence, trying to understand.

"If it were me," he whispered, "I'd start flashy. Psy-chedelics are a good choice for One—you heard that woman."

She stroked his nape again. "Mmm. Visions."

"If they're ready to jump to that conclusion because no one's thinking drugs, it'd be easy to slip in something else."

"Something subtle." Her voice dropped to a whisper, too. "What would you use, if you couldn't afford to create a martyr?"

"There are a hundred things no one would test for. Things no one uses anymore." It would have to be a drug that was fast and deadly, that would stop the heart with a minimum of fuss and leave everyone believing that God had simply called their golden boy home. "Digitoxin, prob-ably. It fits his symptoms, and you don't even have to get it from Five. The glycoside is extracted from the foxglove plant. You could grow it in your backyard, bypass a paper trail altogether."

Jade pressed gently against his shoulder, urging him to face her. "You intervened in time. Mad will recover."

He couldn't look at her, couldn't see that quiet cer-tainty reflected in her eyes. "It's not that simple."

"Dylan."

He finally met her gaze and almost flinched. "What if we hadn't been there?"

She laid her hand on his cheek. "Then Gideon Rios

would be dead. Because I don't think Mad would have stayed without us."

Gentle words, but they twisted in the pit of his stomach like a knife. He'd spent years letting strangers depend on him only in the most fleeting, superficial of ways. And now, not only did he have Jade looking at him like he could move heaven and earth, but there was Mad to think about. Mad, who sometimes looked at him the same way, who made Dylan want to be as good a man as he obviously thought he was.

The only one of them with any sense was Scarlet. She looked at him and saw danger, pain. Smart fucking girl.

He turned his head.

Jade sighed. "You always do that. Turn away, as if you can't stand to let me see you."

"What if I can't?"

"What are you afraid I'll see? Too much darkness, or not enough?"

There was a solemnity about her tonight, an exhaustion that seemed to permeate her soul. So he gave her an honest answer. "I wouldn't worry at all if I was sweetness and light, like Mad or Scarlet. But I'm not. And neither are you."

"Neither am I," she agreed softly. "So don't hide from me, Dylan. You can't show me anything that will shock me."

She believed it to be the truth, so he let it lie. "What do you suggest, Jade? What's our next move?"

She turned back to face the row of vials and brushed her finger over the top of one. "We use the darkness inside us to protect them."

"How?"

"We find out who would want Gideon dead." When she looked up at him, he saw death in her eyes. "And we take care of it before he tries again. Or succeeds, and leaves Mad with Sector One around his neck like a noose."

The possibilities were as endless as the multitude of

drugs someone could have used to stop Mad's heart. An angry sector leader. Eden. A jilted lover. A true believer who thought Gideon was fucking up the Prophet's legacy. Or, as Jade had pointed out, someone who wanted Mad in control of Sector One, for whatever reason.

The last possibility made Dylan's blood run cold. It was the last thing Mad wanted—hell, when he thought he was dying, his last, frantic thoughts had been about the spectacle One would make of him. But he would do it if he had to, if walking away meant suffering, or another civil war.

Dylan sat back and held up both hands. "You're the expert in human behavior, but motive is tricky. Know what's not?"

"Opportunity." She tilted her head. "Anywhere else, I'd say it was easy. The leaders in Eden barely know their servants exist. I managed to subvert the loyalties of half my patron's household by my second month. But Mad's family knows their people. Even *he* knows them."

"You know what Scarlet would say." He laid his hand on Jade's hip. For a moment, all he could see was Scarlet's hand in the exact same spot, skin on skin, and arousal tightened in his gut. "Fuck it. Gideon won't rest until he finds the bastard, we know that. So we leave the manhunt to Rios and his rage, and we take care of Mad."

Jade traced her fingertips over the back of his hand. "And Scarlet."

And Scarlet. Her discomfort during the boisterous family scene had been achingly apparent. Whatever her life had been like, Dylan was sure it had been lonely. But her distress paled next to her terror at Mad's medical emergency. She hadn't panicked, but she hadn't been able to hide her agony, either. It was seared onto Dylan's memory, another glimpse behind her tough façade. "She loves him, doesn't she?"

"She doesn't believe so." Jade's smile was sweet and a little sad. "I think I'm safer for her to care about. I'm not a

prince in exile who might have to take up the crown someday. I'm not going anywhere."

He turned his hand and wrapped his fingers around
hers. "Don't be too hard on her—or yourself."

"I'm not." She lifted one shoulder in a tired shrug. "It's
who they are. Sweetness and light. I want to see them
shine together."

He tugged her into his lap. The stool rolled, and his
back hit the edge of the metal counter, rattling the vials.
Dylan ignored it. "Don't forget how much they shine for
you."

"For us," she countered, leaning against him. She was
soft and warm, and something more—easy, maybe, in a
way she hadn't been before. The subtle tension, the arti-
fice, was gone. She wasn't lying with her body anymore.
"They're so bright. Are you ever afraid you'll get burned?"

"Not at all." He didn't have room to worry about that,
not with every bit of emotion, of *feeling*, licking over his
soul like flame. Everything in the world already burned.
At least he could make them—Mad, Scarlet, even Jade—
burn with him.

Scarlet spent her vigil counting Mad's breaths.

She never meant to. At first, it was instinctive, a way
to reassure herself that the silent rise and fall of his chest
was steady, reliable. Slowly, it evolved into a way to dis-
tract herself. If she spent the quiet hours at his bedside
replaying the scene at Gideon's estate in her mind, she'd
go insane.

So she counted. One after another, until the numbers
blurred and ran together and the silence became so loud
that she had to break it. So she opened her mouth and began to sing.

Softly. Nothing that would disturb Mad's rest, just the
silly tunes and lullabies she'd heard as a child. When she

ran out of those, she made up more, nonsense rhymes that almost made her smile.

Almost.

But a good lullaby was about more than the melody or words. It was about the vibrations, a tactile rhythm of human contact. There was just enough room in his hospital bed for her to climb in beside him. She stretched out on her side, curled around him, pressed her chest to his shoulder and her lips to his temple, and started all over.

"Buzzing bees?" Mad's voice was as rusty as his laugh. "Have you ever seen one?"

Relief stole her voice for a handful of choked, painful seconds. "No. Have you?"

"I saw a whole farm full of them once." He turned his face to hers. "Thousands and thousands. I should take you sometime."

"We've got to get you back on your feet first." The words trembled, and Scarlet squeezed her eyes shut.

"Keep singing to me." He covered her hand with his. "I could hear you."

She shook her head. Staying here felt selfish, too much like hiding. "Dylan will want to know you're awake."

"Dylan will come check on me eventually." His hand tightened, surprisingly strong for a man in a hospital bed. "Don't leave me, Scarlet. Please."

The plea shredded what was left of her resistance. "I won't." She brushed her lips over his temple and snuggled closer. "Tell me about the bee farm."

"It's big. Bigger than the warehouse where we hold our fight nights. A giant greenhouse. They keep the bees inside because they're so rare—people try to steal them. And inside it's just rows of sunflowers and clover and hives..." His voice drifted off as he rubbed his forehead against hers. "It's magic."

Hiding. They could talk about the honey farm, stay away from everything real, but it wouldn't change anything. "Someone tried to kill your cousin."

"The cup." He sighed. "What was in it?"

"I don't know. Dylan and Jade are working on it."

"Where's Gideon?"

"Looking for his own answers." Scarlet slipped her hand from beneath his and laid it on his chest. "I was so scared, and I'm ashamed of myself."

"Ashamed?"

"Because I shouldn't tell you," she explained help-lessly. "You're hurt. This—none of this is about me. It's about you."

"Hey." He moved carefully as he rolled to face her. "You can talk to me. You can always talk to me."

Always, but it wasn't enough. There were others who were worried, people who meant more to him—his family, Dylan. Jade. "I'm just glad you're okay."

"Scarlet." He cupped her cheek, brushing away the tears she hadn't realized were falling. "Don't worry about me. I'm hard to kill. People have been trying my whole life."

"Amazingly, that does *not* make me feel better."

Mad grinned with morbid amusement. "At least they weren't trying to kill me this time?"

"Hilarious." But seeing him smile brought the relief rushing back, and Scarlet found herself mirroring his ex-pression.

"That's it, sweetheart." He stroked her cheek again. "We laugh or we cry, and I decided a long time ago I wasn't going to let them see me cry."

Them. He said it like she should understand, like they had a shared enemy. But what the fuck could a street rat from Three have in common with a runaway prince?

Not a whole hell of a lot. Just an adoptive sector—and the tattoos around their wrists. "Dallas is gonna lose his shit," she whispered. "Completely. Lex won't be able to contain him this time—not that I think she'd try very hard. Not after this."

Mad took a slow breath and closed his eyes. "He'll

keep his shit together. Because something bigger is going on."

"What, you mean the bombing in Two?"

"More than that." He slid an arm around her, his fingers tracing up to sink into her hair. "We have to head back to Four soon. Dallas is calling everyone together for a vote."

Something in his tone raced up her spine, bringing with it a cold jolt of awareness. "About Eden. About going to war with the city."

"Yeah." His voice dropped. "It scares the shit out of me, but so does what happened in Two."

Only an idiot wouldn't be terrified, because the two things were intimately entwined. When Eden's leaders felt threatened, whether actively or just by someone's radical ideas, they lashed out. "Better to go down swinging than let them stomp you like a bug."

"We won't be the only ones swinging." He stroked her hair with steady hands. "Eden can't destroy all of us. They need Five and Eight, at least. And the crops..."

"And Four?" She almost didn't ask, because she already knew the answer—Sector Four's liquor was worth far, far less than Dallas O'Kane's head on a silver platter.

Mad finally opened his eyes, and he looked tired. *Haunted.* "I'm the worst kind of asshole. I want you and Dylan and Jade to stay here."

Because it would be safer. Scarlet snorted. "If you think I'm gonna punk out when things get tough—"

He shut her up with a kiss.

She'd kissed him before, in the tent and during the stolen, dreamy hour when they'd all come together. This kiss held a different kind of desperation, not a physical hunger that would no longer be contained, but a silent plea. For understanding, for connection—she didn't know.

All she knew was the soft graze of Mad's tongue against hers, his hand on her jaw, his slow, careful exploration—like he was learning her, memorizing her.

He broke away to kiss the corner of her lips, and then the tip of her nose. But his words were serious. "I need to do something before we go back to Four."

She couldn't stop her hands from tightening out of worry. "Mad..."

"It doesn't involve killing," he assured her. "Exorcising, maybe."

"Can I help?"

Mad closed his eyes. "I need you to. All of you. I need to..."

She cradled his face. "What is it?"

He took a deep breath, then another. Slowly, like his body was aching. Like his *heart* was aching. "Dallas and Lex know. Ace does too, some. Cruz and Bren have probably figured it out. But I've never—I've never told anyone. And I need to, so I can let it go."

"Tell us?"

His eyes drifted open. "How Adrian Rios died."

10

T HE SHRINE HAD spilled out of the building that had once contained it and onto the surrounding structures. Most of them were abandoned, walls crumbling, roofs destroyed in a civil war that had threatened to tear a sector apart.

Mad had abused his Rios privileges to have the entire area cleared. The Riders had swept through, urging pilgrims and worshippers to leave their offerings and finish their prayers. By the time the sun kissed the hills in the west, the only people left were Dylan, Scarlet, and Jade.

And him. Adrian Maddox Rios, grandson of the Prophet, son of Santa Adriana. Tragic hero of a civil war—but not in the way anyone believed.

The building wasn't much. It hadn't been much then, either. Cement and chipping mortar and long-broken windows. He remembered them being covered in thick curtains, hiding the rebels inside—and the hostages trapped in the basement.

But the building wasn't the point. The shrine was what mattered—two decades' worth of flowers and candles and charms and offerings. Someone had covered the east and south walls in planks of wood that glittered with milagros in the last sunlight.

Everything had ended here. His innocence, his faith in his grandfather—nearly his sanity. He'd run to Sector Four, and when that hadn't been far enough, he'd talked Dallas into letting him head out west, all the way to the Pacific Ocean. As far south as the old border with Mexico, and far enough north that he'd seen the sky light up in a riot of color—greens and blues and purples and pinks.

Running hadn't done him a damn bit of good, and he was tired of being a coward.

"This is where it happened," he said. Slowly at first, but the words came faster and faster, like he could rip off this bandage if he just kept ahead of the pain. "The civil war had been going for several months. A few outright fights, but mostly bloodless political posturing. They wanted my grandfather to abdicate. They thought he was corrupt, that he was abusing his power."

A valid enough complaint, except that the rebels hadn't been outraged at the abuse. They'd been jealous of it, and willing to do whatever it took to get their piece of the Prophet's expansive pie.

But that was the easy part, the stuff most people already knew. He swallowed and fixed his gaze on the flickering flame of a candle, because he'd never said these words before, and he couldn't get them out if he had to face Jade's gentle sadness or Scarlet's worry or Dylan's tense concern.

"They kidnapped my mother and got me as a bonus. They dumped us in the basement in this shitty little house and held us in the dark."

In the dark. As if the words encompassed the terror of it. The dank scent of dirt and mildew. The drip of water from leaky pipes. The way his eyes had strained to adjust but couldn't, because there was no relief from that inky blackness. He'd been thirteen. Old enough for a man's duties and responsibilities, according to his grandfather.

So shame had mingled with his terror—but not enough to keep him from clutching his mother's hand while she stroked his hair and murmured for him to be brave and promised they'd get out.

Only one of them had.

"We were there for days," Mad said hoarsely. "Barely enough water to survive. Stale bread to eat. They sent my grandfather a ransom demand."

Dylan took a step toward him. "Mad—"

Scarlet cut him off with an angry, incoherent sound. "And the bastard paid it, right? He paid it, because he sure as hell had the money."

Painful laughter shredded its way out of Mad's chest. How differently would the story have ended if his grandfather had practiced what he preached? If he'd valued family over power? If he'd chosen love over his own pride. "It wasn't about the money. It was about being challenged and giving in. He couldn't. So he decided to have a vision."

Her glower deepened. "A vision?"

"Like Abraham." And because they probably wouldn't have a fucking clue what that meant, he elaborated. "God was demanding proof of his faith, Scarlet. A willingness to sacrifice what he treasured most if that was the price for the safety and sanctity of Sector One."

"Oh, Mad." Jade touched his shoulder, and her sympathy scraped him raw. No wonder she hated the pity he'd been choking back every time he looked at her—hers made him feel naked and vulnerable. It made him feel small.

He fought it off with another laugh. "The rebels didn't believe his vision. So they came down to the cellar to prove they *would* hurt us. But none of them could bring themselves to touch my mother, just in case it was all true. So they shoved a gun against my head and told her—"

His voice cracked. This was the nightmare, the one that could still jolt him out of bed screaming, struggling, tearing at anyone who got close because if he could just go back, if he could do *something*...

But it always played out the same. The gun against his temple, mean, digging into his skin. The knife in his hand, his entire body shaking with the desire to *use* it, to spin and plunge it into the nearest man and damn the consequences, because that's what a man would do, should do, *had to do*.

The voice, cruel and heartless and cold, giving Adriana a choice that, to her, was no choice at all. *"Your finger or his corpse. We're sending your father one or the other."*

Mad swallowed the memories of his helpless fury. "They put the gun to my head and told my mother she could convince me to cut off one of her fingers for them, or they'd send my grandfather a dead grandson instead."

"No." Dylan reached out, then jerked his hand back, sorrow and horror warring on his face.

Sorrow—for him. As if he deserved it. He'd been the one to cave in, to scream as he carved the knife into her flesh. Adriana had suffered in silence, no doubt trying to spare him. "I should have stabbed the guy instead, and she would have been free. They weren't desperate enough to hurt her yet. If they'd killed me, she could have walked out without anyone laying a hand on her."

"Oh, sweetheart." Dylan breathed a sigh so heavy it almost sounded like a groan. "If they'd killed you, she wouldn't have walked out at all."

"That's not how mothers work." Jade stroked his shoulder. "Not the good ones. Believe me, Mad. All she wanted in the world was to get you out alive."

He closed his eyes. "I know. But knowing doesn't make it easier."

"Could anything?" Dylan asked. "Maybe...some things aren't supposed to be easier. They stay with you forever, because you need to remember."

He'd never forget her. She was still vivid in his mind. A memory, a hallucination. A ghost. But for the first time, he was sharing her with people who knew him as Mad. Who cared about who she'd been to him, not who she'd been to an entire sector. "That's why living here is hell. They tattoo her on their skin, but they don't even know how or why she died. Just the story my grandfather sold them."

"So tell them," Scarlet muttered, somewhere between a whisper and a flat, stark command. "The truth. He can't stop you now, and Gideon wouldn't. You could tell them all what really happened."

It was so simple, so inconceivable, that it stole his breath. "People would fall apart."

"So fucking what? If that's all it takes to shake their world view, maybe it's not such a great one."

"Scarlet," Jade whispered.

"No, she's right." Mad shoved his fingers into his hair and pulled until his scalp tingled. "But I'm scared. With all the shit that's coming, we need everyone. Even people with a shaky world view."

Dylan sidestepped a cluster of candles. "What shit? What's coming?"

Mad glanced at Scarlet. She was fierce and fearless, and there was no way to keep her out of the war to come. But Dylan and Jade—they were healers. They needed to be protected, safe, because they were the ones who'd have to pick up the pieces when it was all over.

Scarlet held his gaze. "The fight, Doc. The big one."

"Eden," Jade said, and oh *God*. The ice in her voice. Scarlet would burn and rage, but Jade's fury was fresh and vast, and if he fought to protect her the way he'd been trying to protect her, she'd cut through him on the way to her vengeance.

There was no keeping any of them safe. The best he could do was keep them together.

He turned his back on the shrine and its offerings to

face them, the people who mattered more to him than all his ghosts. "We leave for Sector Four tomorrow. Dallas is holding a vote, but you know it doesn't matter. No one will back down. We'll be at war, and the only question is how long it'll take Eden to figure it out."

Dylan's face was inscrutable. "And the rest of the sectors?"

"Everyone who matters is already in. One, Five, Eight. Not the leaders of Six and Seven, but the people who control the food production."

"So it's already decided," he said flatly. "The people at the top say it's time to revolt, and fuck what happens to the little guys. You know, the ones who suffer when things go cold because they don't have solar converters. The ones who die when the shells fall because they don't have nice, safe bunkers to hide in."

The bitterness sliced deep, and Mad clenched his fists. "Come on, Dylan. You know Dallas. He won't sign on to something like this and then ignore his people. *Any* of his people."

"And neither will your cousin. But can you say the same for the other leaders?"

There was nothing to say. They all knew the answer. The leaders of Six and Seven were useless. Ryder was an unknown quantity, and Cerys was in the wind, leaving no one to speak for what was left of her sector. And Jim—

Jim had been planning this from the beginning. Only a fool would underestimate how far he'd go and how much he'd sacrifice.

"Dallas and Lex aren't stupid," Jade said, sliding her hand into Mad's. She squeezed, her deceptively fragile fingers warm and strong around his. "And they aren't shortsighted. They won't stop caring about people because of a sector boundary."

Dylan ran his fingers roughly through his hair. "Look, I—"

Scarlet stepped in front of him, her voice low and

pleading. "It's worth it. You of all people know it's true, Dylan. No matter how bad things get, they can't be worse than the way they are now."

He stared at her for an eternity, then held up both hands in surrender. "All right, all right. It doesn't matter, anyway. No one's exactly asking for my input."

"Because, in the end, we're not the ones who decide." Mad's heart thumped hard, and it was a struggle to choke out his next words. Even with part of him hoping Dylan would take the chance to run as far and fast as it took to get to safety, it was a struggle. "But you don't have to wait around for the fighting. None of you do."

Scarlet crossed her arms over her chest. He could practically hear her words echoing through the space between them—*if you think I'm gonna punk out*—but she remained silent.

Dylan eyed him, as well, but with confusion. "What are you saying?"

Run. Hide. Be safe. Christ, he was selfish. He couldn't urge Dylan to leave. He could barely offer freedom. "Just that we all have a choice, and I'll support yours. All of you. No matter what you decide."

He saw the moment understanding dawned in Dylan's gaze. His eyes shuttered, and his shoulders stiffened. "I see."

Shit. He'd fucked it up, and with Scarlet and Jade watching. Maybe if it had just been him and Dylan, he could have found the words to fix it. Or no words—they did better with hands and mouths, communicating through pleasure and pain.

Tonight. He'd make it right tonight. Because if he could stand on the spot where his parents—and his childhood—had died and lay his heart bare without the world ending...

Fuck. He could survive anything.

11

SCARLET HAD NEVER considered herself a particularly good person. But now she knew she'd been overly generous with herself, because she was a bad person, a *terrible* person. One who was going straight to hell.

Ever since their visit to the eerie shrine where Mad had poured out his heart as well as his painful past, he and Dylan had been on edge. There was a tension simmering between them—not quite hurt, and not quite anger—that twisted in Scarlet's belly, scraping over her nerves and raising her awareness.

She was definitely going to hell, because only a sick fucker would find that tension erotic.

Mad shrugged out of his jacket and tossed it across the back of the couch. His movements were lazy, almost relaxed, even though there was so much energy coiled inside him that it turned his walk toward the minibar into a prowl. "Who wants a drink?"

Dylan stood by the door, as if he hadn't quite convinced himself yet not to turn around and walk back
through it. "I'm game."

"Plastic cups and fresh bottles." Mad lifted one—an
amber bottle with a label declaring it one of Nessa's exclu-
sive batches—and rubbed his thumb over the unbroken
seal. "Maricela isn't taking chances."

"Do you blame her?" Scarlet kicked off her shoes.
Across the room, Jade was doing the same, her appraising
gaze flickering back and forth between the two men.

"I suppose not." He dragged four cups into a line and
cracked the seal, spilling a double's worth of liquor into
each one. "We might as well enjoy it. This is a good batch.
It's so rare in Four because Gideon got half of the bottles
in exchange for growing the juniper."

No one gave a fuck about the gin, not even Mad. But
talking to fill the silence was how most people dealt with
the kind of pressure that pervaded the room, a strain that
could snap at any moment.

Mad set down the bottle. As if taking pity on him, Jade
joined him and picked up two—but when she carried one
to Scarlet, she realized it wasn't pity at all. Jade had
neatly removed them as a source of distraction.

And Mad knew it. His jaw clenched as he grabbed the
remaining cups and approached Dylan. He held one out,
silent and challenging.

Dylan grabbed his wrist instead, sloshing the clear
liquor onto the woven rug. "Don't ever do it again."

"Dylan—"

"I mean it." He glared at Mad. "Don't ever talk to me
like I could just walk away from you, because I can't. You
should know that by now."

Mad closed his eyes with a frustrated growl. "I don't
want you to walk away. I want to hide you somewhere safe
so you don't risk your fucking life."

"My life?" Dylan echoed with a laugh. "*My life* doesn't
mean a goddamn thing—not without you in it."

The world froze. This was a personal moment, an intensely private one, and Scarlet willed herself to look away. But she couldn't. She was a part of this already, and she could only watch as Mad drained the second cup and let it drop to the floor.

It bounced softly on the rug. The thump of Dylan's back hitting the door was louder. Mad groaned and kissed him, wrapping his fingers so hard around Dylan's upper arm that they bit into flesh.

Scarlet's smoldering arousal burst into flame, kindled not by the kiss, but by the desperate ferocity behind it. She'd never thought that Dylan could feel this much, this hard. Mad did, of course—it was who he was, just like Jade—but Dylan had always seemed vaguely cold. Bored.

He wasn't bored now. He gripped the other man's hips and dragged him closer, close enough to tear his mouth away and sink his teeth into Mad's shoulder through his shirt. Mad slammed his free hand to the door and ground against him. "Then stay with me. Stay with *us.*"

Dylan urged him back, away from the door—and toward the bed. "All this talk," he murmured, "and you still don't listen."

Mad jerked at Dylan's belt. "We've never been good with words."

Dylan captured his lips again, and Jesus Christ, was Mad ever wrong. Because even with their mouths fused, they were saying *so much.* Scarlet watched as every touch stripped away something—a piece of clothing or an inhibition, a hesitation or a doubt—until they were naked in front of her. Completely exposed.

Growling, Mad threaded his fingers through Dylan's hair. One rough jerk dragged Dylan's head back, the raw possessiveness evident as Mad closed his teeth over the other man's pulse.

They moved in concert, drifting across the room. When they stepped close enough to the bed, Scarlet didn't think, didn't second-guess what she should or even could do.

She reached out. Her fingertips drifted across Mad's side and down to Dylan's hip. From darker skin to pale, the contrast mesmerizing, but not as much as the heat they shared. Both of them burned, and she needed to *taste* it.

She leaned in blindly, drawing her tongue over taut skin and hard muscle, and her breath caught when Mad tangled his free hand in her shirt and tumbled back to the mattress, hauling them both with him.

They landed in a sprawl, Scarlet half trapped between them, and Mad dragged at her shirt, pulling it up.

Just like this. The words were silent, released only on her sigh of pleasure as Dylan's nails scraped her nipple through her bra. Right here, right now, it didn't matter how long they were willing to share their heat with her and Jade. All that mattered was drinking in as much of it as they could.

Mad tossed her shirt from the bed as his teeth skimmed her jaw. "Pants," he rasped, but it was Jade's familiar fingers that tugged at the button on her jeans. Her hair fell across Scarlet's shoulder, and she tangled her hand in the long, sweet-smelling strands.

Mad trembled under Dylan's touch, but Scarlet trembled under his gaze. He was watching her with a challenging glint in his eye, almost as if he was daring her to feel more, do more. To reach out.

So she covered Dylan's hand with hers and urged it lower. Mad tensed as they brushed his abdomen, and when Dylan's fingers curled around his cock, he groaned and thrust up. The sound shivered down her spine and snagged on the heat of Jade's hands as she stripped away denim and delicate lace, leaving Scarlet naked except for her bra.

Dylan bent, his cheek rubbing her bare hip as he licked the head of Mad's cock.

"Fuck, yes." Mad was already drunk with pleasure as

he pushed up into Dylan's mouth. Scarlet's pussy clenched, and again when Jade nudged the piercing above her clit.

"Soon," Jade whispered into her ear. "Soon you'll be the one he's pushing into. I want to watch you take his cock for the first time."

Scarlet turned her head, tumbling into a hot, open kiss. Jade's mouth was so familiar that she couldn't remember a time before its sweet warmth. At the same time, this was brand new, an uncharted world of desire and sin where absolutely nothing tasted of guilt.

Jade's touch between her thighs vanished. Scarlet broke their kiss and watched Mad drag Jade's fingers to his mouth. He licked the wetness from her fingertips without looking away from Scarlet. "I don't know what I want more. My cock in her, or my tongue."

Dylan rose with a lazy half-grin, one that should have looked smug and self-satisfied. Instead, it looked like a promise. "You just have to trust me."

"Always." One word, raw and rough around the edges, the answer to the tension that had been sparking between them since their visit to the shrine.

Dylan knelt behind her, his hands blazing shivering paths all the way up her legs. He gripped her hips and whispered, "Say yes."

"Yes." The answer came without thought. It had to, because if she gave herself time to think, she'd have to wonder what it meant to give your trust to a man like him.

His fingers tightened, biting into flesh, and he lifted her. Mad moved, and so did Jade, all three of them focused on just one thing—the lazy thrust of Mad's hips as he rubbed his shaft teasingly over Scarlet's clit.

"Christ," he breathed. "You burn so hot, so fast."

"So beautiful," Jade added, stroking a finger around Scarlet's nipple. "Watch her eyes the first time you really fuck her deep. You'll be drunk on her for days. I was."

Scarlet couldn't look away, because there was no-where to look. She was surrounded, caged by the same lust that lit Mad's face.

Dylan pressed his chest against her back, and she swallowed a moan at the heat and hardness. "You want him." It was a declaration, not a question.

She answered anyway, her voice shaking with truth. "I want him."

He hummed his approval and lowered her, just a lit-tle. "Then take him."

She tried, but Dylan held her fast, forcing her to wait, shivering, as Mad rubbed up against her again. Hot and hard, his shaft slicking past her outer lips to torment her with grazing pressure on her clit.

Then his thumb nudged her piercing. His other hand gripped his cock, positioning the head as his thumb made careful circles. "Take me, Scarlet."

Even as he whispered the plea, he was thrusting up—slowly, taking all the time in the world. She whimpered, desperate for more, and it was Dylan who gave it to her. He pushed her hips down *hard*, turning the careful ad-vance into a quick, violent possession.

Yes. Fuck fuck fuck *yes.*

Mad gritted out a curse and rolled his hips. "Right there—keep her *right there.*"

"Thought you said you trust me." The words blew across the back of Scarlet's shoulder, followed by the lazy glide of Dylan's tongue over her skin.

Mad growled and thumped his head back against the pillows. "You and your dark, twisty fucking mind. It shouldn't be half as hot as it is."

"But it is." Dylan pressed an open kiss to the base of Scarlet's neck and lifted her again.

She gripped his flexing arms, but he held her steadily, moving her hips not only up and down, but in a gentle rock. Pleasure pulsed through her, an inescapable flash echoed by Mad's moan, and she jerked in Dylan's grasp.

He held tight with a soft, soothing murmur. "I can let go, or I can show you how good it can be with him."

It meant nothing—they were just filthy words meant to crank Mad's arousal higher—until she looked down at Mad. Really *looked*, and holy Christ, the intensity vibrating off him was spellbinding. Every muscle tensed, the one in his jaw ticking as he reached out and traced a path up the center of her body to stroke her throat.

The prize wasn't getting off harder instead of faster. This was her reward—*their* reward—a passion that bordered on religious in its fervor. Being worshipped, adored.

Loved.

Mad continued to caress her, letting Dylan control her movements as he focused on his slow exploration. He followed the line of her jaw up to the curve of her cheekbone. Smoothed a few strands of hair from her temple. Ran a fingertip along her brow and dragged it down her nose.

His thumb pressed to her mouth, gentle but somehow lewd as he used it to part her lips.

Jade trailed kisses up Scarlet's throat, each a whisper-soft caress. "This is what you do to me. What I never have the patience to do to you, because I can't deny you anything."

A shudder seized her, and Scarlet groaned as that tiny movement rippled through her like a shock.

Dylan began to shift her hips again, the same slow, smooth rock—only this time he moved with her, like he was doing more than controlling the speed and rhythm. Like he was the one fucking them both.

That muscle in Mad's jaw jumped again. He edged the tip of his thumb between her teeth and met the next rock of their hips with a quick, hard thrust.

Her vision blurred as pleasure spiked. Instead of crying out, she bit down with a growl.

Mad smiled. "You can bite me all you want. We'll still fuck you until you can't take it anymore."

Her hand moved on its own, and she raked her nails

across his chest. He hissed out a curse and grabbed her hand, trapping it over his heart.

Dylan pressed his teeth into the back of her shoulder with another low hum. "We understand each other, Scarlet," he whispered softly. "Better than you realize."

Then he released her.

For a heartbeat, Mad watched her, a silent battle playing out behind his eyes. Then he jerked her wrist, dragging her forward until her face hovered over his. He leaned up, dug his teeth into her lower lip, and licked the ravaged spot. "Take me, Scarlet."

Nothing could have stopped her—Dylan's steely hands, a plea from Jade, even the fire burning in Mad's eyes. She braced herself on his shoulders, breathed his name, and began to move.

Hard, fast. *Pleasure* was a thing of the past, a weak word that didn't come close to describing the rough, sweet friction. He met every desperate thrust with one of his own, fucking deeper into her with each passing heartbeat.

It was a revelation, and she reached blindly for Jade, twining their fingers together as Dylan spread one hand between her shoulder blades, pushing her closer to Mad.

Mad seized her mouth again, his kiss as wild as the rhythm of their bodies. Advance and retreat, soft and hard, pleasure and the whisper of pain when he tangled his fingers in her hair.

That little flash of sensation ignited the tense heat. It flared in an instant, tipping her over the edge, and she came with a shudder. Instead of releasing her, Mad drank in her cries, keeping her mouth trapped to his as he fucked up into her.

Hard. Intense. *Unrelenting.*

More. She couldn't say it, not with Mad's tongue gliding over hers, but she felt it in every cell of her body. It vibrated through her like a plucked bass string, powerful enough to shake her even when it should have faded away.

His fingers clenched tight, sparking fire all along her

scalp. He dragged her head back just enough to watch her eyes and thrust up again, hard enough to arch her back as the swirling pleasure coalesced into another growing blaze.

Hands skated over her skin, the demanding pressures so alike that she could barely tell them apart. Jade, gripping her hips. Dylan, sliding his around her body to cup her breasts.

He plucked at her nipples, twisting lightly. The hint of promise in the caress left Scarlet clenching around Mad's cock, and his choked groan of surprise spurred Dylan to pinch her harder. To make it hurt.

"*Fuck.*" Mad ground up into her again, his eyes wild. "Is that what you need, sweetheart? A little bit of pain?"

She needed *this*, to be overwhelmed, so surrounded by lust and pleasure that nothing else existed. "Please," she rasped, with no fucking idea what she was asking—no, *begging* for.

But they knew. Dylan hauled her upright, still cupping her breasts, his fingertips plying sensation with masterful precision. And then Jade's joined them, not on her breasts but skating down her trembling abdomen to stroke her clit in a knowing rhythm.

Mad was the one who anchored her hips, holding her above him so there was nothing left for her to do but let them support her as they teased and pinched and stroked—as Jade's tongue slipped over and between Dylan's fingers, as his mouth centered on the spot between her neck and her shoulder.

As Mad rode her, utterly intent, utterly in control, even flat on his back.

Scarlet lost it. Before she could scream, Dylan pressed Jade's fingers hard against her clit. The whole world tumbled away, blotted out by ecstasy, by exquisite relief, by Mad's hoarse whisper as he drove up into her a final time.

Her name, maybe, but she couldn't be sure. All that mattered was the way he pulsed inside her, filling more

than her body. Filling her heart, her soul, all those empty
places no one but Jade had ever touched.

Jade savored Scarlet's trembling more than she
wanted to.

There was an art to taking someone outside of themselves. Some people went their whole lives enjoying
pleasurable sex without brushing those lines, those dangerous and seductive boundaries. Others withered
without it, because for them it was more than especially
intense lovemaking.

For them it was a need. A drive. Fulfillment.

Catharsis.

Scarlet's shivers triggered something dangerous in
Jade as she nuzzled the other woman's neck, licked her
throat, and smiled at her shuddering pulse. The last time
the four of them had fallen together, Scarlet had come
hard and fast. Easy. She was always like that—bright and
hot and so easy to get off.

But this was more. And Jade was drunk again, just
like she'd been the first time her careful control had
slipped. Too much liquor and too much teasing, and the
door on her darkest fantasies had cracked open. She'd
knelt for Scarlet that night, so eager to please—and she
knew so many, *many* ways to please. She'd been trained
for it, after all. Trained to spin ecstasy into the sweetest
trap, to kneel as a prelude to conquest.

She wanted to please tonight. To stalk pleasure and
claim triumph, her submission a naked blade that only a
fool would try to grasp, because she was all predatory
edges with no safe grip.

Dylan dragged his hand down the middle of Scarlet's
back, his fingertips sliding easily over her sweat-slicked
skin. She arched under his touch and leaned against Jade,
then slumped to the bed with a blissful smile.

So beautiful. Jade loved the contradictions of her, Scarlet's sharp angles and soft curves, and especially the places where they met. She liked it even more when Mad dragged Scarlet to his side, one muscular arm decorated in vivid ink dropping across her bare abdomen.

A prince in exile and an orphaned street rat. They were already a fairy tale, and they didn't even realize it.

But Dylan did. He stared at them for a moment before shifting his intense gaze to her. Beneath the panting breaths and his hard, jutting erection, he was serious. Almost solemn.

Waiting.

Dylan was fool enough to try to hold her, and she was drunk enough on wanting to let him. And what could it hurt? Nothing felt quite real, in this giant bed in this fairytale house she'd likely never see again. Nothing had to be.

She licked her lips and gave her consent. "I trust you."

His gaze sharpened. "Do you?"

The darkness wound lazily through her, and she couldn't stop her slow smile. "If you think you can handle me."

He didn't answer. Instead, he hauled her into his arms, against his chest—

Against *all* of him.

As erections went, his was impressive. It was impossible to attend the O'Kanes' parties without developing a passing acquaintance with what the men of Sector Four had to offer. Besides, women talked—probably more than their men realized. There was certainly no shortage of quality cock to be enjoyed.

And she still suspected Dylan had them all beat.

He held her there, the hard ridge of his dick prodding her belly, and slowly licked her lower lip. "I can see it, Jade. All the things you want but shouldn't. Everything you hide."

The hell of it was, she didn't have to hide anything.

People who knew her past made their assumptions—just like Mad, making all the wrong ones for all the sweetest reasons. No one but Dylan was dark enough to understand that the skills you developed out of necessity could resonate with the deepest parts of you. That you could loathe yourself for acting under duress and still crave the very things you'd done.

Free will mattered. But she still felt like she was opening Pandora's box when she tilted her chin up and bared her throat in calculated surrender. "I'm not hiding tonight."

She caught only a glimpse of his satisfied smile before he turned her around—and bent her over Mad and Scarlet.

They were tangled together, damp and *glowing*. Mad drew absent patterns over Scarlet's skin as she smiled with such lazy bliss that Jade's heart skipped another beat.

Dylan laid one hand on her hip, low enough to curl his fingers around the front of her thigh. "How long have you craved that?"

From the first moment she'd realized that passion could be more than a tool, more than clinical drawings and dry strategy. "Forever."

"Mmm. So you watched it. Maybe felt a little of it." His fingers tightened. "Now taste it."

Jade clenched her fingers in the rumpled sheets, one hand near Mad's hip and the other near Scarlet's. As close together as they were, it still spread her arms wide and forced her face low. The dizzying musk of sex and sweat overwhelmed her as she inhaled shakily and fought a swift battle against a stab of shame.

No, all things considered, perhaps she shouldn't want this. But she did, and this was a fantasy. Instead of fighting the shame, she embraced it, let it feed her illicit satisfaction when she drew her tongue up the inside of Scarlet's thigh.

She tasted like pleasure. Like Mad. Even more so when Jade reached her pussy and traced gently over her sensitized clit. Scarlet hissed in a breath and started to move, but Mad spread his fingers wide and held her in place.

Poor Scarlet. She was strung out, floating. Crashing her back into pleasure too quickly would overload her senses—tempting, perhaps, but fleeting. Instead Jade licked lower, soothing and savoring as she used her knowledge of Scarlet's body to lull her into relaxing.

And she did, slowly, her head easing back into the pillows. The flush returned to her skin, visible proof of Jade's success that fed her own arousal as she worked her tongue deeper. Mad's taste intensified, and she was twisted enough to love the perversity of it—the salty tartness on her tongue a preview of what it would be like when she wrapped her lips around his cock and sucked away Scarlet's sweetness.

Because she would. Scarlet was already trembling again, her hips arching restlessly—seeking instead of trying to escape now. She needed more and Jade would give it to her, so softly and gently that Scarlet wouldn't realize how close she was until she was screaming.

Dylan could still stop her. The clever hands resting so low on Jade's hips had turned into the lightest of leashes. A reminder of his presence, a slow burn of anticipation. She half-expected a hand in her hair or at the back of her head, pushing her forward or hauling her back. But even when she worked her way back up to Scarlet's clit and coaxed the other woman to the shuddering edge of pleasure, his grip remained easy.

So she gave in to her own desires and sent Scarlet flying.

There was no time to savor Scarlet's screams. The moment her first sharp cry split the air, Dylan tightened his grip on Jade's hips—and drove into her.

Dear *God*, he was big. Even though her thighs were

slick with arousal, it almost hurt, an ache and a stretching pressure that left her muffling a cry of her own against Scarlet's pussy. Every nerve seemed to fire at once, wildly and randomly, as if the surprise of it was simply too much to handle.

She felt it in her fingertips. In her curled toes. All along her scalp, as if he'd gathered her hair in his fist after all—and she was so drunk on the feel of him that it took her a confused moment to realize someone had.

Mad. He gathered the strands and wrapped them around his fist, his dark gaze fixed on her as if seeing her for the first time. "What does she want that she shouldn't, Dylan?"

He answered through gritted teeth. "Go on, love. It's his turn. Shall we show him?"

Mad's cock was already mostly hard again, putting lie to everything her trainers had ever told her about the re-fractory period in men over thirty. It glistened, slick and wet from when Scarlet had come all over him.

The last time Jade had gotten on her knees before Mad, he'd hauled her upright with guilty horror in his eyes. How could he handle the knowledge that she would gleefully part her lips for him now? That she'd revel in having him close his fist until she was trapped, until the decision of what to do next was simply to either swallow him whole or let him choke her?

Her heart beat faster, and she closed her eyes. "Does he really want to know?"

"More than he wants his next breath," Dylan mur-mured.

Jade didn't know if she believed him. But she trusted him.

The moment her tongue found Mad's shaft, his hand tightened. Precisely—she had walked that line too many times not to recognize a master. Just enough pull to tingle all over, to raise the hair at the back of her neck in antici-pation.

It gave her the courage to meet his gaze as she licked her way higher and paused with his crown balanced against her lower lip. "I could taste you inside Scarlet. I want more."

He hissed out a rough curse, and dangerous satisfaction slipped through her as lust darkened his eyes. "How much more, Jade?"

In answer, she swallowed half of him.

Dylan began to move—gently, at first, while she taunted Mad with her fluttering tongue and careful suction. She let Dylan control the pace and depth, moaning every time a slow, deep thrust rocked her forward onto Mad's cock.

But Mad held back, his body rigid, his expression tense, the muscles in his arm standing out as he followed the sway of her body with the fist in her hair, always tight but never pulling, never trapping, never *forcing...*

Doubt crept in, and she swatted it back. Told herself this was enough. Dylan pushing into her, his cock so thick and hard that even a slow rock provided enough friction to drive her wild. Mad on her tongue, making those low, harsh noises every time she took him, as if he couldn't handle how good it felt. Scarlet, watching with blissful, drowsy eyes, sparking a new level of arousal simply by being there.

Maybe she'd whisper about this later, while she worked as many fingers as Jade could take into her body. Tell her how she'd looked with Dylan buried in her pussy and Mad in her mouth. Scarlet wasn't much for dirty talk, but she knew how to use just the right lewd words to make Jade come that much harder.

It was enough. And as soon as Jade had talked herself into believing it, Mad ruined everything by meeting Dylan's next thrust with one of his own.

The fist in her hair turned to steel. Mad drove deep, and she wasn't ready for it. The head of his cock bumped the back of her throat, stealing her breath as her mind stuttered to a halt. Tears stung her eyes—a physical reaction she couldn't quell, but desperately wished she could. Because if Mad saw, if he *stopped*—

Dylan rocked forward with a grunt, pushing Jade up the bed. And then it didn't matter, because even if Mad wanted to stop, she was trapped between them, carried along by the rhythm of their thrusts. So rough, but still so *precise*—every time her vision swam they eased apart long enough for her to take an unsteady breath before filling her again.

Somewhere in the midst of the storm of pleasure, Scarlet touched her—a familiar, firm hand at the small of her back. It could have been nothing more than comfort, a way to center Jade so she wouldn't fly away—until one slippery finger slid down to prod at her ass.

Yes. She would have screamed it if she could, and the enthusiasm of the thought truly did shake her. Bad enough that Dylan had cracked her armor to expose the eager woman who reveled in skills she should have rejected. But this...

Helplessness shouldn't feel this good.

"Deeper," Dylan growled. Scarlet obeyed the command instantly, and Jade struggled to relax, to accept the touch. And Scarlet *knew* her, knew just how to fuck her, when to go easy and when to push, and it didn't matter that it was only one slender finger. Not with Dylan filling her so completely that Jade could barely take him, much less more.

One of Dylan's hands left her hip, and then Scarlet echoed her moan, low and muffled. Instinct had Jade trying to turn, but Mad held on to her hair, dragging her gaze back to his.

"He's kissing her," he rasped, still pumping lazily up into her mouth. "It's hot. But so are you. Is this what you want?"

She fought his grip to nod, even though the painful pull stung fresh tears in the corner of her eyes. Her heart stopped when he reached out to brush one from her cheek with his thumb, but he didn't pull back. "You can take more, can't you?"

Yes, she could take more. She could take everything he had to give, more than he ever would. She nodded again, and he gritted his teeth and pushed her head down. This time, she didn't let him choke her. She tilted her head and took all of him, let him plunge deep into her throat, and counted his tight, desperate groan as her victory.

Dylan kept fucking her, spurred on by Scarlet whispering filthy encouragement. "Harder." Her voice was velvet, honey. Sex itself. "Make her come and don't stop."

No one had to *make* Jade come this time. Pleasure was within her grasp, a pulse she could either resist or give in to. It was habit to disassociate, to think too much as a counter to feeling too much.

This, she wanted to feel. The heat. The fullness. She let them in one by one—the slick glide of Mad's cock as he thrust deep and held, his whole body shaking with the effort not to succumb too quickly. The erotic friction of Dylan's as he drove deeper, his hips losing their perfect rhythm when she clenched tight around him. Scarlet's finger, as dark and teasing as her words.

So close. But she wasn't ready to let go. Not until she conquered.

Mad was close, too. She could feel it in every line of his body, and in his short, too-controlled thrusts. She sucked harder and moaned with every retreat, and soon he dragged her head up, his chest heaving. "Where do you want me to come?"

She licked her swollen lips. "Wherever the hell you want."

Dylan groaned as he leaned over her, his skin hot against her back. The position forced Scarlet's finger deeper, and she bit the back of Jade's shoulder when Dylan groaned again. "Come on, give it to her."

"Give it to me," she echoed, a plea and a challenge

wrapped into one. And she still wasn't sure he would, not until he curled those strong fingers around his shaft and jerked up, hard and rough. A groan tore free of him, but he held her gaze as he did it again, and again.

The first spurt hit her chin. She parted her lips, dizzy with triumph as he groaned her name and pumped his fist, spilling across her lips and tongue without looking away.

Scarlet nuzzled her ear, moving with her as Dylan fucked her faster, his rhythm furious and desperate. Hard, each quick thrust slamming through her, until she couldn't hold herself above the sensations.

The orgasm started deep, a swift, hard clench that burst into shivery heat. She gasped in a breath that still tasted like Mad, and that tiny detail unraveled her. She buried her face against his hip as the shudders took her, and the fingers that had twisted in her hair loosened now, stroking and soothing.

Panting, Dylan rode her orgasm, his hands grasping her tighter and tighter. He hauled her back roughly into one final thrust and came—shuddering, her name on his lips, his nails biting into her skin.

She'd have marks there. Tiny crescents, little reminders of this moment. This glorious, debauched, shameless moment. She turned her head, found Scarlet's mouth, and shared a lazy kiss that provoked another full-body shudder when Scarlet licked the last drops of Mad from her lips.

And that moment—that helpless, shuddering, *blissful* moment—transcended everything. It filled all the hollow places, the distant, empty craving she'd expected to carry with her for the rest of her life, because that was what surviving the addiction they cooked up in Sector Five meant. A life where nothing ever touched you the way the drugs had touched you.

But they had—Scarlet and Mad and Dylan, all together. Jade's eyes stung anew at the impossibility of it, at the relief. The sheer, drunken *joy*.

The moment passed—moments always passed. But the glow remained, lending a new edge of rediscovered hope to the familiarity of Scarlet's kiss.

"Bath," Mad said hoarsely. "Let's go recover in the bath."

Jade laughed against Scarlet's mouth. "I can't. I can't walk."

"We'll all drown," Scarlet agreed.

"Plus one of us would have to get up to fill it." Mad groaned and threw an arm over his head. "Maybe we should just stay in bed for a couple days and get our energy back."

Dylan didn't move. He knelt right where he'd been, his chest heaving, and braced his fists on his thighs. "We have to go back to Four."

Even in blissful afterglow, he was so practical. It took supreme effort, but Jade managed to turn onto her back. She bumped Scarlet with her elbow and nudged Mad in the stomach with the back of her head, but the glorious tangle of bodies only made her smile wider. "We will. Tomorrow. This is still tonight."

After what seemed like forever, Dylan nodded. "You're right."

Scarlet poked him with her foot until he fell over beside them. "Stop thinking."

"He can't." Mad stroked his fingers absently through Jade's hair. "Dylan's brain is always working. Usually about three steps ahead of mine."

"Too bad," Scarlet countered. "It doesn't belong here, not tonight."

Finally, Dylan unbent enough to smile. "Yes, ma'am."

She was right. Nothing harsh and real belonged in this moment. The first time they'd come together had been intense, desperation seething beneath every touch, and reality had intruded just as intensely in the aftermath. This was different. Soft focus. Safe.

Jade closed her eyes and sank her fingers into Scarlet's tangled hair. "As much as I love Sector Four, I have to admit I'll miss this house. And this bed. Scarlet doesn't kick me at night in this one."

Scarlet nipped at the inside of her arm with a low laugh. "Because I can't find you in it."

Jade stretched her other arm out, across Mad's body, until her fingertips brushed Dylan's shoulder. "Are any of the beds in Four this big?"

Mad laughed softly. "Dallas's is close."

"And yours," Dylan rumbled.

Just like that, the world snapped into sharp focus. Tomorrow they'd be back in Sector Four, under the curious eyes of their O'Kane brothers and sisters. There would be no conveniently shared bed, hidden away from gossip and consequences.

If Jade and Scarlet slipped into Mad's oversized bed, it would mean something. It would mean too much, because they'd already used up casual and convenient. They were scraping past the surface layers, brushing against fantasies and fears.

When she'd dangled the possibility in front of Scarlet all those months ago, she hadn't really meant it. She'd known Mad wanted her, and that he came from a place where wanting and taking and loving more than one person wasn't a sin.

She simply hadn't believed Mad could bring himself to take *her*.

Now, dangerous possibilities taunted her. Dangerous because they sparked too hot, and there were so many ways for two people to implode, much less four.

Dangerous because if they didn't fall apart, if it *lasted*, they'd find their way under Jade's armor. And if war between the sectors and the city was coming, she needed it more than ever.

ashwin

H E DIDN'T KNOW how she'd gotten out of the city.

Watching from the shadows as Dr. Kora Bellamy tended to her current patient, Ashwin Malhotra found himself plagued by the unfamiliar sensation that events were sliding out of his grasp.

He wasn't supposed to be here. The Base had recalled him immediately after the bombing of Two. The orders he'd received were detailed, precise, and of paramount importance. But he'd programmed these alerts years ago, after the first moment he'd come face-to-face with Kora and realized who she must be.

What she must be.

Ashwin was ruthlessly thorough, and so were his alerts. Eden was full of cameras and checkpoints, especially in the restricted-access medical and government buildings, and Ashwin had mastered network infiltration by the age of ten.

An accounting of Kora's movements appeared on his personal tablet every twelve hours. Where she went, how long she stayed. The names and ranks of everyone who crossed her path, from the lowliest of servants to the Council members themselves. An algorithm he'd built processed the data, analyzed it for warning signs.

Disappearing from Eden's surveillance systems entirely was more than a warning sign. It was a potential crisis.

Because Ashwin was thorough, and because he knew who she was—and *what* she was—he'd had little trouble locating her. Left to her own devices, Kora would always drift toward the highest concentration of pain, driven by instincts she couldn't possibly understand to assuage that suffering. Until now, he'd counted on Eden's restrictions to check her tendencies, but his assessment of the various forces in play had been flawed.

Another unfamiliar sensation.

At least he'd found her quickly enough. Of course she was here, in the makeshift hospital Gideon Rios had erected in his sector. Compound fractures and lacerations presented little challenge to a woman who could reconstruct vital organs on a cellular level, but Kora wasn't like other city doctors. They fought over who got to perform the flashiest procedures in order to pad their egos and attract Council attention.

Not Kora. She fought pain in all its forms, and there were so many ways to measure human suffering, calculations that were alien to him. He'd been trained to construct a personality profile based on observed data and known psychology, and he still frequently failed to properly account for the most reliable variable of all—the sheer irrationality of human emotion.

Maybe this was his first taste of it. Ashwin had subjected himself to enough brutal self-assessment to recognize irrationality when it presented itself in his own behaviors. It wasn't entirely unexpected—Makhai soldiers who left the Base for long periods of time often destabilized. That could explain why he was standing in One, watching Kora, instead of executing his mission objectives.

If he admitted his own fallibility to the generals, they'd assign him a domestic handler, a woman who would provide him with the necessary sexual outlet while also tending to his less demanding physical needs. She'd be a spy, of course, trained to seek out fractures in his psyche, to bring them to the surface when she crawled into his bed and report them to the Base so he could be recalibrated as needed.

Perhaps it wouldn't be all bad. His recent duties had prevented him from undertaking the tedious social negotiations involved in obtaining a sexual partner. A domestic handler would already be aware of his particular needs, and most had been so poorly treated that it was only marginally difficult to subvert their loyalties. Even in the face of overwhelming proof to the contrary, a woman could remain stubbornly susceptible to the fantasy that she, and only she, could stir the emotions of a Makhai soldier.

But subverting loyalties took time. It came naturally to some of the soldiers—Ashwin's training partner had been particularly adept. Every handler the Base ever tossed his way had ended up in love with him within a month. He had charm, and the ability to mimic affection. Women melted the first time he touched them.

Women never melted for Ashwin. Oh, they came to him willingly enough, but even those with weak instincts sensed the danger in him, the icy reserve untouched by emotion. They came to him, their hearts pounding with lust and nerves in equal measure, and he worked them over with the same dedication, skill, and unflagging attention to detail he afforded all his missions.

Pleasure was a powerful tool. More powerful than pain, if you had the patience for it. Even the women who feared him usually returned, and in time they forgot everything but the haze of bliss. They confused his willingness to pleasure them with true feelings, because they'd been neglected, if not outright mistreated.

Ashwin watched Kora rise, her movements graceful even though she was exhibiting several symptoms of exhaustion. She placed both hands at the small of her back and stretched, and Ashwin's gaze catalogued the curves of her body by habit. The line of her jaw, the arch of her neck. Her breasts, her hips, the flare of her ass. She was small, but not delicate. Strong beneath all her softness.

Untouched.

He never allowed himself to wonder how she would come to his bed. The moral blankness where his heart should have been balked for some reason, even as he admitted to himself that he had a proprietary interest in every untouched inch of her. He'd watched her halfhearted attempts to date. He'd calculated, with idle curiosity, the number of bones he'd have to break in each suitor's hands to keep him from touching her in the way men in Eden touched women—clumsily, coldly, cruelly.

But she'd known better than to let those men into her heart or her body. She'd known for all the same reasons she'd come here, because of who and what she was.

Because of those reasons, Ashwin would keep her safe. Even if it meant she someday looked into the darkness inside him and knew better than to have anything to do with him.

12

M AD HAD NEVER seen the party room looking so damn solemn.

Every O'Kane with ink was assembled in the middle of the room. Fully clothed, which was different. But Dallas hadn't called his people home for a celebration, and the expressions on the faces closest to Mad were grim.

No surprise, when Dallas had just finished outlining everything they'd learned in Sector One. The stark facts were even more chilling now, since more than a week had passed since the bombing, and Eden was still acting like nothing happened. No propaganda, no excuses or explanations.

They'd killed thousands. And they didn't care enough to lie about why.

"So we're at a crossroads," Dallas said from the dais. He held up his right fist, displaying the O'Kane ink around his wrist—the first symbol Mad had ever truly believed in.

"O'Kane for life," he continued, skimming the crowd. "That's the promise. But we made it in a different world."

Dallas's gaze clashed with Mad's for a heartbeat, then landed on the spot where Flash stood with his arms around Amira, who had sweet little Hana balanced on her hip. The only child on the compound, who could be an orphan—or worse—if this war went wrong.

Mad had known Dallas long enough to read the same thought in his leader's eyes. "This is a guilt-free out, folks. A pass. And I wouldn't blame a goddamn one of you for taking it. You can grab what you need to get clear of the sectors and up into the mountains. All you have to do—" he gestured to the right side of the room, "—is walk over there."

Lex was already standing against the wall on the left-hand side of the room, her arms across her chest. "The alternative," she said slowly, "is to stay and fight. But like Dallas said, it's dangerous. And it's not necessarily what any of you joined up for."

"It's war," Dallas told them flatly, still watching Flash and Amira. "Some of you have people depending on you."

"Yeah." Amira pressed her lips to the top of Hana's head and rocked her gently. "And we're not teaching our daughter to walk away from what's right just because it's easier. Flash?"

The man that Mad had first met all those years ago would have tossed his lover and their daughter into the closest car and driven like hell for safety, whether she agreed or not. The man standing next to him now flexed his fingers before planting them firmly at the small of Amira's back and steering her toward Lex. "For life, Dallas."

"For life," Noelle echoed, giving Jas a look that dared him to protest before she crossed to Lex's side.

Jasper shrugged slightly as he started after her, an easy movement that belied the tension in his voice. "What can I say? I've got to see what you come up with, you crazy bastard."

Six didn't say a damn thing. She started moving at the same moment Bren did, as if neither had to question the other's answer. Tatiana looked at her baby sister and then the empty right wall, but Catalina was already joining the slowly moving river of bodies.

Zan. Noah and Emma. Hawk. Ford and Mia. Jade cast a long look over her shoulder at Mad before following Scarlet to stand with Trix and Finn. Lili was already there, proud and defiant next to a stern-faced Jared.

Dallas remained stoic—until Nessa took a step to the left.

She cut him off pleasantly, before he could say a word. "Fuck you. You'll be broke in a year without me. Plus you'll be sober, and none of us want to be sober tonight."

A smile tugged at Mad's lips in spite of himself. Dallas didn't need to take a vote—and he was the only one who didn't realize it.

The urge to smile vanished when Rachel started forward to join the crowd. Cruz caught her arm, holding her in place in the middle of the room. "Rachel—"

"No." Her voice trembled, but there was no mistaking her resolve. "You are *not* sending me away."

Cruz's tension worried Mad, but Ace was the one who really scared the hell out of him. He'd seen him look more cheerful with a gut wound. "Not here, Cruz."

"Why not here?" Rachel protested. "This is our family. *His* family." She dropped one protective hand to the flat slope of her belly. "I'd rather die than have this baby in a world where Eden bombs whole fucking sectors and no one—no one fights—" She burst into heavy, wracking sobs that shook her whole body.

Silence swept through the room as Ace wrapped her in his arms, and Mad knew he wasn't the only one remembering the joy and laughter that had followed Amira and Flash's announcement. Rachel, Ace, and Cruz deserved the same celebration.

Instead, they were getting tension and tears.

Mad reached out, but Dallas was already moving. He hopped off the dais and covered the intervening space in three long strides. Cruz went rigid when Dallas stopped in front of him, toe-to-toe in his personal space. "Her call, Cruz."

Cruz eyed him bleakly. "You'd feel the same way I do."

"Of course I would." Dallas raised his voice. "How many fantasies for getting you to the mountains did I cop to, Lex? Was it three?"

"Something like that." The words wavered, and she cleared her throat. "I've had my moments, too."

"See?" Dallas braced a hand on Cruz's shoulder. "We all feel it. And then we nut the fuck up and get the hell out of their way, because that's what we're fighting for. Everyone's right to choose how they fight for what they love."

Cruz's expression remained blank, but Mad felt the conflict raging through him. Or maybe it was just projection, the devious, unattractive part of him that was still trying to figure out the right approach.

He'd watched his grandfather for years. He'd watched Gideon, too. You didn't have to drag or command if you knew how to use someone's natural instincts. A little bit of maneuvering, and he could talk Jade and Dylan out of the line of fire, as long as he was coaxing them toward people who needed them. And Scarlet—her weakness was Jade. He could work with that, too—

—and be as bad as his grandfather, using people's noblest impulses for his own gain.

But damn it, they'd be *safe*.

Cruz turned away from Dallas and cupped Rachel's cheeks, his thumbs gentle as he wiped away her tears. "I'll make any world you want for our baby. I just want to keep the three of you safe."

She wrapped her fingers around his wrists so tightly that her knuckles turned as white as her face. "Then we have to win."

"We will," Ace replied firmly. His hands covered Rachel's, stroking until her grip relaxed. "C'mon, lover. You always knew we were never gonna leave you. You're ruining Dallas's big dramatic moment."

Cruz's sigh held a lifetime of affectionate irritation. "You're impossible."

"That's why everyone loves me." Ace took a step back, bringing Rachel with him, and Cruz followed. Of course he followed. Love bound them together as visibly as the ink around Rachel's throat—their names twined together into a single work of art.

And then they were lost in the crowd, and it was just Dallas and Mad in the middle of the room with an empty wall to their right and a silent declaration gathered to their left.

"I could have saved you some time," Mad murmured. "This was always going to be their answer. They're as loyal as anyone in One."

"No," Dallas replied just as softly. "They're more loyal, because they have a choice."

And that was the crux of it all. The rift between the sectors and Eden, between Dallas and the other sectors. He wasn't in the market for obedient soldiers or worshipful followers. The O'Kanes were individual people with their own lives, their own hopes and dreams. And they'd fight so much harder because of it.

Hell, they'd fight *smarter* because of it.

Mad nodded to acknowledge he understood the difference—and made his choice. Five steps brought him into the crowd, and pride swelled as he turned to face Dallas. He would love his family by blood for all his days, but standing with his O'Kane brothers and sisters would always mean coming home.

"Alright, you crazy motherfuckers." Dallas broke into a wide, feral grin. "Let's tear down the walls of heaven and let a little sin in."

The O'Kanes loved a good party. It didn't matter whether they were celebrating or mourning, focused on sex or laughter or drinking. Dylan had often joked that they would revel even if the world was ending. Again.

Turned out, he was right.

He stood at the edge of the room and tracked an appraising gaze over each smiling face. Who would be the first to fall? They were all so damn protective of each other that it could be anyone, at any time.

He didn't pity the ones who would die fast, though. They were lucky—no pain, the whole fucking thing over and done before they even realized what hit them. No, what Dylan dreaded the most was finding out which ones would survive long enough to die under his hands. Sweet-faced little Nessa? Bren, his stone façade shattered by agony?

Lex?

Dylan snorted and closed his hand around the small case in his pocket. The tablets inside rattled reassuringly. If he let Lex die, he'd be better off climbing onto the gurney with her, because Dallas would kill him, too. Kill him slow, make it hurt.

Maybe Dallas could read his mind. The man appeared out of a crowd of dancers and headed straight for Dylan, his expression so pleasantly lazy that anyone who knew him would have recognized the warning signs.

Dylan had seen that expression plenty. Every time Dallas tried to recruit him.

"Not gonna join the dancing?" Dallas asked as he leaned back against the wall next to him. "Jade's been eyeing you all night."

Jade was worried about him, a distinction that was easy to miss. Dylan shrugged one shoulder. "I'm not in the mood to dance. I'm thinking."

"Oh yeah?"

"Yeah."

Dallas watched him for a second, waiting for more. When he failed to elaborate, Dallas just smiled. "Maybe I can give you something else to think about. An offer."

Jesus Christ. "You don't waste time, O'Kane."

"Not membership." Dallas huffed. "I figure you know by now that I'd have inked you years ago if you'd let me. I'm talking bigger, Dylan. Something that wouldn't have been possible with Fleming running Five. A hospital."

"You'll need one, if you're going to war." He couldn't quite keep the acid out of his words.

"Maybe even before we go to war," Dallas replied easily. But he cast Dylan a sidelong look. "I take it you don't approve."

He said it as if it was a simple thing, as if his choices were to approve of death and destruction or of Eden's status quo. "My opinion is pointless. You don't need it, no one does."

"You're one of a handful of people in this room who has lived on both sides of the wall. I need all of your opinions."

"All right, you asked for it." He faced Dallas squarely and pinned him with a look. "I was just wondering how many of them I won't be able to save. Statistically speaking, the number's pretty fucking high."

Dallas didn't flinch, but his eyes betrayed his pain. "I know. Even though it's been a couple of years since we buried one of our own, it used to happen too fucking much. But we didn't have resources then. We didn't have allies. So tell me, Dylan. What do you need to save more of them?"

A miracle. "You never asked why I said no. All those times you tried to get me to join up. Aren't you curious?"

"I guess I figured that after Eden, you weren't ready to start taking orders again."

Taking orders was the least of his concerns. There were things he'd resolved never to do again, of course—if he got another order to torture someone, or to save them so they could be tortured more? He just wouldn't do it. Execution was preferable to losing what was left of his soul. But O'Kane? Nothing he could order Dylan to do would come close to the hell he'd already lived through.

"I don't care about authority," he muttered. "I care about right and wrong. If what you tell me to do is right, I'll do it. If it's wrong, then fuck you."

Dallas tilted his head. "Okay, now I'm curious."

Dylan looked back at the crowd. Ace twirled Rachel in a laughing circle until she thumped her fist against his shoulder in protest. Nearby, Cruz watched indulgently while he chatted with Bren. Six and Scarlet were dancing, and Noelle whispered something to Jade that chased the worry from her gaze as they joined them.

They were all so fucking *alive*, even the ones with an edge of desperation under their cheer.

"My job is difficult," he whispered finally. "Even before the Flares, working in medicine had its problems. Higher risk of alcoholism, suicide—" He hesitated. "Drug addiction. Maybe you can only watch people suffer so much before it drags you under. And it's hard enough when you don't know them. When you do...it's impossible."

"You needed distance," Dallas murmured. "And I've been chipping away at it for years."

"No, not you." On the other side of the room, Mad was standing with Flash and Amira, holding their daughter while she tugged his hair and grasped at his nose. "You have a good thing here, O'Kane, and you're as protected as you can possibly get. Are you sure you want to fuck that up?"

"If I thought we could stay like this forever? No fucking way." Dallas sighed. "It's going to happen, Dylan. With us or without us, rebellion is coming. Do you think Eden will leave us alone if I hold up my hands and swear we had nothing to do with it?"

"I don't know." It wasn't his *job* to know. It was his job

to trail behind the carnage, cleaning up as best he could. "But you have to be prepared to lose some of them."

"I can't. You don't prepare to lose your family. You fight like hell to protect them, and you never get over it when you fail."

He didn't look frightened or sad. He looked like a man poised at the edge of a chasm—unsure of what would happen when he jumped, but beyond certain that the landing would hurt like hell. "Fair enough. Tell me about this hospital."

"We're thinking Sector Three." Dallas leaned against the wall. "We have a few buildings that might work once we've cleared them out. Gideon will provide the labor, Ryder will provide the supplies."

"And you?"

"Security." Dallas lifted an eyebrow. "And hopefully a highly trained doctor who can highly train a few new doctors."

For the first time, his immediate impulse wasn't to say no. Instead, he studied Dallas's carefully composed veneer—such a thin, thin layer over the anxiety that colored everything. He was getting desperate, but not desperate enough to lie.

It was a start. "You gave yourself the hard job. Security's trickier than you think. You build a hospital right before you go to war with the city? You may as well paint a giant bull's-eye on it."

"True enough. We thought about the tunnels under Four and Five but..." He shrugged a shoulder. "Noah could lock Eden's people out, but that's a bell we can't unring. Once he starts fucking with their systems enough for them to notice, the clock starts ticking."

"What about the tunnels under Three?"

"Half of them are caved in. Hell, more than half, for all I know."

"So use all that beautiful labor you were talking about." Dylan looked around the room again, then tipped his head toward the crowd. "You asked me what I need to save more of them. This is it."

"Alright." That simple, as if he could request anything, and Dallas would make it happen. Maybe he would. "I'll talk to Gideon. Maybe Noah can divert the power we need. If not, we have generators."

"Make it work, O'Kane." He took a step away, then stopped and glanced at Dallas. "I'm in, but only if you give me a safe place to work. I'm not going to save them all just so Eden can blow them to hell and back anyway. It's wasteful." *And heartbreaking.*

"It's a deal."

13

JADE SAT CROSS-LEGGED on her tiny bed and worked a comb through her damp hair. "Am I shallow if I admit I miss that bathtub?"

Scarlet threw her head back with a throaty laugh. "If you said you *didn't* miss it, I'd think you were lying. It was the size of my whole room."

The only reason Jade couldn't say the same was timing. She'd had the good fortune of needing a room right around the time Six had decided she'd rather spend her nights *and* days with Bren. "The Rios estate reminded me..." She trailed off, but the usual wariness didn't grip her. Sector One seemed like a dream now, but some of the peace of it lingered. "Before I went to the training house, I lived someplace like it."

The bed dipped as Scarlet slid behind her and took the comb from her hand. "You did?"

"Mmm. My father's house." She'd often wondered if

childhood memory painted the house as grander than it really was, but Jade had accompanied Cerys there once as an adult—a matter of the debt owed by her father for his newest girl.

He'd stared through Jade without a hint of recognition. "He was my mother's patron. We lived with him until I was seven."

Scarlet drew in a deep breath and began pulling the comb through Jade's hair. "What happened?"

"My mother got sick." The memory of her tired, gaunt face came too easily. She'd still been so beautiful to a daughter's adoring eyes—but a patron paid extravagantly for perfection. "My father did what people do with broken possessions. He replaced her."

The sure hands drawing the comb through her hair faltered, then resumed their smooth movements. Her only comment was low, short. Vicious. "Bastard."

"I know." Even though Jade agreed, a perverse, twisted part of her still felt the childlike need to defend him. "I spent years trying to make excuses for him, because I thought he loved her. I thought he loved us."

"You don't throw away someone you love. If you do, you're not worth *having* someone to love."

Pure, simple truth. Her father might have said he loved Jade, but her mother had shown her the truth of real love. "She had money saved up. It might even have been enough to get us out of Two. But she was dying, and without expensive treatments she wouldn't have lasted more than a couple of years. So she made a deal with the devil. She took me to Rose House."

Scarlet was silent for a long time, her fingers constantly moving through Jade's drying hair. "I don't know," she said finally, "what my dad would have done if he'd had some kind of warning that he was going to die. Impossible to know, I guess."

"He would have done his best." Jade leaned back against her. "That's what the people who love us do. Their best."

She moved, pulling Jade into her lap, and rested her chin on her bare shoulder. "That's why it seems wrong to whine about my dad. I was fourteen when he died—practically grown up. And he was a stand-up guy, you know?" She sighed. "I got lucky compared to a lot of people here, not just the orphans."

"That's how I feel," Jade admitted. "My mother held on until I was fifteen. And every damn day she told me I was loved, I was strong, that I deserved the world. Sometimes I try to imagine what Noelle's parents told her every day, and I can't understand how she still has the courage to smile."

"We do what we have to do," Scarlet whispered.

Jade rubbed her cheek against Scarlet's and closed her eyes. She loved being held like this, Scarlet's familiar body warm and soft and safe. In the first weeks after she'd recovered from withdrawal, she'd had dark moments of wondering if pleasure would be tainted for her now. If the sick helplessness of the drugs had done what years of tending to the petty desires of petty men couldn't.

But Scarlet was bright and pure, clean even when she was gloriously filthy. She'd brought joy back to the body that had so betrayed Jade. She was fiercely tender, wildly protective.

Lying in her embrace, Jade hated herself for missing more from Sector One than just the bathtub.

Scarlet smoothed Jade's furrowed brow with the pad of her thumb. "What are you thinking about?"

Jade wished it didn't occur to her to lie. But even with all that joy, with so much *trust*, it was still her first impulse. With effort, she pushed past it. "About how small my bed seems. And...how big."

"You mean how empty."

Not a question. Maybe Scarlet felt it, too. "Yes. How empty."

Scarlet studied her with an expression as inscrutable

as her unspoken thoughts.

How did the people in Sector One do it? God, how did Rachel and Cruz and Ace do it? At least it was expected in Sector One, accepted. Here, it carried the potential to break a heart. Because there was no coming back from *you're not enough*, even if the words were never spoken.

And that wasn't the biggest danger. "What happened was a dream. We're awake now. If we...did something..."

Scarlet sat up a little straighter. "It wasn't a dream, Jade. But you're right—it's different here. At home."

"Yes," Jade agreed, lifting a hand to cup Scarlet's cheek. "I don't want to hurt you by wanting them. That's the thing that scares me most."

"But you do want them, and how I feel about it won't change that. It can't. It *shouldn't*." She hesitated. "Permission, is that it?"

Jade wanted to deny it. She was a grown woman, one who owned her life and her body. She didn't need permission to *want*. But that had always been part of Scarlet's appeal. She'd exploded into Jade's steady, measured life, alive and confident. Bold and sexy as hell.

Scarlet gave so readily, so generously, that Jade hadn't needed to ask for anything. And Dylan didn't wait for her to ask. He'd seen straight into the dark little corners of her heart, and she'd been so grateful for his demands.

Because she didn't know how to ask for what she needed.

Jade rested her forehead against Scarlet's and closed her eyes. "Sometimes I think myself in circles, trying to understand my own feelings. I can never tell what's me and what's my training. And what's both."

Scarlet hummed softly. "Trust me, I know. That's why I have to push sometimes. Because if I tell you I want something, I know you'll do it. Might not even stop to wonder if you want it, too."

Jade smiled. "That's not training. That's trust. You're

the first person who ever deserved it."

"Well, then." She traced her fingers up Jade's arms to the bare upper curves of her shoulders. "I think we have someplace to be."

Not yet. Jade pulled back and met Scarlet's gaze. "If I tell you I need something, I know you'll do it. Promise me that's not all this is."

Scarlet stared back, her eyes alight with warmth. "That's not how I operate, sweetheart."

Jade laughed and gave in to the temptation to kiss those soft, smiling lips. This must be how Rachel and Ace and Cruz managed—by talking and laughing and wanting each other so much that it burned away the awkwardness.

As long as Dylan and Mad felt the same way.

Mad eyed the clock on the side table and swirled the liquor in his glass. "I told you we should have gone to them."

Dylan cut a mild look his way. "You're overthinking it. And if *I'm* saying so…"

As rebukes went, it was gentle. But it landed hard because Mad had overthought a lot of things in his life, but only rarely about who would be tumbling into his bed at the end of the day. Now they had circled around to a mirror image of that first night in One. Dylan was casually certain about whatever the night might bring, while Mad struggled to draw lines around what it all meant.

It had always been easy before. Crashing together, falling apart. Watching his lovers move on to people who could give them everything.

Rachel had asked him about it once, back when Ace and Cruz had still been circling each other as much as her. *"What would you do?"*

"I always do the same thing. Love everyone who crosses my path. Love 'em as much as I can, for as long as

they need."

How clever. How *blithe*. What a goddamn hypocrite he was turning out to be.

Dylan's hand fell on his shoulder, soothing as much as caressing. "Does it matter why they come, as long as they do?"

"Why are you so sure they will?"

"Because they're not finished with us yet."

Mad couldn't maintain his brooding glare. A smile broke through, and he rolled his eyes. "I can't tell if that's hot or chilling."

"Both?" Dylan shrugged and finished his drink in one swallow. "It doesn't have to be sinister. Needing someone doesn't always mean forever. You give what you can, take what you can, and then it's over. We both have plenty of experience with that."

"I guess." Except Mad had never felt so much like he was battling the clock, as if the inevitable end would come before he was ready for it.

He'd never wanted to take this damn much.

A quiet knock on the door scattered his reservations. Relief surged so strongly that Mad choked it back out of instinct, forcing himself to finish his drink before slanting Dylan a teasing look. "So what do you win if you're right?"

In an instant, Dylan's expression went from mild to intense. *Intent.* "Everything."

Mad leaned close, until his lips almost touched Dylan's. "You're hot when you're thinking evil thoughts," he whispered, then kissed him once, hard, before rising to answer the door with the taste of liquor and Dylan still tingling on his tongue.

And of course Jade and Scarlet were on the other side, because Dylan was always right. Jade looked relaxed and sweet, her long hair bound in a loose braid, her body wrapped in a white silk robe. Scarlet was still wearing her clothes from the party—low-riding cargo pants that

hugged her hips and a tiny white T-shirt that barely covered her breasts and shouldn't have bothered, not when
the material was so wash-worn he could see her nipples
through it anyway.

Silently, he pulled the door wide and stepped back.
Jade paused on her way past to rock up on her toes and
kiss his cheek. Scarlet followed, but only looked at him as
she eased by, the very tip of her tongue tracing the corner
of her mouth.

He wanted to lick her there, too.

As he closed the door and twisted the lock, Jade spoke.
"We're going to war soon, and I'm done hiding from the
things I want. I want all of you. On me and under me and
in me, any way I can get you."

"For as long as she—as *we* can get you." There was a
hint of challenge in Scarlet's voice.

Mad stepped up to her and slid a hand around her
bare midriff. Her skin was warm under his fingers, as
smooth and soft as her voice was strong. "Anything you
need, for as long as we can give it."

She gripped his wrist and pulled his hand up, beneath
the hem of that tiny T-shirt, until his fingers brushed the
curve of her breast. Arousal sparked from banked embers,
curling through him as he swept his thumb over the tight
peak of her nipple.

Her heart was pounding beneath his hand. Dylan
stood with Jade, stroking her plaited hair, and they
watched as Mad eased the scrap of cotton pretending to be
a T-shirt up and over Scarlet's head.

He didn't have to rush this time. He didn't have to
hurry in case this was his last chance to touch her. The
clock was counting down, but at least they had more than
tonight.

So he started with her hair. Bleached-blonde with a
blue sheen, darker at the roots. He dragged his fingers
through it to savor its silky softness, then lifted it so he

could kiss the spot where her neck sloped into her shoulder.

Scarlet dropped her head back to bare her throat, her skin pale in the dim light of the room.

His room.

Something shifted inside him. In One, they'd formed a tight triangle around him, insulating him from the uncomfortable reality of all the things he'd fled. He'd been off balance, scraped raw.

Now he was whole. He was *Mad.*

And they were his.

He grazed Scarlet's skin with his teeth. "Are you like Jade? Do you want me on you and under you and in you?"

She smiled—slow, sensual. "Sounds about right."

Dylan cradled Jade to his chest, his hand barely resting on her chin, keeping her gaze focused on them. Her expression was serene, almost dreamy, but her eyes held the same challenging glint he'd seen just before she used her lips and tongue to shatter his self-control.

Mad held Scarlet in place with one hand and used the other to tug open her cargo pants. "What else do you want?"

She shivered. "Honestly?"

"Always, sweetheart."

Her nails scored the back of his hand. "All the shit you were holding back at your cousin's place in One."

He hadn't been holding back any more than usual. He always kept things locked down, because the stakes were so fucking high. It was easier to be a gleeful accomplice—to let Dallas use him to get Lex off, or to obey Jas's growled commands to make Noelle squirm. Because you couldn't let go and *take* without accepting the responsibility that came with it.

There was only one person he'd never been able to hold back with. Mad inched his fingers lower and met his eyes. The corner of Dylan's mouth gradually tilted up, and he nodded.

Let go. It wasn't just permission. It was a silent order, as well as a promise. Mad could burn as hot and volatile as he wanted, because Dylan would be there. Cool. Steely. Unshakable.

Responsible.

Mad spun Scarlet around, gripped her ass, and dragged her up his body until her mouth was level with his. The corner she'd licked before beckoned, and he traced his tongue over it before claiming her mouth with a groan.

She kissed him back, her nails running so lightly over his bare skin that it would have tickled if he hadn't been revved so high. Then, in a flash, a heartbeat, the caress sharpened. She dug her nails into the flesh over his ribs, sparking pain that left him hissing against her lips.

Yes. This was the Scarlet he'd always imagined, the one who played hard and rough and hurt him just right. He tightened his grip and ground against her, cursing himself for not getting rid of her pants first. He could be in her already, working her up and down his cock until his legs gave out and they ended up fucking fast and dirty on the floor.

The distance to the bed seemed endless, but crossing it was worth every heartbeat. He dumped Scarlet on her back and reached for her shoes. As he stripped them off, she tugged at the endless row of buttons on her pants.

Mad knocked her hands out of the way and did it himself, so intent on getting her out of those damn pants that the rest of the world might as well not exist. She reached for him again, this time locking her fingers around his wrists.

Fierce, just like he'd known she'd be. He surged over her, using her grip to drag her hands above her head. He pinned her there with a twist of his wrist, one hand holding her in place while he pulled off her pants with the other.

She fought, not to stop him but to help him. And the second he had her naked, she parted her legs and moaned in desperate invitation.

He'd discarded his shirt hours ago, and his belt with it. He nearly ripped the button from his jeans getting them open, but then the zipper yielded and his cock was free, rubbing between her perfect, eagerly parted thighs. He let go of her hands, desperate to feel her nails in his skin as he thrust into her—

"Mad."

Cool, steely command, and Mad tensed with his cock a mere inch from sliding home. His entire body shook as he lifted his head.

Dylan stood at the end of the bed, with Jade still cradled against him. Her eyes were hazy with anticipation, and her soft noise of disappointment echoed Mad's groan.

He clenched his fists in the blankets and fought for the willpower to obey. "Dylan."

His lips brushed Jade's ear, and he whispered a word almost too soft for Mad to hear. "Go." Then he released her.

She swayed for a moment, dazed, as her fingers drifted to the belt on her robe. By the time she crossed the room, the fabric was slipping from her shoulders, sliding to pool on the floor.

Jade crawled onto the bed, naked, and grasped Scarlet's hands. She kissed the inside of each wrist as she drew them back up, pinning them above her head. "I'm never as rough as she needs," Jade whispered, kissing her way to the inside of Scarlet's elbow. "Don't hold back."

Scarlet arched off the mattress. "Jade..."

"Shh." Jade kissed her temple. "Feel this moment. That's all you can do. That's all you have to do. Just feel everything we give you."

Her whole damn body was trembling. Mad rose to his knees, smoothed his hands down her body, and lifted her hips. Feeling wasn't Scarlet's problem—he knew that from how eagerly she'd fallen apart for them before. But to take pleasure passively, to let herself be *vulnerable*...

This was the responsibility he'd been running from.

Strong, dangerous Scarlet stretched out before him, shivering beneath his touch—

And he was a fucking fool. She was worth it. She was
worth *anything*.

He didn't even have to carry the power alone. As he
stroked Scarlet's inner thigh, he looked up at Dylan, who
leaned in and kissed him softly. Then he touched the small
of Mad's back—lightly, not pushing him forward, not
pushing him at all.

It was enough.

Mad went slow with the first thrust, just to savor her
slick, clenching heat. And her expression—head thrown
back, lips parted, her skin flushing when Jade held her in
place even when she tried to twist free.

He spent another few moments fixing this view into
his memory, from her arched body to her tousled hair. Her
gorgeous breasts thrust up into the air, her nipples so
mouthwateringly tight that he couldn't stop himself from
leaning over her, taking one into his mouth—

She choked out his name, and it was over. He held on
to the blankets and surged into her, fucking so deep she
went tense before melting beneath him. She wound her
legs around him, her thighs gripping his sides as he did it
again, and again.

As he let go.

It wasn't sweet. She didn't want it sweet, and he'd
been waiting too long to go slow. He gave her what they
both needed—deep and hard, with thrusts so powerful
they would have pushed her up the bed if Jade hadn't been
there, holding her in place.

Dylan glided one hand up his back, his fingers digging
into shifting, flexing muscle before sinking into Mad's
hair. He jerked his head back, *hard*, the sharp pain a perfect counterpoint to how Scarlet clenched around his cock
when he groaned.

Stop. That was the silent command. Panting, Mad
stilled his hips, a whole new sort of agony. "Fucking hell,

Dylan, *what?*"

His voice was low and rough, gravel and velvet. "Get up."

For a moment, temptation beckoned. Power. It sung through him and in him, the power of a warrior. A prince. He'd been born to it, bred for it. He could turn on Dylan, drag him down to the bed, and show him what it meant to belong to a prince.

He could show them all what it meant to belong to a Rios.

So tempting—and so fucking wrong. His grandfather's hunger for control was his Rios legacy, and Mad could *not* give into it. Would not. Snarling, he rose to his knees and let Dylan scatter kisses over his shoulder, his chest, down to his stomach.

The first touch of Dylan's tongue on his cock rocketed through him. He swore, tangling his fingers in Dylan's hair as the other man swallowed him, sucking him fast and deep—but in perfect, controlled movements.

"Look at them," Jade said hoarsely, her fingers still twined with Scarlet's. "They're beautiful."

"Beautiful," Scarlet echoed. "And they're *ours*."

"Yeah, we— *Fuck*." Mad's words died when Dylan did something with his tongue that blurred his vision, had him jerking forward hard enough to choke.

Dylan pulled away. Instead of rising, he turned his attention—and that hot, open mouth—to Scarlet. She threw her head back and pulled against Jade's grip on her wrists, but she didn't twist away. She arched her hips toward him, toward his eager lips and clever tongue.

"I know," Mad whispered, stroking his knuckles up her trembling inner thigh. "I know how hot his mouth is. So much pleasure it hurts, because he's methodical." His hand grazed Dylan's chin, and Mad edged past it, teasing her with the tip of his finger. "Relentless."

She whimpered, and Dylan lifted his head only to close his teeth on Mad's arm in a searing, savage bite.

Rough. Nothing held back.

Mad shuddered and gripped Scarlet's hips. "Let her go, Jade."

She obeyed at once, and Mad flipped Scarlet over. He didn't give her a chance to find her balance, just hauled her hips up and shoved her knees wide with his own. Her back formed a perfect, tempting bow, even sharper when he caught her hair in one fist and drew her head back. "Is this what you want?"

"Adri—" The word cut off with a noise that was half moan, half sigh. "*Yes.*"

He drove into her. Deeper this time, pushing forward until his hips ground against her ass. He released her hair and planted his hand between her shoulder blades instead, pinning her in place for his first hard thrust, and she rewarded him with a muffled shriek as she clenched her hands in the sheets.

So he did it again. And again. And this time Dylan didn't stop him from riding her until her cries melded together into a hoarse, helpless moan. Didn't stop him from sliding a hand from her hip to her pussy, where she was so damn wet his fingers slipped over her clit.

She jerked in his grasp then, so close, and he growled his encouragement as he circled his fingers faster. "Show me," he demanded, voice a dark rasp that should have shamed him. But nothing did right now, not when every rough touch made her tighten around him. "Show me how much you like this."

Her legs would barely hold her, she was shaking so hard. Quaking. Then she sucked in a sudden, shocked breath, and all Mad knew was the tight, rhythmic clench of her pussy as she came all over him.

He didn't remember moving, just the abrupt pleasure of her skin against his as he slid one arm beneath her body and dragged her against him. The tempo of his hips was beyond his control. Nothing mattered but closing his teeth on the back of her shoulder and savoring her immediate reaction—another shocked gasp, another round of trembling.

He didn't know if she liked the pain or the possessiveness more, and he was past caring. He bit her neck this time, rough enough to leave a mark, and when she came around his cock again, he slammed deep and joined her.

His heart pounded against Scarlet's back, keeping time with hers as they panted in unison. Then, after an eternity that was probably mere seconds, she sank to the bed with a satisfied moan.

Mad started to follow her, but Dylan's hands locked on his hips, holding him in place. "Jade, love? Top drawer of the nightstand. There's a small bottle with a blue cap."

Oh, sweet fucking *hell.*

The bed barely dipped as Jade moved. The drawer on the nightstand squeaked, something he'd been meaning to fix forever, and anticipation stirred beneath his exhaustion.

Mad hadn't held back. Neither would Dylan.

Dylan rubbed his hip in a gently soothing caress—which only made his words seem more obscene in contrast. "Do you think I can fuck you until you're hard again?"

"You've done it before." Because Dylan's patience and control were seemingly endless. "And you didn't have help that time."

"Mmm." Dylan slapped Scarlet's ass, and she rolled away with a throaty laugh.

Jade returned, a familiar plastic bottle cradled in her hand, but she didn't hand it over. She smoothed Mad's hair back from his forehead before trailing her fingers through his hair and down the back of his neck. His skin prickled under her gentle touch, and he shivered as she drifted lower.

Dylan urged him to bend forward with one hand in the center of his back. He scratched him with the other, tracing fire from his shoulder to his hip. "Scarlet fucking loved it, but maybe you shouldn't have held her hands, Jade. Imagine what he'd look like by now."

"Next time," Jade murmured, following the stinging lines of pain with soft kisses. As heavy as his limbs were, Mad knew he'd be turned on again before Dylan got inside him.

He turned his head and met Scarlet's equally heavy, hungry gaze. She reclined on the bed, one arm folded behind her head, her pale skin still flushed. She drew in a sharp breath when Jade popped open the bottle and poured the oil across her fingers and his lower back, then licked her lips when Dylan dragged down his zipper.

The stiff length of his cock nudged the back of Mad's thigh, and Scarlet's spellbound silence broke with a moan.

Jade was so much gentler than Dylan would have been. Dylan would already have a finger in his ass—hell, maybe two. He'd make Mad groan into the bed until his cock stirred again, then fuck him hard and long.

Jade tormented. She soothed. Her oil-slicked fingertips trailed over his skin, rubbing tension from his back and legs he hadn't even realized was there. His arms weren't heavy anymore—they were boneless. His whole damn body was melting by the time she spilled more oil across his ass and worked the tip of one slender finger inside him.

Hair brushed his arm, and Scarlet's breath whispered over his cheek. "Almost," she promised. "So fucking close."

Dylan sighed, a sound full of anticipation and pleasure—then hauled Scarlet toward him. "Help me," he murmured, a teasing echo of that first night. The first time. "Put my cock in your boyfriend's ass."

His words on Dylan's tongue, and the memory hit him hard—Scarlet's fingers closing around his aching dick, the playful strokes, the impossible fucking hotness of having Jade writhe and beg as Scarlet guided him into her.

Jade was the one making him writhe now. A second finger joined the first, slick and clever, but it was the noise

Dylan made that stirred arousal to life again—a hissed breath, and when Mad squeezed his eyes shut he could envision it. Scarlet, clasping Dylan's shaft, jerking and teasing in turn.

The feral, possessive satisfaction Dylan would feel as she guided him home.

"Filthy motherfucker," Scarlet said, lust and approval dripping from every syllable. "How do you *stand* him?"

"You should know," Mad grated. "You've got the number-one reason in your hand."

"Mmm, it's got to be more than the dick." She paused, and Dylan groaned again. "Jade?"

Jade kissed his shoulder as she slipped her fingers free, then turned to rest her cheek against his back. Watching, and Mad was so fucking jealous he started to turn.

Before he could, the wide head of Dylan's cock pressed against his asshole.

They'd fucked before. So many damn times—fast and slow, soft and rough. In Dylan's bed and in Mad's, and in plenty of other places besides. But it had always been desperate, edged with darkness and pain and all the words they never said.

And the words they had. Their twisted game, conjuring fantasy versions of Scarlet and Jade. But the real versions were here now. Scarlet gripped his hip, her fingernails digging in as she held him in place. And Jade breathed unsteadily, her hand trembling on his back. Fierce and soft, just like they'd imagined—

But so much *more* than they'd imagined.

Mad gritted his teeth against the burn as Dylan began to fuck into him, every movement deliberate and unyielding. Not quite teasing and not quite taking, but with the promise of both.

Not enough. Not tonight. "Don't hold back, Dylan."

Dylan answered his plea with a hitching breath—and a long, hard thrust.

Pain sung along his nerves. Twisted with lingering pleasure. Crashed into the conflicting sensation of Scarlet's nails pricking his hip and Jade's mouth feathering over his back. It was too much, and he needed an outlet.

Jade was still nestled against his side. He reached back, tried to hook an arm around her waist and pull her forward, but Dylan grabbed his wrist. "She'll come to you, love," he rasped. "But you have to ask."

Hypocritical bastard. Dylan never had to ask Jade for a damn thing. He looked at her and she obeyed, as if they'd been doing this for years. As if she already understood Dylan's wants and desires on a cellular level, when Mad had rarely been able to pierce that inscrutable wall around the other man's heart.

Jealousy was a foreign emotion, an unwelcome one. But it barely had time to spear through him before Jade banished it by sliding in front of him, flushed and sweetly pliant. "Mad doesn't have to ask tonight. He can have whatever he wants."

No, he still had to ask. Dylan was testing him, playing their twisted game. He had to own all the dirty things he wanted to do to the lush body in front of him—and this time she'd hear every word.

Not so twisted, anymore. Glorious.

"I want you on your back in front of me," he whispered, staring into her endless brown eyes. "I want your thighs spread wide. I want to see how wet you are from watching us—" Dylan drove forward again, scattering any thoughts but one. "*Fuck*."

Jade didn't look away as she moved. Slow, graceful, stretching out in front of him in silence. But she hesitated with her knees drawn up and together, and he knew he was the one who'd put that wariness there. Every time he'd treated her like a fragile creature, every time he'd assumed she was broken, wounded. That she *should* be broken, and that any desire she thought she felt was a lie.

It would take more than one night to fully earn her

trust. But he would, even if it killed him. He kissed her ankle, her shin, brushed a kiss to each knee and let her see the naked relief that washed over him when Dylan rewarded him with another lazy stroke. "Scarlet doesn't know yet," he murmured against her skin. "How he feels when he's fucking you. So full it should just be pain..."

"But it's not." Jade shivered and let her knees fall apart, baring inner thighs slick with arousal and a pussy begging for his tongue. He checked the temptation to descend on her like a starving man and repaid her trust with soft, slow kisses up the inside of her leg.

It worked. Her legs spread wider, and she stretched with a languid sigh. "It isn't pain. It's perfect."

"Tease." Scarlet stretched out beside her and flashed Mad a wicked grin. "Both of you. You're awful."

"Next time," Jade said dreamily, then laughed. "Oh God, I love those words. I want to do so many beautifully filthy things to all of you. I don't even know where to start."

"Next time," Dylan echoed. It carried the weight of a vow, sworn with the same desperation Mad could feel in the strong, nimble fingers that gripped his hips.

And maybe he knew Dylan well enough, because he knew what that grip meant. Ten magical little points of pressure, a sensation so familiar his body shifted to full arousal in a heartbeat. He had seconds at most before the first *real* thrust.

He used them to smile at Jade before driving his tongue into her pussy.

She arched with a cry, her knees flying up to slam against his shoulders as Dylan drove into him. The pleasure melded together in his mind—soft and hard, giving and taking. He moaned against Jade and licked his way up to her clit. She was so turned on that the first touch of his tongue had her writhing.

He needed more, all of her. He lifted his head and started Dylan's name, but he already knew, he *always* knew. Strong fingers tangled in Mad's hair, dragging him roughly up until he was balanced on his knees, Dylan's body crushed to his back.

Jade gasped when Mad gripped her hips and hauled her down the bed. But her shock dissolved into a moan when he grasped his cock and guided it toward her. She raised her hips, begged him with her body and her shameless, desperate little moans.

Dylan pushed him forward—and into Jade.

She felt so good, his head began to swim. Hot and tight and wet and *bliss*, and Mad barely had the presence of mind to brace his weight on his arms to keep from crushing her as Dylan fucked into him again, driving him down toward the bed and deep into Jade's body.

"Oh—" Her voice trembled as she cupped his face, her eyes glazed and beautiful and so, so open. "You're both fucking me—"

Scarlet smothered the words with a kiss, their tongues flashing as she dragged Jade's head back, exposing the vulnerable curve of her throat.

Nothing to do but give in, to let Dylan set the pace and ignore everything but the places he could kiss and lick before pleasure took over. Jade's pulse fluttered beneath his tongue, quick and frantic like the tightening of her body around his cock every time Dylan thrust forward.

He ground forward even more because Dylan did, his cock huge and hard, perfect in ways that made Mad burn from the inside out. Then Dylan pushed his head down, urging him to take even more—and pressing his teeth into Jade's skin.

A silent command Mad was all too willing to obey. He bit her, set his mark in her skin, and let the guilty thrill rush through him as she moaned and clenched and *came*, pulsing and hot, setting off a chain reaction of lust.

Fire licked up his spine, swept through him, and consumed what was left of his reservations. Scarlet's tongue did the rest, gliding up the column of his neck, and he slammed his head back against Dylan's shoulder with a desperate demand. "Come with us."

Dylan snarled, and the carefully calculated thrusts from before turned into something else, something animal and wild. He fucked Mad faster, pounding his ass so hard and deep that the fire went on and on, endless and over-whelming. Bracing his body against the force of it was impossible, and every rough thrust drove Mad deeper into Jade.

Mad was drunk on it, hazy and unsteady, when his lover—*his lover*—stiffened and froze. Dylan whispered something against his shoulder, but it only registered as heat and breath until he whispered it again. "Fucking beautiful."

That was the damn truth.

Some distant part of him was aware that Jade was beneath them, that he had to move, but his thoughts and his body seemed disconnected. Dylan was the one who pulled him away, and Mad collapsed to the bed, weak-limbed and panting, with the amused thought that this must be what Jade and Scarlet felt when he and Dylan pushed them into that foggy place beyond simple pleasure.

Nothing, and *everything*.

Scarlet curled against his side and traced his parted lips with her fingers. "Still with us?"

He laughed and turned toward her palm. "Not even a little."

"Good," Jade said sleepily, rolling to tuck herself against his other side. "Enjoy it. Dylan will take care of us."

He would. It was one of the few things in which Mad had unshakable faith, even when Dylan didn't. Dylan needed people to take care of—not patients whose lives hung in the balance, but ones he could soothe and hold and stroke and comfort, who trusted him enough to surrender in this one small way.

And maybe, most of all, he needed people who would

care about him in return. And if all three of them did it at once, Dylan would start to understand that he deserved it.

hawk

JADE'S ROOFTOP GARDEN was finally in bloom.
Maybe *bloom* was too optimistic a word, but with the world grinding toward war all around them, Hawk would take his hope where he could find it. And there was hope in watching Jade and Jeni transfer tenderly nurtured plants from the safety of the greenhouse to the raised beds Hawk had spent the last week constructing.

They were still in the first blush of spring, but the weather was warm enough for broccoli and peas and peppers. Tomatoes and onions would join them soon, and carrots and spinach. He did the math in his head by reflex as he anchored a trellis to the bed that would hold beans—but not until closer to summer. They'd be harvesting some of the early vegetables by then. Those could be replanted, would *have* to be replanted, because they needed everything they could can or preserve.

"You've got this now," Jade said, watching Jeni transfer a seedling from the tray to the spot they'd prepared for it in the soil. "Do you think you can finish this row while I check on the greenhouse?"

Jeni tried to hide a smile behind the back of her hand, but it showed through in her eyes. "I'll be fine, Jade. Thanks for your help."

"No, thank *you*." Jade touched Jeni's shoulder as she rose and graced Hawk with the brightest smile he'd ever seen on her usually tired face. "And thank you, too, Hawk. It means a lot to me that you found time for this, even with all your other duties."

He'd discovered the trick to dealing with the O'Kane women. He pretended Jade was one of his sisters and treated her to the same gruff affection he would have given any of them. "I'd be pissed if you didn't ask."

"Noted."

She picked a path between the maze of beds and disappeared into the greenhouse. Then it was just him and Jeni in the clear morning sunlight, and the devil himself couldn't have helped Hawk view her as a sister. Not that the devil would bother. Hawk had no illusions there—the devil was probably laughing at him.

All the bright sunlight didn't help, either. Hawk usually saw Jeni in shadows, in the bar or at parties, or under the blazing lights on the stage at the Broken Circle, where makeup and wigs transformed her into a mysterious, dangerous stranger.

Her hair was naturally red. Not the bright, brassy shade Trix sported, but a deep auburn streaked with rich brown and spun gold.

He'd never before been so damn obsessed with a woman's hair, but hers seemed like an intricate code. It changed as she moved through life, hidden beneath platinum-blonde wigs when she performed, done up in a riot of curls when she worked the bar.

It was straight now, drawn back in a simple, sleek ponytail. A new variation to add to his collection. *Jeni at war.*

She carefully placed another seedling, patting the soil down around it with her bare fingers. "I'm sorry. About the other night."

He drove the final nail into place with more force than necessary, leaving an indention in the wood where the hammer had hit too hard. "For what?"

"For making you uncomfortable." Her answer was matter-of-fact. "I didn't realize my proposition would, but it did, and that's what matters. So I'm sorry."

So it *had* been a proposition. He'd wondered, in the moment, even as caution had him turning it down. But afterwards, alone in his bed, trying not to imagine her there with him, he'd been sure he'd read too much into it. That being an obsessive fucker, watching her so closely that he'd catalogued her favorite hairstyles, had made him turn a friendly overture into something illicit.

And it would be illicit, because she belonged to Dallas and Lex. At least, she *had.*

When she glanced up at him, her eyes were gentle and a little sad. His heart beat faster. "I wasn't uncomfortable. I misunderstood."

"How?"

Hawk tightened his grip on the hammer and moved to the other side of the trellis. Calm, casual movements, as if his words were casual, too. "I heard you had a thing with O'Kane. So I didn't think you were...propositioning me."

She laughed softly, a rough exhalation that was at least as much sigh as rueful amusement. "No. No, I don't have a thing with Dallas and Lex, not anymore. That's been over for a while."

"Oh." It was all he could manage. He was scrambling to replay the last few months' worth of parties in his mind, to pinpoint when he'd last seen her with them. But he'd taken Jas's warning to heart. He'd stopped watching—at least when it was easy for people to catch him at it.

"Yeah." Jeni set the empty seedling tray aside and wiped her grimy hands on her jeans. "Can you hand me the tray of—those—" Her cheeks turned pink, and she shrugged. "I don't know what those plants are."

"Spinach." Feeling like the ground beneath him had finally stopped shifting, Hawk picked up the tray and carried it to her. "If I'd gotten the beds built sooner, Jade could have started these outside. Spinach is tough. Doesn't mind a little cold weather."

She ran one finger along the flat of a slender, curling seed leaf, then traced the rounded edge of a proper leaf that had just begun to grow in. His heart beat even faster, as if she was tracing that fingertip over his skin instead.

One of her nails was chipped, and her hands were covered in dirt. He took one and wiped it clean with the hem of his shirt. "You should wear gloves for this."

"It's just skin." She managed to make the words sound seductive—or maybe anything would sound seductive while they were touching. "It washes."

"The dirt leaves its mark." He turned his own hand over in hers, showing her the roughened skin, the calluses. The dirt under his nails. Earth and engine grease—two things he'd never been able to scrub away completely. "Your hands are soft."

Her gaze clashed with his. She stared at him like she didn't give a shit if his hands were rough or soft as long as he put them on her. And this time he wasn't imagining it—there was no room for doubts or misunderstanding in the bright light of day.

He should say no anyway, because Dallas still might not take kindly to Hawk trespassing on someone so recently his. Because war was coming to Sector Four. Because something worse—starvation—could be for his family back in Six. And Hawk would have to be there, fighting, one way or another.

He should say no. Instead, he rubbed his thumb down the center of her palm and molded his voice into the same sort of velvet-wrapped steel Jas used to melt Noelle's knees. "Put on the gloves, Jeni."

At first, her only reaction was a fine tremor. Then she slowly pulled her hand from his. "You're a tricky one, Hawk. I don't think you misunderstand anything." The words were still hanging in the air when she stretched past him—and picked up her discarded gloves.

"Sure I do. But only once." And he wasn't misunderstanding the satisfaction that stirred low in his gut. It was the biggest reason he should say *no*. The O'Kanes came together casually, easily—and temporarily. He'd tasted enough of fleeting to know it wasn't for him.

Before he took Jeni to bed, he had to learn everything he could about what she wanted and needed. Because when he took Jeni to bed, he had to be ready to convince her to stay there.

14

I T FELT STRANGE to be back in Three.

   Not bad, exactly, but different and familiar, all at once. In a way, it still felt like coming home for Scarlet—the blocked, often-shattered surfaces of the streets, the scent of the mud-and-grass mortar used for makeshift re-pairs to brick and stone, even the way people milled about without ever seeming to come out of cover.

People in Three had long, long memories.

And so did she. She'd gladly volunteered to be part of the labor force clearing some of the more structurally sound tunnels in the sector. It was something she could do, a way to be productive while nearly everyone else she knew was making big plans and even bigger decisions.

But being underground brought those goddamn mem-ories screaming to the front of her mind. The fire, the chaos. Staring down into the gaping crater where the Greer Street facility had once stood, wondering where her father lay in all that filthy rubble.

The nightmares were the worst. For months, she'd woken, silent and panicked, unable to scream, from terrifying dreams of smoke and choking darkness. In sleep, she'd watched her hands turn bloody and raw from scrabbling at debris. From trying to dig herself out of her own grave.

It was hard to get enough air through the mask covering the lower part of her face. She straightened, tugged off her gloves, and yanked the stifling mask away from her mouth. "It's a pretty far cry from our last show, huh?"

Riff's habitually stern expression almost softened into a smile. "I don't know. Crowded, loud, sweaty..."

"This is arguably easier on the hands, though. For you, anyway." She arched an eyebrow at him. "Better watch those magic fingers while you're tossing this shit around. The ladies sure would miss 'em."

"On and off stage." He threw aside a chunk of concrete. "You're pretty damn chipper. Got some ladies waiting back at home for your magic fingers?"

He didn't know. The realization shouldn't have startled her, because *of course* he didn't know. And yet she felt so different, as if she'd changed on some inextricable, fundamental level. Couldn't everyone tell?

Sure, they could. He'd asked, hadn't he? He just didn't know why. "Jade's waiting. And maybe—" She bit her lip. Another thing that shouldn't have startled her—how impossible it would be to explain Mad and Dylan.

Riff raised an eyebrow. "And maybe...?" he prompted. "What, have you gone full-on O'Kane on me, Scarlet?"

"Depends, I guess, on what you mean by that."

"You know." He shrugged and reached for a bottle of water. "You and I have always fucked who we want, how we want, and not given a shit what the world thinks. But the O'Kanes don't just fuck that way. They love that way, the crazy motherfuckers."

His words were circumspect, careful even in their

bluntness. "Is this your delicate way of asking if I've fallen in love?"

"Well, we're underground and you're still glowing, so..." He offered her the water. "C'mon, Scarlet. It's me."

It was Riff, her friend and bandmate. They'd shared everything, from meals to money, sleeping space to lovers. Sob stories and tales of glorious conquest. More than anything else, they'd shared the music, the rhythmic moments of truth that flowed through them and out into the world. They were closer than blood. As close as O'Kanes. So she gave him this truth, silent and still in the dark. "Jade and I have a thing. With Dylan and Mad."

"Dylan?"

Another jolt. "Sorry. Doc, that's his name." When had she started thinking of him that way? By his first name, an intimacy that usually meant nothing, but she'd still never imagined sharing with him?

"Huh." And that was all he said until he reclaimed the water bottle and drained it. "Jade and Mad I get. They're hot. But Doc? I mean, sure, he's headed straight for silver-fucking-fox territory, but he comes off like he'd be a bossy motherfucker in bed."

"He is." And Riff was right for thinking it was the sort of thing that would normally turn her off. Fighting to see who came out on top had come between her and Riff often enough. But with Dylan, all that mattered was seeing how his hard, unbending commands affected Jade and Mad. "Let's just say I'm learning to appreciate the art of compromise."

"Then they must be magical," Riff said, his expression deadly serious and his eyes dancing.

Without thinking, she hurled her gloves at his chest. "Asshole."

He caught them and tossed one back. "Scarlet, honey, you're good at a lot of things. Taking orders has never been one of them."

"That depends on the orders." She shrugged. "If it's

something I want to do, I'm not going to say no just be-cause someone told me to do it. I'm too practical for that shit."

"Fair enough." Riff pitched her other glove at her. "So he's telling you to put your magic fingers interesting places, huh?"

"Aren't you dying to know?" But her cheeks heated, and she didn't move fast enough to cover them.

Riff started laughing. "Goddamn, I take it all back. If the good doctor can make *you* blush..."

"I don't blush." The water bottle was warm, but it still felt cool against her face, proving her protest a lie. "You're the one who asked."

"For old times' sake." Riff's smile faded a little. "I miss it sometimes, you know. As shitty as our lives were..."

"I know." They'd always had each other, and there was a certain comfort and camaraderie in that—us against the world, and damn everyone else. Now, she had a new life in a new sector, and when she came back to Three, she wasn't coming home. She was visiting. "I could talk to Dallas—"

"Hey, no." Riff shook his head. "This is where I belong. I'm not O'Kane material, and we both know it."

"Not being O'Kane material and belonging here aren't the same thing," she corrected gently. "There's a whole wide world out there, Riff."

He tugged his gloves back on. "Yeah. But this isn't a bad place to pass the time for now. A hospital, Scarlet. A fucking hospital."

Even before Eden blew the place up, Three had had to make do with medics and healers, folks who were quick to learn from books or from knowledge passed down from el-ders. They operated out of cramped tenement apartments or drafty, abandoned warehouses, and all too often, their skills had boiled down to little more than apology. Because knowledge didn't matter for shit if you had no medicine or supplies.

Her father had never spoken of it, but their older

neighbors had. Scarlet had been left to piece their mournful whispers—*childbed fever, poor thing*—together with the faded photos her father had hidden behind the loose panel of a kitchen cabinet. Together, they formed verse and chorus of a tragic ballad. Blonde hair, blue eyes, and a smile Scarlet couldn't remember.

Two sectors away, factories hummed night and day, making the antibiotics that would have saved her mother. They might as well have been on the moon.

She shook herself. "It's not just for people in Three. It's for everyone. The lines between the sectors are blurring, Riff. You know what that means."

"Yeah. That it only took about forty fucking years for us to figure out we should be working together."

The truth was even more terrifying, and it could set them free—or get them all killed. Because Eden depended fiercely on the sector leaders being at odds, warring with one another. If they stopped, eight sectors could turn into one. And that one...

The sectors had been built not only as a first line of defense against invasion, but to make goods for the city. Even things like meat and grains that were farmed well outside of the sector limits had to be shipped through them and into the city. If the sector leaders managed to turn against Eden, the city would be surrounded, cut off, damned by their own hubris as much as geography.

Because they'd never imagined this might happen. Riff could talk about how forty years was too long, an eternity, but it was a fucking miracle it was happening at all. Because it was never in the plans.

"I worry," she admitted finally, "that we'll never get the chance to fight. We know better than anyone—Eden doesn't play fair."

"I worry about Four and One," Riff replied quietly. "Eden could put their own men in charge of the factories in Five and Eight, and the workers are so tired they might not even care. But Four and One—that's how I'd take the heart and soul out of the sectors. Take down the people who have something to fight for."

"Shh." It was another thing he didn't know, only this time it wasn't a shock. The O'Kanes held their people tight, and their secrets tighter. "Come on."

Scarlet led him up the gentle slope toward the tunnel's new exit, which was cleverly concealed in a small, concrete building that had been there as long as she could remember. It was the perfect place to hide such an ambitious project.

And the perfect place for a private conversation. "Something already happened in One. An attempt on Gideon Rios."

Riff slumped against the wall. "Shit."

"Either Eden's behind it, or someone has the shittiest timing ever." She paused, trying to pinpoint her roiling unease. It wasn't the anger that flooded her when she thought of Mad's brush with death, a panicked rage that clawed at her throat. This was acid burning a hole in her gut. "It's not right, though. If Eden kills Gideon, his people will still fight. Hell, they'll fight harder to avenge their murdered saint. So *why?*"

"Maybe they think Gideon's the only one who can hold together the sector alliance."

"Could be," she allowed.

"Or they could be crazy motherfuckers planning God knows what."

And it wasn't up to them to find out. They weren't the people holding lives in their hands, sitting in back rooms and conference halls, making decisions and talking strategy. They were here to get to work, to clear rubble and make way for Dylan's vision—a hospital in a safe, secure location.

But she had an undeniable tie now to the people pulling the strings. It would be Dylan's hospital, after all. Mad, whose cousin still ruled One, spent his time at Dallas's side, advising him as well as carrying out his orders.

And Jade didn't talk about it, but she had more money than all the rest of them put together, years of carefully placed investments that equaled practical power, if not political.

Somehow, even though she was no one, Scarlet had ended up surrounded by important people. And important people made excellent targets. "Can you do me a favor, Riff?"

"Anything. Always."

"Keep an ear to the ground, huh? If you hear anything strange—*anything*—"

"I'll be knocking down your door." He grinned. "Unless Bren stabs me before I get there. That crazy bastard does not like me."

Bren didn't do subtle. It was one of the things Scarlet loved about him. "If Bren didn't like you, you'd have a knife in your face already. Just saying."

Riff choked on another laugh. "Christ, Scarlet. Your new friends are a little scary."

"Yeah." She caught Riff's hand—and held on. "But you can back me in a fight anytime. You've always been there for me. I haven't forgotten. I won't."

He gripped her hand so hard it ached. "I know."

Scarlet waited for the wave of nostalgia to sweep over her, to miss her old life so much she could barely breathe. But the pain didn't come.

And maybe this was the real brilliance of what Dallas had to offer—she didn't have to miss her life and her friends in Three, because the O'Kanes had never asked her to leave them behind. She carried them with her, as much a part of her as if she saw them every day.

Still, she clung to Riff's hand. "Come on. We have work to do."

15

T HE REQUISITIONS LIST of hospital supplies on his tablet was endless. Dylan checked it three times, and he was still sure he'd forgotten something huge.

"Ryder will just have to make it work," he muttered to himself.

He should have already had the lists of drugs and equipment ready in case they needed to set up special manufacturing, but he'd been so focused on finding the funding. Money was always his first concern, the great definer of limitations. You didn't get shit if you couldn't pay for it.

Then Lex had blown apart all of his expectations with five little words: *it'll be taken care of.* When pressed for more information, she'd admitted that every sector leader involved in their newly minted revolution had agreed to pitch in to fund the hospitals in One and Three.

Revolution, indeed.

When was the last time he hadn't had to worry about money? Back in the city, he supposed, but even that had come at its own price. He'd been at the beck and call of every councilman and climbing bureaucrat. He'd treated their children's suicide attempts, their mistresses' drug overdoses, all their dirty little secrets. He remembered every single one—and then he learned what happened when you knew too many of those secrets.

They locked you away, and only let you out when they needed someone tortured.

The scent of vanilla spiced with cinnamon wrapped around him, and he closed his eyes to savor it.

"Dylan?" A soft hand touched the back of his neck. "I knocked, but you didn't answer."

Jade. He reached up and held her hand to his skin. "I didn't hear."

"I figured. You've been working so hard."

That made him laugh. "Not nearly. I've been a little distracted, after all."

She brushed her thumb down the back of his neck. "Which only means we're not letting you get enough sleep."

"I won't argue with that." He turned his head just far enough to study her. She was wearing a sweater dress and high boots, and her dark hair was piled on top of her head in a messy knot. "You look nice."

"I'm trying something new." She ran her fingers over the hand-knit fabric. "It cost a fortune and it's not exactly silk robes, but I like it. Though it's warmer than I expected."

"Shit." He fumbled for the environmental control on his desk and almost knocked it off before thumbing the screen to life. "I'm sorry. I set the heat too high and then forgot to turn it off."

"You were focused." She set a basket on the table next to him. "I bet you haven't eaten, either. I considered trying to cook something for you, but I'm pretty sure I could burn water. So I stopped in the market."

"You didn't have to do that." He was hungry, all right, but not for food. Instead, he watched her, drank in the simple grace of her movements as she began to unpack the basket. "I missed you."

"I missed you, too." She set a loaf of bread wrapped in cloth on the table and smiled at him. "Maybe bringing dinner was a little selfish. It's lonely over at the compound today. Everyone who isn't on duty is either over in Three or locked in the conference room for meetings."

"And you somehow escaped?"

"Not entirely. In fact…" Jade drew a tablet from the basket and slid it in front of him. "I spent my morning with Noah and Noelle. Noah thinks he can adapt some of the medical diagnostic software they use in Eden so it'll run on tablets, even the older ones Dallas has piled up in storage. We'll have to have Jim manufacture the accessories, but if you think it's worthwhile to pursue, I'll find the money."

He skimmed the list. Making equipment cheap and portable had never really interested Eden—where the hell would they ever need to take it?—but in battle, it could mean the difference between people making it to a hospital or dying in the field. "I'll go over it with Ryder when we meet to talk about the hospital requisitions. With a little innovation, there's no reason this couldn't work."

"Good." She unloaded the last of the food, but instead of sinking into a chair, she slid into his lap and wrapped her arms around his neck. "I want to help with this, Dylan. Not just with money."

"I know." He'd already loosened his collar, and it slipped down, baring the base of his neck. His skin tingled where she touched him, soft knit fabric and warm flesh brushing over him.

The tingles increased as she threaded her fingers into his hair. "And I want to take care of you. If I'm not there, keeping an eye on you, you'll forget to eat or sleep or turn the heat down when it gets too warm."

"I'm not *that* ridiculous, am I?"

She smiled and kissed the corner of his mouth. "The only reason Mad hasn't noticed is because he's a little ridiculous, too."

Dylan dropped one hand to her knee. Instead of naked skin, he encountered soft, delicately knit tights. Another quiet indication of the wealth she possessed. Nothing finer than thick socks was made in any of the sectors, meaning this was another item of clothing that had been shipped in from far away, like her silk robes or lace nightgowns.

He wondered if she knew any other way, or if her wardrobe was simply left over from her time in Sector Two. The O'Kanes preferred rough denim and supple leather, a baffling mix of mass-produced clothing and lovingly handcrafted items, but that didn't seem much like Jade. Supple, flowing cotton, perhaps, handmade and hand-printed.

She was watching him, waiting, so he returned her smile. "Tell me more about how silly I am."

"Not silly. Dedicated." She smoothed her hand down his neck and across his shoulder. "Strong. Focused."

He felt himself melting under her touch, so he turned his voice to velvety steel. "Jade, did you come here to bring me more than dinner?"

"I told you why I came here." Her hand drifted back up, her knuckles grazing his throat. "It's the thing inside me that made me so valuable. They twisted it all up, turned it into a weapon..." She traced his mouth with one fingertip. "But I still want to take care of you."

"You do, love." Slowly, carefully, he rolled the chair away from his desk.

"It's still a tangle. What I wanted to do, what I had to do..." She pressed her forehead to his and closed her eyes. "Sometimes I wonder if Mad needed me to be a victim because, on some level, he knows what it means if I wasn't."

The fear in her voice shivered through him and

clenched in his gut. "You did what you needed to do to get by, Jade. And it isn't just about surviving, it's about making the most of your situation. Sometimes that's the only way to change it. And Mad knows that."

She pressed closer, her body molding to his with sweet warmth. But her words were dark. "You were an interrogator, weren't you?"

In the past, the question had made him freeze up, colder than the dark of night out in the endless desert. But Jade wasn't just curious—she *needed* to know. "Not exactly. The doctors who attend interrogations are discouraged from speaking. It makes the whole thing that much more terrifying."

"So your job was to make them hurt."

"Sometimes. Mostly, I was there to make sure no one died—at least, not too soon. Not before the Counselors got what they were after." Horror slowly dawned on her face, so Dylan tried to reassure her with a smile. It felt more like a grimace. "I was usually there to facilitate the torture, not perform it. Usually."

"Oh, Dylan—" Her voice cracked, and she buried her face against his throat. "It's sick. It's sick to take the best part of someone and make it evil."

"Don't be sorry for me, love. I made my peace with it a long time ago."

Her fingernails pricked his skin. "Don't lie to me. Not about this."

He'd forgotten how easily she could see the truth, even when she wasn't looking for it. "Fine, *peace* is too generous a word. But I've accepted the fact that no amount of regret can change the past. All I can do is move forward, the best way I can."

"I want to do that. I'm trying. But I can't stop *thinking*." She shivered and pulled back, her dark eyes haunted. "What do I want? Why do I want it? Is it me, or is it them, or is it both? And does it matter?"

"You mean, does it matter to you...or to Mad and Scar-let?"

"To me."

He touched her chin and gently forced her eyes to his. "You're not the only one who can hear lies, you know."

She stared at him forever before wetting her lips nervously. "Does it matter to you?"

"Honestly? A bit," he confessed with a tiny smile. "But only because I'd like very much to believe that you're drawn to me for reasons other than your training."

"I wasn't trained to be drawn to men." She reached for the top button of his shirt and slipped it free. "I was trained to draw them to me. To find out what they were most ashamed of wanting, and to give it to them. The men in Eden had so many layers of shame. They loathed the things they wanted more than I ever could."

"Then you're in luck." He grasped her wrist, stilling her hand. "No one in Sector Four is ashamed of wanting anything."

Jade took a shallow breath, and then another. Her pupils were huge. "You know what I want."

"Yes." He tightened his grip on her wrist until he heard her breath hitch. "Do you need me to make you do it? Is that what this is?"

It took her forever to answer, and even then it was barely a whisper. A sigh of relief. "Yes."

For her, absolute control over herself—her body, her emotions—was a matter of survival, an impossible burden she'd had to carry alone for far too long. For him, it was a gift, a trust he would have to keep earning with every breath.

He loosened his hold on her wrist but didn't quite release her. "Keep going."

She lowered her hands to the next button and then the next, coaxing his shirt open with clever, graceful fingers that grazed his skin as she worked in silence. Dylan slipped his free hand into her hair, dislodging the already messy knot, and soft locks tumbled down to join her hands in caressing him.

He gritted his teeth. His pulse thumped in his ears, and he counted the beats, marking the time until she slipped to her knees in front of him and reached for his belt buckle.

She eased the leather of the belt free of the clasp, her gaze still fixed to his as she rubbed the backs of her fingers over his erection.

He clenched his fingers into a fist, pulling at her hair, though he stopped shy of pain. This wasn't about hurting. "Now, Jade."

She obeyed. No more teasing or testing. Her deft fingers made quick work of the button on his pants, and she gripped his cock, firm and warm, her mouth so close that one jerk of her hair would put her lips on him.

He tugged her head back instead, gently guiding until she met his eyes. "I can give you this, love. As much as you want. But I can do something better, too."

"What could be better?"

He held her gaze. "When I show Mad and Scarlet how to do this. When I teach them what you love about it." Naked hunger filled her expression, fueling the lust her touch had kindled. "Scarlet has already figured it out, at least a little. And Mad—once he understands why it's so good, he'll drive you wild, sweet Jade."

"How?" she whispered, rubbing her fingers slowly up his cock. "Tell me. Please."

Dylan shivered. "*How* is easy. Everything he tells you to do will be a fantasy of his, something he never even knew he wanted until he met you."

She ran her thumb slowly around the crown of his cock. "And Scarlet?"

Mad was a tangle of desires he sometimes couldn't admit. Scarlet, on the other hand, embraced them, wanting it all as hard as she could—but nothing more than Jade.

"You've already seen what she'll do for you. Anything. *Everything*. Even me."

"That's not why she touches you," Jade said softly. "She trusts you. You see all of us—where we fit together, and how, and why."

Maybe someday the words would be true. For now, Scarlet was content to watch him, to make sure he didn't hurt Jade or Mad. And it was heady, the thought that someone could see the weak spots in his carefully cultivated control. Touch them. Shred them. He dreaded that moment even as he welcomed it for its inevitability.

There were parts of him they could tear down individually. Perhaps all three of them could put him back together again.

He brushed away the thought, then brushed Jade's lower lip with his thumb. "Right now, I want to see how we fit. Show me."

She licked his thumb, caught it between her teeth in a quick nip. Then she bent her head, taking his cock into her mouth. Heat sizzled through him, from the wet pleasure of her mouth *and* the exhilaration of her submission.

Take. The word echoed through the darkness inside him, a darkness Jade craved because it matched her own. And, in the end, that was what allowed him to give in—knowing this was what she needed. Why she'd come to him this time.

So Dylan nudged the back of her head, not hard enough to force her to take more of his cock, but just enough to let her know he wanted her to. She responded by squeezing the base of his shaft—firm, almost rough—and sliding her mouth down to meet her hand.

Then she looked up. Her gaze clashed with his, all hunger and satisfaction, as she began to suck.

"That's right." He barely recognized the harsh timbre of his own voice, so he focused on the cadence—soothing, like a rocking ship out on open water. "You could make me come with your mouth, even if I wanted to wait. You could use your lips and tongue and *take it.*" He touched the curve of her jaw. "But that's not training, Jade. That's just how much I want you."

She moaned around him, her eyes glittering. Her touch intensified, her head bobbing faster, as if his words had been a challenge. Not smooth, practiced touches or precise strokes, but grasping fingers and an eagerness to please that cut him to the bone.

The heat was incandescent now, brighter than ever before. It would always be like this with Jade—burning hotter the further he pushed her. In turn, she'd find certain pleasure in pushing *him* beyond his limits.

But not tonight.

Dylan pulled her head up and bent until his mouth was inches from hers. "Now I want to know how much you want me."

"Completely," she whispered.

"Not with words, love." He helped her to her feet, then leaned back in his chair.

After a silent moment, she bent to unzip her boots.

She undressed gracefully. Carefully. Her boots first, and then the delicate, expensive tights. Those she set aside before gathering the heavy knit of her dress in both hands. Underneath was smooth skin and more silk—black panties edged with lace and a matching bra too thin to hide her hardened nipples.

She finished taking her hair down next, tugging the pins free and dropping them to the table. The soft *plinks* disappeared beneath her unsteady breaths as she shook out the full length.

Her hands began to tremble as she reached for the front clasp of her bra. The fabric fell away, baring those taut nipples, and he had to wrap one hand around the base of his shaft to quell the sudden ache that pulsed through him.

Her gaze followed his hand. She licked her lips and eased her fingers under that final scrap of clothing. It took her forever to coax her panties over her hips and down her thighs, until they slid to the ground and she stepped free.

Naked. Aroused.

He rose. Jade gasped when he crowded into her space, his body pressing close to hers. When he reached past her to sweep everything off his desk, she wrapped her arms around him to steady herself. "Dylan—"

"Shh." He lifted her, then leaned her back so she was laid out before him—a vision, an offering. A fantasy come to life.

He could fuck her, hard and fast, ride every orgasm to one deeper than the last. He could make love to her, nice and slow, until all she could do was cling to him as she sobbed with pleasure.

What he wanted was somewhere in between.

He slid his fingers, whisper-soft, up the silky skin of her inner thighs. They parted for him, and she ran her foot up his leg and reached for him in silent pleading.

"I won't make you beg," he assured her, already nudging the head of his cock between the slick lips of her ready pussy. "Not a single *please* or *sir*." He pushed into her, gritting his teeth when she moaned and arched her back. "But I will make you wait for me."

She gripped the edge of the desk, white-knuckled and shaking. "What else?"

Truth—bold and inescapable, just like the pleasure he was about to visit on her body. "I'll make you feel every second of it."

"Yes." She hooked both legs around his hips and tilted her head back. "Make me."

He ran his fingertips up her legs, past her hips, to her sides, the barest touch he could manage with her body so hot beneath him, around him. When she twisted and moaned, reaching out for more, he gave her his nails, dragging hot, pink lines across her skin.

"Oh—" Just a single syllable, caught between a moan and a gasp. Her gaze locked on his, and her pussy clenched around him as she pressed up into his nails. "Yes. *Yes.*"

He moved on to her nipples next, flicking the taut tips until they puckered even tighter, silently begging for more. And he gave it to her, gentle tugs and pinches that turned firmer. Rougher. She'd be sore later, her tits aching from the harsh treatment, but all that mattered right now was the way her skin heated, the way pain turned to molten pleasure.

Her moans became shorter, more insistent. Her body shifted restlessly, and her fingers flexed. "I can't—" Her breathing hitched with another fluttering clench of her inner muscles. Worry filled her trembling voice. "I'm too close."

"That's all right." He laid his hand on her throat, closing his fingers with the tiniest hint of pressure—not enough to cut off her air, but enough to let her know he *could.* And that he never, ever would, not without giving her something transcendent in return.

As soon as her eyes lit with the realization, he began to fuck her with deep, quick thrusts. First to get her off, and then to turn that shaking, screaming orgasm into another, and another.

She released the table and grasped at him. At his shoulders, at his arms, her nails scratching matching lines into his skin as she clutched at him in utter desperation. Her lips parted on another silent scream that turned into a hoarse moan, and then a string of broken, begging cries, one word again and again—a plea and a promise and total, gleeful surrender. "Yes, yes, yes, *yes*—"

She came until she was limp and trembling, beyond thought or even pleasure, and yet still she pleaded with him to go on. She was in that place where nothing existed but giving—giving in, giving herself. Everything.

Dylan drove into her one last time, burying his cock in the unbelievable wet heat of her body. It was more than any mortal man could resist, so he let go. Blood pounded in his ears as his balls tightened, and release ripped through him. He pumped into her, filling her up, giving her his control in return for her precious trust.

When it was over, he gathered her to his chest. Ignoring his weak knees, he carried her to the bed and covered her with a blanket, petting her as she shivered and slowly drifted back to reality.

She was still too raw to hide. He watched the emotions flicker across her face unchecked—the drowsy pleasure in her smile, the dazed wonder in her eyes as her lids fluttered open. And then the tightening of her lips and the gentle furrowing of her brow. Hesitation. Nervousness.

"Tell me," he urged, his voice hoarse.

"It feels so...so *right*," she started, sounding small and lost. "I need it to be mine. Something that's part of me. Not something they—they created."

He touched her flushed cheek. "Would you have given that to just anyone?"

"No." She closed her eyes and leaned into his touch. "Does it get to be that simple?"

"I think maybe it does."

He felt her lips curve against his palm. "I'm not accustomed to sex being simple. That's a blasphemous thing for an O'Kane to admit, isn't it?"

The laugh rumbled up out of his chest with a warmth he didn't expect, but should have. "Somehow, I think they'll forgive you."

"I hope so." She reached up to trace his lips and his nose. His cheeks. "I'm still learning who I want to be. Who I could have been all along. I think we all are, in our own ways. It's less scary like this. Together."

"Mmm." And that was the heart of it, the core of what he could offer her—these moments, free of inhibitions and preconceptions and *control*, where she didn't have to think, only feel.

It had to be enough.

16

THERE WERE SOME things money couldn't buy in the sectors, even when you had as much as Jade did. Delicate chocolates oozing caramel and truffles dipped in cocoa powder were a luxury few people in Sector Four could afford—and most who could had other vices.

But if you were an O'Kane, bartering worked where money failed. An investment in Tatiana's growing business earned Zan's help in supplying the hard-to-find ingredients. A black market contact came through with a collection of pre-Flare cookbooks, which secured Lili's skills in the kitchen.

It was a lot of effort to go through for a basket of chocolates, but every second was worth it when Avery smiled.

Not that the smile lasted for long. It faded as she stared down into the basket on her lap. "These couldn't have been easy to come by."

"Still easier than trying to steal them from underneath Cook's nose," Jade replied, keeping her tone light.
"Besides, you didn't see Lili's face when she got the recipe
to work right. I think she's found a new passion. We'll all
be drowning in fantastical confections soon."

"That's nice." Avery toyed with a tuft of paper wrapping and fell silent.

Jade silenced the part of her that needed Avery's
smile and reached for her friend's hand instead. "It doesn't
have to be nice. You know you can feel however you feel
with me."

"I know. But a lot has happened since those days in
Rose House, Jyoti." She looked away and gently rattled
the basket. "Gordon used to make them for me. They were
horrible—always lumpy or grainy, he never could get
them right. But he knew—" Her voice cracked. "He knew
the trainers wouldn't let me have them."

"Oh, sweetheart." Her heart aching, Jade wrapped an
arm around Avery's shoulders. The right words wouldn't
come, maybe because there were no right words. The
training house had been a place of dubious safety for Jade,
but she'd had her mother as a buffer for those first terrifying years. Avery had only had the trainers and their
determination to prevent her from blossoming into another Lex.

Nothing Avery ever did was right. They criticized her
height, her weight, her lack of grace, and her inability to
quickly master lessons. It didn't matter that she was no
different from any other girl in the house—the teachers
had picked and poked at her until her insecurities turned
it into self-fulfilling prophecy. And so the other initiates
began to avoid her, because no one could afford to attract
the trainers' scorn.

No one but Jade, who had been on the fast-track to
becoming Rose House's shining star.

"It's like a bad dream," Avery whispered, "and it never
ends."

Grief filled her voice. Jade recognized it on a gut level, the same level that tried to reject it. It was an ugly internal battle—Jade's conviction that a man who'd bought you could never love you versus the undeniable proof of Avery's pain.

Pain won. Because whether or not Gordon had loved her, he'd made Avery feel loved. And in the end, he'd protected her—*saved* her—at the cost of his own life. Jade could view the actions cynically as a man securing his property, but that didn't help Avery.

And that was what mattered. Helping Avery. So Jade set aside her dislike of Gordon and pulled her friend closer. "I know."

"But it's not just him. Losing him." Her fingers tightened on the basket until her knuckles turned white. "It's being here. I don't belong here."

Jade wondered how many times those words had been whispered behind the closed doors of the O'Kane compound. "I felt the same way. Sometimes I still do. But that's what makes Dallas special, I think. He's strong enough to let us all belong, even if we shouldn't."

"*No.*" Avery squeezed her eyes shut and laughed, a helpless sound that bordered on hysteria. "I don't know why I keep trying to say it like it makes sense. Of course it doesn't make sense. Why would it?"

"It doesn't have to make sense to be true. You know that."

Tears gathered on Avery's lashes, glittering like jewels. "Four belongs to Lex. She helped build it, and I didn't believe it. I'm here now, I see what this place is, and I *still* don't believe it."

How could she? How could *anyone* who had been trained to see men as easily molded victims of their own basest impulses? It had taken Jade years to understand how the lies she'd learned cut both ways. That absolving men of responsibility denied them the capacity for basic humanity. Sector Four was a fantasy built on the belief that everyone, man and woman, had the power to control their own actions.

Avery's sister had been partly responsible for building that world, but Lex had never been selfish. "Four doesn't belong to Lex. It belongs to every woman who came here bruised and broken who thought, *I don't belong here* and *I don't believe this*." Jade stroked Avery's hair. "But it must be so much harder for you, because she's your sister. And maybe you feel like you should believe and belong already. But you can doubt, Avery. I'd be worried if you didn't."

If anything, her words made Avery tense up even more. She caught Jade's gaze and held it, her eyes wide and worried. "So it's wrong?" she asked slowly. "If I want to leave?"

It would break Lex's heart to think she couldn't make her baby sister feel safe, but Lex *wasn't* selfish. And Jade knew better than most that Sector Four's queen must already be thinking about Eden's next move—and whether or not bombs would be falling on her home soon.

But that wasn't why Jade cupped Avery's face and shook her head. It was because *she* knew, better than anyone, how important it was for Avery to hear something— maybe for the first time. "Nothing you want is wrong. *Nothing.*"

"Are you sure?"

"Absolutely." She pressed her forehead to Avery's. "You're my sister in all the ways that matter. You're one of the only people left who knows my name. I'm selfish and I want you with me, but if you need to go, I'll fight for you. We'll find you someplace that feels right."

"Jyoti—" Avery fumbled for her hands and gripped them both tightly. "What if this part is a lie, too? Wanting to go? What if I don't really feel this way? How can I *know*?"

No easy answers came to her lips. Hadn't she whispered the same thing to Dylan? Indecision tore at her with every step now, because she'd chosen to answer the question for herself by avoiding it for as long as she could. "You don't know until you try," she replied gently. "That's what I'm doing. If something makes me feel better, it's real. If it doesn't... Avery, you can try again. You don't have to get it right the first time."

Avery stared at her, as if her words had been uttered in a completely foreign language. "I don't have to get it right the first time."

"No." Jade smiled. "And you won't, sweetheart. None of us do. But the stakes are a lot lower than they were back in Two."

"For me," she agreed. Her troubled expression melted into one of angry determination, and she'd never looked more like Lex than at that moment. "But that just makes me one of the lucky ones, doesn't it?"

"Maybe." There was such sudden, shining *purpose* in Avery's eyes that Jade whispered a silent plea for forgiveness to Lex. "I might have somewhere you can go. A place where you're needed."

Avery latched on to the words like a lifeline. "Where?"

"For a while now, I've been building homes in Sector One for the girls who escaped their patrons," she confessed. "That's where we're taking the survivors from the bombing. But some of the girls are so young, still children. The women in One, they try to help, but they can't understand where we come from or what we've been taught to endure."

For an endless moment, Avery said nothing. Then, "What is it like in One?"

"Not like they described it during training." The contradictions of One were more subtle than Four, but still hard to describe. She tried anyway. "Many of the people there have incredible faith, but it hasn't turned them cold, not like in Eden. Mostly they believe in love, compassion, and peace. They're not perfect, but they try. I've met the leader and his family. They're good people."

"Gideon." Avery pinned her with an appraising look. "Maddox is his cousin, that's what Dallas told me."

Jade couldn't help it. Her cheeks heated, and she almost squirmed. "This has nothing to do with Mad. I had the houses in One before we...became close. He didn't even know about them."

"Oh."

"No, I mean—" Honestly flustered for the first time in too long, Jade squeezed her eyes shut. "The girls in One need you. Which is a completely separate issue from the fact that I have...feelings. Complicated feelings."

Silence. Then Avery sighed softly. "How do *you* know it's real?"

"I don't," Jade admitted. "But it makes me feel better. With everything going on, maybe that's all that matters. Being with the people who make you strong."

The other woman's distress surged again. "But I'm still the only one who knows your name?"

"I..." What? Every excuse that formed on her tongue tasted like a lie, like cowardice. Scarlet, Mad, and Dylan had chipped away at her armor until it was as insubstantial as mist. She wasn't even afraid of setting it aside anymore, not when the door closed behind the four of them and she lost herself in warm skin and confident touches and enough pleasure to drown a lifetime of pain.

But she was still only setting it aside. As long as she held back that final part of herself, she could slide back into being Jade if things went wrong.

When things went wrong.

It was traitorous and fearful and *weak* in ways that scraped at her pride. And here was Avery, staring at her with such naked fear. She'd see through a gentle lie. If Jade wanted to give her hope, she'd have to give her truth. "I'm going to tell them. Even though it scares the hell out of me."

Avery nodded. "Because it's real."

"It feels real. And I think it's worth the risk to find

out. I don't have to get it right the first time, either."

"Lex got it right." Avery dropped her gaze to the basket in her lap before setting it aside. "Dallas is trying, but the way he looks at me... He's so sure I'm going to shatter. It makes me feel like I can't bend, even a little, or he'll think I'm breaking."

Jade's lips curved up, because she could imagine it so easily. Dallas, the terrifying monster lurking in the nightmares of every councilman, became a blustering, nervous wreck when Lex's heart was on the line. "He knows the kinds of stories you've heard about him. And he knows how much your sister loves you. You probably scare him to death, even if he'd never admit it."

"Because I could hurt Lex." Avery swallowed—hard. "But I don't want to. I never want to. I have to get that much right, at least."

"Never is a long time, Avery." Jade stroked her friend's hair. "You might hurt her, and she might hurt you. But you love each other, so you'll keep trying. That's how you get it right."

"Okay." She took a deep breath. "I grew up in Two. I made it through training. I can do this."

"Of course you can. We're stronger than any of them will ever know." Just like all those girls huddling in One, scared and bruised but stronger than even they knew. If Jade accomplished nothing else as the sectors marched to war, she would find a way to protect the refugees from Two.

"Can I see it?" The determination was back, lighting Avery's eyes until she almost looked the way she had before the trainers at Rose House had broken her. "The place you've built in Sector One?"

"I'm going with Lex and Dallas when they meet the other sector leaders. You should tell Lex you want to come and help."

"Just...*tell* her?"

"Tell," Jade repeated with an encouraging smile.

"Trust me, sweetheart. Telling is going to get you a lot farther than asking around here. Especially with your sister. She doesn't want you obedient. She wants you happy."

"Right." A hint of a smile tilted the corner of her mouth, then vanished. "I'm so used to trying to be both."

Which was why the girls in One needed Avery as much as she needed them. For all their shared training, Jade had never been groomed for obedience. By the time she was fourteen, Cerys had singled her out for a different sort of training. Cerys would never risk breaking her most promising spy, so she'd commanded that Jade be spared the worst of her training, and the head of Rose House had obeyed.

And while Jade was trained to mimic submission, she'd watched helplessly as the trainers broke Avery down into pieces so small that obedience came easier to her than breathing.

"You'll learn." Jade wrapped her in a hug and buried her face in Avery's hair. "I'm just so glad you'll be where I can see you. I've missed you so much."

Some of the tension finally eased from the girl's shoulders. "Me too, Jyoti. It's been too long."

Jade had missed something else, too—the sound of her name on another person's lips. It had been so many years since she'd heard it in anyone else's voice but Avery's. Just her mother's, whispered as she brushed Jade's hair at night. Murmured as she lay dying.

She could imagine how it might sound coming from Dylan. Precise and low, his deep voice curling around it. And Mad sometimes had the softest traces of an accent, as if English hadn't been his first language. He'd rumble her name against her ear and know, as so few people knew, how much power the name you were born with could have.

But Scarlet… She should have already told Scarlet. She'd lost months of that honeyed voice caressing every syllable. Of being known and loved—and of loving enough to trust. Scarlet had earned the truth a hundred times over. Never more than when she'd dragged Dylan and Mad into their lives, willing to fight to give Jade anything she wanted.

If Avery could fight through her grief to face an alien life in an unknown sector, Jade could take off her armor.

Maybe for good.

17

M AD WAS AS good at sucking cock as he was at eating pussy.

Not that Scarlet knew that firsthand, obviously. But watching him kneel in front of Dylan was just like watching him between Jade's thighs, or her own—eager mouth, hungry tongue, grasping hands. And the effect certainly seemed to be the same. Dylan groaned at every touch, his whole body trembling as he stared down at Mad.

Scarlet stared, too. Dylan's dick was still wet from fucking her, and she shivered as Mad licked away the evidence of every delicious orgasm. It wasn't enough to get Dylan off, to suck him hard and fast until he exploded in a rush. Mad had to make it slow, torturous.

So fucking good.

She leaned back against the pillows with Jade draped across her. Scarlet could feel her heart still pounding as she stroked her back, her fingers dipping down to her hips before running up to the base of her neck. Her breathing hitched as Mad finally took Dylan deep, and Scarlet smiled.

Not long now. His trembling had progressed to shaking, and he gave in and gripped the back of Mad's head as he thrust forward, fucking his mouth. Mad stared up at him, his eyes dark and welcoming, and Dylan lost it. He drove deep with a desperate growl that turned into a hoarse, relieved cry.

Mad stroked Dylan's hips until his body relaxed, then eased back with a satisfied smile. "That's what you get for teasing us all night."

"Lies." Dylan staggered to the bed and collapsed on it.

Scarlet reached for her cigarette case, lit one, and passed it to Dylan. "You always have to come last. What is that—a control thing?"

His normally neat hair was in disarray, and a lock fell over one eye, lending him a rakish look as he favored her with a lopsided grin. "Maybe I just like to make sure everyone's had a good time before I get mine."

Scarlet's heart hesitated, then resumed thumping hard enough to make her chest ache. That smile was dangerous—open, unguarded, an invitation to climb past the cold shell separating him from the rest of the world.

Mad had done it, and so had Jade. But Scarlet didn't know if she could.

She shrugged it off and lit another cigarette, taking a deep drag before handing it to Mad. "Has he always been this impossible?"

Mad stretched out beside her with a laugh. "Oh, this is the least impossible he's ever been."

"Christ help us."

Jade stretched slowly and rested her cheek on Dylan's chest. "Don't listen to them. They love it."

He buried his hands in her hair and hummed as his smile faded to an expression of pure contentment. "How could they not?"

Mad exhaled smoke toward the ceiling and passed the cigarette back to Scarlet. "He knows he's a dirty, sexy-as-fuck bastard. It's part of his charm."

"Mmm." Watching them together—Jade's dark curves pressed against the strong, paler lines of Dylan's body—held its own sort of charm. Physically, they were a study in contrasts. But beneath it all, they were so much alike. The rogue doctor and the sector spy.

Delicious.

Jade traced one finger in idle circles across Dylan's chest. She had that *look*, like she had something to say and was mentally anticipating the conversation, searching for just the right words. Like a chess match, where every move had to be planned in advance, with contingencies if the game happened to spin off in some wild direction.

Finally, she sighed. "I talked to Avery today."

Scarlet paused with the cigarette almost to her lips. "How is she?"

"Honestly?" Jade rolled onto her back and stared up into the shadows. "Better than I thought she'd be. And worse. Which shouldn't make sense…"

"She's been through a lot." Mad reached across Scarlet to rest his hand on Jade's stomach. "I've seen my share of women running from Two. Sometimes I think they have it worse than anyone. In the other sectors, it's easy to tell who the bad guys are."

"Gordon," Jade agreed softly. "She's grieving for him."

"For him?" Dylan asked. "Or for what he could have been if she'd met him somewhere else, under other circumstances?"

"I don't know. How do you even separate it when you've been—" She plucked the cigarette from Scarlet's hand, took a drag, and closed her eyes. "You don't know what they did to her because she was Lex's sister. I tried to help, just to be there so she knew someone cared about her, but after Cerys moved me to Orchid House, she was all alone. If Gordon was kind to her, even a little, how could she not love him?"

Scarlet sat up straighter. "Does it matter?" Dylan flashed her a sharp look, and she held up one hand. "It's not like she's still with him. He's gone, and she's free. So she's got time to figure it all out. And if what she figures out is that she really did love him, then that has to be okay. We don't get to take that away from her."

"I know," Jade said, her voice raw. She returned the cigarette and dropped her hand to cover Mad's. "I feel like a hypocrite. I get so angry when people assume I'm a victim...but maybe I'm just terrified. I was never in any danger of loving Gareth Woods."

"You mean well." Mad smiled and stroked her fingers. "So did I. But I was wrong, Jade. You're—"

"Jyoti."

Scarlet blinked. "What?"

"My name." Jade twisted out of their grip and rose to her knees, facing them. "I had this whole thing I was going to tell you... But I've never told anyone except Avery. I had to be Jade for so many years, and maybe that *is* who I am now. For the rest of the world, at least. But here, with you..." The frantic torrent of words fizzled out, and she stared at them, tense and uncertain. "Jyoti. My name is Jyoti."

Scarlet stared at her, shocked not by the revelation, but by the fact that she'd never considered it. Plenty of people in the sectors took new names—to hide, to escape their pasts, even to celebrate overcoming them—but it had never occurred to her that the woman in her bed might be one of them.

Dylan was the first to speak. He held his cigarette between two fingers and smoothed his thumb over his brow. "What does it mean?"

Jade wet her lips. "Light," she said finally. "My mother always told me I was her hope, so she named me after the lights in the temple she went to before the Flares. But when she took me back to the training house, she gave me a new name. Jade was supposed to be a—a persona. A game I played until I'd paid off my debt and could get out."

She looked so anxious that Scarlet wasn't surprised when Mad sat up and rubbed her shoulder encouragingly. "She gave you something to hold on to. Something they couldn't touch."

"Some*one* they couldn't touch," Jade agreed. "But then she died, and Cerys picked me to influence Woods..." She looked at Scarlet, eyes huge and pleading. "I should have told you. But I've been Jade for so long, I didn't think there was anything else left inside me. Not until you made it okay for me to want things for myself."

Something they couldn't touch. Something that Scarlet hadn't been able to touch, either. She took another, longer pull off her cigarette.

"I'm sorry." Jade's voice broke, and her eyes shone with tears she couldn't blink away. But when Mad tried to reach for her, she shrugged out of his arms, her gaze never leaving Scarlet's. "I'm sorry."

"It's not a thing, sweetheart." Scarlet kept her voice carefully even, and backed up the words with a smile. "I like your name. It's beautiful."

"Scarlet—" Jade took a shuddering breath and wiped her face. "Avery said something—that Dallas is always looking at her like she's about to break, and it makes her afraid to even bend. And I'm so bad at this. I don't know how to do any of this when it's not calculated. But if I bend..."

Scarlet's own pain at being shut out of this part of her life was nothing, less than nothing, compared to Jade's agony. So she passed the cigarette to Mad and opened her arms. "Come here."

Jade collapsed into her embrace, hiding her face against Scarlet's shoulder. "You touched her," she whispered hoarsely. "You didn't even know she was there, but you still touched her. Jyoti. *Me.*"

The pressure in Scarlet's chest twisted, and her

shame at her initial withdrawal only made it worse. "Shh, you don't have to explain. It's okay. I'm here." Dylan and Mad watched as she pressed her lips to Jade's temple. "We all are."

Mad gave Scarlet a helpless look before scrubbing his hands over his face. She kept one arm around Jade and lifted the other to him. He curled against her side and gently wrapped them both in a hug.

Dylan stayed where he was, reclined beside them, but there was no distance in the detachment. He was separate but not removed, as if all the contact he needed was in being there, staring at them as they wound together.

"The hardest part of all this, of *life*," he murmured finally, "is learning how to keep going. Even when you fuck up, even when you fail everyone around you. You have to let them forgive you, and you have to forgive yourself."

"Love." The word came, unbidden, to Scarlet's lips, but she didn't have time to be surprised by her declaration. She was too busy being overwhelmed by the truth of it. "That's what it means, right? That you love yourself enough to let someone else do it, too."

"Maybe that's why I'm so bad at it," Mad said, his voice light. "All that Sector One guilt gets heavy sometimes. I'm trying to put some of it down."

"You're not in One anymore," Dylan reminded him.

"That's right." Scarlet caught Mad's chin and urged him to meet her gaze. "We live in Four, and that's forever, isn't it?"

He twisted to kiss her fingers. "O'Kane for life."

That was the true meaning behind everything, the core of who they all were. They might have come from different places, sector or city, but they had all made the choice to leave. And they were here now, right where they wanted to be.

Almost. Scarlet nipped at Mad's ear, then turned to Jade. "I think you and I need a bigger bed."

Jade smiled against her shoulder. "Maybe I'll buy that

one from Gideon."

Mad scraped his fingernails lightly over Scarlet's hip. "You both know you're always welcome in mine."

"Mmm, that won't work in the long run. Unless you want us to move in."

His smile was slow and warm, and it melted something inside Scarlet—the last of her resistance, maybe. "I have plenty of room. And a nice shower. Might even be big enough for all of us."

When Mad smiled at you like that, denial wasn't an option. "That's a sweet offer."

"It's an open one." He kissed her temple before shifting his attention to Dylan. "It always will be."

Dylan returned his smile indulgently and shrugged. "I should probably take my ink before I move onto the compound."

Mad went still and tense. "You're taking ink?"

Scarlet could only think of one thing Dallas could have offered him that had the remotest chance of changing his mind. "The hospital."

"The hospital," Dylan agreed. "Dallas builds it and I run it, but I'm not naive enough to think this is an alliance. It's a first step. It's not a done deal—the ink—but I figure it's only a matter of time."

"A trained doctor is a valuable commodity." Jade shifted in Scarlet's arms and caressed Dylan's cheek. "Dallas will chase you forever. But you don't have to let him catch you."

He touched her hand. "I appreciate the concern, but I'm not afraid of Dallas. And it isn't about him, anyway. The truth is that by the time I've seen the O'Kanes through this—this *war*, then I'll already be one of you in all the ways that matter."

"You are *now*," Mad said, reaching out. "Get over here."

He came to them, sliding close to Jade's back. With the bed as small as it was, he didn't have to move far, but even closing that scant amount of distance was like laying in the last piece of a puzzle. Suddenly, there were no gaps, no spaces. Nothing left unfilled.

Mad rested his hand on Dylan's hip. In return, Dylan touched his arm, rubbing his thumb slowly over the lines of ink just below Mad's elbow. It was a quiet moment, as intimate as a kiss, and Scarlet drank it in—the heat, the tiny hints of movement, the soft murmur of voices blending together in contentment.

Then she closed her eyes and let it lull her to sleep.

18

T he second meeting of the leaders of the sector rebellion—which was what Mad had begun calling them in
his head, if not out loud—began as warily as the first.

They were back in Gideon's sun-filled meeting room,
ignoring the glasses of lemonade Maricela had delivered
with her own hands. The whole house was eerily quiet, as
if the servants had been encouraged to find someplace else
to be. Gideon was clearly taking no chances today, and for
good reason.

Trust was fragile. And the people around the table
slanted heavily toward allegiance with Dallas. More so
than last time, with Jade seated at Mad's left, a tablet lying beneath her folded hands.

They all had tablets. Even Dallas, whose hatred of
tech was the stuff of legend. The lists of resources compiled
on each screen ranged from criminal to treasonous, and
someone had to go first.

Jim Jernigan cleared his throat. "I control most of the large-scale goods manufacturing for the city. Shirts to shoe polish. Inconsequential, unless you plan on a war of attrition, a fight that takes so long they'll give themselves up for a few creature comforts."

"Not a bad idea," Dallas drawled. "Except for the part where they'll bomb us as soon as they realize we're holding back the latest fashion accessory they just have to have. Same problem I have with my hacker friend. Once he starts fucking with their systems, we better be ready to end shit. Fast."

"I can't help you with the bombs, O'Kane. But I can give you something—if you let me borrow your hacker." Jim turned his tablet around. On the display was a cluster of weapons schematics. "The Mark series, handguns to sniper rifles. My people designed them for the military police. Useless without biometric access."

Mad held out a hand for the tablet. "Can I take a look?"

He handed it over. "Be my guest."

Weapons schematics weren't Mad's specialty, but he'd learned enough from Bren to muddle through. He swiped through a few models before glancing at Dallas. "Noah shouldn't have a problem. At the very least, he can disable all the guns at once. With a little finesse—and a bunch of thumbprints—he might even be able to switch the biometric authorizations over to our people."

"Clever." Dallas eyed Jim. "Got back doors into anything else you've built for them?"

"That's the biggest score." Jim's face hardened. "The only purely military one."

He didn't seem pleased with the question. Not that Mad would have expected him to rejoice over the possibility of civilian casualties within Eden—probably. Some sector leaders might have taken glee in it, after all, oblivious to the reality that inequality existed on both sides of the wall.

Knowing Jim wasn't one of them made trusting him a bit easier.

Next to Mad, Jade cleared her throat softly. "I'm afraid what I have to offer isn't so easily targeted at the people in charge. But the leverage could be considerable." She swiped her fingers across her tablet and avoided Mad's gaze. "As of this morning, I own a controlling interest in fourteen of the twenty-three major farms and communes currently supplying Eden. The percentage amongst the minor and illegal farms is lower, but in all it's just short of sixty percent of their food supply."

The words fell into a silence so complete that the ice cracking in Mad's glass sounded like a shot.

Jade continued studiously not looking at him, which was for the best, really, since he was probably gaping at her like an idiot. He'd always idly wondered how much of Eden she actually owned.

He hadn't expected the answer to be *a sizeable fucking chunk.*

"Bullshit," Jim said. "There's no way the Council would let that happen."

"The Council never noticed." She offered Jim a slight, cool smile. "My man of business is resourceful. As far as the Council knows, ownership is spread across almost two dozen different men." She shrugged. "Access to Gareth Woods and his intimate circle gave me certain insights into when and how to focus my investments to avoid suspicion. And maximize their potential."

Dallas shifted forward in his chair and rested his elbows on the table. "Jade and Lex and I had a few heated debates about what to do with this opportunity. Because I think we all know trying to starve them out would hurt the people who are already hurting way before it hurt the people in charge. But there are some alternatives."

Ryder lifted one eyebrow. "Such as?"

Lex inclined her head. "We've been running liquor and beer in and out of Eden for years. Granted, partly because they've let us—but we've still managed to set up some supply routes under the radar. We think we can keep enough food going in. And, more importantly, make sure it gets to the right people."

Gideon finally spoke. "And they'll know exactly who it's coming from."

Ryder leaned back, as if distancing himself from the rest of them. "I can withhold drugs and med-gel. I don't like it, though, for the same reasons you don't want to starve them, and Jim doesn't want to blow up their power centers."

"Because you all have boundaries." Gideon tapped the table. "That's good. That means if we pull this off, maybe we won't be in their shoes a year from now, facing down a revolution of our own."

"*If* we pull this off," Dallas agreed. "Because Eden's not gonna have any reservations about starving, poisoning, or just straight-up bombing the shit out of *our* civilian population."

Lex rubbed at the tense spot between his shoulders. "The upside is that we expect that kind of shit from them. We've been getting it for years. So we're prepared."

"As for the bombs…" Gideon took a deep breath before meeting Dallas's eyes. "Jim and Ryder may be in personal danger, but Eden can't risk their facilities. And the Council has nothing to gain and everything to lose by endangering their closest food supplies in Six and Seven. If they come back with bombs, it will be your people or mine dying. Maybe your people *and* mine."

Dallas didn't need to be told. The darkness in his eyes was beyond anything Mad had ever seen in him before, even in the early days, when death waited for them around every corner. Even in the war for Sector Four, when he'd watched his friends and people die around him and for him.

It wasn't just the weight of the O'Kanes on his shoulders now. It was every life in his sector. Every crafter, every cook, every fighter and dancer and petty thief. Eden would come for Dallas, and the closer you stood to him, the greater your chance of dying a hard, ugly death when that day came.

It would have been easier on him if every last fucking one of the people he loved had run for the hills.

"I know," was all he said, his voice firm and flat. "I have men organizing evacuation and rescue routes, but there's only so much we can do without tipping our hand. The strike in Two gives us an excuse to take some precautions, but..."

It wasn't enough. Nothing could be enough.

"Speaking of Two." Jim slid his tablet away from him. "What are we going to do about it?"

"You said Cerys was gone before the bombs fell," Gideon said. "Judging by the reports from my men, she might not have been the only one. The big river estates outside the blast zone were empty. Offices cleaned out, clothes packed..."

"Eden probably preserved the resources they couldn't replace." Jade's expression was bleak. "The men with the most valuable trading connections. Everyone else was expendable."

"To Eden," Gideon told her softly. "Not to us. We'll find a way to take care of the survivors."

Mad was finally starting to understand Jade, to recognize the subtle shifts in her body language and know what was coming. Which was why his gut twisted when her back straightened and her brow furrowed.

"We can fold them into One and Three," Lex suggested. "Anyone who wants to go. Then, when this is all over, we'll rebuild."

Jim snorted. "You want them to leave a place that was just bombed and go somewhere else that'll probably get bombed?"

Jade's fingers curled toward her palms. Her knuckles

stood out stark and white, and Mad scrambled for a solution, for some way to divert the weight that was so familiar he could feel its ache in his own shoulders.

But there was no simple answer.

Gideon was already agreeing with Jim. "Two is probably the safest place in the sectors right now. And we might as well use those abandoned estates."

"A bunch of traumatized refugees in the biggest looting free-for-all the sectors have ever offered up?" Dallas shook his head. "I know you're a dreamer, Gideon, but that's asking for another disaster."

"It isn't," Gideon insisted. "We can organize guards."

"And pay them with what? Promises? War's expensive, Gideon."

"With money," Jade said, her voice so calm and clear that it broke Mad's heart. "*My* money. The rest of you should stay focused on Eden. I have time to do this. Let me take care of Sector Two. No one knows it better than I do."

It was true. And it would hurt her. Mad met Lex's eyes and begged silently for her to do something. She stared back, her eyes haunted by shadows that deepened with each passing second.

She finally looked away. "Money, Jade. You kick in with that, and we'll handle—"

"Let me do this, Lex." Jade slid her hand to cover Mad's and squeezed it, begging the same thing of him with just a touch. "Cerys kept me in her pocket for all those years. She wanted you to follow her, but she settled for me. I know the people. I know what they need. And I need to do this."

The fierceness of her grip told Mad the truth. She needed this, the same way he'd needed to take them to the shrine where his mother had died. She needed to rip open the scars and hope they'd heal cleaner this time. And even if they didn't, she had to know she'd tried.

His challenge was to let her. To help her.

Lex leaned back and raised both hands in surrender. "I'm not stopping you. I'm just offering alternatives."

"So that would make Jade the new leader of Two, for better or worse." Dallas inclined his head toward her. "Congratulations. And my condolences."

Jade returned his wry smile. "Thank you. I think."

"Don't worry. The gratitude will pass." Dallas sighed. "Most of my men are tied up in Three. Gideon, can you lend us one of your Riders to help Jade manage security?"

"Deacon," Mad said quickly. "He knows Two, and he may still have contacts there." And Deacon would keep Jade safe when Mad couldn't be there—especially once he realized how very much Mad valued her safety.

There were advantages to being a prince, after all.

"I can spare Deacon," Gideon said. "And perhaps a few more workers to help make more of Two livable."

At this, Jim rose, and it was obvious the meeting was over. He buttoned his suit jacket and looked around the table. "Get your shit in order, ladies and gentlemen." He spoke with the air of a general calling his troops to war. "It's been long in coming, but time's running short now. May Gideon's God have mercy on us all."

Especially Mad. Because Scarlet and Dylan weren't going to be happy with him. "Amen."

cruz

T HE WALL IN front of Cruz was seamless cement with a metal sign mounted at waist height. Block letters spelled out EAST QUADRANT with an arrow pointing left, and SECTOR FOUR with an arrow pointing right.

That was it. A cement wall. A metal sign. But the schematic on his tablet—a schematic provided by Noah—indicated a wide tunnel behind that sign. A tunnel that provided a straight shot to Eden.

Cruz handed the tablet to Bren and flicked open his knife. "Let's hope Noah's grandfather wasn't crazy."

"Oh, he was definitely crazy," Bren muttered. "But he was also meticulous with his records."

True enough—thus far. But the revelation that a wall Cruz had walked by a hundred times over the years wasn't a wall at all, but a door—

Cruz worked his knife under the edge of the sign, and the odd placement of it was what made him believe. There were signs in the underground tunnels connecting the sectors to Eden, but most were at major intersections between sectors, not plastered on to walls. He'd always chalked this sign up to the fact that the tunnels hadn't been fully completed before the Flares.

As the edge came up, its true purpose was revealed. The sign hid a tangle of wires and what was left of an access control panel.

Gritting his teeth, Cruz hauled the sign from the wall. The edges cut into his fingers, and the screech of metal was recklessly loud, but tearing something apart with his bare hands was tremendously satisfying.

Bren edged between him and the control panel. "Let me." He reached for the wires and began to separate and twist them together so expertly that Noah must have been giving him lessons on hot-wiring. After a moment, he glanced up at Cruz. "How's Rachel doing?"

Rachel was healthy. Rachel was strong. Rachel was just fine, she assured him, even though she was throwing up half of what she ate and starving when she wasn't throwing up.

And the last time Cruz had expressed rational, *reasonable* concern about this, Rachel had rolled her eyes and finished dressing for her bartending shift at the Broken Circle. "Oh, she's *fine*," Cruz grumbled. "I didn't know a person could puke that much and still be okay, but what do I know?"

Bren made a noise that sounded like a stifled laugh. "It'll subside after the first trimester. At least, that's what Six tells me."

Yes, Six had said the same thing to Ace, who had tried to use that information to reassure Cruz. Cruz didn't know how to tell his lover he was long past being reassured. Rachel was suffering from discomfort that Cruz couldn't stop. She and Ace were both under the threat of danger that Cruz couldn't thwart.

Helplessness was unacceptable, but it was his current, frustrating reality.

At least he and Bren were finally doing something. When Bren twisted the last few wires together, mechanics rumbled behind the door. The surface of the wall chipped in a vertical line from floor to ceiling, followed by crumbling mortar as the painted-over doors slid smoothly apart to reveal a long, straight tunnel.

Bren let out a whistle. "Direction's right. This tunnel might actually run right under the city."

"And it's big, too." Maybe big enough for vehicles, and wouldn't that be a fucking coup? They could truck in supplies to foster rebellion right under Eden's nose—and bring out people who wanted to switch sides. "This could work."

"Yes, it could."

Not Bren's voice, and Cruz had his gun in his hand before the familiarity of the voice pierced through blind instinct. He still couldn't check his turn, but he ended up with the pistol pointed down and to the right of Ashwin's Base-issued military boots. "Ashwin."

"Cruz." Ashwin ignored the gun—and ignored Bren, too. "I need a favor."

The blood pounding through Cruz's veins turned to ice. These were the words he'd been braced for every time Ashwin appeared. The four little words that meant something else entirely, because they weren't a request. They were a reminder.

You owe me one.

When Ace had lain dying, Cruz would have bartered anything to see him safe. His life, his heart, his *soul*. Instead, he'd bartered this. A favor. And Ashwin would expect him to pay.

"All right." Moving slowly, precisely, Cruz holstered his gun. "Can Bren stay for this?"

Bren didn't move, but his shoulders tensed, and he almost smiled. "Bren most certainly will stay for this."

Ashwin's gaze finally flickered to Bren. Just for a moment, but Cruz imagined Ashwin mentally reviewing Bren's entire dossier. "There are some risks associated with knowing. If he's willing to accept those risks..."

"He is," Bren answered stoically.

Ashwin pulled a miniature tablet from his back pocket and handed it to Cruz. It was the kind of tech gadget he hadn't seen since leaving the base—Eden preferred delicate tablets with wide, vivid screens. This one was sturdy enough to survive being knocked around and small enough to fit in the palm of his hand.

He activated the display. Instead of a collection of mission and data folders, there were only two things on the home screen—a custom application and a photo.

Cruz selected the photo. The face that filled the screen was pretty, blonde—and familiar. He'd last seen Kora Bellamy lying in the trunk of a car, blindfolded and trembling because Ashwin had kidnapped her from her cozy Eden life and brought her to the sectors to put a man back together.

To put *Ace* back together.

"She's in Sector One," Ashwin said quietly. "She slipped past her handlers and made it to the hospital there. She's been treating patients for the past week."

"And?"

"I need you to find her. Take her somewhere safe."

Cruz waited for the rest of the favor, but it didn't come. Ashwin simply watched him with a steely blankness that scared the shit out of him, because this was nothing. Extracting a woman from an allied sector and stashing her in a safe house? There was no risk, no danger, no reason Ashwin couldn't have done it himself already.

Chilled, he stared back. "What else, Ashwin?"

"Hide her. Don't tell me where she is."

He tacked it on like it was nothing, an afterthought. But the chill in Cruz's blood spread to the rest of his body as he forced himself to nod. "And if you come back, asking?"

Some Makhai soldiers were good at mimicking emotions. Ashwin wasn't, and he knew it, so Cruz had rarely seen him bother. But he smiled now, with a terrible, false emptiness. "Not telling me is the favor."

"Understood." Cruz barely managed to keep his voice steady.

Ashwin nodded, pivoted, and headed back into the darkness, vanishing around a corner before Cruz had regathered his wits. He still waited, shaking his head, when Bren opened his mouth, silently counting off the steps that would take Ashwin far beyond earshot.

Then he let out his breath in a rush. "Fucking hell."

Bren shuddered. "That guy is terrifying."

Coming from Bren, it was the next step up from pissing himself. "You have no idea."

But because Cruz did have an idea, he closed the photo on the tablet and let his thumb hover over the application. Just a simple blue box labeled ACTIVITY, seemingly harmless.

When he touched it, Kora Bellamy's life spread out before him in precise, methodical detail. Video, audio, surveillance, and schedules. Every person she saw, every patient she treated, every place she shopped...

Bren peered down at the tablet. "Holy fucking Christ."

Cruz paged through the information, each report more damning than the last. "When I was twelve, one of the earliest generation of Makhai soldiers became...fixated on his domestic handler. She'd fallen in love with him, which compromised her judgment as far as the Base was concerned. They tried to remove her, but she didn't want to leave him. So they went after her, and he—"

Words barely existed for the swift escalation of violence. The first man to touch the woman had lost his arm. The next two had their necks snapped before they could get near her. In the end, the Base had to threaten to blow up the entire apartment before the Makhai soldier would surrender.

The handler vanished. And the soldier... "Have you ever seen a man tear himself apart?"

"*Please* tell me you're speaking metaphorically."

He couldn't, so Cruz ignored the question, shut down the tablet, and shoved it into his pocket. "Ashwin can't be too far gone if he has the self-control to make this request. So we'll hide her."

"Uh-huh." Bren raised one eyebrow. "Hiding her isn't the favor, remember?"

Which was why Cruz wouldn't be telling anyone where he stashed Dr. Kora Bellamy. When Ashwin came looking for her—and Ashwin *would* come looking for her—Cruz needed to be the only person standing in his way.

19

THE STREETS IN Two closest to the brothel district made sense to Scarlet. They were—or, at least, had been—laid out in the same grid pattern one could find in Sector Three. Streets ran in one direction, avenues in the other, and blocks were a uniform size that you could use to judge distance as well as addresses.

Out toward the far edge of Two, all that changed. The roads began to meander, weaving in and around fences and wooded areas until Scarlet had to check the sun to orient herself. Finally, she realized that the small forests surrounded by high brick walls were *estates*, but before she had time to do anything but stare, Mad pulled through an open gate and down a long, wide drive.

He stopped the truck in front of a house every bit as majestic as Gideon's home in One. It was fucking *palatial*, with large, ornate columns and a goddamn fountain decorating the circular drive.

And it was Jade's.

Mad didn't seem to notice. He hopped out of the truck and circled to open her door before she could reach for the handle. "I visited Avery's patron's house with Lex once, and I thought that was swank. Guess he was small fucking potatoes."

"I guess." It was a long way from her childhood in the tenements. "I wouldn't know. We had three rooms when I was growing up. My dad let me take the bedroom so I'd feel like I had a space of my own. He slept on the couch."

"I'm sorry, Scarlet."

"For me? Don't be." If anything, she felt sorry for her father—working double shifts at the factory before coming home to try and rest on a lumpy sofa that sagged in the middle. But kids never saw their parents' sacrifices clearly, and she was no exception. "I had it pretty damn good."

Mad slid an arm around her waist and turned her toward the wide glass doors. "Me too, in the beginning. And recently, too, for that matter."

The familiar heat washed over her where they touched, tempered a little this time by her nerves. Jade was already inside this huge, ridiculous house, getting things in order as the new head of Sector Two. "You really think this is a good idea, Adrian?"

"Jade taking over, you mean?" His arm tensed, and he pulled her closer as they mounted the steps. "I don't know. But I don't think telling her she shouldn't is a better idea."

"I just—" She hauled him to a stop in front of the door and faced him, struggling to put the cold knot in her gut into words. "We all have places we can't go again—because they hurt us so much, or we don't like who we were in them. I can't think of a better example of that for Jade than this whole fucking sector, you know?"

"And I thought I couldn't go back to the place where my mother died. I couldn't, Scarlet. It hurt so much." He framed her face with his hands and smiled slowly. "Until

I went there with the three of you. Sometimes you need to go back, but I didn't have to go back alone. And neither does Jade."

He made things sound so easy. "Okay." She gripped his wrists and held his hands to her cheeks. "We can help her."

"Because we don't have to help her alone, either." He leaned in and brushed his lips over hers once, then again. On the third gentle touch, he tilted his head, opened his mouth, and kissed her—deep and hard, until the shocks from each rasp of his tongue over hers began to crash into the next.

The sound of someone clearing her throat broke through the haze of pleasure, and Scarlet jerked away to find an older woman in a neat black dress standing in the open doorway. "You must be Lady Jade's guests. She's expecting you."

"Thank you," Mad said easily, looping his arm through Scarlet's again. And he walked right inside, as if some random woman answering Jade's door and calling her *Lady* wasn't just normal, but the proper way of things.

Scarlet didn't think she'd ever get used to it.

"You're here." Dylan's voice rang out from the second-floor landing above them. An ornate double staircase flowed down from the landing to the open foyer, and Dylan hurried down one side of it. He looked as comfortable surrounded by all this opulence as Mad was, leaving Scarlet the odd one out.

"My last job ran long." Mad didn't release Scarlet's hand as he threw his other arm around Dylan in a rough hug. "How's Jade doing?"

"Hanging in there. Hi, sweetheart." Dylan bent and kissed Scarlet quickly.

When she licked her lips, she could taste him and Mad both, and a shiver ran up her spine. "Where is she?"

"Upstairs. Make a left at the end of the hall, third door on the right."

Scarlet left them in the foyer, muttering to one another in voices too low for her to understand as she
climbed the marble stairs. The upstairs hall was lined
with giant, gilt-framed portraits of stern men and women,
and Scarlet kept her gaze straight ahead, focused on the
light streaming through the huge window at the end of it.

The room Dylan had sent her to was dark, with a massive fireplace and a polished wooden desk that made
everything Dallas O'Kane owned look like he'd dragged it
home from an alley dump. The walls were lined with
shelves, floor to ceiling, and every shelf was filled with
books. Jade stood in the middle of it all, sorting papers into
three stacks on the desk.

She glanced up at Scarlet's entrance. "Maybe Dallas
has a point about tech. It doesn't work as well when your
infrastructure's been destroyed."

"No shit." Scarlet rounded the desk and pulled Jade's
hands into hers. "Hi."

"Hi." There were shadows under Jade's eyes and a
weariness in her grip, but excitement shone in her smile.
"Thank you for coming to help."

"You're welcome." A lock of hair had fallen over her
forehead. Scarlet brushed it back and let her fingers linger
on Jade's temple. "What can I do?"

"Make me take a break." She turned her cheek to
Scarlet's palm and closed her eyes. "There's so much to set
right. But if I can arrange for food and shelter for those
who need it, at least in the short term—"

"Come on." Scarlet began to back up, around the desk
and toward the door, pulling Jade with her. "We'll grab the
boys and have dinner. If there's someone here whose job is
to open the door, surely there's someone who cooks."

"Actually, there's a kitchen staff. A head cook, a junior
cook, and three assistants." Jade laughed. "I don't need
them all, but I can hardly fire them. I was thinking of having them take on more assistants, then they can feed the
people who are helping rebuild. It would let some of the

girls learn a trade."

It would be an utterly foreign concept to the girls who'd grown up in the brothel district, but everyone who hadn't been sold or pressed into prostitution was probably already well-acquainted with the rigors of domestic service. "That sounds like a good idea."

"I have lots of ideas." Jade twined their fingers together and led Scarlet back down the hallway. "There's another manor almost this big on the other side of the river. I want to set up a nursing school in it."

"Jesus, you don't fuck around."

"I don't have time to fuck around. We can clear out the tunnels and build a hospital and fill it with supplies, but that won't do any good if we don't have nurses and doctors who know what they're doing."

"Hey." Scarlet tugged on her hand to slow her down a little. "Pace yourself, okay? All that stuff can't happen overnight."

"I know, I just..." Jade paused at the base of the stairs and turned to look up at Scarlet. "I need to do something big, something they can see. I need to show the girls that there are more types of lives they can live than the one they were trained for."

Mad stepped up behind Jade and kissed her temple. "You're showing them that already. So will Avery and Lex and Mia."

Jade leaned into him without looking away from Scarlet. "In other words, Scarlet is right."

"She usually is," Mad murmured. "It's a good thing she's so cute, or she'd be unbearable."

Dylan was trying to hide a smile behind his hand, so Scarlet flashed him a wink before turning to Mad. "Funny, that's not what you were saying last night."

"That's not what I'll be saying tonight, either, if things go well." He waggled his eyebrows in a suggestive invitation so overdone he had to have stolen it from Ace. "Are things going to go well?"

The sleeve of his black T-shirt had bunched up and gotten trapped under the supple leather of his shoulder holster. Scarlet freed it and smoothed it down, smiling when the muscles in his arm flexed beneath her hand. "One thing at a time, Adrian. Dinner."

"It should almost be ready." Jade slipped past Mad to kiss Dylan on the cheek before tilting her head. "This way. We might as well try the formal dining room once before we decide whether to turn it into something more practical."

Calling the dining room *formal* was a fucking understatement, like calling Jade *kinda smart* or Mad *a little intense*. The cavernous ceiling was crisscrossed with beams that had been plastered and decorated with shit like cherubs and scrollwork, and huge windows let in the last of the fading sunlight.

It gleamed off the long table, which could have easily accommodated two dozen people, and Scarlet was the only one who looked awkward sliding into an ornate chair at one end of it. Her discomfort left her trying to fill the silence, and she blurted out the first thing that came to mind. "What kind of a person really lives in a place like this?"

Jade opened her mouth, then shut it again when a door at the other end of the room opened. Half a dozen people weighed down with silver trays streamed in, led by an older woman with a scarf tied over her hair and a basket cradled between her hands.

The older woman came straight to Jade and placed the basket in front of her. The dinner rolls inside were piled precariously, golden brown and so fresh from the oven they made the whole room smell like baking bread.

"My sweet yeast rolls, just the way you always liked them," the woman told her, and Scarlet swore there were tears in her eyes. "You look so much like her, Miss Jyoti. So much like Lady Radha—"

"Thank you," Jade said swiftly, squeezing the

woman's hands. "It means a great deal to me to know she's remembered fondly."

"You both are."

"Thank you, Molly."

The woman dropped an honest-to-fucking-God curtsy and turned to herd her staff out of the room, leaving Jade staring at the basket of bread.

"My mother's patron," she said, "was the sort of person who lived in a place like this."

Not just her mother's patron, but *her father*. The words reverberated in Scarlet's head, throbbing like a heavy bass line. "You lived here?"

"Not for long. I was seven when we left, remember?" Jade picked up one of the rolls, which steamed when she broke it in half. "On nights when my mother had to help my father entertain guests, Molly would let me sit in the kitchen with her while she planned menus. I think I remember her better than I remember my father."

She said it so calmly, like she was just telling a story about something that happened to someone she once knew. Like she wasn't describing the awful twists and traumatic turns of her own life. "The sector leaders sent you *here* to set up shop?"

Dylan reached for her hand. "Scarlet—"

She shrugged him off. "No, what the hell? Mad and I passed a dozen places just like this on the way. How could they do this? Didn't they know?"

"I don't think they did." Jade tore the bread into smaller and smaller pieces. "I chose it."

"You—" Words failed her, and Scarlet stared at the demolished roll on Jade's plate. "You what?"

"I know it might seem morbid." Jade finally met her gaze. "But I like to think of him sitting somewhere in Eden, right now, knowing that *I'm* sitting at his desk here, undoing everything he ever did. And this house..."

"Should have been yours," Mad finished gently.

Jade's hands curled into fists. "No, not mine. Hers. My

mother's."

So she'd come here for what—revenge? To reclaim part of her past? Scarlet had never begrudged anyone the chance to face down their demons—Christ knew she'd spent enough hours staring at the remains of the factory where her father had perished. But staring into that abyss was hard enough on its own. If you did it when you were already on unsure footing, you could fall. "Be careful, Jade. Please."

"I will," Jade replied softly, reaching for Scarlet's hand. "I can do this, because I'm not alone."

Her fingers were warm, and they trembled the tiniest bit. Scarlet folded hers around them, steadying them. "Promise me."

"I promise."

"Okay."

It wasn't okay, and Jade knew it. Resignation slumped her shoulders and dulled her gaze before she hid it under a too-bright smile. "At least we can all agree that the interior decorations have to go. I could probably fund *three* nursing schools just by selling off the artwork."

"Only if you can find buyers in Eden." Mad's smile was off, too. Determined. "I don't think there's anyone left in the sectors with enough bad taste to buy any of it."

Dylan didn't join them. He stared at Scarlet, his dark eyes full of unbearable sympathy. She looked away instead, and focused her attention on scooping butter out of the tiny silver dish by her water goblet and applying it to a roll.

Polite denial wasn't a skill they taught in Three. It didn't belong in the grungy bars and community halls, and no one practiced it on the front stoops of tenements. If you couldn't say something honest and useful, then you kept your mouth shut.

Pretty manners were for places like this, places with three different glasses, half a dozen kinds of forks, and an individual butter dish for everyone. They were a luxury, just like the feather beds and extra bathrooms. They belonged to people with the time and energy to worry about nothing, to people who didn't have to wonder how they were going to feed their kids.

So Scarlet kept her mouth shut.

20

D OUBT WIGGLED INTO Jade's heart before dawn and lodged itself deep, like a painful splinter.

It wasn't anything obvious. Maybe they'd been too tired for sex last night, but they'd still returned from Sector Two to Mad's bed. They'd fallen between the sheets and into sleep, bodies twisted together...

But still far apart, somehow.

It was Jade's fault. Seizing Sector Two had made so much sense in the moment. She'd been wholly focused on the initiates from the houses, but there were hundreds—*thousands*—of men and women who had supported, and in turn been supported by, the elaborate upper class. People just like Molly, people whose employers had calmly packed their things and abandoned everyone depending on them to die in the bombs or starve in the aftermath.

And the girls. It was only a matter of time before some

ruthless entrepreneur seized the chance to sell the delicate Roses and Orchids and Irises of the training houses to men who resented never having had a chance to possess them. Shutting that down was reason enough to move hard and fast.

But Scarlet was worried, and so was Dylan. If it had just been Mad, who had always underestimated her strength, Jade could have weathered the doubt. But Scarlet had been the one to help her believe she had any strength left to begin with.

The uncertainty drove Jade from the bed while the others still slept. It drove her to her rooms, where she bathed and dressed, and to the quarters Dallas had given Deacon. She was starting to suspect *head of security* meant *personal bodyguard*, but it was hard not to feel secure with Deacon's silent presence towering behind her.

Mad might be irritated she hadn't woken him to accompany her, but today she needed Deacon's watchful silence. Besides, Deacon knew where they were going.

Jade had only visited the houses she'd built in One twice—once to approve of the first construction, and a second time to arrange payment for expansion. They'd been stark then, surrounded by bare earth and filled with quiet, sad girls struggling to comprehend their reversal in fortune.

They'd changed. Jade's heart leapt into her throat and settled there as a lump when Deacon pulled down the drive. The outside walls had been painted in bright blues and golds. Someone had planted fruit trees along the walkway and built a fence around a huge garden, with freshly turned earth and a sea of green seedlings peeking hopefully up from the dirt.

Best of all were the children. A playground sat between two of the buildings, full of screaming, gleeful toddlers racing around on stumpy little legs. Scarlet might think Jade's father's treatment of her had been harsh, but her mother had always been the exception—a woman allowed to keep her baby and raise the child as her own.

The usual reality of an accidental pregnancy was having a patron turn you out on the street—or summon a doctor to take care of the matter, whether you wished it or not. Women who wanted a choice had to find a way out of Two, and faced a hard, hopeless life once they had.

I did this.

This was what she needed to see. The sharp pain in her heart eased even further when Avery ran around the side of the house, hunched over and chasing a group of tiny, screaming kids.

No, not screaming. Laughing, and Jade had to cover her face for a moment and will herself not to cry with the sheer, giddy relief of it.

I did this. I can do so much more.

She wiped her eyes and checked her makeup in the mirror. "You can go inside and get breakfast, if you want."

"I've eaten."

It might have been a lie or the truth, but his implacable expression held the real answer. Deacon would go inside when she went inside, and not before. Considering how much she'd worried her lovers, accepting the presence of a bodyguard with good grace seemed the least of her obligations.

Jade slipped from the car and crossed the grass to Avery. "You look like you're outnumbered. Do you need reinforcements?"

She was out of breath, more from laughing than running, Jade suspected. "I'm fine, I'm fine. It's..." Her laughter died, and Avery shoved her hands into the pockets of her flowing slacks. "It's good to see them here instead of back in Two."

"It is," Jade agreed, watching two girls of only nine or ten years pump their legs, racing to see who could swing higher. Unlike the toddlers, they weren't born to refugees from Two. They *were* refugees, probably two or three years into their training. Still young enough to smile and laugh and run and rediscover what it meant to be a child.

"Miss Rios is inside."

It took Jade a moment to make the connection. "You mean Maricela? Or Isabela?"

"Maricela, of course. She's come to give you a tour of the houses." Avery tilted her head. "And, I suspect, just to see you. She seems awfully curious about you, though it's not surprising, seeing as how her favorite cousin is in love with you."

The word was enough to send heat rushing to Jade's cheeks. *Love.* They'd been saying it all along, because it was an easy word for O'Kanes. Mad loved everyone who came into the circle of his regard, with a heart so big and fearless he never seemed diminished. Scarlet was the same, even if her circle was smaller, her heart fiercer.

But loving wasn't the same as being *in love.* There were nuanced differences, shades of emotion that blurred when you lived as hard and open as the O'Kanes. She and Scarlet and Mad and Dylan trusted each other. They wanted each other. They *needed* each other.

When did love become *in love*? Jade's training certainly hadn't covered that.

Avery's eyes widened, and she rocked back on her heels as the corners of her mouth curved up in an almost-smile. "Sorry. Was that a secret?"

Jade laughed and bumped her shoulder against hers, even as her cheeks grew hotter. "Don't try innocent with me. You're incorrigible. You've always been incorrigible."

"Me? Never."

"Hush." Jade brushed a kiss to Avery's cheek. "Let me deal with my duties, and you can tease me until I can't blush any harder."

She left Avery with her charges and followed the path to the front door. Even though she'd paid for every brick and shingle and stick of furniture, it felt almost intrusive to slip inside. "Hello?"

Maricela popped her head around the end of the hall, followed by three women dressed in white robes fluttering around her. She waved them off and held out her hands. "Jade! It's lovely to see you again. Please, come in."

"Maricela." It wasn't hard to see why Mad adored his youngest cousin. She shone as brightly as he did, but with none of his pain lurking in her huge brown eyes. Jade clasped the younger woman's hands before embracing her. "It's good to see you, too."

"Did you come alone?"

"This time, yes." And she regretted it now. It was so easy to imagine Dylan surrounded again with babbling, happy children, or Mad bouncing a squealing toddler in his arms. And Scarlet would have understood how dear Avery's laughter was, how great a triumph.

Maybe this was the line between love and in love. When everything that gave you joy felt like a dream until you shared it with the people who made that joy possible. Who made it real.

I did this, but I don't have to do it alone anymore.

Maricela didn't notice. "Before we begin, there's some-one who wants to speak with you. She stayed in this morning just to see you."

"Of course."

Jade followed Maricela to a cozy sitting room. The furniture clustered around the fireplace was mismatched but plush and comfortable, and shelves full of books and games lined two walls.

The girl perched on one chair was familiar. Astrid had to be twelve by now, maybe even thirteen. Her long black hair shone as if she'd just finished brushing it her one hundred strokes, and her hands rested in her lap, her fingers laced together. So still and proper, and Jade wanted fervently to see her running with the other girls, her clothes and hair askew.

Instead, she inclined her head in perfect Rose House fashion. "Lady Jade."

"Astrid." Jade sat next to the girl. "Please. Just call me Jade."

"All right." But she didn't, just adjusted her skirt nervously. "I heard that you're—well, that you're in charge of Sector Two now."

"I'm taking care of the people who lived there. Which includes you, Astrid." Jade covered the girl's hands with her own. "If there's something troubling you..."

She tensed but didn't pull away. "It's just..." She trailed off, then finished in a rush. "No one's told us anything, you know? About how long we'll be here, and when we can go home and get back to our training. And I thought—since you're there now—"

Panic sent the blood pounding through Jade's veins, a panic she couldn't even explain. But a lifetime of practice kept her expression smooth, her voice soft. "Nobody's going back to training, sweetheart."

Astrid blinked, and her dark brows drew over her eyes. "I don't understand."

How could she? Astrid had come to them at six, offered up by a desperate mother she probably barely remembered. The trainers had been her parents, the fellow initiates her sisters. She'd lost the only home she'd ever known.

Of course she wanted it back.

Understanding didn't ease the queasy churn in Jade's stomach. "Things have changed in Two. You will go back to some sort of training, but only after you decide what you want to do with your life."

Astrid's look of confused frustration grew. "But... *why?* I'm almost ready to find a patron."

So young. Too young—and not wrong. If Eden had spared Two, Astrid would have been entering her final years of training. She'd be serving at dinners and parties, performing in dances and entertainments. She'd be put on display until some man decided he wanted to own her.

And for every Gordon who clumsily made truffles to

win a smile, there were dozens of Gareths, who wanted only to indulge their whims and sate their lust, oblivious to the spirits they were shattering.

Astrid didn't know any of it. She only knew the dream of beautiful dresses and important dinner parties and earning enough to retire in wealth and comfort. "The patrons are gone. But you're clever and educated, Astrid. There are crafts and trades—"

"What about the parlor girls?" Astrid asked flatly. "That's what happens if you don't find a patron, right? Men will pay for a night. They'll pay more than you can make throwing pots or spinning yarn."

Jade swallowed bile and forced herself to separate. Somewhere, her stomach still roiled, and her heart beat too fast—but a body was simply part of who she was. She had been trained to ignore it and she did so now, keeping her voice gentle and level. "You don't need to worry about making money yet. You're young, and a lot can change, even in a year, Astrid."

Her tiny, thin shoulders squared. "I'm not a child."

"I know." Jade cupped Astrid's cheek and braced herself for the words she had to say. "I'll strike a bargain with you. You live here until you're sixteen. You think about all the things you might want to do. And if you still want to finish your training, I'll help you find somewhere safe, where you'll make good money."

Astrid eyed her with suspicion. "Three more years?"

"Three more years," Jade agreed. "The kind of man you should be letting into your bed won't touch you before then, in any case."

"I'll be behind on my training."

"You were a Rose, Astrid." It hurt to smile, but Jade managed. "You'll be ahead of everyone else they've ever met. You have my promise."

"Okay." She held out her hand. "I agree."

Jade shook the girl's hand and tried to tell herself this promise would never amount to anything. If they survived this war, Astrid would learn how many opportunities the world held. She'd receive her first smile from a handsome farm boy and develop her first crush and come to know that selling her body was a choice she didn't have to make.

She might still make it. And Jade could live with that, but only if she knew it was a choice.

But when Astrid thanked her and slipped from the sitting room, Jade lost her grip on her false calm. The physical sensations from her body roared back, so much worse for being neglected. And the panic—oh, she knew the source of the panic. The dull, hollow thud of her heart as she sat in Dylan's lap and begged him to tell her it didn't matter, that she could *know*.

How many years did it take before you could trust your choices were your own? Even with a mother whispering to her of a wider world, was Jade so different than Astrid? Want and need, training and desire... They were hopelessly tangled together, a snarl made worse by the pressures of survival.

Astrid would have those three years. But other girls wouldn't. They would come to Jade, girls who were old enough to sell their bodies, who wanted the money or the security or the independence of it *now*.

And Jade would have to help them. What was the alternative? To send them into the sectors, into a brewing *war*, to make their way on their own? Let them fall under the influence of whatever entrepreneurial asshole saw opportunity in selling well-trained, sheltered young women?

Forbid them, as if there was shame in exchanging your skills for money? As if Jade's success in doing so hadn't built the house she was sitting in and provided the food they ate and the beds they slept in?

And yet. There might not be shame, but that didn't mean Jade wanted to be the one who vetted their clients and arranged their assignations. The uncertainty would always be there for her, even if from the outside *choice* was as simple as Dylan made it sound. Jade could never view

Sector Two from the outside.

You don't have to do it alone.

It was the only thought that could cut through her panic. So she repeated it to herself as her heart rate slowed, steadied. She rubbed her thumb over her O'Kane ink and knew, with absolute certainty, that Scarlet and Dylan and Mad weren't the only ones who'd have her back.

Sector leaders ruled alone because that was how it had always been done. But she was an O'Kane. Two would never be independent in the way it once had been, because Jade had made her vows to Dallas and Lex, and she intended to keep them. But those promises went both ways.

A soft knock sounded on the door. "Jade?"

Jade smoothed her expression and rose as Maricela opened the door. That painful splinter was still there, a sharp sting in her chest, but she'd have time to deal with it later. She had to tour the houses, and then spend a grueling morning and afternoon in Two.

Jade swore she could *feel* Eden pressing down on them all. Everyone was working faster, harder, longer. As if they could stock enough supplies, prepare enough hospitals, make any sort of plan to counteract the raw truth of rebellion.

When Eden found out, the bombs would fall again.

But they had to try. So Jade fixed her smile in place and let Mad's sweet, earnest cousin lead her through the houses. She took each success, each victory, each smiling face into her heart to combat the pain. She needed to go back to Four smiling and whole, because she knew how Avery felt.

Scarlet was already worried. If she saw Jade bending, even a little, she'd be certain her lover was about to break.

21

THERE WAS A beauty to an elegantly designed circuit board that rivaled anything found in nature. The fact that even thinking such a thing was blasphemy according to the Prophet was probably the reason Mad had fallen in love with tech during his rebellious teen years.

It was the art of it that intrigued him most. The way insignificant pieces could be combined to create function that so far surpassed their individual uses as to be barely fathomable. But you couldn't just smash the components together at random. You had to understand every strength and weakness, the potential for friction and electrical noise, for too much heat or not enough space.

You had to understand the flow of power.

The broken tablets spread out in front of him didn't require much art. Their design had been fixed in place by pre-Flare engineers, women and men with training and certifications that Mad could only dream of. But it took patience to figure out which parts were broken and which could be salvaged, and it took skill to solder the delicate pieces into place.

It was *his* art, his meditation. Only so much more soothing, because when you reassembled all the pieces, there was no ambiguousness, no uncertainty. Tech was concrete and satisfying. Yes or no. On or off.

Fixed or still broken.

"Need some help?"

Scarlet's voice set off a sweet rush of warmth over his skin, and he couldn't stop his smile. Instead of knocking, she'd just come into his room like she belonged here. *Finally*. "I'm almost done, but I could use some company."

She circled the table, and he nearly swallowed his damn tongue when he glanced up. She was wearing one of his shirts, a soft black T-shirt that was so big on her the V-neck was slipping off her shoulder. "Dylan got held up at the hospital. Something about oxygen purifiers."

There was always something demanding Dylan's attention these days, which was a reality they'd all have to get used to. And he wasn't the only one. "Jade sent a note, too. She's dealing with another would-be pimp."

"So we're on our own tonight." Scarlet paused. "Is she all right?"

"I think so." Mad bent back over the magnifying glass, but he couldn't find the same beauty and elegance in the precise placement of circuits. Not when they had to compete with the curve of Scarlet's bare shoulder and music of her voice. "Deacon's with her. He'll protect her like she's a Rios—which means protecting her from herself, if he has to."

"Mmm." She leaned over him, careful not to block the light as she peered down at the board in his hand.

"You're going to get the same treatment, you know." He studied her profile. "Isabela's already demanding I bring you back for a proper visit."

Just before she turned her head, he caught her expression—half wince, half wrinkled nose. "That's not really my scene."

"You mean the kids? I can keep them from climbing on you. We'll just throw them at Dylan."

"No, it's—" Scarlet ran her hands through her hair and toyed with the plastic casing from one of the disassembled tablets. "You know who I am. Where I'm from. Hell, the O'Kanes seem fancy to me. And your cousin—I mean, he has an honest-to-Christ *palace*. It's too much."

Shit. He was usually better at reading people—but that was the problem with losing your comfortable distance. He was so tangled up with Dylan and Jade and Scarlet now that he was missing the obvious.

And what a goddamn thing to miss. They'd been dragging her from one extravagant childhood home to the next with an obliviousness that had to cut deep. Mad shoved back from his desk and rose to wrap his arms around her. "Where you're from is only a part of who you are."

"A big part." She shivered against his chest and traced her fingers slowly over his left shoulder. "Tell me about these."

He watched her fingertip swoop around the skulls, which faced each other over the blade of a sword, and actually *looked* at the tattoo that had decorated his shoulder for over half his life. It was the first he'd ever gotten, his family's emblem. By now, the sector treated it like the centuries-old crest of an ancient dynasty, but Mad's grandfather had designed it himself.

The Prophet had left little to chance when it came to his legacy.

"I got that one when I was sixteen," Mad said, twisting his arm so she could see the wings spreading out from behind the skulls to wrap around his arm. "Ace has touched it up some. I was angry when I got it. Angry at myself, because I was starting to doubt. I was trying too hard to prove I was committed to the family."

Her fingers slowed even further, turning her exploration into a caress. "You were doubting...because of your mom?"

"Because of a lot of things." Words that usually stuck in his throat like glass seemed to come easily when Scarlet was touching him. "Gideon's father took over the sector after the civil war. For a while, I thought things would change. But they never really did, because the people didn't care who was technically in charge. My grandfather was still alive, still their Prophet..."

"And they still listened to him." She brushed a kiss over his collarbone. "I'm sorry."

"So am I." He closed his eyes and slipped his fingers into the soft strands of her hair. "So you're right. Where I come from is a big part of who I am...but it's not the palace, Scarlet. It's knowing that the greed and selfishness that built it could be inside me."

"But it's *not*." She punctuated the words with a kiss. "That's why Dylan loves you." Another kiss. "Why Jade loves you." He could feel her heart pounding. "Why I love you."

Those had to be the most beautiful sounds she'd ever made, and he craved them with a reckless hunger. "Say it again."

"Dylan loves you. Jade loves you." Her hands trembled as they slid down his back. "I love you, Adrian."

She was wrong, sweet and beautiful and wrong to love him. Dylan wasn't here as a safe buffer, a leash to choke back this dangerous rush of need. Mad skated his hands down her back to grip her ass and hauled her up his body. "Again."

"Love you." She gasped when his hands tightened, and her nails bit into the small of his back. "I mean it. I do."

"Even if I'm selfish?" A quick jerk, and he had her off the floor, crushed against his body with his dick grinding between her legs. "Even if I'm greedy?"

Instead of answering, she wrapped her legs around

his hips and licked his lower lip.

Wrong, so wrong, but not even Dylan could have stopped him from biting her in return, sinking his teeth into the softness of her lip as he slammed her back against a wall. "Be mean to me."

A slow, wicked smile curved her lips as the prick of her nails deepened to a hard burn. "Jade should be here," she purred. "To kiss it all better when I'm done."

That was a mental image to savor—Scarlet raking fire across his back while Jade knelt at his feet, waiting for permission to twist pain into bliss with her clever mouth and luscious lips and eager tongue—

"That's right. Doesn't take long to get there, does it?" Scarlet's touch turned tender, coaxing. "Take me to your bed."

He did, crossing the space to the massive expanse of mattress. But instead of dropping her onto it, he fell backwards and brought her with him. She ended up straddling his hips, her ass rubbing against him with maddening pressure. He ignored it and slipped his hands under her shirt—*his* shirt—

She slapped them away. "You told me to be mean. Letting you play with my tits isn't mean, it's a goddamn gift."

The feral gleam in her eyes was hot as hell, but not as arousing as the way his guilt and apprehension shattered. He didn't need Dylan here to slap him down. Scarlet would do it on her own—*had* to do it, because she'd spent so much time locking away any part of her that wasn't about making Jade feel safe.

Maybe she needed this more than he did. But he'd sure as fuck get off on it, too. Meeting her eyes, he smiled lazily. "You think smacking my fingers is going to keep me from touching you?"

"Nope. But I have my ways." She climbed off the bed and kicked off her shoes. Undressing was as much a show as a necessity, and her fingers lingered over her belt, the button on her cargo pants, even her black lace panties.

She left the shirt on as she turned her attention to his jeans, pausing in her task only to rub the heel of her hand *hard* against his erection through the denim. He thrust up into her touch, but she moved her hand and kept undressing him. He was panting by the time she climbed over him again, resuming a position that was so much filthier, so much more tempting now that they were both naked.

Almost naked. Scarlet plucked at the hem of his shirt, tugging it up just high enough for him to catch a glimpse of her bare pussy. "How mean do you want me to be?"

"Wrong question." He clutched her thigh and rubbed his thumb in a slow circle. "How mean do *you* want to be?"

"Mmm." The black cotton inched higher, until it bared the lower curves of her breasts. Then she stripped it quickly over her head. "That *is* a good question."

Her skin was so soft. Like Jade's, like Dylan's even—but for all the strength in both of them, Jade and Dylan had one thing in common. Their hearts were fragile. Careless handling left bruises that could take months to heal.

He was tougher than that, and so was Scarlet. He scraped his nails down her leg, leaving four white lines that would turn pink soon enough. "Whatever it is, I can take it. C'mon, Scarlet. Teach me not to be so fucking greedy."

"You are greedy." She rocked her hips, gliding her wet pussy from the base of his cock all the way up. When the ridge at the head raked over her clit, she shuddered and gripped his wrists. "And you should be careful what you ask for. You might get it."

She stretched up, guiding his arms above his head. She had to slide up his body to reach, and she settled on his stomach as his hands hit the pillows. "Keep them here." The position put her breasts right above his face, and she leaned down until one nipple grazed the corner of his mouth. "Can you?"

He could crouch patiently in the shadows for hours, ignoring the ache in his legs as he stalked an enemy. He could climb into the cage on fight night and take down an opponent as quickly or slowly as whim dictated. He'd once smiled pleasantly for an hour with a bullet in his arm.

He couldn't stop himself from turning his head to lick her nipple. And he couldn't make any promises about staying still with her naked body on top of his. "Maybe."

"Maybe?" she echoed, bowing her back until her hard nipple pushed between his lips. "You're supposed to have an iron will. Control that nothing and no one can shake."

He flexed his fingers, tempted to snatch her up and toss her on her back—but he didn't need his hands to shatter *her* control. He used his teeth instead, scraping them over her soft skin before closing them on her nipple in a precise bite.

A low moan shuddered out of her. "You play dirty." She sat up, leaving him with a perfect view of her flushed, naked body. "I like it."

"I'm good with my mouth." He grinned and licked his lower lip. "Get up here and I'll prove it."

She shook her head and cupped her breast, closing her fingers around the slick peak that was still wet from his tongue. "Tell me."

"I'd be rougher—" His words broke off as her other hand slid down, the backs of her fingers brushing his stomach as she began to stroke her pussy.

Oh holy hell, she was *mean.*

"Rougher," he repeated hoarsely, fighting back with words. "Because Jade is so sweet to you, isn't she? And she's precious like that. What did it feel like the first time she came around your fingers?"

Scarlet's thighs tensed, and she circled her clit slowly with one fingertip. "Like she'd never stop. Like I finally did something right."

"That's how it felt the first time I got Dylan off." If he closed his eyes, he could still see it, but Scarlet couldn't. So he painted the picture for her. "You know how he looks when he's tired, stressed. He puts his hand in his pocket, because he's reaching for those goddamn pills. I pushed him back against the wall and got on my knees and gave him something better to feel. And he got that *look*—"

Her breath hitched, and she laughed softly. "I know the one."

Happiness was still a shock on Dylan's face, as if it was an emotion he'd never had reason to express before. "He had it the first time he touched you. When you were in my lap, squirming all over me while he and Jade fucked you with their fingers."

"Yeah?"

Scarlet was flushed, her fingers slipping easily over flesh he wanted to lick. They were fighting for the top, just like he'd always imagined—and *nothing* like he'd ever imagined, because there were no losers in this game. When one of them broke, they'd both win.

It didn't make the game less fun. He listened to her hitching breaths and built the fantasy a little higher. "I think that might become one of our favorite things to do, you know. All of us together, fucking you until you can't come any more."

"It'd take a while." She rocked back, nudging his cock with the round, firm curve of her ass. "You up for it?"

He gritted his teeth and fought for that iron control. It barely kept him from thrusting up toward her in desperation. "Oh, we'll take our time. You know how it would start. Dylan loves shoving Jade's head between your legs almost as much as she loves being there."

Scarlet stopped moving and leaned forward a little, bracing herself on his chest. "Give me your hand."

"Yes, that's what would happen next." He brought his arm up and teased his knuckles down the center of her body. "Jade would have you screaming under her mouth, but you'd be empty, wouldn't you?"

"Mm-hmm." She caught his hand—and dragged it lower. "So fill me up."

She was so wet, but he took his time, ignoring her insistent grip. It was worth it to watch her body jerk as he teased her clit, stroking back and forth until she loosened her hold on him and shifted her hips instead, rocking into his touch.

"This is how we'd start," he whispered, keeping his touch light enough to make her strain toward him. "But it wouldn't stay slow for long. Dylan might be patient, but I'm not. And Jade's the worst. So greedy for your pleasure."

"She's just hungry."

He twisted his wrist and edged two fingers inside her, gritting his teeth against the lure of her taunting heat. He needed more words, filthier ones, words that could conjure fantasies vivid enough to snap the thin thread of her control. "Have you ever let her have her way with you?"

Scarlet's eyes locked with his, and she slowed her eager, seeking movements. "Not at first. I wanted to be sure, you know?"

Oh, he knew. All about the guilt and uncertainty, all the things that had bound him to caution when it came to Jade. But Scarlet was wrong. "She's not just hungry. It's you, sweetheart. Your flushed skin and your moans—" He worked his fingers deeper, pressed his thumb to her clit, and she choked back a sound that was half-whimper, half-groan. "And that noise right there. That's what she's hungry for. What all of us are hungry for."

But Scarlet wasn't listening. She leaned forward again, bracing her hands on either side of his head. The position trapped his hand between them, leaving him helpless to do anything but watch as she began to fuck his fingers, her clit nudging his palm every time her hips snapped down.

Victory.

And *torture*.

He couldn't even lean up to kiss her. But he got to savor the expressions flickering over her face—her narrowed eyes and parted lips, her ragged breaths, her moans as she gave in and *took*, recklessly and selfishly. "That's it, Scarlet. Use me to get off."

She did, so silently he might not have noticed without his fingers buried inside her. Her hips bucked and her body tightened, pulsing and clenching—

His patience snapped. With a surge of muscle he upended them, spilling her back to the bed with his thighs driving hers wide, his fingers still buried inside her. "Do it again," he growled, bracing his weight on his other hand so he could watch her face. "Use me."

She moaned something that almost sounded like his name and placed her hands on his sides. It could have been a caress, except for the way her nails raked over his skin, carving sharp, bright lines of pain.

He hissed out a breath and let the fire of it burn through him, sweet and clean. "More."

"How careful are they with you, baby?" she whispered. "Everyone in the world."

Most people never got close enough to matter. And the few who did... "Too goddamn careful."

The bite of her nails sharpened. "You want me to be rough?"

"I want you to be *you*."

The pleasure on her face melted into a heart-stopping smile. "What does that even mean?"

He eased his fingers from her and gripped his cock, tormenting them both with one slow stroke before he guided it to her pussy. It was so tempting to thrust into her all at once, but he rocked into her in time with his rasped words. "It means Dylan loves you." Deeper. "It means Jade loves you." *Deeper.*

Mad dropped to his elbows, his body against hers, his face so close he whispered the truth against her lips as he drove home. "It means I love you."

She trembled beneath him—her arms and legs wrapping around him, clinging tight—and the words she sighed echoed his. "Say it again."

He rolled his hips, fucking her without pulling free of her shaking, desperate embrace. "We love you, Scarlet. I love you. When you're mean and when you're nice and when you're everything in between."

"*Yes*." Her teeth scraped his jaw before closing on his neck.

He was past pain and pleasure. It was all sensation, throbbing along with his pounding heart as he rocked into her again. Just a beautiful blur of Scarlet, with only the fleeting regret that Dylan and Jade weren't here to see her like this—writhing beneath him, whimpering against his lips, scratching up his back with abandon, as free as she'd always been but somehow more and better—

But they would see it. For tonight, he let himself believe it. They'd survive the war and this would be their forever. Love and trust until they didn't have to be so careful, because they would know each other and be known. Be *loved*.

Scarlet's nails dug into his shoulder as she shuddered in the grip of another orgasm, and Mad let fantasy guide his mouth to her throat. Her hoarse moan when he bit her was sweet, but not the prize. The mark would be—proof of this moment that he could touch, proof that would take days to fade, each one a promise.

Someday, Ace would set a different kind of mark around her throat, and around Jade's and Dylan's, too. Because Dylan's dominance in bed could only blunt the truth for so long.

Mad was royalty. He had been born to lead, to possess, to protect.

And they were *his*.

The thought was too much. He shuddered as pleasure flooded him, swift and hot and burning like the scratches down his back. He sank into her a final time and groaned against her ear.

Scarlet panted against his cheek, her heart pounding

wildly, somehow still in time with his. "Adrian."

When she wrapped her voice around the syllables, he didn't hate his name. Maybe it could be like Jade—like *Jyoti*—a secret the four of them held behind closed doors. An intimacy reserved for the people he loved. "Scarlet."

Her arms tightened around him, and one leg slid over the back of his. "We could stay here forever. Right here."

"We could," he agreed, nuzzling her cheek. "Jade and Dylan will be back eventually. One of them will bring food."

"That's all we need, isn't it?"

"Pretty much." Jade, Dylan, and a world where looming war wasn't demanding more and more of both of their time. But those thoughts were dark, and Scarlet was warm and soft against him as he rolled to his side and dragged her with him. "I have enough liquor in here to last us through the summer."

He felt more than heard her smothered laugh, and she reached past him for the cigarettes she'd left on his nightstand. "All of our vices covered." She lit one cigarette, and a little of her humor faded. "Have you noticed?"

He smoothed the disheveled hair back from her forehead. "What, our vices?"

She shook her head. "Dylan. Haven't seen him high in a while."

Mad froze with his fingers tangled in her hair and thought back. When was the last time he'd seen those glassy eyes, that sleepy distance? The night he'd gone to Sector Two with Deacon, maybe, but everything after that was a blur. The bombs had fallen, and then Scarlet and Jade—

Jade had needed Dylan. They'd all needed him, and Dylan had always been good at pulling it together when he was needed. But never for this long. "You're right. I haven't, either."

Scarlet exhaled and studied him through the haze of smoke. "That's got to mean something."

"Maybe it just means...we fit." He traced a zigzag pat‐ tern down her arm. "All the broken pieces, all the sharp edges. I tried to protect Dylan from his, but there are some things only Jade can give him. And some things only you can."

"Don't sell yourself short. Jade's coming out of her shell, too. Taking control of her life." She rubbed her cheek against the inside of his wrist and grinned. "You may not be a prince, but you're definitely a fairy tale come true."

He laughed and hauled her on top of him. "Maybe I'm warming up to the idea of being a prince—if it means I get to be greedy about the naked people in my bed."

Her expression softened, and she laid her cigarette in the ashtray on the table. "It's not greed if you're in love."

He tugged her down until her forehead rested on his. "Can I be greedy about something other than sex?"

"Name it."

"Sing for me?"

She blushed, but she didn't refuse. Instead, she began to hum the first notes of a familiar song—the one she'd been singing the night of the concert in Three.

The one she'd sung to *him*.

By the time she started the first verse, Mad could close his eyes and imagine himself back there. The crush of bodies, the heat and the smoke and taste of whiskey on his tongue. The way she'd looked on that stage, clad in leather and steel, crooning like silk.

The way her eyes had met his, and for those intoxicat‐ ing moments, he'd felt seen, understood. Known and loved and forgiven for every goddamn one of his endless list of sins.

Music was its own religion, a spiritual force that bound them together. All of those people crowded into the bar were there to *feel*, because poverty and squalor and danger and the fucking end of the world wasn't enough to alter their fundamental natures.

People loved and lost and grieved and rejoiced, and

Scarlet was as much a priestess as anyone in Sector One, with her husky-voiced reminders that they were all the same, in the end. That they all wanted and needed and *craved.*

That they were all at least a little broken, because they lived in a broken world.

Mad stroked Scarlet's back as her voice wove its spell, relaxed in a way he hadn't felt in more years than he could remember. Since his easy faith had begun to shred around the edges, and he'd tattooed the family shield on his shoulder in a desperate grasp for confidence and security.

His grandfather had played with the idea of God like a sculptor with clay, cutting and reshaping and molding until it reflected everything he needed in a religion tailored to his whims. Trying to form something righteous out of the statue he'd left behind—that was Gideon's battle.

Mad didn't have to fight it. He didn't have to believe in his grandfather to have faith because there were dozens of paths for divinity to take. Scarlet's music. The sound of his nieces and nephews laughing. Things as vast as the beauty of nature and as inexplicable as Dallas O'Kane—a man with the power to be selfish and cruel, but who consistently resisted temptation while the others around him succumbed.

The sight of Dylan and Scarlet and Jade—three people with every right to be shattered beyond the possibility of joy—smiling.

Maybe he still wasn't worthy of their surrender. He'd watched plenty of men make the wrong choices when faced with such power. But he was too damn selfish to walk away now.

So he'd fucking well make himself worthy.

22

FIVE DAYS, FIVE nights. Jade had spent three of them locked up in her new fortress in Sector Two, and Dylan wanted to know why.

The housekeeper seemed intent on denying him. "Lady Jade asked not to be disturbed. She was quite insistent, sir."

The woman had a stone face that would do a dedicated poker player proud. "I'm quite insistent, too, and I'd appreciate it if you'd tell her I'm here."

"I don't think—"

"Oh, it's you!" The cook who'd brought Jade the rolls came down the hallway with a tray gripped in her hands. "Thank goodness. I was going to carry dinner up myself to coax Lady Jade to eat, but you'll do even better."

The housekeeper's expression tightened. "Molly, you know she requested privacy—"

"From outsiders," Molly spoke over her. "You know

this is her doctor friend. I'll walk him up. If she's cross, I'll tell her I insisted."

With another pinch-lipped glare, the housekeeper reluctantly stepped aside. Molly hustled Dylan up the steps. "This way."

"Thank you." He waited until they were out of earshot of the housekeeper before touching Molly's arm. "Have things been that hectic around here?"

"It's been…lively." The cook sighed. "I'm sorry the housekeeper was rude to you, but she's very protective of Lady Jade. If we didn't have a dragon guarding the door, we'd be overrun at all hours with people demanding the lady's attention and fretting her half to death."

Why wasn't Deacon handling the requests? "Is it people who need help and supplies to recover from the bombing, or something else?"

"Oh, I wouldn't know. I just worry when my trays come back untouched." They reached the top of the stairs and the hallway that led to Jade's office. "You'll see that she eats something, won't you?"

"Sure." He took the tray from her and braced it on his forearm with one hand. "Thanks, Molly."

The cook gave him a shaky smile. "It wasn't right, what happened to her mother. Lady Radha was good to us, took care of us. And Jyoti has her mother's heart—" She cut off and shook her head. "I'd best get back. Ring down if you need anything else."

"I will." She headed back down the stairs, and Dylan rapped on Jade's office door.

Nothing.

He pressed his lips into a thin line and opened the door. Jade was seated at her desk, a half-empty bottle of wine at her elbow and a pair of tablets in front of her. "You can set the tray just inside the door," she said without looking up. "I'll get it when I'm finished with this."

Dylan closed the door behind him. "Somehow, I don't believe you."

She jerked upright and spun in her chair, her exhausted expression flashing to joy. "Dylan! What are you—?" That fast, worry creased her brow as she rose. "Are Mad and Scarlet okay?"

"They're fine." He set the tray aside and studied the dark shadows under her eyes. "What about you?"

"I'm..." She attempted a smile. "I suppose you won't believe *fine.*"

"No." He might have, even with Molly's concerns, if Jade didn't look like she'd lost weight. If she hadn't been hiding—or, worse, *stuck*—in this hellhole for nearly a week. "I thought Deacon was supposed to be helping you out."

"He is." She sank back into her chair. "He took some of the men out to deal with a fresh wave of looters. Word's gotten out that not all of the warehouses are completely empty. Not that what's left has much value unless you have black market connections, but..." Her sigh encompassed not just her exhaustion, but the helplessness of fighting sector criminals who'd risk everything for next to nothing.

He had to touch her, *soothe* her. He crossed the room and slid his hands beneath the hair that had loosened from her chignon, massaging the tense muscles of her neck. "We talked about this, Jade. It doesn't matter how much work there is to be done. If you run yourself into the ground, there'll be no one to do it."

"I know." She tipped her head forward, inviting more of his touch. "I thought if I could just stop the worst of it, I'd have time to catch my breath. But I watched Cerys fighting for respect as a leader all those years, and I should have known better."

"You didn't exactly get this place under normal conditions." She'd walked into a ruin of a sector, into the aftermath of the unthinkable, and started restoring order. "Three's still on shaky ground, and how many years has it been since those bombs fell?"

"Three's improving rapidly at the moment, since all the criminals who are scared of Dallas are coming over here to loot." She laughed suddenly, sharp and wry. "I'm going to have to be more menacing than Dallas O'Kane somehow. Or give up and let him do it for me, at which point no one will ever take me seriously again."

"Does that matter?"

"For my ego? No." She twisted to look up at him. "But it makes me less effective. It makes it harder to protect the people who need me."

Power had its own silent language, one that screamed. It combined tiny, effortless shows of arrogance with bigger, louder displays—of wealth, of violence. The thugs who had invaded Two—hell, not to mention the ones who had already been there—understood this language perfectly, even if their attempts to speak it were awkward, messy. Unsuccessful.

How long would it take Jade to learn it? "I'm not arguing the fact that a sector—any sector—needs a strong leader. But you can't give more than you have." He tilted her head back farther with one finger under her chin. "Trust me, love. I know."

"But I haven't given what I have." She stared up at him, eyes dark and cold. "You know what's inside me. I'm more than capable of dragging the next would-be pimp who touches one of those girls out into the street and shooting him in the head myself. Or maybe shoot him someplace that scares men even more than Dallas O'Kane does."

"How much will it cost you?"

"Probably not as much as it should."

"And then what?" He dropped his hand. "You stay here, alone in this house, because you can't stand to look at Scarlet and Mad anymore? Or, rather, to have them look at you?"

She shut her eyes and looked away.

His chest ached. "Don't lose them. Don't lose *yourself.*

It could never be worth it."

"What if this is me?" She wrapped one hand around her opposite wrist, as if blocking out her O'Kane ink—or clinging to it. "I thought being here in this house, where I was Jyoti... I thought I'd remember. But she was just a child, Dylan. It's so much *easier* to be Lady Jade of Sector Two."

He knew better than anyone the seductive nature of *easy*. For years, it had kept him reaching for oblivion, because leaving drugs behind meant facing up to who he was, what he'd done, and *easy* was so much simpler.

And it would be just as easy now to go to Dallas, to tell him that Jade—that one of his people—was spiraling, and he had to stop her. Dylan could put that responsibility on the O'Kanes, because the ink Jade was trying so hard to hide meant it belonged to them.

But it also belonged to him now. That was what her trust and submission meant.

"Come on. Baby steps." He grasped her hand and pulled her from the chair. "First, you eat. That's not nego-tiable."

Her smile was slower to form this time, but it felt real. "That must be the most mundane thing I've ever been or-dered to do."

"You have a short memory." He brushed his thumb over the corner of her sad little smile. "I recall having to ask you to sit down and take a breath when you first came back to Two."

Her eyes softened. "Yes, but you were still pretending to ask back then. Now I know better."

She said it with such yearning that his body re-sponded as if she'd touched him. Only it wasn't sex she craved, but something deeper. More intense.

So he gave it to her. He led her wordlessly to the small table where he'd left the tray, sank into the leather chair beside it, and pulled her into his lap. "Eat."

She relaxed in his arms and lifted the cover from the

first dish. Delicate miniature quiches towered under the dome, warm and fragrant and stacked high enough to feed three. The next dish held hunks of cheese and sliced apples—a priceless delicacy this far out of season.

Jade bit into a piece with a soft hum of pleasure. "I don't know who Molly's contacts are, but they must put Dallas's to shame."

He handed her another slice of apple. "That's what this sector's about, isn't it? Trade?"

"It was. We had trade routes established all across the country." She finished the apple and reached for a piece of cheese. "Eden warned the most influential traders—like my father, apparently—and got them inside the walls. Everyone else was left to their fates, but a few survived. That's what I was doing when you got here. Trying to compile a list of what resources they can access. So much of it is just...frivolous."

"What do you mean?"

She lifted another piece of the apple and held it between them. "This is what Sector Two is. Luxury. You could feed a hundred for what a basket of apples cost. I can get food from the farms I control, but everything else is just like this. Silk and tech and rare coffee and a dozen other things that no one outside of Eden can afford to want. We weren't built for survival."

No one sector was—it was the brilliance of Eden's specialized division of labor. Six could feed itself, but thousands would die every year without the most basic medications they manufactured in Five. And Eight handled everyday items like toilet paper and soap, but without the revenue that came from selling those goods to the city and the other sectors, it would fall apart, too.

Instead of pointing out that they were all stomping around in a house of cards, Dylan turned Jade to face him. "And the girls in this sector were raised to believe all they could ever hope to do was find a patron and please him. Now, they're learning they can do anything they want.

Things can change."

"They can, can't they?" She smiled and offered him a bite of the apple. "You're being optimistic."

He let her feed it to him, then winked as he chewed slowly. "Someone has to be, don't you think?"

"I like it." She cupped his cheek and rubbed her forehead against his. "Maybe we could pack up my dinner and take it back home to share. Scarlet loves apples."

Home. The word meant everything—safety, warmth. Mad and Scarlet, waiting for them. And, somewhere beyond all that, it meant the most important thing of all.

It meant they hadn't lost Jade yet.

23

T HERE WERE BENEFITS and drawbacks to spend-
ing her nights in Sector Four. Jade could list the
benefits easily—security, safety, warmth, love, and the
bone-deep satisfaction of letting the stress of the day fall
away under Dylan's wicked commands and Scarlet's
clever fingers and Mad's eager mouth.

The main drawback was being late every time someone joined her in Mad's spacious shower in the morning.
Though that probably warranted being labeled a benefit,
too. Especially when *everyone* joined her in the shower.

They had this morning, in a slippery tangle of limbs
that had tested her willpower. They'd converged on her as
if rendering her incapable of leaving was the point, closing
in on her on three sides with the tile wall at her back.

And with Dylan there, whispering for her to let them
tend to her, she'd closed her eyes and floated on the stroking hands and caressing mouths and thrusting fingers, her

cries echoing off the tiles as steam made them all slippery...and when her toes had curled and her knees melted, Scarlet had to hold her up while Mad turned on Dylan, a dangerous glint in his eyes—

With *that* vivid memory bringing heat to her face, Jade mentally nudged morning showers firmly into the *drawback* category and forced herself to focus on the tablet in front of her.

At least it was easier to focus—Dylan hadn't been wrong about that. A week of forcing herself to go home every night had produced plenty of more subtle advantages. Eating and sleeping gave her the energy to tackle thorny problems. And being in Sector Four reminded her that she had more resources at her disposal than Cerys ever dreamed of.

She had the O'Kanes.

That list of frivolous items stacked in abandoned warehouses wasn't so frivolous when Six and Bren knew people in Three who could sell it in Eden at outrageous prices. Eden might scramble to reestablish trade contact with the men they'd deemed worth saving, but Jade had the goods *now*, and if the people of Eden were anything, it was impatient when it came to luxury.

All she needed was a list of what she had to offer, and Six and Bren would turn it into money and supplies. Blankets, sturdy clothing, solar converters. Finn would work with his friends in Sector Five to turn some of that money into med-gel and antibiotics—things Sector Two needed far more than silk tights and custom Italian suits and artwork looted from distant museums.

She almost had the inventory organized when Deacon stepped into her office. Well, he didn't step *in* so much as lean one massive shoulder against the doorframe and silently wait to be acknowledged—a strange, stilted courtesy that no number of standing invitations could sway.

"Come in, Deacon." She arranged a few more things in

her spreadsheet before using the connection Noah had rigged for her to send him the file. He'd get it to Six without Jade having to leave her desk—another way the sector boundaries were blurring. "I'm just finishing up."

"We have a situation."

The last of the lingering warmth dissipated as she set aside her tablet and rose. Deacon combined Jasper's easy efficiency with Bren's steely nerves—anything he deemed a *situation* was likely a stone's throw from *crisis*. "What is it?"

"There's a girl downstairs," he rumbled. "She's in bad shape, but I thought you might want to see her before I have someone take her to the hospital in One."

She hurried to meet him at the door—and then hurried even more, because his massive strides devoured the hallway floor. Running wasn't dignified, but the words *bad shape* echoed in her head until she lifted her skirts to race down the stairs.

Deacon hadn't been exaggerating. The girl lay limp and fretful on one of the couches in the sitting room, her skin sallow and her eyelids fluttering. Her expression was so slack it took Jade a moment to recognize Lisa, a sixteen-year-old from Rose House who'd been in her last year of training when Jade left. Golden-brown hair stuck to her sweaty brow and cheeks, but her soft moan wasn't one of pain, and Jade's entire body tightened in recognition.

Smooth, warm, hot. Sliding, melting, burning, flying. Hurt me, cut me, beat me—I'll beg, I'll crawl, just don't take it away—

Sometimes, when Jade saw Finn, her entire body still jolted with anticipation. She craved it, needed it in a part of her she could never entirely lock away—that first bliss of the drugs they'd given her hitting her system, lighting her up in ways words couldn't encompass. Sector Five had mastered the art of customized designer drugs. They could heal, rebuild, regenerate your body and your mind. They could bring you up or down, alleviate pain or flood you with pleasure.

Addiction didn't have to be part of the equation any-more. But with some drugs, addiction was rather the point. Not just the physical dependency but the emotional malleability, the weakness that made you biddable, that bound you to the person who could give.

Who could take away.

Lisa moaned again, but there was an edge to the sound this time, the first taste of loss. Jade locked her own feelings down and crossed the room to lay a hand on the girl's cheek. "Where did you find her?"

"Wandering the old Garden District, too high to know where she was."

"Lisa." Her eyelids fluttered, and Jade patted her cheek gently. "Lisa, sweetheart, it's Jade. I need you to look at me."

"Jade," she echoed vaguely, then huffed out a breath that almost sounded like a laugh. "Not Jade. She's gone."

"I was gone, and now I'm back." Jade put the thread of command the girls had been trained to respond to in her voice. "Look at me, Lisa."

The girl obeyed, but her eyes were glazed and refused to focus.

There was nothing else she could do. A wet washcloth or a glass of water might make her more comfortable, but nothing would bring her back to sense but more drugs— the kind Jade hardly kept on hand. All she had were words and the rage building inside her. "Where were you trying to go?"

It took her a few seconds to respond. "Home. Valerie said to be home by seven."

Her anger spiked higher, and Jade took a careful breath. Valerie had been a trainer at Rose House—an in-stitution, already there when Jade arrived and only digging in deeper with each passing year. She'd enjoyed privileges as a senior trainer, and she'd had a particular flair for breaking the wills of stubborn young girls.

Not that she'd ever tried with Jade. Valerie knew potential power when she saw it. Her deft, frequent flattery might have eventually succeeded in endearing her to Jade, too—if she hadn't spent week after week watching Valerie crush Avery's heart.

Valerie had been through Jade's office twice. The first time had been to deliver a groveling offer to perform as Jade's deputy and reopen the houses. The second time, Deacon's boys had caught her trying to pimp out girls. Jade had slapped her down for that. Hard.

Maybe not hard enough.

But Lisa was flying so high, she might think Rose House was still there and Valerie would be waiting to punish her for an infraction. Jade needed proof, not to let rage guide her. "Where is home, honey? You tell us, and we'll get you there."

A little of the haze cleared from Lisa's gaze again, supplanted by a flash of fear. "If we miss curfew, we miss our dose."

"I understand, Lisa." And she did. Too well, because she should have seen this coming. Should have known that she wasn't Dallas O'Kane, wasn't even Lex—her reputation was built on guile and smiles and knowing how to bend.

They weren't afraid of her. Yet.

Lisa was trembling. Jade coaxed her into a sitting position and wrapped an arm around her slender shoulders. "You're going to be all right. Just tell me where Valerie is."

"The house—" Her voice cracked, failed, and she licked her lips. "I don't want to get in trouble."

Deacon made a rough noise in the back of his throat.

"You can't get in trouble." Jade stroked the girl's tangled hair. "I took over for Cerys, sweetheart. I'm the one who decides who's in trouble. And if anyone tries to hurt you, Deacon and his men will deal with them. I promise."

Lisa stared at her, then squeezed her eyes shut. "Down the street from Rose. The house that belonged to

Setta's patron."

"Thank you." She kissed the top of Lisa's head and rose. "My personal driver will take you to the hospital in One. I'll have Avery meet you there. You remember her, don't you? She'll take care of you until you're feeling better."

"Okay." The girl slumped against the arm of the couch.

Deacon didn't break his stony silence until they were in the hallway, out of earshot, with the door firmly closed behind them. "May I?"

She'd had Deacon with her for long enough to know the real question. Not *May I give my opinion?* but *May I eliminate the problem?* And he would, if she let him. She could return to her desk, like Cerys always had, confident that her dirty work was being performed swiftly and efficiently.

It would be so, so easy to become Cerys.

"Yes," she said, keeping her voice cool. Rage might be writhing inside her, but she didn't have the luxury of appearing angry. An emotional woman was an irrational woman, and inadequate as a leader—as if Dallas wouldn't already be out the door, on his way to strangle the offender with his bare hands. "Of course you can come with me."

He arched one eyebrow. "I can handle it. This is what I do."

Her gaze drifted to the big arms folded across his chest. One was covered with tattoos—tiny ravens whose significance Mad had explained to her. Delicate, elegant penance, each bird marking a life he'd taken. The dirty work he'd performed to keep someone else's hands and soul clean.

Jade's soul had always been her own responsibility. "This time, we deal with it together."

Valerie had picked the perfect house. Right along the ragged edge of the destruction zone, the property had suffered extensive cosmetic damage but still seemed relatively sound. And the worst of the looting had been concentrated along the river and out toward the grand estates, where two generations' worth of hoarded wealth sat, barely guarded. The people here were scavengers, poor and determined, committed to minding their own business.

The edge of total annihilation wasn't the worst place to hide.

Jade didn't argue when Deacon asked her to wait beside the car. This was what he did, after all—and there were advantages to playing the unruffled leader into whose chilly presence a transgressor had to be escorted.

Theatrics. Something Cerys had excelled at, and the only one of the woman's lessons Jade planned to make her own.

She stood with her hands shoved into her coat pockets, ticking off the seconds in silence. At forty-seven, someone inside the house shouted. A muffled crash followed, along with more shouting. An upper window shattered as a man flew through it, his arms and legs flailing until he slammed into the ground with a grunt.

He groaned and tried to roll over. Jade ignored him and counted off another thirty seconds before Deacon came out the front door, dragging a struggling Valerie behind him.

She saw Jade and stopped struggling, pulling herself up to her full height instead. "Really, was the brute necessary?"

"I wanted to get your attention," Jade replied mildly. "And the *brute* is Gideon Rios' right-hand man. Your political instincts are getting rusty."

"Yours are the same as ever." Valerie tried to jerk her arm out of Deacon's grasp, then sniffed and gave up when he held tight. "Someone else's right-hand man. Someone else's sector. Honestly, Jade, don't you have anything of your own?"

The verbal jab landed, but not for the reason the woman undoubtedly imagined. Valerie would have burned with frustration to be so close to total control, yet still answerable to others. Jade, on the other hand, had the wisdom to appreciate just how heavily absolute leadership lay across the shoulders of anyone who claimed it.

And she had something else—something of her own. She had Mad's earnest smile and Scarlet's easy laugh and Dylan's quiet protectiveness. She had the thing that mattered most—people who loved her even when she was weak, even when she was broken.

Jade hoped they could still love her when she was neither.

They were attracting a crowd now—workers from the blast zone, opportunists who had been picking over demolished buildings, and refugees who'd been huddled in nearby structures. No one came too close, but they would hear her words…and repeat them.

Good. "I warned you, Valerie. Twice. I offered you a chance at a new life—"

"At that *hospital?*" She wrinkled her nose in disgust. "I haven't trained my whole life to settle for a job like that. I can do more. I can help these girls."

"With drugs?" She fought the tremor in her voice, because Valerie would latch on to any weakness. "They found Lisa wandering the blast zone, alone and defenseless. Is that how you help them?"

"It's better than uprooting them completely. They can have a bit of their lives back, Jade."

"They can have nothing. They can be used and violated while you pretend they're willing because they keep crawling back to you." Revulsion welled, along with bitter regret. She'd warned Valerie, but it didn't matter. This was what Sector Two *was.* Selling helpless girls to anyone willing to meet the asking price. She could chastise Valerie, punish her, *banish* her, and it wouldn't make any difference.

Until there were consequences for violating these girls, there would always be another Valerie.

There would always be another Lisa.

"You were warned." Jade stepped forward, face-to-face with the woman who'd caused so much pain. "And I told you there wouldn't be a third warning."

The crowd was whispering now, a quiet swell that seemed to bolster Valerie. She tilted her head, a smile in her eyes as she regarded Jade. "What are you going to do about it? Have your borrowed brute take me out back and teach me a lesson?"

Deacon would. Hell, from the look on his face he was *eager* to, which made Jade wonder what further horrors awaited her in the house. More girls, undoubtedly. Wounded, drugged, addicted—maybe even broken, like she'd been once.

Lex had rescued her from that life. Lex would understand this moment—or maybe not, because she would have taken care of Valerie before it got to this point.

A good leader didn't ask people to do things they weren't willing to do.

Jade extended her hand to Deacon. "Gun, please."

He complied instantly, without argument or hesitation, unholstering one of the smaller pistols he always carried. Only someone who'd spent the last few weeks glued to his side could have perceived his displeasure as he passed her the weapon and stepped back.

She'd trained in basic firearms proficiency for two years during her advanced tutelage at Orchid House. Two months under Bren's direction had taught her more. The gun still didn't feel natural in her hand—she'd always preferred knives—but she raised it with confidence.

Valerie was still smiling in amused disbelief when Jade shot her.

The older woman's head snapped back. Time seemed to slow, and the sharp, acrid scent of gunpowder filled the air as Valerie slumped to the ground, dead from a perfect headshot that would have made Bren proud.

Jade waited for horror, for shame—even for satisfaction—but all that came was chilly resolve. She handed Deacon back his gun with a murmured thanks, trying not to look too closely at the blood splattered across his jacket.

Behind her, the crowd had fallen silent. Jade turned to face them and raised one fist in the air. The sleeve of her jacket slid down, revealing her wrist—and her O'Kane ink. More theatrics, but she knew the weight of this moment. If she did it right, maybe she wouldn't have to do it again.

"I'm the leader of this sector," she announced, letting her voice carry through the clear morning. "But I'm also an O'Kane. When I give an order, I expect it to be obeyed. This was Valerie's third chance. The next person who tries to sell initiates from the houses won't even get a second. If you want to earn a living in this sector, you'll do it by selling your own skills and bodies, not someone else's."

Some backed away. Some slipped into the shadows, fear twisting their features. But others stood, watching her, something close to respect—maybe even admiration—on their faces.

She turned her back on them, stepped over Valerie's body, and headed for the house. And finally, *finally* the numbness broke, swept away by serene confidence in her actions. It welled up from the core of her—strength gifted by her mother and nurtured in secret. Her heart felt no conflict.

Valerie had posed a threat to her sector. She'd dispatched that threat and sent a message that would discourage future ones. Perhaps she'd used some of the skills Cerys had forced on her, but even more important were her mother's lessons—how to tell right from wrong, and how to use whatever power she had to protect those who had none.

This was what Jade was made for, to use every scrap of training from Cerys to tear down the world Cerys had built. And she could do it, like no one else could.

Because her mother had loved her enough to tell her she could do anything.

24

POKER NIGHT WITH the O'Kane ladies could be a lot of things—raucous, contemplative, hilarious, even obscene—but it was never, ever boring.

"So I come back from the bar with the shots, and he's got his pants open. Just fucking *open*, with his dick waving around right there in the fucking bar. I mean the table's barely hiding it." Nessa shuffled the cards and started dealing. "And then he says—wait for it—'Thank God you're back, baby. My cock's ready to get wet.'"

Lex made a face and reached for her drink. "Bastard wasn't trying very hard, was he?"

"Oh, trust me, that was the top of his game." Nessa rolled her eyes. "So I dumped the shots in his lap, because you know. Who the fuck wouldn't have? Don't worry, it wasn't the good liquor. But then *Six* notices what's going on…"

"Oh God, I heard this part of the story." Noelle

grinned and refilled her own drink. "The waitresses were laughing so hard they couldn't carry the trays."

Scarlet peered over her cards—a truly, tragically shitty hand she should have thrown in anyway. "What happened?"

Nessa laughed. "Oh, he saw her coming and started trying to put his dick away, but she told him since he was so anxious to show it off, he could just walk out like that. And that table of old-timers was by the door, and you *know* he didn't want to go strutting by them with his junk waggling in the wind because that'd be the end of his rep. So he told her to fuck off and she said in that case, he could wear the shot glass out or he could leave without a dick."

"And it turns out, he didn't like *everyone* looking at his dick." Noelle's smile was downright wicked as she held up a finger and then let it droop. "About halfway to the door, the shot glass hit the floor and he took off running. He's probably in Sector Seven by now."

"If he even stopped there." Trix snorted. "Served him right, not waiting for an invitation to whip it out."

Scarlet could imagine the guy, scuttling out the door with his pants around his knees. "Never mess with an O'Kane, man *or* woman. But if you have to pick one, go with the dudes."

Lex held her glass aloft. "Hear, hear."

Nessa knocked her glass into Lex's and drank. "Okay, someone tell a *good* sex story now so I can live vicariously, because I'm calling it. The only men left in this sector who aren't scared of trying to get in my pants are the idiots. I'm gonna be the first O'Kane nun."

"I could set you up with Riff," Scarlet offered.

"The bass player?" Nessa considered her cards before flopping them on the table with a sigh. "Nah, don't get my hopes up. Bren would just run him off."

"That's the damn truth." Six came through the door looking rumpled and tired, her shoulder holster visible beneath her jacket. Her voice probably sounded casual to everyone else, but Scarlet had known her long enough to hear the edge. "Bren's extra grumpy this week. Too many assholes from Three testing his patience."

Lex considered that. "Do Dallas and our boys need to roll out? Crack some skulls?"

"Maybe." Six tilted her head toward the door. "If you and Scarlet want to sit this hand out, we can talk about it."

Something about the words—and the way she said them—made Scarlet's pulse kick into a higher gear. She could have wanted her input because they were talking about Three, and Scarlet had grown up there, knew it inside and out. But there was something beneath the words, an unspoken trill of tension that stabbed at Scarlet's instincts.

She'd always had sharp instincts. It was the only way to survive in Three.

She threw her cards down. "Didn't have anything good anyway. You ladies have fun."

"But not *too* much fun," Lex added as she rose. "Not until I get back, anyway."

When they were out in the hallway, Six leaned back against the wall and eyed Scarlet. "There's some crazy-ass shit gossip coming out of Two. I thought you'd want to hear it first."

Her stomach twisted. "About Jade?"

A quick nod. "Rumor is, there was a public execution this morning. Some former trainer got a couple girls doped up on some nasty drugs and was pimping them out, and Jade made a statement out of her. Shot her in front of a crowd."

Lex sighed. "Shit."

It sounded far off and vague to Scarlet. *Everything* did, with her ears buzzing and the world swimming. "Where the hell was Deacon?"

"I don't know." Six shrugged uncomfortably. "By now, people are saying she shot a dozen pimps and put out bounties on even more, so details are sketchy. But the main part—I heard that from someone I believe."

Lex laid a hand on Scarlet's shoulder. "She has to prove herself, honey. Show them she means business."

No, she didn't *have* to do anything. Someone else— *anyone* else—could shoot their way through the remnants of Sector Two, reminding everyone that the old days were over. And if Jade's sense of obligation to the sector that almost destroyed her ended up finishing off the job, then Scarlet would—

What? Raise hell? Scream? Kick someone's ass? It wouldn't help, because the damage would be done. Jade would already be gone in all the ways that mattered.

Scarlet locked it down. "I'm sure she can handle it. Jade can handle anything."

"Well, she sure knows how to make her point." The corner of Six's mouth quirked. "And she wasn't shy about waving Dallas in their faces. My guy said she made it clear she might be the new sector leader, but she was still an O'Kane. And they got the message—you fuck with an O'Kane, you die."

"Good," Lex breathed fervently. "She's not in this alone."

Lex believed the words, beyond any and all doubt, that much was clear. And Scarlet wanted to, more than anything. They'd all spilled a little well-deserved blood—it was part of living in the sectors, part of defending those who couldn't defend themselves.

Only this was about far more than killing someone who had it coming. It was about the constant stream of pimps, the desperate girls, all the people who wanted to get back to business as usual in Two. It was about Jade, sitting in her father's cold house, surrounded by a million memories but nothing *good*, every passing moment tearing down a future she'd fought so hard for.

It was about a name that almost no one knew, a name that a little girl had been told to hold tight, because it was all she had that was truly hers.

"I have to go," she mumbled. Lex said something be-hind her, but Scarlet kept walking. She'd walk all the way to Sector fucking Two if that was what it took.

Someone had to remind Jyoti of all the other things she had now.

25

MAD THOUGHT ARRIVING together was a mistake. Not a big one, maybe—and with Scarlet tangled up with worry and Dylan stone-faced with tension, waiting hadn't seemed like a *better* idea. But he'd been trained from a young age to appreciate the nuances of power and how you applied it. The three of them arriving at the home of their lover didn't have to be a big deal, but Scarlet was pale and nervous, and Dylan seemed carved from rock.

Nuances. Jade recognized them, too.

She watched the three of them enter her office in silence, her expression so carefully blank Mad knew she'd been waiting for them. Rumors had hit a fever pitch by dinner, washing through Sector Three and into Four, where reactions ranged from wariness to pride. Dallas O'Kane wasn't just a king anymore. Jade's unflinching declaration had made him more—the king of kings, the ruler of an ever-expanding empire.

She'd won a victory today. But until she let her mask slip, none of them would know how much it had cost her.

Scarlet broke the silence. "We heard what happened."

Jade rose and walked to the bar set under one ornate window. "I assumed word would travel. I hoped it would, in any case."

She set four glasses in a row and began to pour, and the hair at the back of Mad's neck rose at the ice in her voice. He'd seen Jade dissemble, had seen her flat-out lie, but he'd never seen her like this. Shut down, blank. Cold. "We were worried about you, Jade. You should have sent a message so we could help you deal with it."

"I had the situation under control." She picked up a glass and held it out to Scarlet. "It wasn't pleasant, but it's over."

"I don't want a drink. I want—" Scarlet took a step toward her. "Just come home, okay? Let someone else deal with this bullshit."

Jade's hand trembled. She recovered quickly and sipped the drink, but that terrifying emptiness had fractured. "I'm okay, Scarlet. But I can't just go running back to Four tonight. I have to let the message sink in for a day or two, and be here to make sure it sticks."

"No." Another step. "I mean *come home*. It's not worth it, Jade. This place isn't worth it."

Jade went stiff. "The people here are worth protecting."

"Of course they are," Mad said quickly. "No one wants to abandon Sector Two—"

"You just want *me* to abandon it." Her dark gaze swung to him, and it felt like that morning in the hallway, when she'd held a knife to his balls and cursed his doubt in her. "You don't think I can do this."

Dylan shook his head. "No one said that."

She didn't look away from Mad. Her stare burned through him, damning him for the truth that had always lurked between them. He hadn't thought her capable of running a sector without shattering under the hard choices she'd have to make, not even when he'd fought for her chance to try.

And Jade knew it. "So what are you saying?"

Scarlet moved closer—close enough to touch, though she kept her hands closed in fists at her sides. "You can do this, but so can a dozen other people. And they don't have your history with Two, you know?"

"I know." Jade's voice wavered and came back stronger. "That's why it should be me, Scarlet. There's no one left who knows this sector like I do. I'll be good at it. I just need to find my feet."

"But *why?*"

"Because I *want* to!"

Scarlet recoiled as if she'd been slapped. Jade's breath hitched.

Their pain echoed through the tense silence, highlighting the precariousness of the moment. The four of them had managed to come together, and they fit now, jagged edge against jagged edge. But it felt like one wrong move could break them apart again, and this time their pieces might not fit together the same way anymore. Or at all.

Mad took a breath, but Jade was already turning away from them. "I'm good at this, better than anyone else can be. And we're going to *war.* Everyone is making hard choices, and this is mine. I want to make it."

Scarlet cast a pleading look at Dylan, who crossed his arms over his chest. He leaned against the wall and stared down at the carpet, his face still carefully blank. "You don't see what's happening?" he asked quietly. "Scarlet had to hear that there'd been trouble from another O'Kane. Mad picked it up on the street, and *I* didn't hear about it at all."

"I would have sent a message," Jade replied just as quietly. But she was still looking away, out the window. Mad could only see the stiff set of her shoulders and the barest hint of her profile. "I just...needed to think before..." *This.*

She didn't say it. She didn't have to. She'd wanted time to think before they swept in here with their concern and their worry and their overwhelming need to shelter her against all the ways this sector could shred her heart. She'd needed time to don her emotional armor.

Jade was strong. But she'd let their doubts scrape away her certainty, because it was the one thing she'd never been trained to resist—love. They could hurt her as badly as the damn sector, and with all the best intentions.

"I understand," Mad told her softly.

"You understand?" Scarlet echoed. "Adrian, she's barricading herself in this tomb, and the only people around her are ones who think that it's normal that she came back to her asshole father's house. Like, no big deal."

"I understand that she wanted to think first." Mad approached the window and touched Jade's shoulder, urging her gently to turn. When she did, her mask was back in place—her expression placid, her eyes shuttered. He touched her cheek. "You thought, Jade. So talk to us."

She raised her eyebrows. "Will anything I say matter? Do you want me to cry because I killed someone? Because I don't have any tears in me for a woman who purposefully addicted girls to drugs that might kill them just to make them easier to sell."

"Good. She doesn't deserve your grief." Dylan slipped his hands into his pockets, the movement slow. Deliberate. "We don't want you to cry, or mourn, or lose your shit on us unless it's what you need."

"And if I needed to?" She backed away from Mad's touch. "You'd listen to me cry and mourn and lose my shit, and still support me if I stayed?"

Dylan hesitated. "What if something happened and Mad took over One? How would you feel, watching that place grind him into the dirt?"

Even the thought tightened Mad's chest with panic.

But it wasn't a hypothetical concept that he could shrug aside now. Jade was *living* it—so Mad closed his eyes and faced the question he'd never wanted to have to answer.

Would you do it?

The answer had always been *no*. When he'd taken Dallas's ink, he'd sworn his loyalty. He'd made a promise—O'Kane for life. Before now, taking up the throne in One would have meant forsaking everything. His adopted family, his pledge, the brothers and sisters who had brought him back from the brink. The lines between sectors had been rigid, and the risk of crossing them too high.

Things were different now. Chaos and ruins lay between One and Four. He'd have the same option Jade had—to use the resources of the O'Kanes as well as his own. To protect people who would otherwise suffer and die.

Would it be easy? No. It would hurt like hell sometimes. There'd be emotional bruises around every corner, things that scraped him raw and opened old wounds. It would be a sacrifice.

But he'd do it. If that was what it took to get Sector One through the war, he'd do it. And he'd pray like hell that the people who loved him would understand that protecting his heart at the cost of so many lives was just another way to die a little at a time.

Jade still hadn't answered, so Mad opened his eyes. She looked torn, unguarded and exposed, because Dylan *knew* her, knew exactly how to make her doubt.

Mad stepped between them. "That's not fair, Dylan."

"Why? Because it's not the same thing, or because it is?"

"Because it's not the whole question. What if I *did* have to take over One? Is this what you'd do to me? Make me choose?"

Dylan stared back, a fine tremble overwhelming him—the first crack in his steely, careful control. "No," he said finally. "If you got to the point where you felt like you had to *choose* between us and One, then it wouldn't matter. It would mean you'd already made your choice."

"Bullshit," he growled. "*Bullshit*, Dylan. Don't put that on her—"

Jade touched his shoulder. "Mad—"

"No," he cut her off. "No, it's not fair to say that if you won't abandon people to whatever the fuck fate, you've already chosen."

"This isn't about that," Scarlet interjected desperately. "It's not about making anyone choose—"

Mad was too angry now to stop. He was standing at the edge of the chasm that had always separated him from Dylan, the one they'd never managed to bridge without Jade and Scarlet between them. "It's about *us* choosing. Whether to stay and try to protect her from the shit that comes with this job, or leave her to drown in it."

Scarlet squeezed her eyes shut. "No one's *leaving*."

Jade made a soft, pained noise, almost a laugh. "No, I think everyone should leave. Before words are said that can't be taken back."

Dylan turned to her, stricken. "Jade."

She crossed to the door and dragged it open. "You're all fighting with each other, and I can't watch that. I can't be the one who *caused* it."

Mad clenched his fists and forced his temper under control. "I'm sorry, Jade. I just wanted—"

"I know," she interrupted. "You wanted to help. You always want to help. So listen to what I'm asking you to do."

Leave.

This was a challenge he couldn't win. He could stay and fight for her and prove her right, or he could walk away and maybe lose her.

Maybe lose *all* of them.

Scarlet was the first to yield. But she paused in the doorway, her fingers brushing the back of Jade's hand. "You know where I am."

"I do," Jade replied. Soft. *Sad*.

Mad's chest hurt.

Dylan followed silently, his gaze locked on Jade until he cleared the doorway and disappeared into the dark hall.

"Jade—"

She silenced him with a shake of her head. "Take care of them, Mad. Especially Dylan. He won't take care of himself. He needs you."

It sounded so final. Like she was writing herself out of their lives, and he couldn't figure out *why*. There was something growing beneath that polite, perfect mask— some pain they'd missed, some secret she hadn't told them because she was afraid to let them see her weakness.

She wouldn't share it now. She was locked down and resolute, and Mad knew the value of strategic retreat. He nodded and walked past her, out into the ornately decorated hallway, his boots digging into the pristine, priceless rugs.

He'd be back. And if he couldn't coax the truth out of her with kindness, he'd piss her the fuck off. He'd probably end up stabbed with one of his own knives, but he could take it.

He could take anything but losing them.

Scarlet's heart howled, a wounded animal caged in her chest. Her pulse screamed louder with each passing thump, but she made it out of the house, all the way down to the circular driveway.

She stopped beside the huge, ornate fountain. No water flowed from the jugs held aloft by the smiling cherubs, and only a tiny bit remained in the shallow pool at the bottom. Her knees locked at the image, the *imagery*. All of Two was just like that goddamn fountain—pretty and dead.

And they were leaving Jade here.

Her fury boiled over, and she whirled on Dylan. "Why? Why did you do that?"

His jaw clenched, and he shoved one hand through his hair. "I didn't do anything, Scarlet."

"That's *crap*. You poked him on purpose. You did it on purpose, Dylan!"

"He wasn't poking me." Mad stopped across from them and folded his arms across his chest. "He was using me as a weapon. Very effectively."

The nerve of him, acting as though he'd been blameless in the whole stupid mess. "Don't get me started on you," she snapped. "You're just as bad, maybe worse."

"Me? At least I was trying to listen to her!"

"No, you weren't. You two started swinging your dicks, and you made it all about you." The look on his face would have been comical if it didn't hurt so very, very much. "She isn't you, Adrian. This place isn't her legacy or her birthright. She doesn't have to be here because the people think she's some sort of god, walking among them."

"Maybe not, but she feels like she needs to be here." Mad's scowl softened as he stepped closer to her. "Can't you see it, Scarlet? If we make her fight us *and* the sector, we'll just break her that much faster."

She backed away. She had to. "This wasn't supposed to be about fighting at all, remember? We were just going to tell her that we're here for her. Ask her not to shut us out."

"It's too late for that," Dylan muttered.

"Well, *now* it is."

"It already was," he argued. "Her putting that pimp down—you really think that's the only thing she neglected to tell us, Scarlet? The only piece of pain she hid away where you couldn't see it, much less touch it?"

"No." Unshed tears burned her throat, and she looked away from him, only to have her gaze snag on Mad instead—on his beautiful face, on all the emotion he could never bring himself to reveal. "We all hide things. Don't we, Mad?"

"It's the sectors," he replied. So gentle. So sad. "None of us would still be here if we hadn't learned to laugh so no one could see us cry."

Hiding was survival, but only with enemies and strangers, not friends. Not lovers. "What a crock of shit."

"Not to Jade." He jerked his thumb over his shoulder. "You know what she's probably up there thinking? That she was right not to show any weakness because we *still* stared at her like she had three fucking heads when she said she wanted to stay. We just taught her to hide more."

"That's not fair, Mad." Scarlet's shock had been simply that—shock, not horror or revulsion or any of the darker emotions he seemed to want to see. And who wouldn't be surprised, when Jade had spent weeks arguing that this was her duty, that someone had to do it, that she was best suited for the job—

She'd never said she wanted it. Not once. But maybe that was Mad's real point—that just because Jade felt something didn't mean she would share it, and Scarlet was an oblivious asshole for thinking otherwise.

Her vision blurred, and she shut her eyes tight.

Mad sighed. "Scarlet—"

"Stop." Dylan's voice carried a stony edge of something beyond anger. "This isn't her fault. It's ours."

"Yes," Mad agreed. "We've been having this fight forever without saying a damn word. So c'mon, Dylan. Just fucking say it."

"Is that really what you want? Be sure."

"Hiding it hasn't worked out so well for us, has it?"

The sick sensation in Scarlet's gut twisted tighter, and what came out of Dylan's mouth next made her want to cover her ears, run away, anything but listen.

"All right," he said. "You're a liar. You spend your time bemoaning the whole prince thing, but it's all you want. More than me, more than Scarlet or Jade—more than *life*, man. You want to be Saint Adrian, savior of the weak and the broken."

"I want to *help* people—"

"No, you need it. And it took me forever to figure out why, but it's just that, isn't it? Broken. If we're not smashed into tiny bits, you can't save us." He looked at Scarlet, so many emotions swirling in his eyes that she couldn't decipher them all—regret, grief, even envy. "That's why he wants Jade here. Because you don't need him to fix you—"

Mad snarled. "Stop it, Dylan. You leave her the fuck alone."

He acted as though he hadn't heard the words. "—but you need *her*. And if she stays here, if this place shatters her, then she'll need *him*. The transitive property of Adrian Maddox."

The sick feeling spread, until Scarlet had to lean against the fountain to stay on her feet. "So I don't matter?"

"I don't know," Dylan answered helplessly. "Fuck, maybe you matter the most, because you're the one he can only have if the rest of us are in pieces."

Mad's hands balled into fists. For a moment, she thought he'd swing, land a punch to Dylan's jaw and lay him out. But he only stood there, his chest heaving, his eyes wild. "So that's what you see in me. A fucking monster."

"No, not a monster. That'd be easy," Dylan rasped. "You're a martyr. The O'Kanes like to talk about how I'm a suicidal wreck, but I've got nothing on you. You're just waiting to die. And maybe you think that's all you're good for, but you're wrong."

"Oh yeah? Well, if you think I'd break Jade just to—" His voice cracked, came back rougher. "If you think any of that shit, maybe the two of you should go back and save her from me."

He turned and stalked off into the darkness—towards Sector One, thankfully, because Scarlet was planning on walking, too, and heading in the same direction as Mad would completely defeat the point of being alone.

The car keys jingled in Dylan's shaking hand. "Get in the car, Scarlet."

"No." It was the last thing in the world she'd do. She'd drown herself in the two inches of scummy water left in that ridiculous fountain before she got in a car with him. "I don't want to look at you right now."

"Scarlet—"

"Fuck off, Dylan." She walked faster, though she forced herself not to run. It hurt, physically *hurt*, but so did everything.

It was one thing to be reminded that she wasn't important to Dylan. That had been part of their unspoken deal from the start—that they were along for the ride, that they'd tolerate one another as long as Mad and Jade were happy. That they'd put up with each other because it was worth it.

But hearing that Mad saw her the same way? Even if it wasn't true—*he didn't deny it, did he?* a tiny, traitorous voice whispered—it still tore through to the very heart of her, to that place where she knew she was nothing more than an interloper. Where she wasn't good enough for any of them, anyway.

She dragged in a ragged breath, the cold night air slicing through her lungs, and made herself silently repeat the words—*I'm not good enough for them.* Over and over, until they began to sink in.

Truth was truth, and denying it was dangerous. It made room for all sorts of hopes and dreams, the kind that existed only to be dashed against dirty brick walls and cracked asphalt. It made room for fairy tales.

Street rats could fall in love with princes, with queens and heroes, even in the sectors. But happily-ever-afters were indulgences they could never afford.

26

NONE OF HER rituals were working.

Jade bathed. She lined up her oils and lotions and balms—not the mismatched jars she'd left in her rooms in Four, the ones filled with Tatiana's handmade products, but pristine glass containers imported at dizzying expense from somewhere far to the south. She worked the lush assortment of oils and butters into her skin until the scent of vanilla and cinnamon pervaded the room.

When that didn't help, she turned to her hair. A hundred strokes and then two hundred, waiting for the peace and serenity, the slow satisfaction of knowing this moment was *hers*, that whatever else happened was fleeting because no one could touch her heart.

Except Scarlet. Scarlet had become part of the rituals. Her amusement and fondness as she watched Jade return from her bath and settle in front of her vanity. The tenderness in her touch as she took the brush from Jade and started the slow, careful strokes that could send Jade floating on sensual pleasure.

The laughing mischief when Scarlet plucked the lotion from Jade's hands and promised to help, and the shameless desire when her hands smoothed everywhere, until Jade couldn't think, couldn't care, could only sigh and moan and *feel*.

She wanted Scarlet. She wanted to crawl to her, cry on her, wrap herself up in the other woman until Mad and Dylan joined them and the rest of the world vanished. Because it would have to vanish. They'd have to freeze time so Jade could be the things they'd all fallen in love with. Soft and vulnerable and uncertain.

She'd sold them a fantasy, and reality was ruining it.

Power in a woman repels people. You must always possess it, Jade, but never show it.

It had been so long since Cerys's voice had haunted her thoughts. Maybe Scarlet was right and Two would chip away at her like this, with all its ghosts coming back to haunt her.

Or maybe she simply couldn't stop thinking about the woman who had drugged *her*.

The girls Valerie had doped up were in Sector One now, resting under Avery's watchful gaze. The healers were still trying to figure out what they'd been given and how dangerous detox would be. Jade knew the girls had resources she'd lacked—Ryder was an ally now, and if she reached out to him, he'd help—but that didn't diminish the horror of what they were facing.

And there were other concerns, more potential nightmares Jade would have to find a way to help them get through, because some of the girls had shown signs of rough handling. None were in any state to tell Jade what had happened to them, if they could even remember. A well-meaning nurse had assured Jade that perhaps they wouldn't, as if it was for the best.

As if violation was easier to come to terms with when

you had to fill in the grisly details with the worst your imagination could conjure.

Bend, Jade. Always bend. I don't care how petty the request, you yield with a smile. Your job is to be utterly, consistently pleasing. An ill-timed frown could cost you everything.

Jade didn't need imagination. The drugs had fogged her senses and blurred the world, but the cruelty she'd endured always remained in sharp focus. Gareth Woods had loathed her to the very depths of his being. Loathed her because one day he'd made a petty request, and she'd frowned.

It wasn't as if it had been the first disgusting demand. He asked her to do petty things all the time. Sometimes they were meant to humiliate her, sometimes to put other women in their place. He set her against the defensive, frigid wives of his business partners, against tired-eyed whores hired for a fraction of what she cost and considered disposable by the men who would later deny having indulged themselves in such sinful pursuits.

Usually, she would smile and find a way to divert him—repressed men were simple to manipulate. So many desires left unexplored, so much thwarted frustration. But this time, it had been a maid in Woods's sights, a terrified girl whose hands trembled as she poured drinks for him and his inner circle. His booming request to Jade that she *settle the girl's nerves* before she wasted the precious liquor had been so coyly suggestive that the other men had leaned forward with glazed, eager eyes.

And Jade had frowned.

One slip, but it was enough. He'd glimpsed her power. It didn't matter how quickly she adjusted, how smoothly she distracted the other men. This time, he saw the diversion because he knew she wanted him diverted. No doubt he thought back to every time she'd deftly convinced him to alter his desires, how cleverly she'd manipulated him.

She destroyed his ego with that frown. And so he'd set

about reclaiming it.

Maybe it should have spoiled sex for her. She'd certainly met people who felt that way, people who felt *she* should feel that way. But his methodical attempts to humiliate and break her had never been about anything other than power and injured pride. Six was the one who'd given her the words for it, one night over too much liquor. *"I always figured people'd fuck with my body, and whatever. I couldn't stop that. But when the bastard started fucking with my head..."*

The only thing Jade had ever considered inviolate was her mind. But the drugs had altered it, twisted it, confused the way it processed the input from her body, the way it felt pleasure and suffered pain. Even worse, the drugs stripped away her ability to deflect, to dissemble, to protect the parts of her she meant to keep private.

Nobody wants the messy reality of a woman, Jade. They'll love you when you're perfect, but your father taught you life's most important lesson, didn't he? They only *love us when we're perfect.*

Jade tossed aside her brush and dragged her fingers through her hair, as if she could pull the strands hard enough to pull Cerys's voice out of her mind. But she was stuck there now, taunting and victorious.

Cerys never would have shot Valerie in public. It would have been too gauche a display for such a refined woman. Too brutal. Too *masculine*. And it would have damaged her image by letting people know she viewed the woman as a threat. Cerys would have simply arranged for Valerie to disappear.

Just like Cerys had disappeared. Probably with advance notice of the coming strikes and enough money to start herself up somewhere far from the sectors, comfortable and safe and oblivious to all the people she'd put in harm's way.

Jade would never be Cerys. Sometimes she saw that fear in Mad's eyes—the fear that he would become all the things he'd hated in his grandfather—but she didn't share it. Because there was a line she would never cross, a line Cerys had so obliterated that Jade silently promised to spend her whole life teaching the refugees from the houses that it existed at all.

You didn't solidify your own power by selling girls who trusted you to men who would break them.

I let your mother influence your training for too long. I'm sure she loved you as best she could, but you see where she ended up. She wanted more for you. I'll make you a star, if you let me. Alexa is stuck playing queen in some backward slum. You'll be an empress in Eden itself.

Jade's hands trembled. She slipped from bed and found her robe, wrapping it tight around her body. But that wasn't enough to fight the chill, not when she was used to the warmth of three more people curled around her. Loneliness had never troubled her before, but it hollowed her out now, as if her heart was small and weak and every beat echoed in the spaces they'd left behind.

She should have simply told them. She'd been preparing the words all day, laying out her reasons and her arguments, readying herself to send a message and meet their arrival. But then they'd shown up, all three of them, worried and frantic, ready to stage an intervention, so *horrified* because she was their sweet, soft, fragile lover, and she'd been forced to kill.

Even when Mad stepped up to defend her, it wasn't with confidence in her skills and her choice. It was a plea to the others to save her before she *drowned.*

They didn't really know her. And she couldn't blame them—she'd barely known herself, either. For so long, she'd imagined that Jyoti was the confused, sheltered part of her, the part that struggled with her desires, with the darkness of her life and the way she'd lived it to survive.

But that was Jade. Fractured, wounded Jade. Not the armor that protected her heart after all, but the chains she'd been wrapped up in for so many years.

Jyoti was the part of her that fought. The part that was strong enough to stare Valerie in the eye and decide that sparing her life meant too much pain for others, the part that was unflinching enough to pull the trigger and not look back. Because the lives that mattered were ahead of her, all the girls who still had a chance because Jade would shoot and stab and burn her way across this sector until every vulnerable person in it was safe.

Jyoti was the part of her that wanted to run Sector Two. Not needed to or felt obligated to. *Wanted* to. Because she was smart, and she was strong, and she trusted herself to use power for the right damn reasons.

Jyoti was the part of her that loved fiercely. Scarlet first, because she'd sung her back to life. And then Dylan, because he'd walked away from the darkness to be a hero and was the only one who didn't see it. And Mad. *Adrian.* Trapped, just like her, between two lives and two names, torn between the need to fight and the terror of becoming the evil people had to fight.

She loved them all, because they'd let her *see* them.

And when they'd finally seen her? They'd come running in terror, sure she was falling apart. When she'd told them she wanted this, they recoiled. They doubted. They discussed how to save her, because that was what she'd shown them. A woman who needed saving.

Power in a woman repels people. You must always possess it, Jade, but never show it.

Never show it.

Never.

The words pounded in her skull, mocking and cruel, until she drowned them with enough whiskey to let her close her eyes.

With her eyes closed, she could pretend she wasn't crying.

The world was tumbling end over end, spinning so fast that Dylan couldn't keep up. Only the door in front of him was solid, unmoving, even as he beat his fist against it. *Open it. Please.*

Scarlet obeyed, as if she'd heard his silent entreaty— or wanted the blasted noise to stop. She stood there, her hair a perfectly blonde cloud now, all traces of blue and pink and black gone from the silky, luminous strands, and stared at him.

He willed her to smile. Instead, she spoke. "I should have known you'd find your way here."

Dylan leaned against the doorframe, tried to blink through the haze, and grinned. "Because you're that irre-sistible?"

"Because I'm all you have left." The words were flat, delivered more like a description of the weather than a heartbreaking condemnation of them both. "You're high."

She didn't pull punches, God love her. *He* loved her, and he still wasn't even sure why. But it knifed through him as he followed her into her sad, empty little room, the sentiment growing stronger with every step.

She was beautiful, sure. Smart and tough. All traits he admired, but it didn't come close to explaining the panic that seized him when he thought of her silence, of her turning away and slamming the door in his face instead of letting him in.

He couldn't say it. Not until he figured out why, so that it could be a statement of fact, a declaration, instead of a desperate, clumsy apology offered in his defense. "I'm high. Is that a problem?"

"Not for me. I'm not your mama." She dropped to the low couch against the wall. Rather than half-empty liquor bottles, it was covered with pens and scattered sheets of paper, some half-filled, others crumpled and tossed aside.

Letters. It was quaint and a little wasteful. Paper wasn't easy to come by, even for an O'Kane, and a digital message could be written and sent in the blink of an eye.

But there were things on those pages that wouldn't translate into email. The trembling lines, words scratched out when her mind had worked too quickly for her fingers to keep up. The blurred spots where tears had fallen onto the paper and smeared the ink.

He really was a bastard, wasn't he?

His throat ached. "I came to—"

"Shut up," she cut in, then tilted her head to the couch beside her as she gathered up the papers. "Sit down."

The cushions smelled like Jade, along with a softer floral scent that took him too long to place. It made him think of floating, of warm water and cool breezes, and when he closed his eyes, all he saw was a wash of bright pink edged with yellow.

Hibiscus. He'd only ever seen them in hothouses, and he opened his eyes to ask Scarlet where she'd found the fragrance, only the words dissipated like smoke, because she was *watching* him, sad and hungry all at once.

"I'm so angry with you," she whispered.

I know. He almost said it, along with *I'm sorry* and *I swear I'll do better*. But what came out was, "I didn't mean it, Scarlet."

"Yes, you did. Every single word."

He had and he hadn't, but it was all so mixed up that he could barely wrap his own head around it, much less explain himself. So he opened his mouth and let the confession come, without thought. "I wanted to hurt him."

She waited, watching, her eyes the clearest, deepest blue he'd ever seen. Fathomless, like the sky or the sea, and full of things he longed to discover.

Dylan took a deep breath. "He hurt me. When I mentioned him taking over Sector One, he didn't say—he was supposed to say—"

"That he wouldn't," she finished, a tear slipping down her cheek. "I know."

Mad was supposed to choose them. Dylan had always known that he wouldn't be enough to sway him from his grand, divine destiny, but being with Scarlet and Jade meant things were different. They were enough, they were *everything*—

Scarlet moved closer and touched his face, her hand cool against his flushed cheek. "Can I ask you something?"

He'd never believed in God, but that one touch—welcoming, calming—was changing his mind. "Anything."

Closer still, until he could feel the warmth of her breath on his skin, see the tiny flecks of gold that rimmed her pupils. "You could have made them stay. You know you could have." Her breath hitched. "So why didn't you?"

Her pain was his, magnified. Reflected. "Because...you can't, okay? You can't make someone do something like that, not if they don't want to. It isn't worth shit if you do."

She leaned her head on his shoulder. "That makes sense."

It was a deceptively casual gesture, one that made something in his chest lurch into place. He hadn't come to her room expecting forgiveness, but here she was, offering it to him just the same, and without any of the groveling apologies she deserved.

That was Scarlet—open, not only about sex or love but the darker things, too. The rest of them would hide their faces, let their doubts beat them down, but Scarlet accepted people as they were...and moved on.

He wanted to comfort her, to be the man who deserved this generosity. "It'll be okay. It *will*," he insisted when she made a soft noise of denial. "I'll sober up, and we'll go see them both in the morning. I'll make it right."

"I hope so." Her rich voice sounded thin, lost. "They're...the very best parts of everything I ever wanted to be."

It hit him like a sucker punch to the chest, the perfect description of the Mad- and Jade-shaped holes in his heart. "Yeah. Sounds about right."

Scarlet stroked his arm. "How's the hospital coming

along?"

There it was again, that stab of panic, only this time it was entirely practical. "Too slowly. It needs to be done before things get really bad."

"If you need help—"

"I know." He lifted her hand and kissed her knuckles. "You're here."

"I'm here."

 dallas

T HERE'D BEEN A time when Dallas refused to roll out of bed before noon.

Those had been the good times. After they'd gotten established enough that the sector ran itself on an average day, but before they got so much power that everyone in the godforsaken world was banging on his door. The days of hard fighting, lazy drinking, and fucking that went on until dawn.

Preparation for war was fucking with his sleep. *And* his fucking.

But some things were worth dragging his sorry ass out into the early morning sunlight. The hospital qualified, especially now that they'd shifted from clearing out the tunnels to actual construction.

Not that you could tell from above ground. Some of the ways they'd gotten supplies in without being obvious were ingenious, and Six was having the time of her life pointing them out as they made their way from the Sector Three headquarters with Bren a step behind them, watching their backs. "We're staging supplies in the warehouses to the south, since most of it's coming from Five. And when they drag rubble out, the shit they can't use goes in the warehouses to the north and east. All through the tunnels, all invisible."

"Clever," he murmured, and that was all it took to win him a grin. Six had come a long way from the girl who'd stumbled into his life in chains, which meant Lex was right. As usual.

Someday soon, he'd have to hand Three over to the woman who'd fought and bled for it, who'd earned the right to rebuild it. Six would rule the shit out of this sector.

Bren would go with her, consort to his queen. Always O'Kanes, but more than that, because together Bren and Six could be a force of nature and powerful allies. And Dallas would learn to let them go, just a little. He'd have to let them see how damn high they could fly.

They turned a corner, and Dallas spotted a man down the street leaning against the building, one boot propped up on the brick and a hand in his jacket pocket. Everything about his posture screamed *casual*, but Dallas's instincts screamed louder. The hair on the back of his neck stood up, and his spine prickled with the sick sense that something was off, wrong—

By the time the man pulled the gun from his jacket, Six was already shouting. A heavy pressure hit Dallas square in the back—Bren, slamming him down to the ground, covering Dallas's head with the large bulk of his upper body.

Gunfire cracked in the alley. Bren's body jerked on top of his, but when Dallas tried to lift his head, Bren shoved him back down.

Two more shots went off close together, and then after a moment, a third. Dallas heaved his body, driving Bren

up in time to watch Six kick the gun away from their attacker's limp fingers. Blood bloomed on his chest and
against the wall in a messy trail where he'd slumped to
the sidewalk, and part of his head was gone.

Bren climbed to his feet, his pistol in his hand. "Are
there more?"

"If there are, they chickened the fuck out." Six
frowned at Bren. "You're bleeding."

He glanced down at his arm, assessing the damage
with a shake of his head. "It's nothing. Are you all right?"

"Fine. Dallas?"

"Fine," Dallas grumbled, pushing himself to his feet
and dusting gravel and debris from his body. His ego was
a little tattered around the edges at ending up facedown
in the dirt, but Lex had already laughingly warned him to
get used to the price of power.

Until this war ended, he was too important to die.
Which meant being too important to have any goddamn
fun.

With Bren standing guard, Six holstered her gun and
crouched in front of the body. She studied what was left of
his face and frowned. "I don't recognize him."

"Yeah?" Bren nudged the corpse's wrist with his boot,
pushing the blood-spattered jacket sleeve up far enough to
reveal a city bar code. "How about that?"

Wordlessly, Six reached into her pocket and pulled out
a handheld tablet. It was a big improvement over the old-
school bar-code scanners, another upgrade Noah had
brought to their lives. She snapped a picture and waited
for the beep before pursing her lips. "Classified."

Of course it was. Dallas traded a look with Bren, who
nodded. "We don't have our encryption in place yet, but I'll
send messengers to the other sector leaders. Just in case."

"Just in case," Dallas agreed, turning back toward the
car. He wasn't going to make Bren say it. If there were
assassins crawling out of the city, the hospital could wait.
Dallas needed to park his ass somewhere Eden couldn't

get to him.
Someone had to lead this damn rebellion.

ryder

"**Y**ou really think that crazy bastard can pull this off?" Ryder tossed his napkin onto his cleared plate and eyed his mentor. Jim Jernigan had been more than a boss to him over the years. More like an uncle—and if you listened to the stories his mother liked to tell about the early years, that was nearer to the truth than anything else. Jim and his father had been as close as brothers, but with the kind of bond that was stronger because it was choice, not blood.

Sometimes Ryder thought that must be why Jim admired Dallas O'Kane so much—because he hadn't stopped with one best friend. He'd made a whole fucking family for himself.

"I don't know," he answered finally. "It's a little late to worry about it, though, isn't it? All the pieces are already in play."

"You know better than that. We can stop worrying

when we're dead." Jim finished his drink and eyed Ryder over the rim of the glass. "Will the hospital be ready?"

"Stocked and supplied. The rest is up to Dr. Jordan."

His distaste must have shown on his face, because Jim laughed. "Don't count the good doctor out, Ryder. Once upon a time, he was Eden's brightest young star."

"A shooting star, maybe." He'd sure as hell burned out like one. "I don't trust people who can't handle their business without crawling into a bottle of *anything*."

Jim rose to his feet. "That doesn't leave very many people."

A gentle admonition, but Ryder took it to heart. He had to get better about that if he was going to be working with the other sector leaders. Not everyone had spent years infiltrating Mac Fleming's regime, watching him do things with drugs that were barely human, much less humane. "Sorry, you're right."

"So are you." Jim clapped a hand to his shoulder. "That's why you're the only one I could trust with Five. You'll make the right calls."

"I'll try—" The door slammed open, cutting him off with a tremendous bang as the solid wood rebounded against the wall.

"Get down!" Even as Jim shouted the words, he was shoving Ryder out of his chair. It tipped over and crashed to the floor. His head hit the leg of the conference table, and he saw stars—bright, blinding, *loud* as fuck—

Not stars—gunshots. Ryder rolled off the floor, his gun already in his hand, training taking over for his bewildered, aching head. He fired—once, twice, three times, and when the assailant fell to the plush carpet, another bullet for good measure.

"Ry—" His name disappeared in a wheezing cough.

He whirled around. Jim had fallen against the window, the blinds buckling under his weight. Four bright blotches of red had seeped through his white dress shirt, soaking the starched fabric as they slowly spread.

"*No.*" Ryder lunged for him, caught him just as he collapsed, but he knew it was too late. There was no life left in the sightless pair of pale blue eyes that stared up at him.

Jim was gone.

gideon

MARICELA FRETTED WHEN Gideon didn't finish his breakfast. It was the only reason he was still pushing the eggs around his plate, pretending he had any intention of eating them.

Mad had arrived in the sector by foot after nightfall, crashed in the Riders barracks, and torn out before dawn on a borrowed motorcycle. The fact that he'd avoided the house and his comfortable bedroom in favor of sleeping in Deacon's empty bunk was telling. Undoubtedly, it had everything to do with the rumors winding their way through the sectors—rumors that Jade had taken her first bloody stand as a sector leader.

Deacon had been displeased. Not that he'd said so in as many words, of course. To the Riders, Jade was already an extension of the Rios family. They wanted to protect her the same way they sheltered Isabela and Maricela, the way they fought to shelter Gideon. To them it was that

simple—they'd accepted damnation and an afterlife de-
void of forgiveness, so what was one more drop of blood on
their hands?

The fact that Jade didn't see it that way gave Gideon
hope. Hope that he now had another ally who saw leadership as a responsibility, who wouldn't ask for what she
wasn't willing to give.

It would take time for Mad to see it that way, but Gideon had to believe he would. Mad deserved the peace that
came with love, perhaps more than anyone Gideon had
ever met.

As for what *he* deserved... Gideon would push the
damn scrambled eggs around his plate all day if it helped
him avoid thinking about it.

The click of his office door opening stole even that distraction. Sighing, he let the fork clatter to the plate and
rose as one of the workers assigned to the kitchens stepped
in. "Do me a favor, Donny, and scrape the plate before it
gets back to the kitchen. Maricela will scold—"

It was as far as he got. When he glanced up, Donny
was staring at him, his blue eyes bloodshot and red, his
expression tortured. Gideon's vision narrowed to the gun
in his shaking hand, shock slowing everything to a crawl.
He *saw* Donny's finger squeeze the trigger, saw his hand
jerk.

The crack of the shot snapped the world back into focus as pain exploded through his abdomen. Hot, grinding,
nauseating pain so intense he fell back into his chair.

Or maybe that was the surprise. Of all the ways he'd
imagined leaving this world—and he'd imagined so many,
too many, sometimes with an air of anticipation that
would have scared the shit out of anyone who knew him—
this had not been among them.

Shot by a follower racked with silent sobs so intense,
he couldn't even take him out cleanly.

Tears streaked Donny's cheeks, and words tumbled
from his lips, words Gideon had to reach for through the

pain. "—sorry, I'm sorry, I didn't want to, I didn't, but—"

"But someone in Eden threatened your family," Gideon guessed. It wasn't a very clever guess—the man was clearly here under duress—but Gideon was who he was. He uttered mundane logic, and true believers heard the prescience of a god among men.

Donny paled even more, his fingers twitching as if he wanted to cross himself. "They have my eldest son," he whispered. Begging for forgiveness, with his eyes and voice and the tears that made his words waver. "I thought, the wine—it would have been painless. I just wanted it to be over. But I moved too fast, and they punished *him* for it. I have to get it right this time."

Moved too fast. Those words were important, more important than his lingering anger over Mad's brush with death, more important than his own pulsing agony and the blood drenching his fingers. They implied a timeline. Coordination.

Sector leaders. Kill enough of them all at once, and chaos would sweep through their territories. Any glint of rebellion would die. The O'Kanes might hold it together if Lex or enough of Dallas's inner circle survived, but Jim had held absolute power in his own two hands, Five would fracture into factions without Ryder, and Isabela and Maricela...

They'd be fighting to quell a holy war, maybe even fighting to *start* one. Unless Mad survived to help them, but Mad would be...

"Gideon, what's—" Maricela hovered in the doorway, a look of disbelief frozen on her features. "Donny?"

Donny began to turn toward her, and panic lent Gideon the strength to stand. "Maricela, get out."

The disbelief vanished, overtaken by horror. "*Santa Adriana*—Gideon!" She rushed into the room, straight to his side, and he bit back a snarl of frustration as she pressed a trembling hand to his blood-soaked shirt. "What happened?"

"Maricela, *please*." Donny's hand trembled as fresh panic filled his eyes. He was strung so tightly, his finger still on the trigger, but Maricela ignored the danger. No, not ignored—she was *oblivious*, because they'd sheltered and cosseted her so completely, she simply couldn't fathom a world in which her life hung by a thread as fragile as a desperate man's terror.

"You." Trembling with anger, she spun to face that desperate man. "How could you do this? *How?*" She rounded the desk, each step taking her closer to death.

Donny would pull the trigger. As soon as he realized he was already damned for Gideon's murder, he'd salvage the only thing he could—his son's life in exchange for two deaths. Gideon tried to lunge after Maricela, to pull her back, but his knees buckled after two steps. He crashed to the floor as fresh pain spasmed through him, graying the edges of his vision.

Maricela reached for the gun, still bold, still oblivious—until Donny slapped her away, his cry of alarm nearly drowned out by the blood roaring in Gideon's ears. He caught one glimpse of Maricela's face—shocked, a splash of angry red spreading over her ashen cheek.

Then she screamed, not in terror but in sheer, righteous *fury*, and threw herself at Donny.

Gideon must have had one foot already in the grave, because he heard a whole damn symphony in that scream. An opera, an *awakening*. Shattered innocence and thundering rage and grief clawing at her heart, and Gideon prayed to every martyred relative in his family tree and the God his grandfather had profaned, prayed that Maricela would survive and Isabela would protect her, and Mad—

Moved too fast.

There was no mercy in the blackness swimming up to claim him. Because someone was killing sector leaders.

And Mad would be with Jade.

27

THERE WERE ADVANTAGES to being a Rios.
There were also disadvantages.

Currently, the largest disadvantage was standing between Mad and the door to the gardens. If life had turned out a little differently, Mad might have held the place Deacon did. Right-hand to Gideon. Leader of the Riders. Steeped in the same amount of blood, etching reminders on his skin, and facing a bleak, lonely future.

Well, that last part might not turn out so differently if Deacon didn't *move*. But he stood there, solid and implacable, every second ticking him closer to outright disobedience.

No, that wasn't fair. Deacon wouldn't consider a refusal to move disobedience if he truly believed that keeping Mad from Jade meant protecting Mad from himself. Mad simply refused to agree with him. "I have to see her, Deacon."

Deacon folded his arms over his chest.

"I need to apologize. For *both* our sakes."

"She doesn't want to see anyone. Sir."

Mad couldn't stop the wry smile from curving his lips. "Which one of us are you protecting?"

Deacon answered with a rueful grin of his own. "What, it can't be both of you?"

Of course it would be. Because who could watch Jade, witness her passion for protecting this sector, and not feel the pull of loyalty? Jade was everything Sector One revered—a warrior for good.

"I won't push her," Mad promised quietly. "But I hurt her, Deacon. She needs to know I believe in her, and I need to tell her."

For a few agonizing heartbeats, Mad didn't know if the man would relent. But he finally did, with a terse nod and a jerk of his head. "I'll be inside."

Mad waited for him to turn the corner before stepping through the metal gate.

The gardens were extensive and pristinely maintained. Hedges were trimmed to perfection, flowerbeds sat turned and tended, and carefully raked gravel paths wound between shaded arbors climbing with vines, stands of trees, and a fountain that was the twin of the one in the front yard.

The only thing missing was the workers. Dozens should have cluttered the paths, busy with the spring chores of weeding and planting. Jade's desire for solitude must have been absolute, which only wrenched the guilt in Mad's gut into tighter knots as he followed the path toward the edge of the woods.

Jade was on her knees next to a raised bed, dressed simply in a homespun skirt and cotton blouse. Her hair was piled on top of her head in a sloppy ponytail, and dirt smudged her cheek and forehead. A pair of discarded work gloves lay at her side as she sank her fingers into the earth, digging a row of neatly spaced holes for the seed-lings in the tray next to her.

Mad had rarely seen her in anything but elegant silks—unless she was stripped naked. And he'd rarely seen her without her hair perfectly arranged—unless she was fresh from his shower or panting for breath after a screaming orgasm. This woman with dirt under her nails and a total disregard for perfect presentation could have been a stranger.

Then she looked up at him, her brown eyes seething with hurt and challenge and the tiniest hint of mocking acknowledgment, as if she knew precisely what he was thinking.

Jyoti.

She would expect an apology. He had come prepared to give her one. But that *look* stirred a deeper memory of the first time he'd laid eyes on her. It seemed like a million years ago, that meeting in Cerys's house where Dallas had ended up with control of Sector Three—and Lex in his bed.

Cerys had sent Jade to them. To him and Bren, more accurately, no doubt with orders to coax O'Kane secrets from brutish bodyguards who would get stupid the instant a pretty lady touched their dicks. And Mad had been so noble, so full of righteous anger, so ready to see her as a helpless victim.

She'd seen through him from the first. Her lips had quirked, her eyes had filled with that wry, mocking chal-lenge. And before he had a chance to be honorable, she'd dismissed him and dragged Bren off for who knew what sort of kinky fuckery without a backwards glance.

He *had* to stop underestimating her.

She tilted her head. "Are you just going to stare at me?"

"I was thinking about the first time we met. At Cerys's estate."

"Oh." Jade sat back and reached for a towel. "That seems like a different world, doesn't it?"

It did, more than a little. There was nostalgia there, a yearning for a time when life as an O'Kane had been simple. When he'd been shattered beyond hope, because there was an easy comfort in knowing you had no chance for something better. It seemed like the more he fit pieces back into his heart, the shakier the ground beneath him became.

But it was worth the fear. *They* were worth the fear. "A different world, but I keep doing the same stupid shit. I looked at you and saw a victim. I'm sorry."

Jade took her time wiping her hands on the towel before slowly, reluctantly nodding. "You looked at a woman in Sector Two and saw a victim. You were wrong, because it was me. But if it had been someone else—almost anyone else—you might have been right."

It was a hand extended across the chasm between them, and more absolution than he'd expected. "Jade—"

The wind shifted, and a thrill of warning shot up his spine. The hair at the back of his neck stood up, and he was already moving when his brain caught up to tiny clues his instincts had neatly put together. Eerie silence from a forest that had been alive with birdsong while he argued with Deacon. The soft crack of a branch just inside the tree line.

The *feeling* of being watched.

Sunlight glinted off metal as something sailed out of the trees and bounced toward them. Gut-level recognition had him lunging for Jade as a *pop* sounded, followed by a gentle hiss. Colored smoke billowed from the sphere, and the sudden sickening sweetness on his tongue answered the question Mad's mind still hadn't had time to ask.

Not just smoke, but some sort of gas. Tear gas, nerve gas—he didn't know, *couldn't* know. Not until it had them choking or puking up their guts or seizing on the ground.

Jade opened her mouth. Mad covered it with his hand and shook his head. Her thin cotton blouse was feeble protection, but he pulled it up over her mouth and nose and turned her toward the house, keeping his body between her and the woods. "As fast as you can," he told her, hustling her forward. "Try not to breathe it in."

She nodded her understanding and quickened her pace as much as she could in the rising haze. The wind was at their backs, pushing the smoke after them like a pack of hunting hounds. Mad pressed closer to her, trying to breathe as shallowly as possible, all of his focus on outrunning the cloud of smoke.

Jade stumbled, and Mad jerked her off her feet and hauled her clear of the encroaching smoke. The house loomed ahead of them, twenty feet, fifteen... The back door flew open, and he'd never been so fucking glad to see Deacon in his life. He staggered the last ten feet and shoved Jade at him. "Get her to safety. I'll deal with this."

"*No!*" Jade's hand shot out, her fingers tangling in his jacket. "Come with us, Mad."

"I can't." It risked shattering their moment of understanding, but Jade's survival trumped everything. "You're a sector leader now. Your job is to get someplace secure so you can keep protecting the people depending on you. Just like Dallas would." He cupped her cheek. "My job is to take care of the problem."

She hesitated, her eyes shuttered. Then she wrenched free of Deacon's grasp to grab Mad's hair, hauled him down, and kissed him hard. "Come back," she whispered hoarsely. "Come back, or Scarlet and Dylan will never forgive me."

Scarlet and Dylan would never forgive *him* for playing the martyr, for sinking a blade of guilt into Jade's heart. If he died today, like this, the wound would bleed forever.

So he wouldn't fucking die.

He kissed her again, but Deacon pulled her away. "Watch your ass," he said tersely, then slammed the door.

By the time he turned, the wind had brought the great billows of smoke to him. But he could still breathe and control his muscles, which meant the grenade was probably filled with some sort of psychoactive agent. Soon, he'd be tripping higher than a Sector Five junkie, but at least the smoke offered some cover. He wouldn't make for an easy target.

He drew his pistol and crept slowly into the pale cloud. The earth tilted beneath him as he listened for footsteps, for the slightest hint of his attacker's location, but all that filled his ears was a high-pitched whine that swelled and receded like the tide.

He couldn't trust his eyes, either. Shapes flitted in and out of the smoke, formless and fleeting, and he edged closer to the wall that surrounded the garden. It was something solid, maybe the only thing he could rely on with the ground itself trembling under his feet.

A shot cracked through the air, hitting the wall next to him. The brick splintered, and sharp pain sliced across his cheek, but he didn't care. He didn't care because it gave him a direction. He charged forward, firing at the shadow that darted past him. He was rewarded with a grunt of pain before the smoke swallowed the figure, but he kept firing, following the crunch of gravel under boots.

Too fast. The thought came a second before he squeezed his finger down a final time, emptying the magazine. A rookie fucking mistake, and he made another one by groping for the spare ammo he wasn't even carrying.

This time, the bullet tore past him so closely that he felt the heat of it along his arm. He dove to one side, hissing as he hit the gravel hard, and came up on his knees with his thoughts racing in a hundred directions, too warped to be trusted and too slippery to hold. He'd be dead before he formulated a plan to keep from dying—

Unless he stopped trying to think.

A sound came from his right. Soft, a muffled footstep. Mad rolled to his feet and rushed it. The figure appeared from the smoke a heartbeat before Mad barreled into him—tall, clad in black, his face distorted and hidden by googles and a mask. Mad crashed into him, and they both went down in a heap.

Metal skittered across gravel—a gun. Mad had only a split second to process that before the man swung hard, snapping him in the jaw with a solid blow that rolled him onto his back.

Oddly, the pain helped. It was purely physical, completely familiar. His body knew the dance of a bare-knuckle brawl. A hundred nights in the cage came back to him as the man slammed into him again, fighting to pin him to the ground.

He twisted his head out of the way of the next punch, letting the guy's hand smash into the gravel. Mad trapped his arm and returned the attack, but not with a punch. He ripped the mask from his attacker's face and tossed it away into the smoke. Panic flooded the hazel eyes staring down at him, a heartbeat's worth of hesitation.

Plenty of time for Mad to land a good right hook.

The man's face whipped to the side. He tried to recover, but Mad moved on pure instinct. He wrapped his legs around the man's waist and rolled, gaining the upper position. His opponent bucked, trying to throw him off, but Mad already had his boot knife in his hand.

He buried it into the side of the man's throat and yanked hard. Blood sprayed in a glittering rainbow, gushing over his hands and arms, splattering his clothes. It should have been red—he *knew* it should have been red, the same way he *knew* he couldn't just sit there, staring at the man who'd tried to kill him—but instinct faded along with the light in his opponent's eyes.

The smoke still surrounded him. The wind caught it, played with it, set it drifting as Mad rolled free of the dead attacker and sprawled onto his back. His arms and legs were too heavy to move. The earth itself was growing denser, dragging him down to its surface.

He'd get up. As soon as gravity righted itself.

"Adrian."

It was a man's voice. Low, deep. Familiar. But not

Deacon. This voice bypassed the fog in his mind to sink into his heart.

Why did he always have to be haunted so *literally?*

"You have to get up, son."

Mad opened his eyes and faced his ghost.

Carter Maddox was tall and broad-shouldered, the only two things Mad had inherited from him. Carter had auburn hair, blue eyes, and freckles across a nose that had been broken exactly once—during a training exercise with Mad's mother.

He'd lost count of the number of times they'd laughingly told the story. The princess of Sector One and her trainer-turned-bodyguard. Their forbidden romance. The love against which he measured all love because it was the only example he'd had—the kind of love where nothing could stop you from fighting to your last breath. The kind where you risked everything.

No order from the Prophet could have prevented Carter from coming for his family. Nothing short of God coming to earth with all of his angels could have stopped him. He'd kicked through the door of their dark little hell, bringing light and hope with him. And for a brief, shining moment, Mad had believed in hope and happy endings.

Carter Maddox didn't obey orders from the Prophet. But he obeyed them from his wife. With the panicked cries of reinforcements echoing through the floor, she'd snatched the gun from Carter's hand and shoved Mad into his father's arms, changing his world forever with the last words he ever heard her speak.

Go. Get him to safety. They're still afraid to hurt me.

Carter got Mad to safety. And then he turned around and went back for Adriana, because their love was the kind where you never gave up. Where you died, if that was what it took.

Mad was going to die if he didn't get up.

He tried. He focused on lifting his arm, just one arm,

but the second it left the ground, the world dipped side-ways and his stomach swam. He rolled to his side and stayed there until the colors stopped throbbing so brightly they blurred out everything else.

His father was still there, waiting. "I can't," he rasped. "I can't do it."

"Yes, you can," Carter insisted. "You're a fighter."

Mad choked on bitter, bruising laughter. "I'm not a fighter. I'm a Rios. I'm a *martyr*."

His father crouched beside him. "You have Rios blood. Your mother's blood, and she was the strongest person I ever met. The best damn fighter you could ever hope to see." He gripped Mad's hand. "So *get up*."

"You're not real," he muttered, squeezing his eyes shut. But the hand gripping his felt as real as anything else in the world.

Jade was waiting for him. Scarlet, with her angelic voice and her bright eyes.

And *Dylan*.

Dylan was the one who brought him to his knees. Dylan and all the words between them, all the bitter, an-gry words they'd finally given voice. Those couldn't be the last words.

He had to fight.

His stomach churned as he climbed to his feet. He swayed, almost went back down. The wind stirred his hair, blowing straight at him, and he knew if he could just put one foot in front of the other, he'd find the edge of the heavy cloud of smoke.

"You're almost there," his father's voice whispered, distant and hazy, as if he was fading along with the smoke. Not that he should be, because Mad broke into clean air and was still high as hell, but his staggering footsteps held no ghostly echo.

He made it up the path and braced himself against the side of the house. The door swung open, the darkness behind it vast and disorienting after the bright sunlight.

He toppled forward and slammed into a slightly less hard surface.

"I've got you." Deacon held him up, practically dragging him inside the house. "Help me. Is any of this blood his?"

"I don't think so." Jade touched his face, cool and soothing, before sliding down his arms and across his chest. "We need to get him to Dylan."

"He's already on his way to One. We can meet him there."

"Mad." Jade's face filled his vision, beautiful and worried, with a gold halo shining behind her head, like a painting of a saint. "It's going to be okay. We're taking you to Dylan. Just close your eyes."

He didn't have a choice. The light behind her was so bright it made his eyes water. The blissful release of passing the fuck out beckoned, and Mad welcomed it, even as Jade's final words chased him down into darkness.

"I'll tell him about Gideon when he wakes up."

28

THE BATHTUB IN the guest suite at Gideon's house was as lavish as Jade remembered, but Jade picked the shower this time. She stood under the hot spray until she'd scrubbed the last of the blood from her hands and arms.

None of it was Mad's, thank God, but he'd been *covered* in it. By the time they got him to Sector One, so was she. Maricela had taken one look at it and broken down in sobs, weeping until Isabela finally took her away.

There was nothing else Jade could do. Mad was sleeping off the drugs under a healer's supervision, and Dylan was working on Gideon. She hadn't even tried to shove her way into the room to assist—one look at her own wide pupils in the mirror told her she was still unsteady herself.

But she was also safe, whole. And when she wrapped herself in her robe and slipped from the bathroom, Scarlet was standing there, so familiar and necessary to life that a sob caught in her throat.

She opened her arms, and Jade flew into them. Scarlet held her close, rocking her gently as she pressed her lips to her wet hair. "Oh, baby. Are you okay?"

"I'm fine, I'm—" She clung to Scarlet, pressed so tight she could pace her slow, steadying breaths by the beat of the other woman's heart. "Mad didn't let him get near me. But he was in that gas for so *long*."

"He'll be all right," she soothed. "Dylan already consulted with Ryder, from Sector Five. It's a short-acting hallucinogen. It won't hurt him."

Jade pulled back far enough to read the truth in Scarlet's eyes, and relief nearly melted her knees. "I shouldn't have let him do it. I just kept thinking—if this is how he dies, for *me*..."

"I know," Scarlet whispered, then touched her cheek. "But any of us would do it, no hesitation. It's part of loving someone."

Jade swallowed tears and tried to be brave enough not to look away. "I should have talked to you, but I'm terrified. I'm so scared that you'll realize who I am and you'll hate me for it. That you *deserve* to hate me for it because I didn't show you everything."

"No." Scarlet stared back at her with eyes as clear and sure as the sky. "I know you, sweetheart. This is who you've always been—the woman strong enough to do this."

"Only because of you." She buried her face against Scarlet's throat again. "Gareth Woods broke me," she whispered, admitting it to herself for the first time. "Maybe only a little, but the bruises are still there. If I keep pretending they're not, I'll hurt all of us."

Scarlet sighed. "All I need is for you to talk to me. That way, I know you're not holding it all in, letting it build up and fuck with your head."

Talking terrified her only moderately less than assassins, which would make it so easy to put off. To murmur promises and then brush it aside and tell herself she'd start later, when the crisis was over. She'd mean well. But Jade could play herself almost as expertly as she played other people.

She backed toward the bed, tugging Scarlet with her, and perched on the end. "I didn't know how I'd feel about killing someone. And after it was done...I felt okay. But Deacon was angry with me for not letting him do it, and you were all so worried..." She twisted her fingers through Scarlet's. "Maybe I started to feel like I wasn't supposed to be okay."

Scarlet snorted. "Deacon was probably pissed because you offended his sense of honor or something. The rest of us..." She shook her head. "I don't know about Dylan and Mad, but for me? It's not as simple as killing someone and feeling okay about it. Even if it was right—even if it was *righteous*—sometimes that shit sneaks up on you. And you may not even realize it's happening until it takes you down."

Scarlet was right, and Jade knew it. Cerys had absolved herself of guilt by sending others to do her killing, but Jade couldn't fix it by blindly doing the opposite. She had to walk her own path, make her own choices—and talk about them with someone who loved her enough to give her hard truths.

Like Lex did for Dallas.

"I want to run Two," she told Scarlet softly. "Not because I feel like no one else can, and not because I have to. I want to do it because someone is going to create a new world for the people who live there, and I think I can make it a good one. But if I had to choose between Sector Two and you, I'd choose you. All of you, every time."

Scarlet's sudden smile was brilliant, as bright as sunlight streaming through a window, as warm as the trembling kiss she pressed to Jade's lips.

So sweet. Sweet and open and vulnerable, and Jade sank her fingers into Scarlet's hair and savored the impossible contradiction of a kiss that was both comfortably familiar and achingly new.

She might have kissed Scarlet forever if the soft *click* of the door hadn't intruded. Jade pulled back with reluctance only to find Mad hovering in the doorway, swaying with exhaustion, one hand still gripping the doorknob as if he was considering backing out of the room.

Scarlet rose, reached for him—then pulled her hand back and pressed her fingers to her lips. "You look like hell."

His lips curved in that quintessentially *Mad* smile—the one that laughed in the face of his own broken heart. "Funny, 'cause I'm looking at heaven."

He'd stand there forever if they let him, half-dead on his feet and too proud to impose. Jade moved past Scarlet and wrapped her arm around his waist. "Sit down before you fall over. You're too heavy to carry."

He walked mostly under his own power, but when they reached Scarlet, Mad dug in his feet. He touched her cheek with a trembling hand. "I'm sorry, Scarlet."

Tears glittered in her eyes. "Don't. Don't apologize to me."

"Too late." He slid his hand down to her back and tugged, pulling her against them. Jade put her other arm around Scarlet, holding them both as Mad rested his forehead against Scarlet's. "I walked away angry. We don't get to do that, not during a war."

"No, you were right." Her voice broke. "I don't understand the pressure, or what you two have to deal with. I've never had people depending on me."

"Bullshit," Mad said, low and intense. "Your band always depended on you. And before any of us even met you, Six talked about you like you made the damn moon rise every night. You know what it means to take care of your people."

"You take care of us," Jade agreed, stroking Scarlet's hair. "You tell us the shit we don't want to hear—that we *need* to hear. That's a thankless job."

"It's annoying," she countered, "and more than a little mean."

"It's annoying." Mad kissed her forehead. "But only when you're right. And then it's not mean at all."

She met his gaze as the first tears slipped down her cheeks. "I'll always sing for you. I promise."

Mad's smile this time was new. Brilliant, shining—so real that it made Jade's eyes sting. Scarlet was the heart of them. Loyal, fearless, loving them all so joyfully that she could heal just by forgiving them.

Mad bent toward Scarlet and overbalanced, and Jade caught him before he brought them all down in a tangle. "Bed," she commanded, urging Mad toward it. "You can ask her to sing once you get there."

"Yes, ma'am." He let Scarlet get her shoulder under his other arm before leaning close to her. "I think Dylan's rubbing off on her. She's getting bossy."

"Or she doesn't want you to wind up back in the hospital. Or infirmary." Scarlet wrinkled her nose. "However that works here."

Mad huffed a laugh as he tumbled to the bed. "I think how it works is Dylan yells at me."

There was so much raw vulnerability in the words, but Jade couldn't soothe it. Only Dylan could relieve the last bit of tension keeping Mad coiled tight even as Jade and Scarlet curled up on either side of him.

They fit together in so many different ways, and for so many different reasons. The way Scarlet proved with every breath that a woman's strength could take whatever form she damn well pleased, then challenged Jade to believe it. The way Mad looked at the world with the same determination in Jade's heart, refusing to believe he couldn't make it better.

The way Dylan cut through the tangle of her desires to remind her that trust should be at the heart of everything—and that you didn't reward people with trust. You rewarded them *for* it, because there was nothing as valuable in a dark and broken world as someone who believed in you enough to let themselves be vulnerable.

It was the way Dylan looked at Scarlet and found hope. The way Scarlet's music brought Mad peace. The way Mad loved all three of them so fiercely, so brightly, you could almost believe he really was touched by a higher power.

It was all of them, together. And she could hold Mad close and stroke his hair while Scarlet sang him to sleep, but they wouldn't be complete. They wouldn't be whole.

Not without Dylan.

Dylan couldn't remember the last time he cried.

Probably when he was a boy, denied something by his parents for reasons no childish brain could ever fathom. A punishment, perhaps, or because he wanted something they couldn't afford.

It wasn't uncommon. Both of his parents had jobs—his mother cleaned wealthy people's homes, and his father sold gloves and boots at an upscale shop in the city center—but there never seemed to be enough money. They never went hungry, but they went without plenty of other, less important things.

It wasn't until he was older that he realized how much his parents spent on his education. Between school fees and the bribes necessary to get him into the right classes, the sum was astronomical. But they'd been obsessively determined that he would grow up to do more, to *be* more.

He climbed the stairs toward the room where Scarlet and Jade waited. Mad was probably there by now, too, because following instructions was unthinkable to him. The thought of the nurses trying to keep him contained brought a smile to Dylan's face as he stopped in front of the bedroom door.

And stood there, his hand hovering over the knob, his eyes dry and burning.

During his school breaks, his mother would take him to work with her. Never when her employers were home, of course, and he had to be very careful not to touch any-thing. He'd sit, just so, on a pristine white sofa or chair and look around, fascinated by his luxurious surround-ings. By the artwork, by the technology, by all the *things* those people had.

And when the novelty of those beautiful apartments wore off, he'd read a novel or work ahead in his textbooks. Sometimes, he'd stare at his mother as she worked—par-ticularly her hands, red and raw from the harsh chemicals she used. The ones she never let him touch, even when he tried to help her.

He remembered one sunny, clear day—standing at the window of a high-rise apartment, looking out over the city and the sectors beyond. That high, he could even see the desert, ringing the whole thing in arid shades of brown.

His mother had come up behind him, laid her hand on his shoulder, and made a soft, satisfied noise. "One day, Dylan. It can be yours, as much of it as you want."

He'd failed her. In so many ways, and finally in that, because he never amassed the fortune they planned for him. He wanted no part of the city. He'd walked away from it all, and everything he wanted, *everything*, was behind this door.

He opened it.

They were on the bed. Mad and Scarlet were tangled together, sleeping, and Jade sat with her back against the headboard, her fingers stroking idly through Mad's hair.

Her eyes met his. Her fingers stilled. She extended her other hand, reaching for him in quiet invitation.

He kicked off his shoes and slid onto the bed, curling as close to her as he could, wrapping himself damn near around her. The contact eased some of the tightness in his chest, and he managed a deep breath. "Gideon's going to make it. I held him together long enough for the regen tech—for Kora—to help him."

She slipped her arms around him and brushed a kiss to his forehead. "I knew you would."

Her faith in him was heartwarming, but she had no idea how close a call it had been. "He was barely hanging on when I got here, Jade. He almost died."

"People die sometimes." She cupped his cheek and forced him to look at her. "But when you're around—"

"I'm not doubting my abilities." He lowered his voice. "I'm saying Gideon nearly died, but Mad—Mad's the one we almost lost. He would have had to stay here, and it's not like your work in Two. You know it isn't. It's different for him."

Jade watched him forever, her thumb gliding back and forth across his cheek. Then she nodded. "Yes, it's different for him here. But that doesn't mean we almost lost him, Dylan, or that we *will* lose him if something happens to Gideon. He'll have to decide what he can live with doing and not doing, and we'll have to help him...but the sector lines are blurring. He doesn't have to stay, and we don't have to go."

"Maybe you're right." He and Mad had left things unsettled, perhaps even broken between them, but for Jade—for Scarlet—

"I know I am." Jade stroked his cheek again with a soft smile. "The only way we lose one another is if we stop coming back after we argue, because we're going to argue. Too many important things are happening to avoid that."

He closed his eyes. "You don't know what I said to him, Jade. It was unforgivable. The only reason Scarlet's still speaking to me is that heart of hers."

"And you think Mad's is any smaller?"

"Hell, no. But I think I can hurt him more." He hesitated. "Scarlet never wanted to love me."

"But she does, Dylan." Her lips touched his, her whisper almost a kiss. "It's scary, trying to feel worthy of hearts that big. But we owe it to them to do our best, because they love us."

"We can hear you, you know," Scarlet murmured, her voice husky with sleep.

"Shh," Jade replied, but her lips curved against Dylan's. "Or you won't hear all the other good stuff I was about to say about you."

A hand slid over Dylan's, prompting him to open his eyes. It was Mad's hand, warm and reassuring as he twined their fingers together. "You better be getting to the part about my badass rescue."

Scarlet propped up on one arm, just enough to peer up at Dylan over the bulk of Mad's body. "Nah, I think Dylan was getting to the part where he's sorry for what he said to you."

"I *am* sorry." He could barely choke out the words. "You don't know how hard I wish I could take it back."

"Don't." The mattress dipped as Mad rose to his knees and crawled up behind Dylan. He settled there, dragging Dylan back against his chest, one hand coming around to rest over his heart. "It hurt, but I needed it to. I needed to wonder if it was true."

Now it was Dylan's turn, even if Mad didn't realize it. He braced himself for their shock, their pity, and reached for the words. "My father worked in a shop that sold handmade shoes and belts. The owner bought them from artisans in the sectors and communes and told his customers they'd been imported from places like London and Milan." He tried to laugh, but what came out sounded more like a sigh. "He made a fortune, and my father died at forty-eight. Heart attack. The kind of thing that modern medicine is supposed to prevent—assuming you can afford access to it, I mean."

Jade's brow furrowed. "Who?" she asked in a chilly, dangerous voice that hearkened immediate financial ruin for his father's former boss.

"Oh, it's too late for that, love." His reassuring smile felt more like a grimace. "It was my first stop on my way out of the city." He'd strangled the man with a very nice tie, one stitched with the label *Crafted in Paris* that had probably been made in the wilds beyond Sector Eight.

Scarlet slid closer. "Dylan—"

"My mother," he interrupted, "was a sadder story. She was a maid, the kind who cleaned for people who couldn't quite afford proper housekeepers. When Dad died, she tripled her workload. She was exhausted all the time. I guess that's why she didn't realize she was sick until it was too late."

Mad spread his fingers wide on Dylan's chest, as if sheltering his heart. "How old were you?"

"Twenty-four. I'd just finished my medical training. She—" His throat closed suddenly, and his eyes burned worse than ever. "She didn't tell me anything was wrong, didn't ask me for help. She didn't want to disrupt my studies."

Jade was the one who knew enough of Eden to understand. "Because she'd worked so hard to give you that chance."

"By then, it didn't matter how many favors I called in. No one could help her." Everything hurt—pins and needles, like warming up after being terribly cold. "I didn't know what to do with myself at first, so I kept working. Then, after a few years, it got to the point where I was... I was *glad* they were dead. It meant they'd never have to find out what kind of miserable, hellish life they'd bought for me."

Jade slid her hand over Mad's, her fingers slipping between his to press against Dylan's chest. "That's how Eden's built, sweetheart. To keep people in their place. The rich built a wall around their world, and your parents slipped you through an impossible crack. They couldn't have known what was on the other side. That's why the wall is there."

She was right, and he hated that fucking wall. Everyone saw the one separating the city from the sectors, but no one ever saw the invisible one inside, the one erected by the rich and privileged to ensure that what was theirs remained theirs. It was an intangible barrier, but it might as well have been stone, three solid feet thick.

"My parents didn't know," he agreed hoarsely. "I understand that now, and it's better. I don't have to hate them anymore."

Scarlet sat on his lap and wrapped her arms around his neck. Her face was hot against his, and he tasted her tears on his lips. "I love you," she whispered. "You've endured so much, and you haven't let it crush how much you care."

He couldn't have stopped caring entirely, not about a world with people like her and Jade and Mad in it. And he could finally give voice to all the things he'd wanted to tell her the previous night. "I love you because you don't know how to say something's impossible. You just stare at it until you figure out how to make it happen."

Jade leaned into his side and kissed his cheek. "She made us happen. All of us."

The gentle caress combined with Scarlet's mouth on his twisted the relief at sharing his story into something else, no less desperate but *hungrier*. Immediate.

He held on to Scarlet as he rose from the bed, then turned and laid her on it, bent over her, his lips still fused to hers.

As she returned his kiss, Mad stroked his back, his shoulders, slipped his fingers down and under Dylan's shirt in a feather-soft caress up his spine. "Let her love you, Dylan."

Jade sank her fingers into Dylan's hair. "Let us all love you."

For the first time in his entire lonely, fucked-up life, he said yes.

29

*Y*ES.
The word was still vibrating against Scarlet's lips, a heady buzz of desire and acceptance, when Mad slid his hands between them and hauled Dylan upright. Over his shoulder, Mad smiled down at Scarlet, his gaze almost feverish. "You heard her, lover. This time you have to let *us* love *you.*"

Dylan sucked in a sharp breath and trembled in his embrace. "You want me to do nothing?"

"I want you to feel this. I want you to wonder what Jade will do to you when she can do anything she wants." Mad's clever fingers danced down the buttons on Dylan's shirt before dragging the fabric back—and his arms with it. "I want you to wonder if Jade won't do anything until Scarlet *makes* her, because then we'll all get off, won't we?"

Control. Dylan needed it so much—but Mad was finally ready to take it. Scarlet licked her lips, sat up, and brushed a quick kiss over the center of Dylan's chest. "What do you have in mind?"

Mad buried his fingers in Dylan's hair and pulled his head back. Jade leaned in as if summoned, dropping soft kisses to Dylan's throat as Mad sought Scarlet's gaze.

She recognized the look there. She'd seen it before, the moment before Mad had upended her world and seized control from her. Dark, bottomless hunger, a challenge—not to fight against him this time, but with him.

She ducked her head to hide her smile and toyed with the buckle on Dylan's belt. "Will you need this?" she asked innocently.

"Maybe," Mad rumbled, his mouth against Dylan's ear. "I don't know if I trust him not to touch you."

Dylan's head fell back again, this time of his own volition, and his strong throat worked as he bit off a groan. "*Fuck.* Keep talking."

And say what? The words were on the tip of Scarlet's tongue, and she chased them away by licking a slow path from his navel up to his sternum. "You can't do it, can you? Just turn it off and let us fuck you?"

He looked down at her, his eyes burning with banked lust, and Scarlet had never wanted anything more than to stoke that fire to life and let it burn all four of them to the ground.

She unbuckled his belt. Jade clasped one end of it and tugged, dragging it free of one belt loop after another with methodical patience. When it slipped from the last one, she folded the leather in half and traced it down Dylan's arm. "This is what you need, isn't it? To be set free, even if it's only for tonight. To know we want you for more than making sure we all get off."

He shuddered.

Jade leaned closer, her lips tracing over his shoulder. "It's okay to want that. Because you wouldn't give it to just anyone, would you?"

For some reason, that made him laugh, though the sound was muffled, crushed, when he dipped his head and caught her mouth with his. Mad let him, releasing Dylan's hair to take the belt from Jade. His gaze found Scarlet's again, warm and lazy as he stripped Dylan's shirt away and bound the man's arms behind him with his own belt.

Dylan's cock strained the fabric of his pants. Scarlet freed him carefully, then gripped the base of his shaft, relishing his deep groan. "Jade, sweetheart?" she purred. "I need to borrow your tongue."

She broke from Dylan's kiss with a soft sigh before turning to lean into Scarlet. She nuzzled her cheek, her ear, dropping slow kisses all along her jaw to the corner of her mouth. "What should I do with it?"

Scarlet slid one hand into Jade's unbound hair and twisted it tight. "You can tease him, but not me. Not yet."

Mad hummed his agreement as he wrapped an arm around Dylan's body and traced his fingers down. "Let me hear the magic word, Jade. Let *him* hear it. What are you willing to do to get him off? What should we *make* you do?"

A tremor rocked Jade. Mad's words were darkly demanding, promising an unyielding dominance he'd always held back. She licked her lips and fought Scarlet's hold on her hair. "Anything."

"You hear that, Dylan?" Mad closed his fingers over Scarlet's, where they still gripped the base of Dylan's cock. "She'll do *anything*."

"Jesus Christ." His muscles flexed as he strained against the leather binding his wrists. "Please."

Scarlet let go and bent her head, meeting Jade's open mouth right at the tip of Dylan's cock for a leisurely, wet kiss. Jade moaned, her tongue gliding around the crown and then into Scarlet's mouth, carrying the taste of him with her. Then she returned to Dylan, working her way obediently down to Mad's fingers with slow, careful licks that left his cock glistening.

Even in obedience, she was teasing him. Because Scarlet had said *tongue*, that was all she'd give him.

Unless Scarlet made her.

She bit Jade's earlobe and placed her hand on the back of her head. She nudged her forward—gently, giving her plenty of time to open and take his cock.

Dylan wasn't the only one who groaned as Jade's lips slid slowly down his shaft. Mad growled and scraped his nails across Dylan's chest. "Look at her. Getting her mouth around your dick gets her so hot, she's shaking. That's how much she wants your pleasure."

"Deeper—"

"Uh-uh." Mad nipped at Dylan's ear as his fingers drifted up to settle on Dylan's throat in a light, warning grip. "You can beg all you want, but we're not going to rush her, not when she's having so much fun. And you are, sweetheart, aren't you?"

Jade hummed in agreement, and Dylan jerked. Mad made a noise low in his throat. "You should show him how wet this is getting her, Scarlet. Let him see it. Or taste it."

The belt on Jade's delicate silk robe had loosened, and the sensuous white fabric clung to her curves like a lover's hands, revealing as much as it concealed—the slopes of her breasts and hips, the tight pucker of her nipples.

Scarlet didn't pull it free. Instead, she eased her hand beneath the silk, biting her lip when she encountered the wet heat slicking Jade's inner thighs. "You have no idea," she breathed, then edged her hand higher, until her fingers brushed the outer lips of Jade's pussy. "No fucking idea."

Jade shuddered under her touch and lifted her head. "He always stops me before he comes. He holds back."

"To take care of our pleasure." With one hand still collaring Dylan's throat, Mad used the other to slowly stroke the man's cock. "Tell her what you want, Dylan. What you need."

His chest heaved. "I want—"

Scarlet cut him off by shoving her wet fingers between his lips. He growled and bit her, then held her gaze as he licked each one.

"You filthy fucker." Mad touched Dylan's chin, tilting his head back. His tongue joined Dylan's, slipping over her fingers before she pulled them away and left the two of them in the hottest kiss she'd ever seen—mouths fused together, Mad swallowing Dylan's moan as Jade returned to her task with renewed eagerness.

Scarlet eased the front of Jade's robe open, baring her breasts. She cupped them, pushing them together, pinching her nipples between her fingers until Jade released Dylan and threw her head back.

And Mad understood. He knew—damn him, *bless* him—without a word every dirty, delicious carnal thought that popped into Scarlet's head almost as soon as she did. So he guided Dylan's cock, thrusting it between Jade's luscious, ready breasts.

Dylan gasped. Jade did too, arching her back. Scarlet gripped Dylan's hips, urging him on, but Mad was already there, grinding against his ass, guiding his thrusts as he murmured obscene encouragement. "See what you taught me, Dylan? To listen instead of assuming. Sweet, pretty Jade wants dirty, dirty things, doesn't she?"

"Yes," Jade moaned, squirming in Scarlet's grasp, because even having Mad acknowledge it triggered wild arousal. "I want to fuck. I want to fuck all of you."

Leather creaked as Dylan fought his restraints, and the muscles in his stomach and hips flexed as he drove forward, gliding his cock so far between Jade's breasts that the head nearly brushed her chin.

But he didn't utter a desperate command this time. He kept silent and let them touch him without interference, without grasping for control, so Scarlet rewarded him with a quick lick. And the next time he thrust forward, it was into her waiting mouth.

"Oh, God." He shuddered again, and the taste of his

frantic arousal bloomed on her tongue.

Fingers threaded through Scarlet's hair, too big to be Jade's. Mad cupped the back of her head, linking them all together as his words coiled around her. "No holding back this time, lover. Come for them."

Dylan choked out Mad's name as he began to shake. Two more thrusts and he came in Scarlet's mouth, spurting hot and thick across her tongue, so much and so fast that she could barely swallow.

Jade joined her, fighting her for the last shudders of Dylan's orgasm, kissing her long after it was over, after Mad eased Dylan back, until it was just the two of them, entangled in a kiss that might have lasted forever if leather hadn't tickled up Scarlet's arm.

When she broke away, Mad had freed Dylan's arms and was languidly rubbing one while Dylan panted for breath. He clutched the belt in his free hand, his eyes glinting as he quirked one eyebrow. "Her turn?"

Scarlet looked at Jade. Her cheeks were flushed, and there was no mistaking the lust that sparked in her dark eyes. "I think so, don't you, Jyoti? Oh, yeah."

Jade's lashes fluttered as her head tipped back. "Say it again," she whispered.

"Jyoti." She whispered it in her ear, against her jaw, the perfect curve of her shoulder, then finally into her mouth. Jade sighed against her lips and melted for her, exquisitely pliant as Scarlet guided her onto her back. Jade ran her fingernails lightly up Scarlet's spine, then put her arms over her head, twisting her hands together above her in anticipation.

Scarlet broke the kiss and had to drag in a deep breath to quell her thumping heart. "I need the belt."

Mad handed it over. "I think someone's eager to be ravished."

"Desperately," Jade replied huskily. Her eyes were full of lust, but also bright, mischievous challenge. Her smile curved wickedly as she raised her eyebrows, daring

Scarlet to take control. So different from the solemn, almost absentminded obedience Jade had offered in the beginning, and so full of *joy.*

"Let me?" Dylan asked hoarsely, his outstretched hand still trembling.

Scarlet brushed Jade's cheek with the warm leather. Being the one to bind her meant something to him, something utterly lost on Scarlet. Sure, it was fun, and seeing Jade's reaction was as arousing as every other naked thing they did. But it didn't reach inside her, clasp a hand around her guts, and drop-kick her in the throat the way it did Dylan.

She handed him the belt.

It was like watching something sacred. Jade stared up at him, her lips parted, her breath coming faster and faster as he wrapped the leather carefully around her wrists. Even Mad seemed hypnotized, his only movement the slow glide of his fingertips up and down Scarlet's spine.

When Dylan buckled it in place, so tightly that Jade could only wiggle her wrists helplessly, she closed her eyes and exhaled on a shudder.

Dylan lay down beside her, his face close to hers. "You're beautiful like this."

She smiled. "Only for you. Only for my lovers."

"That's right." Mad stroked the graceful line of her extended arm. "Scarlet, why don't you look in the drawer next to the bed? There's something there we might want."

She found a tiny bottle, not the plain plastic ones that Tatiana used for her goods in Sector Four, but a delicate glass vial swirling with color. The craftsmanship was remarkable, and Scarlet rubbed her thumb breathlessly over its surface. "What is it?"

"Something you can use for all sorts of things." He tickled down Jade's arm and circled one nipple until she arched restlessly. "It warms against the skin. And it's safe to put anywhere."

Scarlet pulled the stopper free and drizzled a tiny bit on the inside of Jade's thigh. The oil was slick, and it heated Scarlet's thumb as she worked it into Jade's soft skin.

"Oh *God*," Jade moaned.

"Yeah, sweetheart." Mad leaned down to grip her chin and forced her to look at him. "We'll give you everything you want. Everything you can take. But that's a game we play carefully. Okay?"

She nodded shakily.

"Good." Mad turned her face toward Dylan. "You need a safe word, sweetheart. Dylan's going to watch you and be here with you, taking care of you. And if it's too much, you tell him your safe word. Promise us."

"I—I promise."

"Good," he repeated, touching her lips with his thumb. "What's your word?"

Jade didn't hesitate. "Eden."

Scarlet stretched out, propping herself over Jade's leg. It gave her perfect access to Jade's bare, wet pussy—and a perfect view of anything Mad did to her.

She held up the bottle and arched one eyebrow. Mad smiled and released Jade, trailing his fingers down the center of her body. He stopped to stroke lightly over Jade's inner thigh. "I remember the first time. You said she likes it slow and intense, almost more than she can take."

"Mmm, but you weren't quite ready to give it to her."

Mad smiled and plucked the bottle from her fingers. "Show me what she likes," he murmured as he poured the warm liquid over her fingers. "And then we'll find out how much she can take."

Scarlet started slow, drinking in every restless shift and tiny noise. Jade was so turned on that barely brushing her clit brought her hips off the bed, so she moved on to gently opening her pussy.

One finger, then two. She pumped them slowly, curling them to stroke over Jade's G-spot. Jade rewarded her with a gasping moan and renewed squirming, because she was so *easy* to please it was a crime almost no one had ever bothered before.

Mad watched for a moment before lifting the bottle again, drizzling it over her nipples this time. "Touch her, Dylan."

He complied, working the oil into her skin with long, lazy strokes. Then, suddenly, he tugged at both of Jade's nipples, and the shock of the caress—or the pleasure mixed with pain—made her inner muscles clamp tightly on Scarlet's fingers.

"Not enough." Scarlet pulled her fingers free. "Come on, Adrian. No holding back, remember?"

Mad tipped the bottle again, coating two of his fingers. When he stroked them into Jade, she gasped and twisted. Her arms came up, but Dylan pressed them back down to the bed with a soothing hum.

Jade panted, trembling harder than Scarlet had ever seen her, as if the leather around her wrists had unlocked something wild. Mad held her there, his thumb hovering over her clit but not touching. "Do you remember your safe word, darling?"

"Yes," she whispered.

"Do you want to use it?"

Jade shook her head frantically. Mad withdrew his fingers and thrust back in with three. His eyes met Scarlet's, and she knew what he wanted without words.

She bent her head and flicked her tongue over Jade's clit. She could taste the oil and her arousal, a heady combination that made the world spin, especially when Jade bucked her hips and Mad groaned and she knew that meant Jade was close, squeezing around his fingers in delicious, pulsing flutters.

She knew Jade's body. Knew the tempo and pressure it took, knew what her hitching breaths and sounds meant. She knew when to suck gently to elicit a hoarse cry, and Mad choked on a curse and pumped his fingers as

Jade came for them.

Working together, they could have dragged it on and on. But Mad slowed his touch until the bucking of her hips subsided before saying, "Watch her, Dylan."

Scarlet's breath burned in her lungs, a mix of anticipation and longing. Seeing Jade come was one of her favorite things, and she already knew that witnessing the moment when Mad pushed himself beyond his own boundaries would be another.

He could barely fit three of his long, beautiful fingers inside Jade. But when Dylan whispered his name, Mad slowly—slowly—worked in a fourth, moving carefully but intently. Insistently, until he had damn near his whole hand inside her.

He stayed there, buried deep, his other hand stroking soothingly over her abdomen. "Stay with us, Jyoti."

She sobbed out another moan, her fingers flexing helplessly, only one word falling from her lips. "Yes."

Mad hauled Scarlet up by her hair until they were face-to-face and licked Jade's arousal from her lips. "Don't stop this time until Dylan says so."

The command made her pulse with an empty ache. As soon as he released her, she obeyed, sucking Jade's clit into her mouth and nudging it with her tongue. It didn't matter what she did with Mad fucking Jade like this— soft, hard, even a graze of her teeth. Orgasm after orgasm gripped Jade, until her skin burned and her whole body was quaking.

And they didn't stop. Even when she cried out, even when she *screamed*, not until Dylan stroked a hand over the back of Scarlet's head and then touched Mad's wrist.

"Enough," he rasped. "She's had enough."

Mad eased his fingers free—gently, so gently. He stretched out beside Jade and cupped her pussy, his lips tender against her temple. "So strong. So sweet. I love you for both."

Jade turned into his touch and kissed him.

It was another sacred moment that stole Scarlet's breath, an intimacy that bordered on divine. Maybe Mad didn't want to be a prince or a saint, but here, in this bed with them, he was both.

She exhaled a ragged breath, something close to a sob. "I don't understand," she whispered. "I don't know how I can possibly belong here, but I do. I feel it."

Jade lifted her bound hands, reaching for her with a yearning that transcended words. Dylan dragged her down, and Scarlet turned from one kiss into another—from Jade, soft but desperate, to Dylan, who wove entire poetic apologies and promises with just his tongue.

And Mad, who kissed her as if he'd saved her for last because she was the one who wanted him like this—aroused to the edge of control, mere seconds from falling apart.

As if he finally trusted her to love him even when he was greedy.

Metal clicked, and Scarlet turned her head just in time to see Dylan free Jade's hands from the confines of the belt. But instead of bringing it to her next, he tossed the leather aside and grasped her wrist in an iron grip.

"No belt," he told her. "The only thing holding you will be us."

"Mmm." Mad stroked her other wrist and up her arm as he shifted to his knees. Across her shoulder, down her spine, so slow and deliberate she was trembling by the time he grazed the curve of her ass and then brushed her pussy. "So patient. Are you tired of being empty, Scarlet?"

She couldn't stop her back from arching, or the eager moan that slipped free. "Yes."

His touch vanished, and she could only follow his movements by the clues. The dip of the bed as he settled behind her. The click of his belt and the whisper of his zipper.

Jade sank her hands into Scarlet's hair and forced her to meet her eyes. "Are you going to let us love you?"

The truth shining in her eyes was undeniable. Inescapable. "You do," she said. "You love me."

"More than the rest of the world combined." Jade tugged her down for a kiss, soft and unhurried, a gentle contrast to the hard fingers suddenly gripping her hips.

Mad gave her no warning. He didn't ask or tease. He held her in place and drove into her, all the way in one long thrust that curled her toes and sent the first shivery tingles of pleasure singing up her spine.

"Already?" Dylan licked her shoulder and smiled against her skin. "He hasn't even gotten started, love."

Jade wrapped her arms around Scarlet and pulled her closer, trapping her at such a sharp angle that Mad's next thrust felt even deeper. He groaned and did it again. "She's going to come any second, isn't she? I can feel it."

"Yes," Jade breathed against Scarlet's lips. "Because she never holds back."

"Never." Dylan traced slick fingers over the small of her back, leaving her skin hot wherever he touched. More of that lube, and she understood why as soon as he reached the curve of her ass.

He circled her asshole with his fingertips, a caress that warmed and then burned as he pushed deeper. It was another silent promise—next time, he'd fill her with more than his fingers. It would be a plug, or even his cock buried deep inside as Mad fucked her.

She couldn't breathe. She could only push back, driving against Dylan's fingers and Mad's steady, relentless thrusts. Then Jade's hand snuck between their bodies, her fingers light and knowing on Scarlet's clit.

They were touching her *everywhere*, inside and out. It wasn't the first time the four of them had fallen together, but it was different. Not just the things they'd said, but the way they said it—Jade's soft lips at the hollow of her throat, Dylan whispering against her shoulder. Mad's fingers biting into her skin as he growled and shook behind her.

It was a whole language, one only the four of them could ever comprehend, their new native tongue. The thing that would hold them together in tough times and bring them back when they'd fought with one another. It would shelter them, give them strength, show the world what they meant to each other.

Love.

Scarlet fell apart, her entire body pulsing with a bliss and completion she could only describe with a scream. Dylan sank his teeth into her skin as Mad shuddered, his hips jerking against hers, and she knew he was right there with her, coming with her, falling with her.

Loving with her.

She didn't have to collapse to the bed. Jade was already cradling her, and Scarlet buried her face in her neck as Dylan petted her and Mad dropped on their opposite side. His hand joined Dylan's, rubbing her back as he panted against Jade's shoulder, all of them trapped in a moment of perfect, easy satisfaction.

Jade was the one who broke it. "I like being Jyoti. Do you think it's too late to...be her?"

Dylan made a rough noise in the back of his throat. "It's never too late, love. I think I'm living proof of that."

Scarlet slipped her fingers through his hair. "I think we all are."

"We get to decide who we are, and what our names should be." Mad tilted Jade's face to his. "If the O'Kanes can learn all the crazy-ass nicknames we come up with for each other, we can learn to call you whatever you want."

She smiled shakily. "Does it mean less if I don't just share it with you?"

Mad kissed her nose. "It means plenty that you shared it with us first."

"It's your name," Scarlet reminded her. "Yours. You can do whatever you want with it."

"I want to use it. Because it *is* my name." She closed her eyes and nuzzled Scarlet. "And it's not the only thing that's mine anymore. Not even close."

Only one thing still intruded on the peaceful calm of the moment, and one look at Mad told Scarlet he was thinking of it, too. "What are you going to do?" she asked quietly.

Mad threw his arm over both of them and closed his eyes. "I'm going to sleep," he said firmly. "And hope Gideon's feeling well enough to talk in the morning."

30

MAD'S COUSIN WAS so pale and weak that even sitting up in bed left him exhausted, but Gideon was whole. Not just healing, but *healed*, because Dylan had held him together long enough for regeneration equipment to arrive.

As far as Mad was concerned, Dylan had performed the first true miracle Sector One had ever seen.

Gideon reached for the water on his bedside table and winced. "Is it supposed to feel this much like getting run over?"

"Hey, quit whining." Mad picked up the glass and handed it to him. "You practically died and came back to life. Did you think that was gonna tickle?"

That earned him a scowl and Gideon's best Lofty Prophet glare. "I see the drugs haven't worn off yet. Or your sense of propriety is worse than ever."

"My sense of humor, too," Mad retorted with a grin.

"But you love me this way."

"I do." Gideon smiled, though it faded quickly. "I wish you'd use some of that humor on Maricela."

Any urge Mad had to smile dissipated. Maricela was sleeping off a sedative Dylan had provided, but waking up would bring her no relief. His sheltered baby cousin had received too many abrupt shocks—including stabbing Gideon's attacker.

Taking a life for the first time was bad enough, but Maricela had been raised from birth to believe that killing blackened your soul, even if done in self-defense. And killing someone she *knew*, someone she'd laughed with, prayed for, someone she'd trusted...

"She'll be okay." If Mad said it confidently enough, maybe he could convince them both. "She's tougher than you know. And she saved your life. Maybe that will help her come to terms with it."

"Maybe." Gideon shifted and winced again, clutching his side. "The wound is gone, but I swear I can still feel it."

"Ace says it takes a while to go away." It was the segue he needed. *Speaking of going away...* But it had been easier to imagine upstairs, surrounded by Jade and Dylan and Scarlet, his future warm and bright with promise.

This was the hard reality—staring into the eyes of a man who'd narrowly escaped death, who had still lost so much, and saying, *I can't be here for you. Not really. Not ever.*

It felt so fucking selfish.

"It's okay, Adrian." It was the first time Gideon had used his name in years. His cousin's eyes were dark and understanding, so *ancient* that the hair on the back of Mad's neck rose. "Sector One has taken enough from you. The only person in the world who still thinks you owe this place more blood and tears is you."

"Gideon—"

"Don't. Not unless you're going to tell me the damn truth."

Mad exhaled roughly and sat back in the chair. "Fine. You and Maricela and Isabela are my family. If you need me as family, I'll come. But you have to take me out of the line of succession. Officially. You need to have a plan in place for who's going to follow you, because it won't be me. I have other responsibilities now."

The words lay there between them, echoing in the silence. The guilt of saying them was miniscule compared to the sheer, throbbing *relief,* as if the rocks crushing his chest had finally vanished. He could take a full breath again.

And when Gideon said, "You're right," he actually did.

"You're right," Gideon repeated. "I've been irresponsible. That's something you recognize pretty fast when you think you only have thirty seconds left to live. If we don't get through this war in one piece, it won't matter. But if we do..."

He trailed off into silence, his eyes unfocused, and goose bumps joined the raised hairs on the back of Mad's neck. Most of the time, he thought Gideon's displays were just that—conscious theatrics. A useful way of influencing the devout.

And sometimes Mad thought he wasn't the only one in the family who ended up arguing with ghosts when shit went to hell.

"Church and state," Gideon said abruptly, as if simply continuing his thought. "It solves all our problems rather neatly, don't you think?"

Mad blinked his confusion. "You're already the church. And the state."

"I know. That's the problem. Too much damn power, Mad. And what have you always told me?"

Maybe you mean well, maybe your kids will. But it won't take long for someone to come along who sees all that power and thinks it would be fun to abuse the shit out of it.

It was true of every leader, maybe, on some level. But

in Sector One, they didn't hold power through money or violence or even legacy. Theirs was the power of belief, of faith. The threat of ruination not just in this life, but for eternity.

The faithful of Sector One wouldn't give up their beliefs easily. Gideon knew that from trying to change them. But if the walls came down and the sectors changed, not everyone in One would be part of that faith anymore. Gideon would have to build a new sort of sector, one where the leader of the government and the leader of their grandfather's religion worked together—or, if the worst happened, checked each other's power.

And he knew, in his gut, which type of power Gideon would choose for himself. "Who are you thinking of for the new religious leader?"

"Isabela." Gideon smiled. "She's the traditional one, anyway, and she loves the rituals. That's what they want. Someone who can give them that comfort. She'll take the best parts of what faith should be and do good with it. Especially if she doesn't have to worry about running the sector."

"She will." Mad might not agree with his cousin's worship of their grandfather, but he'd never doubted her heart. And the sector adored her for upholding the traditions of the Prophet. "It's a good idea, Gideon."

"I'm glad you think so." When Mad started to smile, Gideon shook his head. "I'm serious, Mad. You've lived in O'Kane's back pocket all these years. He's done this right. And you watched him do it."

He had. And he'd bit back criticism of Gideon every time he came home, because it wasn't his place, and because too much lay between them to ever meet in the middle when it came to religion.

But leadership and loyalty... "You want my advice?"

"Yes."

Mad thrust out his wrist, showing off the ink that wrapped around it, along with the O'Kane logo. "Every time the Riders get another raven, you remind them how little their souls are worth. Dallas only marks us once, and it's to remind us how much we have to live for."

Gideon stared at the ink forever before meeting Mad's gaze. "But that's not all you're living for now."

He was living for the three exhausted people still tangled together in a giant bed, no doubt holding each other a little closer just in case. Just in case guilt or obligation overcame him, and he turned Dylan's terrified words into prophecy and chose to be a living martyr instead of a man in love.

"No," he agreed quietly. "There are different sorts of marks we use for that, ink I hope they'll accept from me. Because they're mine, Gideon. My responsibility. I'll protect them from anything."

Understanding stood in his cousin's eyes. "Even yourself."

"Even myself. And there's only one way to do that."

"I know." Gideon extended his hand and clasped Mad's in a surprisingly strong grip. "Then go do it."

A handshake wasn't enough. Mad leaned in and hugged his cousin. Then he left, nodding to the Rider guarding the door and the second stationed at the foot of the stairs. No one was taking chances anymore, which only spurred Mad on as he took the steps two and then three at a time.

Scarlet, Jade, and Dylan were where he'd left them, talking sleepily. Their voices faded into silence as he slipped through the door and walked to the end of the bed.

His whole damn life he'd fought against letting people need and depend on him. Maybe it all went back to that cold, dark little basement and the choices he'd made—and the ones he hadn't made.

How much guilt had he carried for living when his mother hadn't, for giving in to her pleas and hurting her to save himself? Reliving it over and over, the refrain always the same—*I should have died to spare her that pain.*

But he wouldn't have been sparing her pain. He would have been deciding what sort of pain she had to live with, deciding *for* her that her life would go on just fine if he wasn't a part of it.

His parents had died to give him the life he had now. He owed them too fucking much to throw it away recklessly. Especially with three shining reasons to embrace life staring at him.

They were nervous. Jade and Scarlet only a little, but Dylan was still bruised, still raw from baring his heart. So he was the one Mad smiled at, the one whose hand he reached out to squeeze. "Get dressed. We're going home."

dallas

THEIR REVOLUTION WAS looking ragged around the damn edges.

As what remained of the sector leaders settled into seats around his conference table, Dallas took a mental tally of the devastation.

Colby and Scott were gone, taken down in the wave of assassinations. Dallas hadn't had much use for the leaders of Six and Seven while they were alive, but they were somehow even more annoying dead. Better the incompetent devils they knew than whatever mess those leaderless sectors would face now.

Gideon looked like shit three days warmed over, and Dallas almost felt guilty dragging the bastard out of his home. But no one wanted another meeting in One until they were sure Gideon had straightened out the loyalty problems with his staff—even Gideon.

Jade had taken the seat next to him. No, not Jade.

Jade was gone, burned up in whatever trial by fire had gone down in Sector Two over the last few weeks. Only Jyoti remained, a woman who sat with the casual confidence of a billionaire and the chilly ruthlessness of a person deeply in love and willing to do whatever the fuck it took to protect her people.

The look was plenty familiar. Dallas saw it in his mirror every day.

But the scariest eyes in the room belonged to Ryder. On a practical level, freaking the shit out over Jim's loss was hard to avoid. He'd been the backbone of this rebellion, the driving force, the man who'd plotted it for dozens of years. They were in deep shit without him, and they all knew it.

That was practical. Personally, Dallas had spent years cordially loathing the bastard and years more circling him warily, unsure if he was looking at a potential friend or a crafty enemy. Ryder's pain was grief, pure and simple. And grief was dangerous, because people fought hard and smart to protect the living.

People got themselves—and everyone around them—killed trying to avenge the dead.

Six sat on Ryder's other side, damn near vibrating with nervous excitement. She knew she'd been tapped to speak for Sector Three today. She didn't know they'd be making it official soon—if they were still around in a week to make *anything* official.

Which was the point of the damn meeting. He gathered everyone's attention by rapping his knuckles on the table. "So. Eden tried to take us out."

"Motherfuckers," Ryder muttered.

"We knew they'd make a move eventually," Lex said flatly.

"It was well-coordinated," Jade—*Jyoti*—added, tapping one fingernail on the table. "And well-informed, too, to target me so soon after my...promotion."

Gideon barely managed to hide his flinch. "I'd like to

think the contents of our meetings were confidential, but obviously I had a spy who saw everyone who was coming and going."

"Doesn't mean that's how they knew about Jyoti." Six shrugged. "Street kids know everything about twenty minutes after it happens, and there's always a few willing to get bought off by the MPs."

"Security, then." Ryder scrubbed his hands over his face. "It's time for all of us to get serious about it."

"Security doesn't answer the real question," Dallas drawled as he exchanged a look with Lex. "They came after us with guns instead of bombs. What do they know that we don't?"

"Everything," said an unfamiliar voice from the door.

Even knowing that Cruz and Bren were holding down the hallway, Dallas went for his gun, and he wasn't the only one. Six already had hers drawn, and Ryder even made it out of his chair, his pistol pointed at the newcomer's forehead.

Dallas had never met him, but he'd seen pictures of Ashwin Malhotra. The pictures showed a stone-faced, frozen-eyed man with medium-brown skin, dark-brown eyes, and black hair, coldly handsome even when he looked likely to murder you.

Compared to the reality, the pictures were warm and fuzzy.

Cruz slipped in after him and nodded to Dallas, so Six relaxed back into her chair. But Ryder stayed where he was, his arm and his aim steady. "Who's this?" he asked.

Ashwin studied Ryder for a moment and then dismissed him, turning back to Dallas as if having a gun pointed at his head was such a common damn occurrence that he didn't even give a shit. Considering how much Dallas's fingers still itched for his pistol, he'd wager having guns pointed at him *was* a normal day for Ashwin.

"This is an informant," Dallas said carefully. "One with access to high-level information within Eden."

"And outside of Eden," Ashwin corrected. "Which is the relevant detail in this case."

Lex sighed. "What the fuck does that mean, Malhotra?"

"It means Eden didn't bomb you because they can't." He said it casually, like he was issuing a weather report. "They've lost the support of the Base."

The words might as well have been a bomb themselves. They crashed into the silence with an audible boom, and Dallas was so fucking stunned he didn't realize he was hearing a *literal* boom until the power flickered.

And went out.

That got people moving. Chairs squeaked and people cursed. Dallas reached instinctively for Lex and found her hand reaching for him. A heartbeat later, light flared as Cruz cut on the flashlight from his belt. "Blackout?"

"No," Ashwin replied, and that one word kicked Dallas into action.

Other people were heading for the roof, too—it was the best place to assess the extent of a power outage. But a hushed murmur of confusion greeted Dallas when he stepped out the access door, Lex's hand still gripped tightly in his.

As far as the eye could see, the sectors were dark—even Five, which *never* lost power. Bits of light that looked like fires flared here and there, but a dark stillness had settled.

Only the city still glowed.

"What the fuck?" Jasper muttered beside him. "What the actual—?"

A loud buzz that seemed to vibrate through Dallas's bones cut off the words, and he watched as the tall wall surrounding Eden came alive with hundreds of tiny lights.

"Holy shit." Rachel shook free of Ace's restraining hand and stepped forward. "Is that—?"

"They turned on the juice," Bren confirmed. "The wall's hot."

"Lockdown," Dallas murmured. It was urban fucking legend to everyone but the old-timers. With the wall electrified, anyone who got too close to it would get slammed with enough voltage to fry their brains. Useful in sieges.

Or when the sectors turned against you.

Eden was going to war. Not from the sky with drones and bombs, but from behind their precious wall. A knock-down, drag-out war of attrition with their population growing more restless by the day and their every supply route leading straight through the sectors.

Dallas would have laughed if it hadn't been for one tiny detail.

With Jim dead, Eden was going to war with *him*.

ABOUT KIT

Kit Rocha is the pseudonym for co-writing team Donna Herren and Bree Bridges. After penning dozens of paranormal novels, novellas and stories as Moira Rogers, they branched out into gritty, sexy dystopian romance.

The Beyond series has appeared on the New York Times and USA Today bestseller lists, and was honored with a 2013 RT Reviewer's Choice award.

ACKNOWLEDGMENTS & THANKS

Not a single word of this book could have been produced without the enthusiastic participation and support of an expansively large group of people: our editor, Sasha Knight; our proofreader, Sharon Muha; Lillie Applegarth, queen of timelines and bibles; our assistant, Angie Ramey; Jay and Tracy, the best mods in the entire world—no, make that the universe; and our friends and family, all the people who've been with us through the course of this crazy journey. Thank you all so much.

Special thanks to Alisha Rai and Suleikha Snyder for the help with Jyoti's name, and to Jeanne for the endless chats about the evolution of tattoos. Your patient answers to our questions shaped this book—and the future of the series—more than even we realized at the time. Because names, like tattoos, can mean everything.

And, finally, we'd like to thank all the O'Kanes out there. We may not live in Sector Four, but our hearts are always there, and that's what counts.

O'Kane for life.

OUR BOOKS

Beyond Shame
Beyond Control
Beyond Pain
Beyond Jealousy
Beyond Addiction
Beyond Innocence
Beyond Ruin

Beyond Ecstasy
(coming later in 2016)

OUR NOVELLAS

Beyond Temptation
(novella — first published in the MARKED anthology)
Beyond Solitude
(novella — first published in ALPHAS AFTER DARK)
Beyond Possession

44359425R00219

Made in the USA
Middletown, DE
04 June 2017